MAFIA AND ANGEL

ISA OLIVER

MAFIA AND ANGEL

Copyright © 2023 by Isa Oliver

All rights reserved.

No portion of this book may be reproduced in any form without written permission from the publisher or author, except as permitted by U.K. copyright law.

This book features an Italian Mafia arranged marriage romance, enemies to lovers, an age gap, and some dark romance content.

Contents

DEDICATION	VI
AUTHOR'S NOTE	VII
CONTENT NOTE - SPOILERS	VIII
MAFIA FAMILIES	IX
FACEBOOK GROUP AND ARCs	XI
1. CHAPTER 1	1
2. CHAPTER 2	8
3. CHAPTER 3	18
4. CHAPTER 4	24
5. CHAPTER 5	29
6. CHAPTER 6	37
7. CHAPTER 7	42
8. CHAPTER 8	45
9. CHAPTER 9	53
10. CHAPTER 10	58

11.	CHAPTER 11	60
12.	CHAPTER 12	64
13.	CHAPTER 13	70
14.	CHAPTER 14	74
15.	CHAPTER 15	77
16.	CHAPTER 16	82
17.	CHAPTER 17	85
18.	CHAPTER 18	88
19.	CHAPTER 19	99
20.	CHAPTER 20	105
21.	CHAPTER 21	111
22.	CHAPTER 22	116
23.	CHAPTER 23	125
24.	CHAPTER 24	134
25.	CHAPTER 25	139
26.	CHAPTER 26	144
27.	CHAPTER 27	148
28.	CHAPTER 28	152
29.	CHAPTER 29	157
30.	CHAPTER 30	162
31.	CHAPTER 31	167
32.	CHAPTER 32	172
33.	CHAPTER 33	180

34.	CHAPTER 34	187
35.	CHAPTER 35	193
36.	CHAPTER 36	196
37.	CHAPTER 37	199
38.	CHAPTER 38	202
39.	CHAPTER 39	206
40.	CHAPTER 40	210
41.	CHAPTER 41	214
42.	CHAPTER 42	217
43.	CHAPTER 43	224
44.	CHAPTER 44	231
45.	CHAPTER 45	237
46.	CHAPTER 46	242
47.	CHAPTER 47	251
48.	CHAPTER 48	256
49.	CHAPTER 49	259
50.	CHAPTER 50	264
51.	CHAPTER 51	269
52.	EPILOGUE	277
53.	SNEAK PEEK	291

DEDICATION

For my beautiful family.
I love you to the moon and back, always and forever.
xoxox

Acknowledgements: Thank you so much to my family for allowing me the time to write and your love. A huge thank you, Magan, for all your invaluable help and for the giggles over Anni's first chapter. Chrisandra, many thanks for your help and the kind words of support. And also thanks to Peachy Keen Author Services for being so amazing. I also want to say a big thank you to the beautiful and very talented Trishaa for the gorgeous picture edits she made on Instagram (@tri_book_reads). I have been truly humbled by all the extremely kind people I have met in the book community who have been so generous with their time and support for a newbie author like me, so a heartfelt thank you to all the readers, bloggers, and reviewers who have helped me on my writing journey.

AUTHOR'S NOTE

Dear Reader, different books in this series have different darkness levels. While this particular book is **NOT** a dark romance, it does include some references to sensitive elements. Specific topics are listed on the next page. The events in this book take place shortly before the events in Mafia And Captive (the latter being Marco's story). Love Isa xxx

Marchiano Mafia Series (all can be read as standalones):
Mafia And Captive
(An Age Gap Dark Captive Romance)
Mafia And Angel
(A Single Dad Age Gap Arranged Marriage)
Mafia And Taken
(A Dark Mafia Romance)

CONTENT NOTE – SPOILERS

Topics referred to include:
...
...
...
Mafia violence
Suicide
Depression
Postnatal depression
Murder
Death

MAFIA FAMILIES

<u>Veneti Family: Imperiosi Mafia, New York</u>
Napoleone Veneti (Capo)
Fantasia Veneti - Napoleone's wife
Christian Veneti - Napoleone's son and heir
Leoluca Veneti - Napoleone's son
Fidella Veneti - Napoleone's daughter
Annunciata Veneti - Napoleone's daughter
Priscilla Veneti - Napoleone's sister
Benny Veneti - Napoleone's nephew

<u>Marco Marchiano: Fratellanza Mafia, Chicago</u>
Marco Marchiano (Capo)
Alessio Marchiano (Consigliere) - Marco's brother
Camillo Marchiano - Marco's brother
Danio Marchiano - Marco's brother
Debora Marchiano - Marco's sister

<u>Lorenzo Marchiano: Fratellanza Mafia, Chicago</u>
Lorenzo Marchiano (Underboss) - Marco's cousin

Aloysius Marchiano (Captain) - Lorenzo's brother
Rita Marchiano - Lorenzo's first wife
Clara Marchiano - Lorenzo's daughter
Clemente Marchiano - Lorenzo's son
Cosima Marchiano - Lorenzo's mother

FACEBOOK GROUP AND ARCs

Facebook Group: 'Isa's Angels & Mafia Books'
https://www.facebook.com/groups/1409806332760996

Would you like to receive a free 'Advance Reader Copy' of Isa's next release before anyone else? Please see here:
https://isaoliverauthor.com/free-arcs/

CHAPTER 1

Santa Adelina, Madre di Dio, prega per noi peccatori, adesso e nell'ora della nostra morte.
Holy Mary, Mother of God, pray for us sinners now and at the hour of our death.
— the words every Made Man recites upon a death.

ANNUNCIATA

"Okay, I've finished my math now," I said, as I slammed my book shut and leaned back in my chair at the antique table, stretching out my arms. It should have taken at least an hour to complete my assignment for college; however, as usual, it had only taken me a fraction of the time.

I was glad I'd finished before Ma got home. She thought I was too serious—getting good grades and doing my homework on time were not traits looked for in a good Mafia daughter. I knew I was a bit of a nerd, but I loved math and figures.

"So, Wilbur, that means I've got time to give you a tummy rub."

The fluffy white cat gracefully leaped up onto the seat of the chair next to me and rolled onto his back, curling his front paws under his chin while he gazed at me with his large blue eyes.

I was in the dining room of my papà's Staten Island mansion. Set high on a hill with the bright lights of the city glittering across the water, my papà had sought to provide us with the most opulent home.

Its shimmering chandeliers and gleaming marble columns shone fiercely in an attempt to distract us from the glare of the silver bullets that my family shot from their guns. Because my papà, brothers, uncles, and cousins ran the Imperiosi Mafia in New York, and each one of them could give Hades a run for his money when it came to ruling the underworld.

"You really are a handsome boy," I cooed to Wilbur, as I ran my hand over the soft fur of our family pet.

"If you keep talking to him like that, Anni, everyone's going to think that you're a crazy-cat-lady," said my older sister, Fidella, as she walked into the dining room. She carried a dish she had borrowed from Ma yesterday. Even though she was married, she and her family still spent a lot of time at our place.

I grinned at her. "I have to do something to pass the time. It's not as if I have a wide circle of friends I can spend time with. You know what it's like, Fee. Our social circle is pretty much confined to Mafia families. Even at school, the non-Mafia kids avoid us connected kids like we're the Cullen vampire family from *Twilight*."

Just then, Wilbur decided it was time for a nap and stalked over to the dark green chaise longue, curling up on the end in a patch of sun.

As I watched him, I ran my hand over my blonde bob.

Fidella eyed me critically. "Jeez, Anni, Ma's going to have a coronary when she sees that your hair is even shorter."

"The stylist only took off two centimeters exactly when I had it trimmed earlier today."

"Ma still hates your short hair. She thinks it's going to massively affect your marriage prospects."

I divided my hair into two and started to put each side into a French braid. "I think she's getting used to it. She's definitely complaining less about it. I mean, I did cut it over two years ago. I didn't think she would hold a grudge against it for quite so long."

My hair skimmed the top of my shoulders, so it wasn't super short, but it was much shorter than most Mafia girls and women wore their hair.

Our institution was traditional, and many still believed that the main role of women was to look attractive for their husbands. The traditionalists held a non-negotiable view that females should wear elegant dresses, high heels, a full face of make-up, and have long swishy hair.

I pulled a hair tie around my first completed braid. "Anyway, Ma knows I've always wanted to study math at college. And since Papà is allowing me to do that, there's absolutely no way that I'm going to be a Mafia wife at the age of twenty. I've got a brain and I'm going to use it."

"You've always been so determined about it, I'll give you that," chuckled my sister.

My ma said that a woman in the Mafia world having ambition was akin to opening Pandora's box: it would lead to conflict, destruction, and ruin. If you asked me, I thought Ma was being overdramatic. Anyway, many people seemed to miss the hidden potential in what Pandora had done. She'd been forbidden by Zeus from looking inside the gilded box; when her curiosity, however, meant that she'd opened it and unleashed a tyranny of unforeseen problems upon mankind, she had also revealed everlasting hope. Hope could be seen as good or evil. Personally, I liked to look on the bright side.

And so, for me, ambition and my college degree were a ticket not to problems, but to hope—and my hope was to use my talent for math and put it to good use.

"I'm sure," I carried on, "that I'll eventually manage to persuade Papà to let me help in the business on the paperwork side."

"Ma will hate that idea as well."

"All done," I said, as I put a tie around the second completed braid and checked my reflection in the dining room mirror. "What do you think?"

"Cute," grinned Fee, as she walked out of the room and headed for the kitchen.

I wandered around the house and finally into the backyard. There I found that someone hadn't tidied up after their shooting practice, instead leaving out empty beer bottles and a revolver on the patio table.

Wilbur scampered outside and leaped onto the table, deciding to keep me company instead of having a nap.

I picked up the revolver and loaded it. This would do to pass the time. I mean, what harm could it possibly do?

LORENZO

I was in a car with my cousin, Marco Marchiano—he was Capo of the Fratellanza in Chicago, and I was one of his Underbosses.

Together with Marco's brothers, we were known as the Kings of Chicago, running the city with a brutality and ruthlessness that had propelled the Fratellanza to being one of the most powerful Mafia families in the United States.

We'd come to Staten Island today for a meeting with our new ally, Napoleone Veneti, Capo of the Imperiosi in New York.

I was exhausted and tried to distract myself from my tiredness by taking in my surroundings. "This is my first time in New York in years," I remarked, watching out of the window. Marco had set up this new alliance only a month ago, so the relationship was still in its early stages.

As we drove toward the Veneti mansion in the Todt Hill area, I saw a large glossy sign announcing that we'd arrived in Venetiville. "I thought this was Staten Island?" I said, a frown of confusion tugging at my brow.

"Yeah, it is," replied Marco. "But this little corner of Staten Island has been renamed by Napoleone Veneti."

"Renamed—what, after himself? What a self-obsessed moron." I wasn't in the best of moods today. I was thirty years old and a single dad. Being a single parent, with two young children who woke every night, was far from an easy job.

I was tired and irritable, and I didn't see that improving anytime soon. And the way things were going, I didn't see my four-year-old daughter, Clara, ever getting over the death of her mom. At least my son was younger and barely remembered his mother.

Marco looked across at me. "Napoleone might be a self-obsessed moron, but he's *our* self-obsessed moron now. This alliance between our families will increase our overall power and help get the Bratva off our backs. They've gained too much power and territory recently, and this is our best way of fighting back."

After clearing a security checkpoint, we entered the gated community.

I stared around myself. 'Gated community' was an understatement. Venetiville was surrounded by an electrified perimeter, barbed wire, and look-out towers complete with machine-gun-toting soldiers.

As we drove up to the Veneti mansion, however, the whole ambience changed, and it was like I was in a holiday resort. I saw tennis courts, a huge outdoor pool, lush green lawns, and magnificent homes which any Made Man would be proud of.

"What's that place?" I pointed to a large building next to the tennis courts. It was white stucco, with white shutters around the windows and pillars on either side of the doors.

"It's the clubhouse."

"The clubhouse? For what?"

"The Venetiville Country Club."

I looked at Marco in disbelief. "The Imperiosi Mafia have their *own country club*?"

"Yeah. Fucking hilarious, isn't it?"

"Hilarious is one word for it," I muttered.

We pulled up in front of a mansion. It was a grand, colonial-style house built from dark bricks, and it looked to have three main floors.

As I got out of our black Mercedes and stood on the front lawn, I had a direct view of the nearby church whose roof was adorned with one of the largest crucifixes I'd ever seen—this was what Napoleone Veneti saw every time he left his house.

"The church is called St. Napoleone's," chuckled Marco.

"He is just being fucking ridiculous now," I griped. "Who the fuck names a church after themselves? I'm surprised that Napoleone hasn't replaced the Jesus on the crucifix with an image of himself."

"The crucifix emphasizes Jesus's sacrifice: his death by crucifixion," remarked Marco. "But I doubt Napoleone would ever sacrifice himself, as Jesus did, for the redemption of mankind."

"True," I admitted grudgingly. "Like most Made Men, Napoleone loves killing others just a bit too much to give up his own life."

Napoleone greeted us at the dark-stained oak door of his mansion. "Welcome to Venetiville," he boomed—as if we hadn't already figured out that we were in his territory. "Come in, come in," he welcomed.

We stepped inside the wood-paneled hallway.

"Would you like coffee?"

"That would be good," replied Marco, with a shark-like smile. I nodded as well, being parched after our trip here. After this meeting, we also planned to drive into the city to pay a visit to Napoleone's illegal casino. It was a highly profitable income stream for him, particularly since he had local law enforcement in his back pocket.

"Fidella! Anni!" he called out, but no one answered. "My daughters must have gone out," he sighed. "If no one else is home, I won't be able to operate the damn new coffee machine, but come to my study and I will fix us a whiskey instead and we can get down to business."

Another car with some more of our soldiers had also parked up, and those men would keep guard while we were inside. The alliance was still in its infancy, and we weren't taking any chances.

The study was suitably grand, as befitting the Capo of the Imperiosi. Its centerpiece was an original oak and stone fireplace, while the large windows were topped with smaller panes of antique stained glass.

After the drinks had been poured, Marco and I settled back into the comfortable leather armchairs. I took a sip of my whisky and let the smooth, smoky liquid slide down my throat and soothe my mind.

As I was about to take another sip, gunshots rang out from somewhere in the house.

Pop! Pop!

What the fuck? Napoleone had said no one was home. That meant someone had broken in and was trying to kill the Marchianos, Napoleone Veneti, or all of us.

I flung my tumbler to the floor as I sprang to my feet and drew out my revolver.

I was nearest to the door. I ran over to it and threw it open. Napoleone and Marco were close behind me.

I heard Napoleone shouting into his cell phone for backup.

I sprinted toward the back of the house where the sound had come from. Our soldiers were also running through the house toward the gunshots.

Pop!

Hearing another shot come from the backyard, I saw a flash of movement through a window and caught a glimpse of someone holding a gun.

I ran through the open back door, pointing my gun at the intruder.

The person with the gun spun on their heel as they turned their body toward me. And, with a gun raised in their hand, they aimed straight at me.

CHAPTER 2

ANNUNCIATA

Fuck! A scary looking man was running out of the house with his weapon aimed at me!

I told myself to stay calm as I pointed my gun at him.

My finger squeezed the trigger.

Pop!

I missed!

I aimed again.

Before I could shoot again, Papà ran into the yard and yelled at me. "It's okay, Anni! This is Lorenzo Marchiano." Papà hurried over to me and caught my arm, just as some soldiers ran into the yard. "It's fine," he called to the soldiers. "It's just a misunderstanding. Everyone's just got a bit carried away."

Suddenly, I went very still. "Marchiano?" I repeated slowly.

I had never met the man; however, of course, I had heard of him. He was an Underboss in the Fratellanza. And, as a Marchiano, he was now one of our allies—not an enemy as I'd first thought when he'd burst into the backyard and aimed his revolver at me.

Uh-oh. I was going to have to change my name, move to Costa Rica, and fake my own death for good measure.

"I didn't know who he was," I said quickly.

Up behind my papà came the Fratellanza Capo, whom I had previously met. But I had never met Lorenzo before.

"Lorenzo, this is my daughter, Anni."

I looked at him properly for the first time. He was tall, good-looking, and looked ruthlessly fit under his expensive suit. He had dark, almost-black hair, while his eyes were deep brown and glinting fiercely as they glared at me.

Despite the beautiful proportions of his face and the sort of body women would sigh over, something in his expression hinted at the darkness within him. And a sense of raw masculinity and danger rolled off him in waves as his stare on me intensified.

Goosebumps erupted on my arms under his piercing gaze. He was notorious within the underworld: he was the devil dressed in Brioni and black, and his darkness dimmed the bright lights of the city he ruled with his cousins.

And now his ruthless attention was fixed on me.

I licked my lips. "Papà, I didn't know he was one of the Marchianos. He was going to shoot me. I was just killing some time by practicing my shooting."

"Do you always just shoot at random strangers?" Lorenzo growled at me, stepping closer so that he towered over me with his threatening presence.

I glared at him. "What were you so scared of that you needed to pull your weapon on me? I mean, *I'm five-foot-nothing and a girl.*"

"Look, everyone just needs to calm down," soothed my papà, trying to defuse the tension. "Anni likes to practice her shooting skills from time to time. It's good for a girl to know how to protect herself."

"You let your daughter *fool around* with guns?" Lorenzo's words hurtled through the air. "She tried to kill me!"

My blood heated at his condescending tone. "I'm not used to shooting running targets. But if I'd been given five more seconds, I would have *definitely* killed you, trust me." I knew I should keep quiet at this point, but my mouth just kept on babbling. All the while, Wilbur still sat on the patio table, watching with interest what all the commotion was about and cleaning his paws at the same time.

"Anni..." Papà admonished gently. I had never dared to speak like this to a stranger, especially not to one who was also a Made Man. "I still don't understand why you shot at him?"

I took a deep breath, attempting to steady my racing pulse. "The bottles and guns were out. I was bored, so I decided to do some firing practice. Then he came out of nowhere and pulled his gun on me. What did you want me to do, Papà, call 911? You know you always tell us never to call the authorities and that we can handle any dangers by ourselves."

My dad ran his hand through his gray hair. "I meant that the *men* can handle any dangers, Anni. You should have called for me if you were scared."

"There was no time," I exclaimed. "He already had his gun aimed at me, and he was about to kill me."

Lorenzo took another step closer and grabbed at the gun in my hand. "Give me that before you hurt yourself."

I wasn't going to give him my weapon, so before he could take it, I jerked my hand away. And Wilbur, sensing Lorenzo's tension toward me, simultaneously swiped at him with his sharp claws.

"What the fuck?" snapped Lorenzo, yanking his hand back and staring at the lines of bright red blood spreading over the back of his hand. His eyes darted up at Wilbur, and he growled at him with a murderous look gleaming in his eyes.

Before Lorenzo could hurt Wilbur, I snatched up our pet and hugged him to my chest while at the same time dashing to the other side of the patio table so that it was a barrier between us.

But Lorenzo clenched his jaw tight and took another stride forward while giving Wilbur a menacing look.

Without further thought, I raised my arm and fired my weapon.

The bullet skimmed his upper arm before hitting the wall of the house behind him.

"Fuck!" Lorenzo snarled, his hand flying to his right arm.

"Don't even think about killing the cat," I said icily as he examined the hole the bullet had burned into his jacket. "That was a warning shot. I deliberately only damaged your Brioni suit. Come any closer and my next bullet will take out the lateral cutaneous nerve in your forearm."

Lorenzo's eyebrows shot up.

"Yeah," I nodded, "my brothers have taught me where best to aim if I want to disarm a man."

"Anni, what are you doing?" Papà asked in confusion.

"He wants to kill Wilbur!"

"Anni, dear, of course he won't kill our cat," reasoned Papà. "This is all a big misunderstanding."

"Didn't you see the look in his eyes when Wilbur scratched him? And he *growled* at the cat." I had grown up around Made Men, and I knew murderous intent when I saw it.

"Jesus Christ," gritted out Lorenzo. "She might be your daughter, but she's batshit crazy."

I bet he would kill the cat if given half a chance, I thought to myself. He looked like the type who got off on hurting poor innocent souls.

My papà might have trusted him, but I certainly didn't.

LORENZO

I glared at the girl in front of me.

Her tousled white-blonde hair was styled into two short braids around a face that was free of make-up. Her doe-like green eyes gave her a softness that belied the feistiness I'd just witnessed in her.

She was wearing jeans and a weird top that was white, flowy, and had sleeves that looked like batwings.

We heard the front door open and then footsteps in the hallway before female voices wafted through the house toward us.

A lady wearing a leather mini-skirt and low-cut red top tottered into the backyard on the highest of heels, chewing gum as she made her way toward Napoleone, loudly asking what was going on. We all still had our weapons drawn, although they were now at our sides rather than aimed.

Napoleone started to explain to her what had happened.

"Is that hooker her mother?" I murmured to Marco in horror.

"Nope. That's her Aunt Priscilla." Marco kept his voice low. "That other woman, Fantasia Veneti, is her mother." He nodded toward another woman who had just stepped into the backyard.

The mother had an over-ample figure which was clad in a black dress. She also wore ridiculously large gold earrings and carried an enormous black purse. I couldn't stop my eyes from staring at her shock of carrot-colored hair, which seemed to be a dye job's bad attempt at a shade of auburn. At least the tacky mom was a slight improvement on the trashy aunt.

Jesus fucking Christ. This family was supposed to be rolling in money, yet these women were dressed like trash and hookers.

What ensued was a conversation on how to make right what had just happened. Soldiers from both the Fratellanza and Imperiosi had witnessed the whole incident.

"It's a sign of utter disrespect toward the Fratellanza for your daughter to have fired at my Underboss," growled Marco. He was beyond pissed, and his infamous short temper did not bode well for the future of this alliance.

"I can assure you that Anni meant no disrespect," Napoleone blustered, the girl standing at his side. "It is all a big misunderstanding. She never meant to fire the gun or hurt anyone."

"Like hell she didn't," I said tersely.

"Whatever she meant, the fact is that she did shoot at one of my Underbosses." Marco's tone was severe. "You know that can't go unpunished."

"To punish her would be too harsh," Napoleone wheedled. "Why not have a marriage between our families instead, as a gesture of goodwill and to solidify the alliance? Anni can marry into your family, and we can demonstrate to our respective organizations that all is well between our families."

Anni's eyes widened as she heard her father's suggestion, but thankfully the girl kept her mouth shut.

I could see Marco considering the idea before he looked at me. "She should marry you, Lorenzo. That will show our men that she's been brought under control and tamed by us."

I stared at my Capo like he had suddenly grown two heads. "I'm not sure the girl is tameable." I curled my lip. "She's like a wildcat."

Marco turned to our host. "Lorenzo and I need to talk privately if we are to consider such a marriage."

"Of course, I understand completely. Use the drawing room. I'll make sure no one disturbs you there."

***

We made our way to the drawing room.

As soon as the doors were closed, I turned to Marco. "There's no way in hell I'm marrying that girl. She's not wife material."

"If she's married off to you, she'll have to settle down and stop messing around," said Marco. "Being a wife, plus raising a two-year-old and a four-year-old, will be no walk in the park for her." Marco looked at me with a hard look in his eyes. "Lorenzo, you need a wife. Rita has been dead for over a year."

What he really meant was that some people thought I still wasn't over my dead wife, and that made me look weak in the eyes of my men. And he was right that I wasn't over what had happened. Fury still raced through me every time I thought about Rita.

I sighed inwardly. I was thirty years old, a widower, and I was raising two children by myself.

My mother now helped with looking after the children. Even still, being a single dad was more work than I'd ever imagined. I was muddling through the physical side of looking after them day-to-day, but I had no idea of how to deal with the emotional side of helping the kids through their mother's death, nor how to banish my own demons.

After the whole shitshow with Rita, I'd swore I'd never get involved with another woman again.

"You're barely coping with looking after the kids," Marco added, not letting this topic go.

Normally, I would do anything for my Capo, but when shit like this came up and people started interfering in my personal life, then I started to feel resentful.

Weariness suddenly consumed me. My role as an Underboss was demanding and left little time for child-rearing. Perhaps Marco was right? If the girl was my wife, she would have to submit to me and obey me.

"Maybe the girl wouldn't be too bad as a wife," I said thoughtfully. "She's probably the way she is due to a lack of discipline from her parents. Her father didn't even seem that angry with her for shooting at me—I mean, what the fuck?"

"There's the wellbeing of the alliance to consider," Marco carried on. The Fratellanza's interests were mainly in the drug trade, laundering the dirty money through our legitimate businesses of hotels and clubs, the net result being that we had become extremely wealthy. "There's always someone trying to muscle into our territory, and currently that someone is the Bratva, which means that our alliance with the Imperiosi is crucial because it will unite our organizations against our common enemy."

We talked about this some more, although I still wasn't entirely convinced. We returned to Napoleone to discuss the matter further, however, with the critical aim of preserving our fledgling alliance with the Imperiosi.

***

As we talked some more in the study about the possibility of a marriage union, Mrs. Veneti came in with a tray of coffee.

"She's not old enough to marry," I said. "She still wears her hair in pigtails."

"They're not pigtails," the girl interrupted. "They're French braids." She continued standing at her father's side. I wasn't sure why she was still even here—this matter was between her father and the Fratellanza.

Her response riled me further. "The girl is completely out of control," I gritted out. "No girl in my family would dare shoot a gun at a Made Man."

Mrs. Veneti interrupted. "It was the shock—you know, of having a weapon aimed at her. She was staring down the barrel of a gun. Annunciata is the sweetest, most obedient girl you could ever meet—*an absolute angel.*"

The way her mother spoke, anyone would think that the girl spent all her spare time polishing a halo.

As Mrs. Veneti batted her fake eyelashes at me, I wondered if I had judged the girl too harshly. I *had* probably scared her when I pulled my gun on her, and the girl had probably been in shock when she shot at me the second time. If Mrs. Veneti was saying that her daughter was obedient, then I knew I could take her word for it—after all, I knew that Mrs. Veneti wouldn't lie to me, especially not in the presence of her husband.

"She's still a teenager," I observed. The obvious age gap between us was a concern for me.

"Annunciata turned twenty last week," announced her mother, as if one week made a world of difference.

"Papà, I don't want to get married," interjected the girl.

"Anni, dear, you've always known that you would have an arranged marriage," Napoleone responded in a soothing voice. "It's just come a little sooner than expected. You are of age now, and he will make a good husband."

Why the fuck was he talking to her in such an appeasing tone, as if he were trying to *persuade* her to marry me?

He should be commanding his daughter to do her duty, not pussyfooting around her sensitivities. No wonder she was so out of control—she was spoiled and her parents pandered to her whims.

I looked the girl over. With her blonde hair and eyes that sparkled like emeralds, she was pretty in her own way. I liked that she didn't have that overtly flirtatious manner that many young girls from Mafia families adopted when they were looking to snare a husband, although I wasn't sure I liked her feistiness.

She just needed someone to take control of her, I told myself. As my wife, she would no longer have time to waste on doing irresponsible things like running around and shooting guns.

And Marco was right—I needed to remarry at some point so that my children would have a mother figure in their lives. And this was particularly important given how much the kids were currently struggling, especially Clara. If I needed to remarry, I might as well marry someone who looked vaguely attractive. "Very well. I will marry her."

Everyone gave a sigh of relief. The marriage would avert a war breaking out between our organizations, and our alliance could continue intact.

"My daughter is going to be married!" shrieked Mrs. Veneti. "We should set the wedding date today."

"There's no rush for that, Mrs. Veneti—" I began.

"You're part of the family now. You're to call me *Ma* Veneti—I insist!"

"Ma Veneti?" I exclaimed in horror.

"He'd be honored to call you that," interrupted Marco, a fucking smirk plastered across his face.

I really didn't want to have to call this woman 'Ma'. But this crazy family was determined to get their claws well and truly into me.

Dear God, what the fuck had I let myself in for?

ANNUNCIATA

The Marchianos departed shortly before dinner.

I was dying to talk to my papà, to persuade him that the marriage was a ridiculous idea. I hadn't dared to say anything more in front of the Marchianos. My papà was kind to me, but even he drew the limit at being disobeyed in front of company.

I had no desire to give up my current life, my college degree, and the relative freedoms I had. And especially not when it meant that I would be under the thumb of a man like Lorenzo Marchiano—a man who was arrogant, bad-tempered, and condescending.

The way he'd spoken to me today kept running through my mind—I couldn't believe the nerve of the man. He thought that women shouldn't handle weapons. He probably also thought that women didn't have the brain cells to study for a college degree and instead should spend all their time chained to the kitchen sink.

I sat at the dinner table with my parents and Aunt Priscilla. Also present were my two older brothers: Christian and Leoluca.

"You really fired a gun at him?" Christian chuckled, greatly amused at Aunt Priscilla's retelling of events. "I'm pissed now that I missed the meeting—I would love to have seen the look on the Marchianos' faces."

"The only important thing is that the alliance remains intact now that we have agreed on a marriage between Anni and Lorenzo Marchiano," said Papà in a serious voice.

I couldn't keep quiet any longer. "But Papà, surely you can't expect me to marry him? He's a murderer!"

"You won't have to see that side of his life, Anni." Papà took a sip of his wine as he spoke to me. "He'll keep his work life separate from his home life, in the same way me and your brothers do."

"I'm not talking about the Mafia stuff, Papà. I mean that he wanted to kill Wilbur. I bet he enjoys killing cats in his spare time—he looks like just the sort of man who would enjoy committing moggycides."

"Anni, dear, I know the man," Papà said in a placating voice. "Apart from extortion, drug dealing, and weapons trafficking, he's a good man. He's never killed a cat in his life. He only kills humans."

"Are you sure, Papà?"

"Yes, I'm sure. There are no moggycides, my dear. The only things he commits are homicides."

Talking about deaths, my thoughts drifted to his late wife, Rita. It was said that she had died of pneumonia. Not much else was known about her, but that wasn't unusual given that Mafia families were notoriously secretive about every aspect of their lives.

I chewed on my lower lip. Lorenzo Marchiano was rude, condescending, and overbearing. "It's not as if I have a real choice in the matter, do I?" I asked glumly.

"No, Anni, you don't," said Papà in a steely voice. I knew that he wouldn't be persuaded otherwise. This was business for him.

I sighed in defeat. "I'll guess I'll have to marry him then."

CHAPTER 3

LORENZO

I had fallen into an uneasy sleep, dreaming about the events from one year earlier...

Rita was dead. May God forgive me...
Now I had to break the news to the children.
When I saw a car pull up outside, I went out to get three-year-old Clara and one-year-old Clemente. They had spent the day at my mother's house and had just been brought home.
"Dadda," greeted Clara in her small, shy voice, giving me that special smile of hers. It never failed to touch my heart—I could see in her face her love for me. And I knew that would change after she heard what I had to say.
I scooped them up, one in each arm, relishing the warmth of their tiny bodies as they perched against my cold body.
I brought them inside and sat them down next to me on the couch. They both had my dark hair and my brown eyes—and now those eyes were solemn as if they sensed something might be amiss.
I explained to them in the best way I could that their mother was dead.

Clemente was too young to understand, and as soon as I had finished speaking, he toddled off to play with his toy cars.

Clara sat very still as she listened carefully to me. Although she was having difficulty understanding what I was saying, she could sense from my tone that something was very wrong. She clung to me, holding tightly onto my arms with her small, chubby hands, and asked in a small voice, "When Momma come back?" Her big brown eyes brimmed with fear.

"Momma isn't coming back," I said.

As I looked at Clara and Clemente and watched the wretched tears tumble from my daughter's eyes, my heart clenched with guilt.

I had taken their mother away from them.

I was a monster.

I woke up with a start. It took me a moment to realize that I was in my bedroom. I sat up and checked the clock. It was only 3 a.m.

I collapsed back onto my pillows. I had been dreaming of that day again: the last day of Rita's life.

I let out a sound of frustration. Nothing had been the same since that day.

The only things I wanted in life now were to be successful at my work and to raise my children. I certainly didn't need any other complications in my life. And that's what Anni was: a complication.

But I knew it was too late to change my mind—the success of the alliance was what mattered.

I hated how much my life had changed since Rita's death. Clara had withdrawn into her shell. I hadn't seen her smile once since that day. Instead, there had been tears: so many tears and so much grief.

And it was all my fault.

ANNUNCIATA

Two weeks later, I was in the den watching television, trying to take my mind off tomorrow's engagement party.

My thoughts, however, kept wandering to Lorenzo.

I knew next to nothing about him except that his first wife was dead and he had two children.

I exhaled in frustration. I'd always planned to at least finish my college degree before I had to marry. My major was in math, and I enjoyed studying. I was sure I could be of use to Papà in his business, but no one had mentioned my college course when the engagement had been decided upon.

I decided it was best to keep quiet about it: if Lorenzo didn't know about my degree, he couldn't forbid me from carrying on with it.

All my study was by distance learning anyway—since there was no way that Papà would ever allow me to physically attend a college campus. So once married, all I had to do was find some time to squeeze in my studies when Lorenzo wasn't around. I was sure I would be able to manage that.

Ma came into the den, hugging a large bowl of popcorn to her chest.

Popcorn in front of the TV was one of Ma's favorite past-times, picking up the habit when she arrived in the States from Italy twenty years ago. She snatched up the TV remote and flicked the channel over.

"Ma, I'm watching a program about the workings of international stock markets," I exclaimed.

"There's no need to watch such nonsense." She waved a hand dismissively at me. "It has nothing to do with us." *Because we earned our money illegally.* "That isn't real life."

She turned over to her favorite reality show: The Real Housewives of Sunset Beach.

"We can watch this together instead," Ma said.

"But I really wanted to watch the other program," I protested.

Ma narrowed her eyes at me—and then burst into tears. "You d-don't want to spend some q-q-quality time with your Ma before you get married?" she sobbed.

"I didn't say that, Ma—"

"Yes, you did!" she snapped. "You'd said you'd rather watch that other program because you know I won't stay and watch it with you."

"Ma—"

"It's always the same with you, wanting to watch these stupid money programs you know I can't understand. I don't think you love me anymore," she wailed.

"You're being silly," I sighed.

In between her tears, she slid her beady eyes over to look at me. "And you probably already love Lorenzo more than you've ever loved me!"

I most certainly did *not* love Lorenzo. And I wasn't going to fall for a sinner. Because you couldn't catch feelings for a bad guy…could you? Anyway, I definitely didn't want to talk to Ma about such things. "Okay, okay, we'll watch the Real Housewives…"

At my words, the tears stopped—a bit too quickly, I thought with suspicion.

The opening credits of the latest episode began, and Ma sighed with pleasure as she watched the show and shoved handfuls of popcorn into her mouth.

Aunt Priscilla, dressed in an orange, leopard-print mini-skirt, came in and sat next to Ma. "These American women dress so trashy," she uttered in horror as she looked at the screen.

"This is what living the American Dream must be like," Ma said wistfully. "American women have no worries apart from wondering what to wear, which party to go to, and what bitchy things they should say behind whose back."

Ma still considered herself Italian. To her, Americans were an alien species, their habits to be observed and commented upon.

"What happened on the last episode?" I asked, resigning myself to the fact that I wasn't going to get to watch the rest of the stock market program.

Ma's eyes lit up as she revealed the latest goings-on. "Brayden is going to propose to Briana today because she is his one true love, and then they're going to have perfect babies and live happily ever after."

"Are you sure, Ma?" My tone was skeptical. "Brayden's been banging Briana's half-sister, Hailey, as well as the neighbor with the big boobs."

"Yes, I'm sure," Ma nodded manically. "Those floozies were just a phase. He's grown up a lot since that episode last week, and I'm sure I just heard him swear his undying love to Briana." Ma's saucer-like eyes were glued to the screen as she slowly brought another handful of popcorn up to her mouth.

"Ma, he didn't just say that—"

"Yes, he did. Didn't you hear him?" Ma looked at me like I was a complete idiot.

"Uh huh," I murmured, somewhat disbelievingly. Ma had a tendency to lie about what had actually happened when I asked her for a catch-up on an episode.

She said it was because they spoke too fast, and her English wasn't good enough to keep up with what they were saying.

I thought, however, that she liked to have various unspoiled scenarios playing out in her mind. And in those scenarios, life was perfect: no one cheated, no one stole, and absolutely no one killed one another. As I'd gotten older, I noticed that she also ignored all the ugly details in our own lives. This made-up world playing out in her mind was the complete opposite of her real life; however, her deliberate oblivion kept her seemingly happy.

As I watched the episode, I couldn't stop myself from thinking about Lorenzo.

He was tall, handsome, and powerful. The man could get it, and everyone knew it. But he was also arrogant and obnoxious—making him, most definitely, not my type.

Ma, as if sensing my thoughts, patted my hand. "Don't worry about your marriage. I hear he kills a good amount of men every month, so he'll be a husband you can be proud of. Your papà wouldn't marry you off to any *stronzo*."

"Gee, thanks Ma. That makes me feel so much better."

***

That evening we were sitting around our dinner table: Me, Papà, Ma, Christian, Leoluca, Aunt Priscilla, and also my cousin Benny.

All talk was about the party and engagement contract signing tomorrow. The Italian Mafia was a traditional institution, and our families still followed the custom of signing an engagement contract. The marriage was a formal business arrangement between the Imperiosi and the Fratellanza, and I would be expected to sign the contract along with Lorenzo.

Christian turned to me. "I'm proud of you, Anni."

"What, for being obedient and marrying him?" I couldn't help the glum note in my voice.

"Nah, for not killing him when you pulled the gun on him. Lorenzo Marchiano is an annoying fucker sometimes—you showed great restraint."

"Yeah, well, if I was better at shooting running targets, then I wouldn't have to be marrying him now."

"Just don't say anything *at all* during the party tomorrow, Annunciata," ordered Ma. She was one of the few people who insisted on calling me by my full name. "That way, nothing will go wrong."

Ma consulted the seating plan and then turned to my cousin, Benny. "Benny, you'll be sitting opposite Annunciata at the party. If she talks, if she says absolutely anything, kick her."

"Sure thing, Aunt Fantasia," replied Benny. "Whatever you need, you can count on me."

I sighed. I was sure I could get through one measly party without incident, but my parents appeared to be taking no chances.

CHAPTER 4

ANNUNCIATA

It was the day of the engagement party.

Before I had to play the role of a dutiful Mafia daughter tonight, I had most of the day free—and I intended to make the most of it.

I was due to play a game of tennis with friends, and I'd also planned to sneak over to my cousins' house to watch the latest season of 'Jersey Shore'. My siblings and I had been forbidden from watching this, my parents fearing that we would be corrupted by the antics of the party-loving American-Italians on this reality show.

Ma's biggest fear was that I'd turn into the opposite of what a good Mafia daughter should be: obedient, well-behaved, and demure. Ma most definitely didn't know that I had secretly watched all the past seasons. Quite honestly, their lives, as portrayed on the show, looked relatively tame compared to what went on in my household.

LORENZO

I arrived in Staten Island. It was early evening, and the party wouldn't start for another hour; however, I had arrived earlier than the rest of my family for the signing of the engagement contract.

Marco and some other members of our family would be arriving in about an hour. Clara and Clemente wouldn't be here today—I wanted them to have some time to get used to the whole idea of the marriage before introducing them to Anni.

Napoleone greeted me in his mansion. "Welcome, Lorenzo. You're right on time. I've got the engagement contract set out in the dining room, and it's all ready for your and Anni's signatures."

I looked around and frowned. "Talking of the bride-to-be, where exactly is she?"

"She was spending the afternoon at the country club." He gave a small frown. "She should have been back by now. No matter, I will get a soldier to show you to her, and you can both sign the contract in your own time."

For God's sake. The girl knew that we were signing the contract at five o'clock. Instead, I was having to go find her and drag her ass back to the house to get her signature.

Her father didn't even seem to care that his daughter had failed to show up on time for the contract signing.

A soldier walked me to the clubhouse.

As we approached, I wasn't sure what I'd been expecting, but I certainly hadn't expected to find her on the tennis courts, acting as if she didn't have a care in the world.

She was wearing a pure white, sleeveless tennis dress, and her blonde hair was pulled into a short ponytail which bounced from side to side as she ran around the court.

Sweat glistened around her neck, and lean muscle flexed in her long legs as she stretched into a backhand.

I narrowed my eyes, not liking how she was dressed. The dress made her look virginal and was an unwelcome reminder of how much younger she was.

She was playing a doubles match with a young girl and two teenage boys. I felt my blood rush through my veins. What the fuck were those boys doing pissing around playing tennis? They should have been busy doing fight training or killing someone.

As Anni flew across the court and hit a forehand shot, the very short skirt of her white tennis dress flipped up, revealing her white lacy panties and the tempting curves of her ass.

And if I could see her ass, that meant that every other man here could see it as well—including the boys playing with her and the numerous soldiers who were on guard duty. I had the unwelcome thought that being on guard duty at the clubhouse was a job the Imperiosi men probably fought over.

"Enjoying yourself?" I growled, making her head whip around. "I've come to collect you to get ready for our engagement party."

"Lorenzo." Her face fell when she saw me, but noting my expression, she didn't argue. She turned to her companions. "Sorry, guys. I have to go. But I'll see you later at the party."

She walked silently next to me as we made our way back to her parent's house.

I caught her upper arm, pulling her to an abrupt stop in front of me.

I gave her shoulder a caress with my fingers, tracing her skin through her sweat-dampened dress.

Feeling my hand on her body, she let out a rushed breath, her green eyes widening.

I raked my eyes slowly over her body. Her hair stuck to the back of her slender neck, beads of sweat trailing down her skin and disappearing into the front of her dress's V-shaped neckline.

I dropped my eyes, taking in her tanned legs and pausing at the top of her bare, shapely thighs.

"You won't wear that tennis dress ever again," I gritted out. "Not unless you want me to spank your ass and then kill every man who looked at you."

Her mouth gaped open. "Is this what my life is going to be like from now on—you dictating everything I can and can't do? What am I supposed to wear when I play tennis?"

"Sweatpants and a hoodie," I barked. I didn't want any other Made Men ogling at my wife-to-be.

As soon as we arrived back in the house, she headed for the staircase. As she put her foot on the first step, she turned her face toward me. "I'm going to take a shower."

I took hold of her wrist and pulled her back down the stairs. "Not so fast. There's still the matter of the contract you need to sign."

The door of her father's study was open, and I could see he was on the phone. But I wasn't going to permit any further delays.

I put my hand against the small of her back and pushed her reluctant body, urging it toward the dining room where the contract lay waiting.

She looked over her shoulder, probably seeking out someone in her family who could get her out of this.

"Your father had agreed to this. There's no way out."

When she reached the table, I pulled out a chair, but she hesitated.

I pushed down firmly on her shoulders, forcing her to sit down at the antique table.

I stood behind her, my hands resting heavily on either side of her neck. I stooped down to be closer to her, inhaling the scent of her hair and noticing the damp tendrils that had escaped from her short ponytail.

I shoved the contract so that it was in front of her.

"Sign," I ordered.

She looked around at me; meeting my eyes, she took a deep swallow and quickly turned back to the table in front of her. "Look, I'm sorry for what happened and for firing a gun at you," she said slowly. "I understand that I shouldn't have done what I did. So, there's no need for you to insist on this marriage."

My fingers tightened around the back of her neck. "There's every point."

Her eyes remained glued to the table and contract in front of her. "I've apologized, so why do you even still want to go ahead with this?"

I bent down so that my mouth was right next to her throat. "I don't like being questioned." My lips almost pressed against her ear, making her close her eyes tightly as if to protect herself from me. "You won't question me again. You know, don't you, what curiosity killed...?"

"...the cat?" she finished in a whisper, her breaths shallow.

"Exactly. I'm not a patient man. Now sign."

Her slender fingers flexed as she picked up the pen.

After she had written her name in the required place, I reached into the pocket of my dark suit and pulled out a small, black velvet box.

Flicking open the hinged lid, I took out the diamond engagement ring, which was nestled in the satin lining.

Taking her wrist, I pulled her to her feet and tugged her hand toward me. Feeling the rapid flutter of her pulse under my fingers, I pushed the ring onto her finger.

Her eyes stared down at it. She looked confused, as if not knowing how to feel or what to say. Then she snatched her hand back and stepped around me to make her escape.

Before she could leave, I lifted an arm and pressed my large hand against the doorframe, barring her exit from the room. I wasn't finished with her yet. "You're to wear it at all times and never take it off. You're mine now."

"I'm not a possession."

I turned my body toward her and placed my free hand against the wall behind her, trapping her between my muscular arms. "You're mine now, and that ring proves it."

She exhaled and her heavy breaths filled the air as she pressed her back as far against the wall as she could, but there was nowhere for her to go. "I'll have to take it off when I shower," she retorted.

She watched my hand as I lifted it slowly to her face.

I caressed a thumb across her cheek and let my stare drop to her lips for a few long moments before flicking it back up to meet her eyes. "No, you won't," I said roughly. "When you're naked, whether in the shower or under me in bed, I'll still expect you to be wearing that ring."

She scowled at me, despite the deep blush rushing up her face.

Letting my hands drop from the doorframe and her face, I finally allowed her to squeeze past me and hurry up the staircase. I'd gotten what I'd needed from her—for now, at least.

CHAPTER 5

ANNUNCIATA

I finally escaped up to my room.

My blood rushed through my veins, hating how he'd stood so close to me, all six feet and four inches of him towering above my body.

I wouldn't admit it to anyone, but I found his whole presence intimidating, my body heating uncomfortably every time he was close.

As I stood under the refreshing shower in my attached bathroom, I looked down at the large ring on my finger. I had almost taken it off with my other jewelry as I'd undressed, but then his command ran through my mind, and I'd left it on.

I told myself that the huge diamond was tacky. If I hadn't been so reluctant to marry, however, I might have been able to admit that the design of the ring was, in fact, gorgeous, the shape of the Asscher-cut diamond lending a vintage look to it.

After shampooing my hair and washing my body, I got out of the shower and wrapped my white robe around me. As I stepped into my bedroom, a knock sounded at my door.

I opened it—to find Lorenzo standing there.

His large frame took an uninvited step into my room, making me take a hasty step backward.

"You can't be in here." My voice came out hoarsely as I tightened the belt of my robe and retreated to the other side of my bed. "It's not appropriate."

He ignored me, prowling further into my bedroom, taking a good look around himself.

I licked my dry lips. "I'll scream," I threatened.

"Your papà gave me his permission to be here so long as the door stays open. You're my fiancée now, so you're mine." His voice dripped with authority and dominance.

The air grew thicker, and the walls closed in around me. My bedroom suddenly seemed too small with him in the room. I didn't know what he wanted, and I couldn't get any more words out as he stalked across to the bed.

His gaze on me was heavy, burning my skin as his eyes coasted from my wet hair down to my bare legs and feet.

A shiver skated down my spine. I didn't know why his presence was so unnerving.

"I told him I would be confiscating this," he drawled, picking up my tennis dress from my bed. "Although I think I'll also take this and this." He picked up my discarded panties and bra, and running his fingers thoughtfully over the white lace.

Jesus, he'd just run his fingers over my panties.

I took a step toward him and tried to snatch them back from him, but he held them out of my reach.

He had a complete lack of boundaries, and his very presence was suffocating me. Trying to hide how flustered I was, I turned away from him and sat down at my vanity, picking up my hairbrush.

As I dragged the brush through my wet strands, my hand shook, and I prayed to God that he wouldn't notice.

Lorenzo silently came up behind me. He was wearing a fitted black suit, white dress shirt, and black tie. His clothes had been tailored to be a perfect fit for his tall, muscular body.

I held my breath as he lifted his fingers and ran them slowly over my hair. His lazy touch made my body flinch and my scalp tighten.

"Relax," he breathed, a low sound of satisfaction rumbling from him as his rough fingers trailed from my hair down the side of my damp throat, leaving a hot trail burning along my skin.

In the reflection of the mirror, I couldn't help watching his large, tanned hands, noticing how they led to strong wrists with a dusting of dark hair that disappeared into the sleeves of his dress shirt.

His touch was intimate—too intimate.

Every stare from him was too hot and too heavy. Heat ran up my neck and I couldn't breathe, his proximity stealing the air from my lungs.

"I like a woman to have long hair." His voice was smooth and smoky like a fine whiskey. "You won't have enough time to grow it by the wedding next month. Maybe you'll have to get hair extensions put in."

"Hair extensions?" I managed to get out. "I don't think so. Absolutely no way." I wasn't going to look like a blow-up Barbie doll for him or any other man.

His eyes caught mine in the reflection, his gaze like a predator who had just snared his prey. "You are my fiancée now. You've signed the contract, giving yourself over to me. You should want to please me."

My mouth gaped open. "If you make me get extensions, I'll shave my head before the wedding," I shot back at him as I smiled to myself, knowing that I'd got the last word in.

"I want your hair long enough to wrap around my fist when you're in bed with me," he replied in a low voice.

Jesus Christ. I sucked in a tight breath. And as his words made my core clench, I inwardly cursed at him.

He said nothing further, and I watched as he casually sauntered out of my bedroom.

After I managed to calm my racing pulse, I dried my hair and tried to keep my mind off what had just happened. Just the thought of it made it hard to breathe.

I looked through my make-up drawer. I normally didn't wear much make-up but chose mascara and a nude lip-gloss for the party.

I knew that Lorenzo would be expecting me to wear a dress tonight. I found many dresses too formal and tried to avoid wearing clothes that I felt were too prim and proper.

Looking through my closet, I decided upon a black dress with cap sleeves—I had customized it by hand since I enjoyed sewing. I completed my outfit with my favorite ballet flats, which were red and had small bows at the front.

I checked my reflection in the mirror. Unlike most of my family, who had dark hair, I took after my mother's side of the family with my blonde locks. To delay having to see Lorenzo, I decided to style my hair. I divided it into two and then twisted and pinned each section so that two small buns sat on top of my head.

When I couldn't put off going downstairs any longer, I gathered up my courage and headed downstairs.

LORENZO

As I waited in the drawing room for my fiancée while she finished getting ready, I checked e-mails on my phone and made a few calls.

I didn't really care about the length of my fiancée's hair. When I'd suggested hair extensions, it was more because I hoped that if she looked more like a stereotypical Mafia wife, then maybe she'd also act like one—instead of acting like a feisty, spoiled princess.

Although something about her defiance also made my loins stir... I couldn't wait to make her scream under me in my bed.

I fingered her lace panties which were tucked in pocket of my pants. And liking the feel of them, I decided that I might have to keep them close at hand.

I finally heard light footsteps running down the grand mahogany staircase, and a few moments later, Anni stepped into the drawing room.

I looked up from my phone. And my eyes traveled down her outfit.

She came to a stop in front of me, but I couldn't take my eyes off what she was wearing.

She had on a black dress which had red cat-shaped buttons down the front. But the worst thing was the red pockets on the front of her dress, each pocket being in the shape of a cat face.

No, the cat pockets weren't the worst thing—her hair was. It was in a style which resembled two fucking cat ears.

"What are you wearing?" I growled.

"A dress," she replied calmly.

"Why the hell does it have cat-face pockets on it? Can't you wear something more appropriate? You'll soon be my wife, and those clothes you're wearing are not how I'll expect you to dress."

"Look, I don't normally wear dresses, but I wore a dress tonight *for you*. If you prefer, you can give me back my tennis dress, and I'll wear that tonight instead."

"I've already burned it," I announced with satisfaction.

Her eyes widened. "Seriously?"

"Yeah. I used the kitchen stove."

"Well, you can't stop me from buying another tennis dress," she snapped.

I felt my muscles tense. "My mansion doesn't have a tennis court."

"Chicago must have plenty of public courts. I'll find one."

"No, you won't. I don't want to see you dressed like that ever again." My words whipped through the air. "That dress was not decent."

"You can't stop me from playing tennis or wearing what I want."

"Yes, I can," I gritted out. "I need *obedience*. And one way or another, I'm going to get it from you."

Her eyes sparked at me. "No, Lorenzo, what you need is *therapy*."

My mouth dropped open. But before I could respond, our discussion was interrupted by Anni's mother clomping into the hallway on very high heels.

"Your papà has already gone to the clubhouse," she said to Anni. "He was going to drive me there—I can't possibly walk there in these shoes." She looked at me expectantly.

I barely suppressed a sigh. "I can drive you," I said.

"What car do you drive?" Ma Veneti blurted out.

"Excuse me?"

"What. Car?" she repeated slowly, as she did an impression of a crazy person maneuvering a steering wheel.

"A Mercedes."

She snorted. "*Real* men drive Cadillacs," she said, her tone making clear that she was not impressed by my choice of vehicle.

In the hope of cutting short this ridiculous conversation, I ushered Anni and her mother out to my car.

As I drove the short distance to the clubhouse, I heard Ma Veneti sniff loudly. "Lorenzo, these leather seats smell dreadful. If you had a proper car, then it wouldn't have this smell."

"All leather smells the same," I gritted out, attempting to suppress my irritation with the woman.

I watched in the rear-view mirror as she crossed her arms over her chest. "Caddies don't smell bad like your car," she retorted.

I opened my mouth to argue but then clamped my lips shut, realizing that it was impossible to have a rational discussion with a lunatic.

When we arrived at the white-stucco clubhouse, we went inside, and Ma Veneti led us to our table in the middle of the room.

One half of the table was filled with Napoleone and other Veneti family members who were all wearing…*sombreros*? While the other half of the table was empty, obviously left for my side of the family.

We took our seats. Anni was by my side, and I looked at her, wondering what the hats were about; however, she was too busy putting on her own sombrero to notice my questioning looks.

I glared at Mr. and Mrs. Veneti. Those fucks hadn't said anything about having to wear goddamn sombreros tonight.

"Anni," I barked.

"Hmm?" she replied absently.

"What's with the hats?"

"Papà thought it would be nice to have our engagement coincide with the country club's monthly Mexican night."

"You have monthly Mexican nights?" I couldn't help my incredulous tone as I looked around at the clubhouse which was strewn with brightly colored papel picado.

"Yes. Papà loves Mexico."

Just then, my side of the family arrived. The Marchianos consulted the seating plan and then took their seats around tables across the clubhouse. I was joined at my table by various members of my family, including Marco, my mother, and my brother, Aloysius. Aloysius was a Captain in the Fratellanza; as well as being my brother, he was my right-hand man, and I could trust him with anything.

Next to Anni sat her parents, her two brothers, and her cousin, Benny.

The seating plan put equal numbers of people from the two families at each table. But with the Mexican hats all on one side, and all the empty heads on the other side of the table, the stark contrast made it impossible to claim ignorance that our families didn't really like one another.

I couldn't help but notice Anni's papà giving me a strange look when he realized that none of the Marchianos were donning the provided hats. I looked across at Marco, who looked as pissed as I was feeling.

"Anni, has your papà ever been to Mexico?" I asked carefully.

At that moment, a band struck up with lively Mexican music. "No. We can't go there on holiday obviously—you know, because of the Cartels and stuff."

So, Napoleone Veneti supposedly loved all things Mexican, even though he had never actually visited the fucking place. And he looked at my family like we were the crazy ones?

"When will you leave for your honeymoon in Italy?" Ma Veneti asked me, interrupting my thoughts.

"There's no time for a honeymoon."

"But our family always honeymoons in Italy," exclaimed my future mother-in-law.

"I'm too busy with the business."

Ma Veneti started bawling—extremely loudly.

I looked in horror toward her, wondering what I'd done to make her so distraught. My eyes flicked across to Anni, but she appeared unperturbed by her mother's behavior. "Anni?" I asked, wondering if she knew what was wrong.

"Ma wants us to go to Italy in a private jet so that we can bring her back more *credenze*," she responded casually, paying little attention to her mother. I racked my brain, finally remembering that this Italian word meant 'sideboards'.

She was crying about...sideboards?

I remembered when I was in the Veneti drawing room earlier, waiting for Anni. I had passed the time by counting the eleven sideboards in the room, their sheer number and large size giving the room a claustrophobic feel.

"Ma, you don't need any more credenze," Christian protested.

"But I do," she wailed. "I only have nine in our dining room!"

She was batshit crazy—I knew it. "Why don't you just get one shipped over?" My tone was terse. Her crying was getting on my nerves.

"No, they get s-s-seized by customs," she sobbed. "You know, when they get their sniffer d-d-dogs out. I still haven't got over that original 1970s credenza I lost two years ago!"

She'd completely lost me now. "Er, Fantasia, why would customs seize a sideboard?"

Anni sighed. "It was our cousin's fault."

"The problem with our family is how many fucking cousins we have and all the issues they cause," muttered Christian. "I spend all my time dealing with one *stupido* cousin after another, clearing up their shit and trying to put things right."

"Our cousin collected Ma's sideboard from the seller and delivered it to the freight shipping line in Naples," Anni explained. "What we didn't know was that he'd used the top of it to cut his lines of coke on..."

"Ma, I keep telling you," Christian interrupted, "we're in charge of all the ports in New York State now. We can get any credenza you want shipped in freight from Italy, and I'll make sure that it bypasses customs."

"Nooo," she bawled, "I *need* Annunciata to go to Italy and b-b-bring me back three more c-c-credenze on Lorenzo's private plane..."

Jesus, the woman was a loon. Who collected *sideboards*? And who needed so many in one house?

I wasn't sure how much more of this fucking family I could take.

CHAPTER 6

ANNUNCIATA

The celebratory meal was long and exhausting, and I was frustrated at having to keep quiet as per Ma's instructions.

Ma's cousins openly gawked at Lorenzo's good looks, annoying me with their lack of subtlety. You'd have thought at their age that they would have known better.

The Marchianos all looked miserable. Their Capo, Marco, looked like he'd rather cut off his right arm than actually try to enjoy himself. The Mexican food at the clubhouse was always delicious, and I really wasn't sure what their problem was.

We were having quesadillas for the second course, the soft corn tortillas filled with beef and cheese. As I ate, I looked around at the clubhouse, which had been decorated for Mexican Night with papel picado. The sheets of tissue paper were cut into intricate designs and their bright colors glowed around the room.

Lorenzo sat on my right-hand side, and I loathed that I had to be so close to him. His masculine scent seemed to surround me, his nearness making my skin prickle with unease.

As he reached for some more water, the sleeve of his dark suit brushed against me, the fabric feeling rough against my bare arm. My whole body felt oversensitive and hyperaware of each movement he made and every look he gave me.

As a distraction, I began to ask Lorenzo about his children. "How old did you say your children—"

But then Christian interrupted. "What the fuck?" he snapped, glaring at our cousin, Benny. "Why the fuck did you just kick me, Benny? Have you got a death wish?"

Benny looked sheepish. "I was trying to kick Anni like your ma told me to if she said anything."

I sighed. My cousin was such an idiot. If he couldn't even kick straight, what hope did he have with a gun?

I gave up trying to make conversation. Instead, I gave in to the thoughts that had been running through my head all evening. There was no way Lorenzo and me would ever manage to be friends and have a tolerable marriage. He wouldn't even put a fricking sombrero on his head. We had absolutely nothing in common.

I didn't want much out of a husband. I mean, I hadn't even asked him about his family, friends, GPA, hobbies, or criminal record. But the one thing I did want, and that was non-negotiable for me, was someone who wouldn't look down on my family and me.

I looked at him, his superior expression making it clear that he thought he was too good for our Mexican night. He also kept looking at Ma like she was a bit strange.

I just knew that I couldn't be married to a man like him, and I had to find a way to make him not want to marry me. The only way to do that would be to make it clear to him that I wasn't into this marriage idea as much as him—despite the contract that had been signed and the gigantic diamond rock he'd just given me.

***

Once the dinner was finally over, limoncello and more champagne were served in the outdoor area next to the pool, allowing people to mingle.

The night air was warm, and the outdoor lights made the water of the pool shimmer. It might have been romantic if I was actually happy to be marrying this man.

I spotted Lorenzo talking with his Capo. Not that he was difficult to find: I could sense his invasive gaze scorching me all evening, tracking me wherever I went, monitoring everyone I spoke to. His tall frame towered above most other people here; what really made him stand out, however, was the brooding aura that smoldered from him.

He replied to something Marco had just said to him, but his eyes remained on me as he spoke. I glanced down at the ring on my finger—it felt strange to be wearing it, especially as I rarely wore jewelry. I hated that he saw it as a sign of his ownership of me: just like a dog collar. What man in his right mind saw an engagement ring as a sign of owning someone? His ring, and his views, were beyond tacky.

I remembered again how he'd commanded me to never take it off, and how he'd told me earlier that he expected obedience from me...

If I took off my ring and 'lost' it on the very day he'd ordered me to never remove it, then that would definitely show him I was not a woman who would blindly obey him.

I discreetly slipped off my ring when Lorenzo wasn't watching me, dropping it into the pool. If this didn't make my refusal to obey him and my opposition to the marriage crystal clear, then nothing would.

Just then, I heard the sound system start up and looked over to see Benny on the turntables. He was wasted and had obviously decided to liven up the party.

As the opening beats of House of Pain's 'Jump Around' started, I walked over to where Lorenzo was standing, walking up behind him so that he didn't notice my approach.

"What's with the hellish music?" Lorenzo griped to Marco, finding yet another reason to find fault with this evening. "Doesn't anyone in this family have any taste?"

At that moment, Ma let out a loud screech as she caught sight of yet another one of her seven hundred cousins.

And I heard Lorenzo comment, "Christ—Ma Veneti and the whole fucking family are insufferable."

I cleared my throat and took another couple of steps forward, stopping in front of him. My face made it clear that I'd heard what he'd just said about my mother and family.

Noticing my scowl, he spoke to me. "You weren't supposed to hear that."

"That's okay then—you were only talking *behind our backs*."

I deliberately wrapped my ringless left hand around the stem of my champagne glass, so that my bare finger was facing him. Let's see how observant he actually was.

He began to speak again but stopped mid-sentence. "Where's your ring?" he said tersely.

"Oh, I think it dropped in the pool."

A muscle in his jaw tensed. "I told you to never take it off, so how did you manage that?"

"I was bored. I took it off and was fiddling with it and it dropped."

"Where?" he barked. Good, I could tell he was angry.

"Um, I can't remember," I said. "Somewhere over there." I waved vaguely to the huge pool, indicating the opposite end to where I had dropped it.

He marched over to the area I had pointed out, arching his neck to look into the water. "I can't see it," he snapped.

"Well, that's where I dropped it..."

I wondered how long I could drag this out for. His fury was growing by each second that went by. By the time he managed to find it, he would be well and truly raging—and that was exactly what I wanted.

And then I had an idea.

I pushed him.

Hard.

And ran for my life.

Hurrying away, I heard a large, satisfying splash and the echo of him spluttering and swearing.

As people noticed what had happened, I reveled in the combined gasp that reverberated around me.

I chuckled to myself in glee: *Take that, asshole,* my mind shouted, as I strutted a catwalk-style stride along the edge of the pool, drawing even more attention to my misdeed—and thus maximizing Lorenzo's humiliation.

He was so mad that there was absolutely no way he'd want to marry me now, I thought in triumph.

Ha! Take that, Mr. Lorenzo too-cool-for-a-sombrero Marchiano!

CHAPTER 7

LORENZO

I was raving mad. "This girl is not wife-material!"

We had abandoned the party and swiftly returned to the Veneti mansion. I was now standing in Napoleone's study, still dripping water from my expensive black suit and my handmade shoes squelching noisily with every movement. I hoped the chlorine from the pool water was ruining Napoleone's fucking antique rugs, I thought bitterly.

Marco stood next to me, also clearly pissed at the evening's turn of events.

It was clear as day that the girl's actions had been deliberate. First she'd shot at me, now she'd pushed me into a pool.

Anni and Ma Veneti stood on either side of Napoleone as he sat back in his leather chair behind his desk, acting as if nothing out of the ordinary had happened.

"Your daughter's behavior is unacceptable," I snarled, my hands clenched in tight fists. "She's obviously too young and too irresponsible to be a good wife and a mother to my children." What the hell had I been thinking agreeing to this bond?

"It was an accident," exclaimed Ma Veneti. "I saw it all with my own eyes—Annunciata was leaning over the pool and lost her balance, pushing into you."

I looked at Ma Veneti carefully as she gazed at me with her guileless eyes.

Had it been an accident? On the way back to the house, I had asked Marco what he thought, and he had said that even after witnessing it himself, it was impossible to say if it had been deliberate or an accident.

"Anni would *never* do such a thing deliberately," carried on Ma Veneti.

Perhaps I had been too rash? I unclenched my fists and rolled back my shoulders. "Accident or not," I said forcefully, "some people within the Fratellanza may still have their doubts. Therefore, your daughter's actions cannot go unpunished. The wedding is due to take place in two months. I suggest we move it up to two weeks' time; that should satisfy our people."

Marco nodded at my suggestion.

"Very well," Napoleone agreed. And upon hearing this, Anni's face dropped.

"Well," I said, trying to gather my shreds of dignity back together, "at least Annie Oakley here didn't pull a gun on me this time."

"It's Anni without an 'e'!" snapped my fiancée. She turned to her father. "Papà, why are you making me marry a man who can't even get my name right?"

My blood roared through my veins. Her reaction and words made me think the pool incident probably hadn't been an accident. The matter, however, had been settled now; we would marry in two weeks, the revised timeline being her punishment.

"Anni," her papà said tersely, making it clear that this was an end to the matter, "why don't you show Marco and Lorenzo out?"

"I'll be with you in a minute," Marco said to me, hanging back to discuss another matter with Napoleone.

Anni reluctantly complied with her papà's request and walked me to the front door.

As she opened the heavy oak door, I turned to face her. "You know pushing me into the pool was childish, right?"

"You know refusing to wear your sombrero was childish, right?" she said, mimicking my tone.

"Next time you try to push me into a pool, I'll drag you down into the water with me." My tone was harsh. "And don't think that I won't. Because know that I can't wait to see you *dripping wet* in front of me."

Her face fell at my last sentence—it was clear from my voice that I wanted to see her wet in more ways than one.

And I knew I'd got my point across.

Walking over to my car and opening the door, I sighed as I sank into the driver's seat.

The girl definitely had homicidal tendencies—she was a murderess wannabe. Rather than being an angel as her ma had claimed, I was beginning to think that the girl was, in fact, a hellcat.

CHAPTER 8

LORENZO

The last two weeks had sped by, and it was already the day of the wedding.

I stood at the front of the altar at St. Napoleone's—of course, Anni's papà had insisted on having the wedding at his namesake church.

I wore a black tux, as did my younger brother, Aloysius, who stood at my side. He was three years younger than me, and today he would act as my best man.

"Do you think she'll turn up?" Aloysius asked with a chuckle. He thought Anni's actions to date were hilarious.

"She will unless she has a death wish," I muttered.

Marco approached us. "I wish they would hurry this up," he gritted out. "I'm fed up of having to make pointless small talk with people I don't even like." His arms were crossed over his chest and he was scowling—he didn't even attempt to mask his body language, which shouted loud and clear that he was annoyed he even had to be here in the first place. "There better be a fuckable bridesmaid or two to relieve me of my boredom before this day is out, otherwise I'm going to have to shoot somebody."

"Screwing the Veneti virgins is hardly conducive to a good working relationship with the Imperiosi," I pointed out, but Marco clearly wasn't interested in my opinion.

I looked across at my children who sat with my mother in the pews. When, in my anger, I had brought forward the date of the wedding after the pool incident, I hadn't considered that it would give Clara and Clemente even less time to get used to the idea of it.

But then, no amount of time would ever be enough to allow them to get over the loss of their mother, particularly for Clara.

When I had sat the children down to explain that I was going to be getting married again, Clemente hadn't really understood. He was only two years old, and he soon became restless and bored with the conversation, running off to play as soon as he could, shouting, "Car, car!" He was obsessed with cars, and that was his favorite word at the moment.

Four-year-old Clara, on the other hand, had sat very still, looking even more lost than she normally looked.

I knew she'd been trying hard to understand what I was saying and what was happening. For the last few weeks, people kept saying to her that she was getting 'a new mom'. My own mother, in particular, kept repeating this, although I had asked her not to phrase it in such a manner—because every time someone said that, I could see that it drove home harshly to Clara that her mom had been ripped from their lives and was never coming back.

My mother was over the moon that I was getting remarried. She thought it was high time that I got over Rita and her betrayal, and she kept saying that I needed to overcome my anger for the sake of the children.

But just as I didn't think Clara would ever get over her grief, I knew that nothing would ever allow me to banish the anger that raged so fiercely inside me.

I watched Clara as she sat quietly. I couldn't look at her without guilt piercing my heart. She was wearing an off-white satin dress with a tiered skirt, while Clemente wore a blue and white sailor suit. Clemente was doing everything he could to try and get down from his grandmother's lap—he was an energetic toddler who was into everything and never sat still.

Ma Veneti scurried down the aisle and took her seat, and I knew this meant that my bride had arrived.

A hush descended over the guests as the music started up.

The Venetis had arranged all the music, including a string quartet, to play in the church. As the deep, soulful notes of the cellist rang out, I closed my eyes for a long moment. They were playing Johann Pachelbel's Canon in D—the tune to which Rita had walked down the aisle during my first wedding.

The Venetis couldn't have known this, but it still sent a shot of pain and bitterness through me. As the first violinist began the sweeter tones of the melody, I mentally shook myself out of my memories, banishing them to the recesses of my mind as I opened my eyes.

Then, as the second violinist joined in, flower girls appeared, scattering rose petals in front of them. They were closely followed by Anni's older sister and another girl, who entered as the third violinist began to play. They were the bridesmaids and were dressed in burgundy silk dresses.

I tried to let the sound of the quartet soothe me.

Then came the moment I had been waiting for, and all tension left my body as I saw my bride appear at the top of the aisle on the arm of her papà.

Anni looked absolutely exquisite, and, in that moment, she did look like an angel.

As she slowly made her way toward me, I couldn't take my eyes off her.

Her white dress was made of fine lace embroidered with small pearls. I ran my eyes up the full skirt, over her narrow waist, and then to the strapless fitted bodice. Her green eyes were solemn, and she had left her white-blonde hair down and it shone through her sheer veil.

Her lace neckline dipped into a 'v', emphasizing her shapely breasts and making my loins stir.

I couldn't wait to have her under me tonight, using my body inside hers. She wouldn't be able to disobey me then. It would be just me and her, all alone.

She carried a bouquet of burgundy flowers. As was the Italian tradition, I had sent the bouquet as a gift to my bride-to-be this morning.

Napoleone looked like he would burst with pride. He was very fond of his daughter, and I could tell by the way he looked at her that he loved her very much. That in itself was unusual for Made Men of his generation—they tended to keep their emotions hidden. The Venetis, however, seemed to do everything in their own way.

As she walked toward me, she kept her eyes straight ahead and avoided my gaze.

When they reached the altar, Napoleone slowly lifted her veil, revealing her face to me, and placed her small hand in mine.

She looked up at me, not flinching as I stared back at her. She was indeed beautiful, and I felt lucky to have her as my bride.

As I held her warm hand tightly within mine, the Catholic priest began the wedding ceremony.

"Lorenzo and Annunciata, have you come here to enter into marriage without coercion, freely and wholeheartedly?"

I replied, "I have," and then looked across at my bride.

She replied, "I have," and I gave a silent sigh of relief. At least the girl had some sense of self-preservation.

"Are you prepared, as you follow the path of marriage, to love and honor each other for as long as you both shall live? And are you prepared to accept children lovingly from God and to bring them up according to the law of Christ and his church?"

I replied, "I am."

"I am." Anni's voice was strong and firm.

"Since it is your intention to enter the covenant of holy matrimony, join your right hands, and declare your consent before God and his church," decreed the priest.

I turned to Anni to make my vows to her. "I, Lorenzo, take you, Annunciata, to be my wife. I promise to be true to you in good times and in bad, in sickness and in health. I will love you and honor you all the days of my life."

Then it was Anni's turn. "I, Annunciata, take you, Lorenzo, to be my husband. I promise to be true to you in good times and in bad, in sickness and in health. I will love you and honor you all the days of my life."

Hearing her say these words willingly made me think that perhaps our marriage could work and be a happy one.

The priest asked for the rings, and Aloysius passed me the wedding ring he was looking after.

I took Anni's band and slid it onto her finger. "Annunciata, receive this ring as a sign of my love and fidelity. In the name of the Father and of the Son and of the Holy Spirit."

Anni then took my wedding band and repeated the same words to me as she placed it on my finger.

When the priest announced that I could kiss my wife, I pulled her against my chest and pressed my lips against hers.

A small gasp escaped from her mouth as if she hadn't expected the kiss, and I let my warm breath caress her perfect lips.

As I pulled back, I looked deep into her eyes. My kiss had been hard and possessive. She was mine now, and I felt a sense of satisfaction surge within me, as well as the flames of desire stirring my loins.

The string quartet struck up Schubert's Ave Maria. As I held tightly onto Anni's hand, we turned to face the congregation and made our way back down the aisle.

Outside St. Napoleone's, we stood on the stone steps as people congratulated us, and the photographer snapped away.

"Congratulations, bro," said Marco, shaking my hand and giving a rare smile. "I'm happy for you, I really am."

I thought back to our previous conversation where he'd told me that my kids needed a mother. I'd known in my heart of hearts that he was right. "Hey, you're twenty-seven now, so you should be married soon as well."

"Yeah, we'll see," was all he said. He wasn't a man to be tied down—he was a cold, ruthless monster who lived for power and bloodshed.

Once the photographer had got what he needed, I put my arm around Anni. "Come. I'll drive us to the reception."

ANNUNCIATA

Lorenzo gripped my hip possessively and ushered me to his black Mercedes to drive me to the reception.

This would be our first opportunity to talk alone, I thought, but then Ma insisted on also traveling in the car with us. As Lorenzo drove us the very short distance to the Venetiville Country Club, Ma prattled on endlessly about how beautiful the service had been, not letting anyone else get a word in.

We reached the clubhouse, and as we walked inside, Lorenzo gave what sounded like a sigh of relief. "Thank God it's not Mexican-themed and there's not a fucking sombrero in sight."

Ma shot him a dirty look.

Jesus, he could be a real Prince Charmless.

We made our way to the head table, where we were seated with our closest family members. Lorenzo's mother, Cosima, was there, looking after the children.

Cosima got up as we approached, leading the children over by their hands. When they got nearer, Clara ran over to her father and Clemente followed her.

This was the first time that I was meeting the children. Although I'd been told that they had seen a photograph of me, Lorenzo had not brought them to the engagement party, thinking that it might have been too much, too soon. And, of course, my papà wouldn't let me go anywhere near Chicago until I was married.

"Clara, Clemente," Lorenzo said softly, "this is Annunciata."

"But you can call me Anni," I added quickly. Despite my long dress, I carefully crouched down to the height of the children. "Annunciata is such a long name to say, and most people call me Anni anyway."

Clara clung to her father's leg and used it to hide behind, peeking from behind it to get a glimpse of me. Even though she seemed to want to look at me, she only gazed at me briefly from the corner of her big, brown eyes—eyes that were the same color as her father's. She tightened her grip on Lorenzo's leg but said nothing.

"Say hello to your new mommy," Cosima said. I saw Lorenzo wince as he heard her refer to me as their new mom.

Clara remained silent while Clemente chuckled and shouted, "Car! Vroom, vroom!" He pointed to a car outside the window. I could tell that Clemente didn't really understand who I was.

Probably realizing that this was the best reaction we could expect from the children for now, Lorenzo gestured toward the table. "Why don't we all sit down?" he suggested in an attempt to ease the awkwardness.

Lorenzo gently removed Clara's hands from his legs and lifted her into a seat next to him, while I sat on his other side.

Soon after we sat, waiters arrived to serve champagne, along with antipasti consisting of a charcuterie board with Italian meats, cheeses, and breads. This was followed by the first course of seafood risotto. Each course was accompanied by fine wines and more champagne.

Cosima put food on the plates for the children, and Lorenzo encouraged them to eat, although they appeared to me to be a little overwhelmed by the occasion.

All too soon, it was time for the first dance, and as Lorenzo led me by my hand to the dancefloor, I thought to myself that this was the first opportunity I'd had today to talk to him without any of our family members around.

As the music started and he took me in his arms, his touch feeling too hot and my heart drumming too fast. He looked down at me. "You looked beautiful today, Anni."

"Thank you," I croaked out, slightly surprised to receive a compliment from him. Arranged marriages, by their very nature, were not a romantic scenario, particularly in the Mafia world.

The string quartet from the church was now accompanied by a pianist and was playing Hoppípolla by Sigur Rós. Fidella had chosen the music, saying that it was suitable for the occasion of our first dance as a married couple.

"You left your hair down," he remarked, raking his rich brown eyes slowly from my lips upward.

"To remind you that I haven't gotten, nor will I ever be getting, hair extensions." My voice was soft and without aggression as I let my body sink into his hold. His aura was intoxicating, his scent suffused with masculinity and power. The music was beautiful and uplifting...and it was hopeful. It made me think that things were maybe going to turn out okay.

One side of his lips quirked upward. "Your short hair is actually quite sexy." His words made my cheeks flush and my breasts heavy.

"Everything has gone well today." I spoke quickly, deliberately changing the subject. "Though the children have been rather quiet," I observed.

"It's a big change for them obviously," he said stiffly, "and it will take them a little while to adjust."

We remained silent for the rest of the dance, the flash of intimacy from a few moments ago disappearing as our conversation turned to the children.

I didn't find Lorenzo the easiest person to talk to—we hadn't exactly gotten off on the right foot. Added to this, I felt uncomfortable, sensing that everyone in the room was watching me, their eyes burning into me. Not only were they watching our first dance, but they were probably also gossiping about what would happen tonight: I would be expected to have sex with my new husband, and he would confirm to his family tomorrow that I had bled for him and had been a virgin.

If the marriage wasn't consummated, then it could be annulled. And an annulment would be a disaster, given that the marriage was a strategic business arrangement between the two families.

It was my duty as a Mafia daughter to consummate my marriage tonight, despite the fact that Lorenzo was practically a stranger to me.

Yes, he was good looking with his tall, dark looks and powerful demeanor. But that didn't mean I could forget everything that had happened and why this marriage had been insisted upon: to show the Fratellanza that I had been brought to heel by Lorenzo after daring to insult him.

CHAPTER 9

LORENZO

As the music ended, Anni's papà came over to claim her for the next dance.

I went over to my mother as it was my turn to dance with her now.

"I would love to dance with you, Lorenzo, but my hip is troubling me today," she said apologetically. "I'm afraid that I will have to sit this one out."

"No matter, Mother, you rest. The children have been keeping you on your toes. It just means that I will get my dance with Clara even sooner."

I looked across at Clara. "May I have the pleasure of dancing with my beautiful daughter?" I gave a mock bow and held out my hand to her.

She gave a slight nod, and placing her small hand in mine, I walked her to the center of the dance floor. She was tiny compared to my large frame, so I scooped her up and held her in my arms as I moved around to the music, causing her to giggle.

She had always loved music, and I could feel her small body relaxing into mine as the melody played around us. And then she rested her head on my shoulder, snuggling into the crook of my neck.

It wasn't often that she let me hold her like this. The only real time was at night when she'd wake up crying and would seek comfort from me. But then her cries would tear at my soul and eat away at my conscience, meaning that I couldn't enjoy her closeness.

When she was in my arms like this, I felt that I could protect her from everything—from all the bad things that had happened so far in her short life, to anything else that might threaten her in the future.

The music came to an end too quickly. I wanted to carry on holding her and dancing with her, but I knew I had my duties to fulfill. It was my turn to dance with Ma Veneti, and I could not insult the Imperiosi by ignoring her. I carried Clara back over to her grandmother, setting her in her chair and planting a kiss on the top of her dark curls. "Thank you so much for our dance, Clara. It's been the highlight of my day."

After Anni and I had danced with the required people, the main course was served. This was followed by more dancing and the remaining courses of salad, cheese and fruit, zeppole for dessert, then espresso and limoncello. It was a celebratory feast, and no expense had been spared by Napoleone.

Much of my time at the reception was consumed by business duties. Our alliance with the Imperiosi was in its infancy, and today was the perfect opportunity to talk business with several of Napoleone's men. Anni may have expected me to spend time with her, but business came first for me, and she would have to get used to that.

When the hour became late, I signaled to Marco and Aloysius that I was ready to make a move. I would be taking Anni to a nearby hotel for our wedding night.

I came up behind her chair and put my hands on her bare shoulders, making her flinch slightly.

"I didn't hear you come up behind me," she said in a breathy voice.

I bent my mouth down to her ear. "It's time for us to make our way to the hotel."

She avoided my eyes but gave a small nod.

I bent down and kissed the children. They were spending the next couple of days with their grandmother. Aloysius was taking our mother and the kids back to Chicago tonight, meaning that they would miss the brunch tomorrow, but I thought that the children had probably had enough by now. That, and the fact that I didn't like the children at too many large family gatherings like these: I didn't like the risk of them hearing salacious gossip about the demise of their mother.

Anni was hugged goodbye by her parents, sister, and various other members of her family, while her two older brothers shot threatening stares at me—silently warning me to treat their sister well tonight. They could go to hell as far as I was concerned. Anni was mine now, and I could do to her whatever I wished.

Once we were in my car, I switched on the radio to fill the silence. The sat-nav directed me to the hotel which Aloysius had hired out for our people. The Fratellanza had turned out in force to attend today's wedding, and from a security point of view, it was better to have us all staying in the same hotel and for that hotel to be hired out exclusively to us.

I stole a gaze at Anni. I could tell that my virgin bride was nervous.

I had been with a few women since Rita's death, but no one that I had been attracted to. I was, however, attracted to Anni. Her doe-like eyes, blonde hair, and perfect body, made me long to take her and derive pleasure from her body.

Her mother would have made sure that Anni knew what was expected of her tonight. I was already looking forward to making her submit to me and having her writhing body pinned underneath me in bed.

Arriving at the hotel, I checked us in, and we took the lift up to our room.

Using the keycard, I held the door open to allow Anni to enter first, her body brushing against mine as she went in.

The bedroom was decorated in dark, intimate tones. I put our bags down and went to the windows to close the drapes.

Anni stood in the middle of the room, looking unsure of what she should do. "Can I use the bathroom first to get ready?" she asked hesitantly.

I strode across to the champagne which awaited us. "Why don't you have a glass of champagne first? It will help to relax you."

"Um, maybe later. I'd like to freshen up first."

"Very well," I nodded. We had the whole night ahead of us, and there was no way that she could avoid the inevitable. She was my wife now, and she knew that she had to fulfill her marital duties tonight.

As I drank my champagne, I heard the shower run. My dick stirred again, imagining Anni's naked body in the shower. I would have preferred to have taken off her wedding dress myself, but no doubt she would wear a suitably sexy negligee that I could remove instead.

Finishing my champagne after answering some work messages on my phone, I heard the lock turn in the bathroom door. A moment later, Anni emerged, wearing a silk robe over her nightdress. She'd removed the light make-up she'd been wearing today, making her pretty face suddenly look younger.

I itched to rip her clothes from her body, but instead I handed her the champagne that I had poured for her. Refilling my drink, I clinked my crystal glass against hers and toasted us. "Here's to a wonderful night together."

She said nothing as she took a sip of her drink, her emerald eyes luminescent in her face.

I took a quick shower, and returning to the bedroom, I found Anni already lying in bed under the covers.

I switched off the overhead light but kept on the more subtle mood lighting in the room.

I was wearing only my boxer shorts. As I prowled to the side of the bed, Anni ran her gaze over my naked chest. She took in the tattoos covering my torso, plus the tattoo at the top of my left shoulder which depicted the symbol of the Fratellanza: a knife piercing a hand.

Her gaze moved down to the obvious bulge in my shorts before darting back up again, a faint blush coloring her cheeks.

Getting in, I propped myself up on one arm, and as I bent my head over her, I spoke to her in a low voice. "You look gorgeous tonight." I ran the back of my hand against her hair which hung loose around her neck. "I've been looking forward to being alone with you."

She didn't say anything but kept her eyes on mine as I spoke to her.

I pulled the sheet down, revealing her ivory nightdress to me. It was made from thin silk and had delicate spaghetti straps.

I moved my hand down to the sensitive skin at the tops of her breasts, just above the edge of her nightdress, enjoying the softness of her skin under my touch.

Slowly I bent my head to hers, watching her throat swallow as I moved my mouth toward hers.

Pressing against her luscious mouth, I suppressed a groan as I felt her take a sharp breath. She moved away slightly, but I brought my free hand up to the back of her head and grasped her short, silky hair to keep her in place.

Taking my time, I coaxed her lips until she opened her delicious mouth to me, and I inhaled the sweet sigh that escaped from her as she tilted her head upward.

Slipping my tongue inside, I stroked her tongue firmly, imagining how I would soon be using my tongue to caress her pussy lips and entice her wet juices from her core.

I ran my hands over her hot, silk-covered breasts, feeling her nipples harden under my fingers. I wanted my touch and my tongue to scorch every inch of her delectable body.

Her tongue started to surrender to me, the tip giving a small brush against my mouth. Her pupils were dilated from arousal and her breaths ragged.

I wanted her body, all the tension from the last few weeks making my body tight with need and coiled with desire. I pressed my rigid dick up against her stomach.

She reached up with her hands, giving me a small push against my chest.

My little virgin was being a tease.

I knew that once my fingers delved between her thighs, I would find her wet for me and needing my cock. I squeezed my fingers around her erect nipples, feeling them grow harder and bigger as she squirmed under me.

"No!" she panted, pushing me away harder and grabbing something from under her pillow.

She aimed a small canister of something at me, making me freeze.

My eyes widened. "Is that...?"

"...Pepper spray," she finished for me.

CHAPTER 10

LORENZO

My nostrils flared. "Where the hell did you get that?"

"Ma gave it to me in case you do anything I don't want. She knows I wouldn't be afraid to use it—even against a Made Man."

Her ma? That was the same woman who had looked at me with wide eyes and assured me that her daughter was 'an absolute angel', yet here she was, equipping her with a weapon to use against me.

"You know what's supposed to happen tonight?" I snapped.

When she didn't answer, I got out of bed and marched over to the dresser. Grabbing Anni's purse, I rummaged through it, thinking that she might have a gun as well, but thankfully found nothing else that could be used as a weapon.

I looked back at my feisty wife and scowled at her. "Why have you got pepper spray when you know how to shoot a gun?"

"Ma wanted to give me a gun for tonight, but Papà wouldn't let her. My dad thinks guns are dangerous," she shrugged, as if bringing a gun or pepper spray to your wedding night was completely normal.

I grasped her wrist tightly, and removing the spray from her hands, I confiscated it. "You'll end up hurting yourself with that," I spat.

"I'm not sleeping with you," she said firmly.

"You know I will be asked tomorrow to confirm that you were a virgin? I can't answer that if we haven't had sex."

"I'm sure it won't be the first time in your life you've had to lie." She turned her back to me, and turning off her nightstand lamp, she settled down to sleep.

Watching her, I could tell by the tension in her slim shoulders that she was worried that I might insist on my rights and try to force her.

I had never forced a woman in my life, and I wasn't about to start now.

I clenched my jaw. I would give the Fratellanza the answer they expected tomorrow, that Anni had been a virgin, preferring to lie to my own organization instead of being humiliated by Anni yet again.

CHAPTER 11

ANNUNCIATA

It was the next morning. I was tired after yesterday's long day, and I hadn't slept well last night. It was the first time I had slept in the same bed as a man, and I had sensed every sound and movement from him during the night, not to mention the angry waves coming off him after I'd refused to have sex with him.

It would have been easy to give in to the fact that he was insanely handsome and had the perfect body. But we were strangers. And irrespective of our customs and traditions, I wanted to know something about a man before I slept with him.

Lorenzo and I didn't speak much as we got ready, although he didn't hesitate to glare at me when he saw that I was wearing white pants with a pale pink silk camisole top.

"Don't you have a *dress* that you can wear?"

It was clear that he expected me to dress like a typical Mafia wife. "I prefer this outfit," I shrugged.

He scowled in response but said nothing further.

We met my family back in Venetiville so that I could say my goodbyes. The Marchianos were also present since their Capo, Marco, would ask Lorenzo to confirm that I had been a virgin for him.

When we walked into the clubhouse, my family greeted me, led by Ma and Fidella.

"How did you find last night?" asked Fidella when we had a moment to ourselves.

"It was fine." I couldn't really talk about it with so many people about.

"Really?" she asked, looking at me with concern.

"It was as fine as it could have been," I shrugged, not knowing what else I could say about something that hadn't actually happened.

Her voice was quiet. "He didn't do anything you didn't want, did he?"

"No, he didn't." At least that was one thing I could be truthful about.

When asked, Lorenzo confirmed that I had been a virgin for him. This was technically the truth—it's just that I shouldn't *still* have been a virgin this morning.

I looked around the clubhouse, recalling all the good times I'd enjoyed here: family functions, Mexican nights, tennis, and swimming with friends from other Imperiosi families.

I wasn't looking forward to moving to Chicago. I was really going to miss Venetiville and Staten Island. This was the only home I'd ever known.

Some people referred to Staten Island as New York's 'forgotten borough'—it was the third largest of the boroughs in terms of land size, yet also the least populated. That's what gave it so much room for family homes and green spaces. Papà liked it here and thought it a good place to raise a family, particularly since attitudes were more conservative here than in the other boroughs.

Venetiville was located within the Todt Hill neighborhood, and the mansions had stunning views since this part of the island was over 400 feet above sea level. The Imperiosi families also benefitted from a high degree of privacy here, as our gated community was secluded and self-sufficient. My childhood in Venetiville had always felt safe, privileged and happy.

I remembered when I'd first been considered old enough to take the Staten Island ferry without my parents—although I'd still needed to take one of my brothers or cousins as a bodyguard. As a child, I'd always loved going to the St. George Ferry Terminal to make the thirty-minute trip to the Whitehall Terminal in Lower Manhattan. There were so many fond memories of time spent at other local places too, like Staten Island Zoo and Silver Lake Park.

I knew that some people might find my family to be a little loud or over-the-top, but they were warm, generous, and loving people.

Lorenzo was the complete opposite: cold, brooding, and unforgiving.

At least Lorenzo now knew I wasn't going to just roll over and be a subservient wife to him. Although I was under no illusions about the challenges I would face. An arranged marriage was one thing; but an arranged marriage to a widower, who also had two kids, and who lived hundreds of miles away in a different state, was a whole other ballgame.

As I said goodbye to my family, I couldn't hold back my tears. Ma, Fidella and Aunt Priscilla were inconsolable. And, although Papà kept on his business mask, I knew from the way he hugged me very tightly that he was going to miss me too.

I wished that I'd been able to marry someone here in New York so that I could have stayed close to my family, just as Fidella had. Instead, I was going to be alone, without family or friends, in a strange city, among people who had until recently been an enemy of the Imperiosi.

After the goodbyes were complete, Lorenzo drove us to a private airfield from where we would board a Fratellanza jet. As we crossed the Verrazzano-Narrows Bridge, I resisted the urge to look over my shoulder at Staten Island as I left it behind. I had crossed this bridge so many times, but today's journey felt so final.

By the time we arrived at the airfield, I was feeling somewhat calmer. I told myself that I had to be strong to get through what lay ahead.

The jet was fueled and ready for our journey, and already on board were Marco and some other members of the Marchiano family. Lorenzo ushered me to a seat and then sat down next to me.

The flight was only three hours, but sitting on the plane next to a virtual stranger made it seem much longer.

After eating supper on the plane, we arrived in Chicago at 7 p.m.

Lorenzo and I said goodbye to the other family members and took one of the waiting cars for Lorenzo to drive us to his mansion.

After sitting in silence for the first fifteen minutes of the drive, I switched on the car radio and flicked through the stations until settling on one I liked.

Lorenzo took his dark eyes off the road for a moment to glance over at me. "What on earth are you listening to?"

I frowned. "It's a country and western station."

"But you're from *Staten Island*."

I looked across at him as he scowled at me. "So?"

"So, you come from a family of murderers—why in God's name would you want to spend your time listening to wailing cowboys?"

I took a deep breath. "It's good for my soul. You should try it sometime," I said pointedly to him.

"Christ," he muttered, "this must be some more Staten Island shit I don't understand."

Ignoring him, I sat back in my seat and let the music wash over me.

However, after listening to the soothing music for only another sixty seconds, Lorenzo snapped the radio over to the 24-hour news station.

I sighed. He was just like all Made Men: if he wasn't murdering someone, he had to, at the very least, be listening to how someone else had been killed. He could really do with chilling out a bit.

CHAPTER 12

LORENZO

We pulled up outside my mansion in the late evening. I was glad to be home and to have all the wedding frivolities over with. All I wanted was to get back to my work.

My housekeeper greeted us at the door.

I addressed Anni. "This is my housekeeper, Adelina. She will show you to our bedroom. The soldiers will be here in a few minutes with your belongings."

Anni's things had been packed in numerous bags and boxes, and they had been loaded onto our jet before we left New York.

"You can unpack and then go to bed whenever you want. Don't wait up for me—I have work matters to see to."

Anni looked surprised, but I turned on my heel and left her to it, not wanting to engage in further conversation. The children would be with their grandmother until tomorrow. My mother had thought I'd enjoy some time alone with my new wife to get to know her, but after her behavior last night, I just wanted to immerse myself in my work and occupy my mind with something other than her and this marriage. At least with my work, I was in total control, and none of my men dared to defy me.

Half an hour later, a soldier at the gate rang my cell as I worked at my desk in my study.

"Boss, Fantasia Veneti has just arrived."

I paused for a moment in confusion. "What do you mean?" I barked.

"Um, apparently, she's just flown here in the Veneti's private jet, and one of the Veneti soldiers has just driven her here from the airfield."

"Ask her what the fuck she wants," I ordered. We'd only left Staten Island today—it was far too soon for a visit from the in-laws.

I heard my soldier ask her the purpose of her visit in words more polite than I had just used. I hoped to God that she wasn't going to be one of those clinging mothers who couldn't bear to let her darling daughter go.

"Boss, she says she's got some things to drop off for her daughter."

We'd only be home for less than an hour and already the fucking Venetis were all over us. I clenched my jaw. "Let her in." I would have liked to have refused her entry, but she was my mother-in-law now and we did need to preserve the alliance with her husband.

Sitting in my study, which was located at the front of the house, I heard the Veneti car pull up outside the house.

But after a minute, the doorbell still hadn't rung.

Standing up to look out of the study window, I could see Ma Veneti loitering on my front doorstep, upon which a Veneti soldier had just unloaded six boxes.

I exited my study and strode to the front door.

As soon as I opened the door to the woman, she ran back down the front path and jumped into the vehicle driven by the Veneti soldier. I'd never seen her move so fast.

"What are you doing?" I called out to Ma Veneti. "Aren't you coming in?"

"I'm just dropping off some more of Anni's clothes!" she shrieked. Why did she have to be so fucking loud all the time? "I told Anni I'd bring them to Chicago for her because they probably wouldn't fit on the plane!"

"But I've got a private jet," I answered in bewilderment as the Veneti car sped away with screeching tires. Surely she must have realized that I had plenty of room for another six boxes?

I sighed, looking down at the boxes. How many more clothes did one girl need? And why the hell didn't she just bring them on my plane today instead of getting her mother to make a special trip on the Veneti's jet? I would never understand my wife or her crazy family.

I heard Anni's footsteps behind me as she came to see who was at the door. "I thought I just heard my mother…?"

"She's just delivered these boxes for you," I sighed. "She said that they're more of your clothes."

Anni frowned at me. "You didn't invite her in?" Her tone was distinctly accusing.

"She seemed to be in a rush. I don't know why you couldn't have just brought these boxes on my jet." As I began to pick up the boxes, one burst open. "What the hell…?"

Two furry white ears and two glaring blue eyes burst out of the box.

As I looked down at it in disbelief, Anni's face lit up. And I realized that the box did not contain more of Anni's *clothes*, as claimed by Ma Veneti—not unless Anni bred creatures to make into fur coats for herself.

I was beginning to think that Ma Veneti might have problems with the definition of 'the truth'.

"Fuck me!" I exclaimed. "It's that cat!"

Anni rolled her eyes as she scooped up the animal into her arms. "You haven't been formally introduced. This is Wilbur."

"Yeah, I remember him. He was the reason you shot me the second time." The creature had white fur, a round face, and intense eyes. "Why have you given him a human name? He's an animal, for God's sake."

"He's my best friend."

"He's a cat," I replied bluntly.

"Yes, I know. But that doesn't mean he can't be my best friend as well." She looked back down at the animal. "Wilbur, show how lovely and friendly you are by saying 'meow' to Lorenzo."

The creature was resolutely silent as it looked disdainfully at me before flicking its head away and licking its large fluffy paw.

Oblivious to her pet's overt hostility toward me, Anni turned her attention to opening the other boxes. My nostrils flared as I watched the contents being taken out. The boxes contained beds, baskets, bowls, toys, and a multitude of what I guessed could only be various other feline paraphernalia.

"Those items are certainly not clothes. For fuck's sake, your fucking ma is a pathological liar," I spat. "And no one ever said that you were bringing a pet with you."

"Well, technically, he's our family cat. My papà got him for all of us."

"So why is he here now instead of in Venetiville?"

Anni shrugged. "I guess Ma thought he'd prefer being with me in Chicago. Wasn't it sweet of her to think of me and come all this way to bring Wilbur here?"

"Sweet isn't the word that comes to mind," I retorted.

I watched while she fussed over the animal, still smarting over her rejection of me last night. Jesus fucking Christ. I was a King of Chicago, while he was a mere fucking cat—but she still preferred him over me.

"Just make sure it doesn't shit on my rugs," I gritted out. "And keep that stupid creature away from me."

Anni narrowed her gaze at me. "That won't be hard. He doesn't like people who are rude and charmless."

***

After our wedding night, I was in no hurry to go to bed. After delaying for as long as possible in the hope that Anni would already be asleep, I finally went up to bed at around midnight.

Walking into the master bedroom, I was glad to see that Anni was already asleep and her cat was nowhere in sight. Adelina had told me before retiring for the night that Anni had put the cat to sleep in the kitchen.

What I wasn't happy about, though, was that Anni was asleep on my side of the bed.

I knew I shouldn't disturb her, but I really couldn't sleep unless I was on the right side of the bed.

Closing the bedroom door, I padded over to the bed. So as not to disturb her, I didn't turn on the light. After undressing down to my boxers, I gently shook her shoulder. She was wearing another silk nightdress with thin straps, and as I shook her, I felt her soft skin under my touch.

"Hmm?" she said sleepily in a husky voice that stirred my desire for her.

Her blonde hair was tousled sexily over around her face and her lips pouted in her drowsy state. The comforter was gathered around her waist and I could see her nipples pebbled hard under her silky gown in the cool night air.

One thin strap had fallen off her shoulder, exposing the top half of her full breast, although it wasn't enough to give me a glimpse of the tantalizing erect nipple that teased me from underneath the silk.

I couldn't help wondering how short her nightdress was and what lay under it.

"Shift over to the other side of the bed," I growled in a low voice.

Still half-asleep, she didn't open her eyes. She rolled across, making her nightdress inadvertently ride up her thighs and giving me a flash of the matching panties she wore underneath.

After the taste I'd gotten of her mouth on our wedding night, my tongue desired something else now...her sweet pussy.

My fingers itched to rip off her silky panties and then force her thighs apart with my hands, exposing her folds and slit for my eyes to feast upon.

My mouth watered as I thought about having my tongue lap at her wet juices, at making her squirm under me, and at having her beg for me to make her cum. I would love to see her begging me—to have her under my control, her desire dependent on what I was willing to grant her.

Would I let her come on my tongue? Or would her first orgasm from me be at the pounding of my thick cock inside her untouched, virgin pussy, drilling deep into her until her tight channel spasmed around my erection and milked it of every last drop of my cum? There was something primal about the thought of pinning her down on my bed and coating the slick walls of her pussy with my seed—and it made my aching dick even harder as I watched her.

I looked back up at her face.

She had fallen back asleep almost instantly, much to my frustration.

I could have woken her and demanded my marital rights—demanded the virgin blood she had refused to give me last night. But she looked exhausted after all the wedding festivities, and I resolved to wait just a little longer to take her and make her mine. I'd never forced a woman before, and I would wait until Anni wanted me just as much as I wanted her.

I had never been with a virgin before, and just thinking about being the first man inside her wet pussy was chasing away any thoughts of sleep. Adjusting my rigid dick, I climbed into the space she had vacated in my bed, looking forward to sleeping in my own bed again.

I turned over onto my side, my back toward Anni. And as soon as I got comfortable, my eyes caught a glimpse of something different beside me.

Looking more carefully, I saw that she'd put a framed picture on my nightstand—a framed picture of Wilbur.

That fucking cat's face was staring right at me—and he had what could only be described as a self-satisfied grin in the photo.

Sitting up quickly, I snatched up the framed photo of Wilbur and slammed it facedown onto the nightstand. First thing tomorrow morning, I thought, I would shift it to her side of the bed.

Then, closing my eyes tightly, I tried to shut out the smirking face of that cat and attempted to ignore my aching dick as I willed sleep to come to me.

CHAPTER 13

ANNUNCIATA

I slowly opened my eyes, the feel of the strange bed and comforter reminding me that I was in my new home.

I quickly looked around but Lorenzo wasn't here, although I could still smell his scent on the sheets. Sitting up in bed, I realized I was on the opposite side of the bed from where I had fallen asleep.

I vaguely remembered Lorenzo waking me last night to tell me to move to the other side of the bed. I looked over to his nightstand and noticed that my photo frame of Wilbur was face down on its polished top. Crawling over to his side of the bed, I picked up the frame and moved it onto my nightstand.

Was this the bedroom that he'd shared with his first wife? I'd planned on asking him this when he came to bed, but I must have fallen asleep before that.

Standing up from the bed, I walked over to the drapes, drawing them open to let the sun stream in.

Since arriving here last night, I had barely seen my husband. As I looked down at the view of the gardens, I wondered if this was how my marriage would be: Lorenzo avoiding me as much as possible. I imagined that the only thing we would have in common would be the children.

I showered in the attached bathroom and then entered the walk-in closet where my bags and boxes had been left last night. I had only opened a couple of my bags so far and would have to do the rest of my unpacking today. That would keep me occupied until the children arrived home tonight. Adelina had told me that Clara and Clemente would arrive home from their grandmother's just before dinner.

I picked out an outfit, settling on jeans and a brightly colored red boho top fringed with white tassels. I knew Lorenzo had told me that he wanted me to wear clothing suitable for a Mafia wife, but I wasn't a doll that he could dress up. I wasn't going to change who I was and what I looked like just to please him.

I went down downstairs to the dining room, where I saw a place had been laid at one end of the table, while at the other end of the table was a discarded newspaper which Lorenzo had obviously left behind. He must have eaten already, I thought. It would have been nice to have at least have breakfast together so that I could find out if there was anything I needed to do today to prepare for the children's arrival later.

I made my way to the kitchen to find Adelina and Wilbur.

Upon entering the kitchen, Wilbur scampered up to me and wrapped his soft body around my legs. At least he was glad to see me.

"Good morning, Adelina," I said in greeting to the housekeeper who stood in front of the sink. She was a motherly looking woman who I guessed to be in her fifties. She wore a formal black dress covered with a white apron, and her dark hair, which was liberally streaked with gray, was held back in a neat bun at the nape of her neck.

"Good morning, Mrs. Marchiano. I hope you slept well."

"Yes, thank you, I did. And you must call me Anni."

"No, ma'am, that wouldn't be right. But perhaps I will call you Mrs. Anni." She nervously fiddled with her apron. "I'm afraid Mr. Lorenzo has already eaten his breakfast," she said apologetically. Even she realized that a newly married couple should have breakfast together.

"He must have gotten up early."

"And I haven't fed your cat yet. I didn't know what I should give him, and I didn't want to feed him the wrong thing."

"That's okay, Adelina. I've brought down some of his cat food with me. It was in one of the boxes that my ma delivered yesterday. I bet he's been pestering you non-stop for food."

"He's been rubbing against my legs for the last hour." Adelina gave a warm smile. "But I don't mind. He has such beautiful fur. What sort of cat is he?"

"He's a British Shorthair."

"I used to have a cat when I was a girl. This one," she said, bending down to scratch between his ears, "really is a handsome boy."

"Isn't he just?" I said, proudly looking down at him as he stretched his neck toward his new admirer.

"His fur is as white as snow," carried on Adelina, "and those big blue eyes of his are so unusual."

After Adelina had shown me where various things were kept around the kitchen and I'd fed Wilbur, she insisted that I go back to the dining room and that she'd serve me breakfast there. "Mr. Lorenzo won't like you eating in the kitchen," she advised.

After a breakfast of muesli, toast, and coffee, I went to see Lorenzo. Approaching his study, I took a deep breath, knocked, and then slipped inside.

After looking up only very briefly from his papers, Lorenzo addressed me. "What do you need?"

"I thought that perhaps you could show me around the house and property?" I suggested.

"I'm not a tour guide."

"I just thought—" I began.

"If you need anything, ask Adelina. That's what she's here for. I've already had to take two days off because of this whole wedding thing—and work has piled up while I've been gone." His manner made it clear that he thought the wedding had been an inconvenience. "I have urgent matters that need to be dealt with. I don't have time for domestic trivialities."

Not knowing what else to say, I left his study, closing the door behind me.

I went and found Adelina, and she was more than happy to show me around the house and grounds.

"The house is beautiful," I commented as I looked at the various rooms.

"Mrs. Rita decorated it when she and Mr. Lorenzo first married." Adelina flushed as she mentioned Lorenzo's first wife.

"How long have you worked here?"

"I was hired by Mrs. Rita when she arrived here after her wedding. I'm not really supposed to talk about her though," she said in a hurried tone.

"That's okay," I said, not wanting my questions to make her feel uncomfortable.

"Let me show you the children's bedroom," Adelina offered. "Clara and Clemente still share a bedroom. Mr. Lorenzo thought Clara was old enough for her own bedroom a couple of months ago; he tried to move her into her own room, but she was so upset that he had to move her back into here."

The bedroom was painted in a pretty cream color and contained two beds as well as a plethora of toys. Clara's side had lots of stuffed toys, while Clemente's side was full of cars and other toy vehicles.

As we walked around, I thought how Lorenzo was treating me like a stranger, not like a wife. I hoped that things would improve once the children arrived back. They needed something better than a cold, hostile environment around them.

Adelina then took me outside—and as well as the lovely gardens, there was also a tennis court.

I pursed my lips. Lorenzo had obviously been lying when he'd told me that there was no tennis court at his mansion.

After my tour of the house was complete, I realized that I hadn't seen a single photo of Lorenzo's first wife—not even in the children's bedroom.

And that, I thought to myself, was very strange.

CHAPTER 14

LORENZO

Although it was only Anni's second day in my home, I needed to focus on my work. Being away for just a couple of days had meant that work had started to pile up, and, in all honesty, I found it a welcome distraction.

Whenever I thought about my wedding night, I felt anger stir within me. I hadn't been able to take Anni last night, and that had made my frustration build further.

I had gotten up early and spent the entire day holed up in my study, even having Adelina bring my lunch in here. But damnit, despite my best efforts to concentrate on business, my thoughts kept wandering to Anni. Sleeping next to her last night without touching her had been torturous.

Just before dinner, the soldiers at the gate called my cell to let me know that my mother had arrived with the children.

I went to the door to greet them.

"Mother," I said, kissing her cheek. Clara and Clemente ran into my outstretched arms for a hug. "Black car!" Clemente shouted, pointing to the car he'd just ridden in, while Clara stayed quiet, happy just to feel my arms around her. As usual, she was wearing her favorite blue dress, although it was getting a bit shabby and small now.

"Thank you for having the children, Mother; I really appreciate it."

"You know I love having them, Lorenzo. And you needed some time alone with your new wife, of course. I hope things are going well with her?"

"Things are fine," I replied. "Adelina has dinner ready," I said, deliberately changing the subject. My mother didn't need to know that this marriage looked like it was going to be just as much of a disaster as my first one. "Why don't you join us?"

"That's kind of you, Lorenzo. But I'm rather tired after looking after these two, so I think I'll just head home."

After saying goodbye, I took the children into the dining room where Adelina was bringing in the food.

Upon seeing Anni, Clara shrunk back.

"Hello Clemente, hello Clara," said Anni gently.

Clemente smiled up at Anni as he ran past her to his seat at the table. Clara, however, tried to hide herself behind my body.

I looked down at my daughter. "It's okay, Clara. You remember Anni from the wedding, don't you?"

Clara gave a hesitant nod.

"Anni is going to live here with us now and help look after you."

Clara still looked doubtful but let me lead her to her seat.

I sat at the head of the table, with one child on either side of me, while Anni sat on the other side of Clemente.

Adelina had made a pasta dish with a ham and cream sauce, knowing that this would suit both the adults and children. However, Clara refused to even touch the food on her plate, while Clemente was happy to pick up his food but kept throwing it onto the floor.

"Clemente, stop playing with your food," I admonished, fast losing patience with his antics.

Anni kept throwing glances at the children, but she made no effort to encourage them to eat.

"Clara, why don't you try some of your pasta?" I suggested. "You've liked it before when Adelina's cooked it." My words were in vain though, as Clara continued to refuse to eat.

There was a knock at the dining room door and a soldier popped his head around. "Sorry to disturb you, boss, but the Capo is on the phone for you."

"I'll have to take this call." I looked at Anni as I walked to the door. "Can you get the children to eat their dinner," I said as I headed to my study where I had left my cell phone.

After discussing with Marco an issue that had come up, I returned twenty minutes later to the dining room expecting to see that everyone had finished eating. What I came back to, however, was to see Clemente had most of his food on the floor while Clara still hadn't touched a morsel from her plate.

"Haven't you got the children to eat their dinner yet?" I tried to swallow down my frustration over the fact that the kids, especially Clara, weren't eating enough.

"I tried, but I don't think they're hungry."

"My mother told me they haven't eaten anything since lunchtime."

While I was talking to Anni, Clemente used my distraction to slip out of his seat and run away to play.

Clara didn't say anything but looked up at me expectantly. Her food would all be cold by now anyway, so I gave her a nod, and she slipped silently out of her chair and scampered away.

"If they were hungry, they probably would have eaten their meal," reasoned Anni.

"Everyone knows that children usually have to be coaxed into eating." As I spoke, I let out a frustrated sigh. I got the distinct impression that Anni had a lot to learn about raising children.

CHAPTER 15

ANNUNCIATA

I looked at Lorenzo's retreating back as he strode out of the dining room.

Then I heard Lorenzo talking to the children, telling them it was time for a bath and then bed.

Walking into the den where the children were playing, I spoke to Lorenzo. "Can I help?"

"Have you ever bathed a child and done their bedtime?"

"No..."

He sighed.

"But I'm willing to learn," I said firmly, determined to start learning my new role.

I stood back but watched intently as Lorenzo saw to the children's bath time. Clara and Clemente shared a bath, and once they were clean, Lorenzo got them dressed in their pajamas. Clara's were pale pink and decorated with unicorns, while Clemente's pj's were Superman-themed, although both children took some convincing to get dressed.

Finally, having gotten them clean and dressed for bed, Lorenzo went to pick a story from their shared bookshelf.

"Panda book?" asked Clara hopefully.

He raised an eyebrow. "Again?"

She nodded solemnly.

"Of course, mia preziosa." *My precious.* He gave a special smile to his little girl before he opened the book and started to read them a story about a panda who was celebrating her birthday by having a party with her friends.

Lorenzo was sitting on Clara's bed, and both children were pressed up against him, leaning against his lap to look at the pictures in the storybook.

I sat in the rocking chair and gave a small smile as I listened to the sweet story and saw how engrossed both children were. Lorenzo surprised me with his patience. I would have taken him for the type to skip pages so that he could get to the end quicker, but instead he took his time to read the story properly and even did voices for all the characters.

When both children started to fall asleep, he got them into bed, carefully tucked the covers around their small bodies, and gave them a gentle kiss on their foreheads. Before leaving them to sleep, he took one final, contemplative look at them from the doorway and then quietly tiptoed out of the room.

Whatever my feelings about Lorenzo, I could see that he truly loved his children, and that somewhere in his icy chest, he had a heart that beat more softly for those he cared about. When he was with his children, I got a glimpse of the real man rather than the cold, cruel Underboss. And seeing what a good father he was made something inside me warm toward him.

Standing in the upstairs hallway, I waited until Lorenzo had closed their bedroom door before speaking to him. "Is there anything else that needs to be done for the children tonight?"

"No. You can relax or go to bed. I've got work to do."

I watched him walk down the stairs and toward his study.

I know he was disappointed that I wasn't more experienced with child-rearing. I sighed. Perhaps tomorrow would be better: it would be my first full day with Clara and Clemente, and I would use the time to get to know them better.

With nothing else to do, I decided to run myself a hot bath and then watch some TV in the bedroom.

Later, when Lorenzo came up and joined me in bed, I switched off the TV and turned toward him, although I tried to avert my eyes as he stripped and pulled on a pair of sweatpants. "I've been thinking and I've decided that I'll call Ma tomorrow and ask her for some child-rearing advice."

Lorenzo scowled at me. "I don't think your ma—"

"I know that she may not be your favorite person right now," I interrupted, "but she has raised four children of her own and should be able to give me some tips. I'll also call Fidella and get some advice from her too."

Without saying anything further, he turned away from me and switched off his nightstand lamp, plunging us into darkness.

As I looked at his back, I thought that at least his bad mood meant that it looked like he wasn't going to try to have sex with me tonight.

I must have been tired because I fell asleep in no time.

Sometime much later, I startled awake to find Lorenzo getting out of bed. "What's the matter," I said sleepily.

"Clara's awake," he said, as I heard a soft cry.

Then another cry sounded, different in pitch to the first cry I'd heard.

"And she's woken up Clemente now as well," Lorenzo sighed. "This is usually what happens every night at least once, if not twice."

I couldn't stop staring at his bare chest and the gray sweatpants that hung low on his hips. My gaze trailed over his defined muscles and the tattoos covering his upper body, making a languid heat spread through my veins. He was handsome when he was dressed in one of his dark business suits, but he was a hundred degrees of hot when he was half-naked.

"Should I get up?" I asked, not knowing what he expected of me. "I want to help."

"Stay here and I'll bring Clara into you."

I lay back against my pillow, watching the muscles in his back flex as he walked out of the room.

A couple minutes later he returned, clutching Clara to his tattooed chest. He bent down and put her on the bed next to me.

"Is she going to sleep here?" I asked in confusion.

"Yes, that's the only way she'll get back to sleep. I'll go take care of Clemente and get him back down. You look after Clara and get her back to sleep."

He walked away before I could ask what I should do to get her to sleep.

Chewing on my lower lip, I gazed at the little girl in bed next to me. "What normally helps to get you back to sleep, Clara?"

I waited for an answer, but she didn't say anything.

I wondered whether I should tell her a story. That had worked for Lorenzo earlier. We didn't have any storybooks in the master bedroom, and I didn't want to go back into the children's bedroom and potentially disturb Clemente when Lorenzo was trying to get him off to sleep, so I decided just to make up a story myself and tell that to Clara.

After thinking for a bit, I decided to tell her a story about a little girl who got a pet cat, basing it on my own story of how I got Wilbur.

By the end of the story, Clara had listened intently to everything, but her eyes were resolutely fighting sleep.

"Do you think that maybe you want to try to shut your eyes and try to sleep now?"

She shook her head, and I noticed that she kept looking toward the door, just as she'd been doing while I'd been telling her the story. It was as if she were waiting for her father to come back.

We lay there next to each other, and I watched her, but she kept looking toward the bedroom door, tension obvious in her tiny shoulders.

When Lorenzo finally returned and walked back into the bedroom, I saw Clara visibly relax.

"I think she's been waiting for you."

"Okay, I'll take over now," he sighed. Getting back into bed, he gathered Clara to him, resting her small body against his chest.

Looking at the tiredness etched around Lorenzo's eyes, I felt a pang of guilt that I hadn't been able to get Clara back to sleep. I'd tried hard, but I was a stranger to her, and she wasn't used to me yet.

"I'm here now, my precious," he murmured to his little girl, as he waited for her to fall back asleep. "I won't let anything bad happen to you."

Lorenzo was gently smoothing her dark curls back from her forehead as she hugged her small hands to him. He continued speaking to her in a low voice, reassuring her that she was safe and that he was there for her.

After a time, her eyelids began to droop, and eventually, she drifted off to sleep, Lorenzo tucking the comforter snugly around her body.

Looking at the little girl who lay between us, I knew I didn't mind her being there. There was plenty of room for her in our huge bed, and I could see how desperately she needed this reassurance from her father.

Clemente woke a further two times that night. Each time, Lorenzo told me to stay with Clara in our bed while he saw to Clemente. Thankfully, Clara stayed asleep on these occasions.

When Lorenzo returned to our bed after seeing to Clemente for the third time, I tried to get back to sleep. And I told myself that tomorrow was a new day, and I would try again to make things work with the children.

CHAPTER 16

LORENZO

The next morning, I was awake for a while but didn't move because I didn't want to wake Clara.

Anni woke up just before the time my alarm normally went off.

She looked across at Clara who was still huddled up to me, with her tiny fists curled against my chest. "She didn't wake again after that first time," she commented. "She likes being near you at night."

Turning off my alarm before it went off, I slid out of bed, careful not to disturb Clara, and headed for the shower.

In the bathroom, my eye caught a packet of pills peeking out of Anni's make-up bag.

Taking a closer look, I saw that they were birth control, and judging by the empty tabs, she had already started to take them. Good, because when I fucked her, I wanted to take her bareback—so that I could feel every inch of her tight pussy milking my dick when I made her come.

When I was done, I wrapped a towel around my waist and made my way to the closet to get dressed, selecting a black suit and a charcoal-gray dress shirt.

As I got dressed, Anni took her turn in the shower.

Then I sat on the side of the bed, replying to some e-mails on my phone, while she got dressed. She came out from the closet wearing jeans and a sleeveless yellow and white geometric-print top which has ridiculous ruffles around the high neck and cap sleeves.

"I really wish you would wear a dress."

"I've already told you that I don't usually wear dresses. Most are too prim and proper for my tastes."

I didn't have time right now to deal with her inappropriate attire. We needed to deal with the kids so that I could leave for work. "Time to get the kids up," I said. "You take Clemente, and I'll get Clara dressed."

After washing Clara's face and hands, I tried to persuade her to get dressed. I'd got a pink dress out of the closet and was holding it out to her, but she was reluctant to wear it.

While I attempted to convince her to put it on, I could hear Anni doing the same with Clemente across the hallway. Through the open doorways, I could see my son sitting on the floor, playing with a toy car and a toy plane, making noises as he moved them around.

He was just as reluctant to get dressed as Clara, although his reason seemed to be that he didn't want to stop playing with his toys. Eventually, Anni managed to get him out of his pajamas and wrestled him into his clothes. At least Clemente thought that the whole thing was like a game and was still smiling at the end of it.

Anni then took his hand and brought him into the master bedroom where I was still struggling with Clara.

I was trying to persuade Clara to put on the pretty pink dress. "Come on, Clara, you need to get dressed."

She gave a small shake of her head.

"I know you want to wear your blue dress, but I forgot to wash it last night, so it's still dirty. You have to wear something clean."

Clara just looked at me with big, sad eyes.

"Please, Clara, put on the dress," I pleaded. "I need to get to work."

Clara shook her head from side to side again.

I was getting irritated, but I was careful not to let it show to Clara. "I know you want the blue dress, but you wear that dress every single day. It won't harm you to wear something different today. You look so pretty in pink—why don't you give this other dress a try at least?"

But Clara continued to refuse to get dressed and remained in her pajamas with tears in her big, brown eyes.

I sat back on my heels and ran my hand through my hair.

"What can I do to help?" Anni asked.

"Can you get the blue dress from the laundry room? It's a bit dirty but will have to do for now." He checked his watch as he spoke. "Breakfast will be on the table now and will be getting cold."

After she had retrieved the dress Clara's tears stopped and she quickly got dressed by herself.

"Let's go down for breakfast," I said, hurrying both children out of the bedroom.

"Don't we need to brush Clara's hair first?"

"No. She won't let me brush it in the mornings. The only time I can get a brush to it is after her hair has been washed, although by then it's got so many tangles in it that she always ends up crying."

We all trooped down to the dining room for breakfast, and I was definitely looking forward to my first coffee of the day.

As I sipped at the scalding liquid, I closed my eyes briefly. When I agreed to marry Anni, I thought I'd be getting a mother for Clara and Clemente. I needed someone who was going to make my life easier, not an inexperienced girl who needed telling how to dress appropriately and how to look after my children.

CHAPTER 17

ANNUNCIATA

Adelina had breakfast on the table and as I sat down, I saw Lorenzo grab a couple of slices of buttered toast and a napkin.

"I don't normally have time to stay for breakfast. Can you get Clara to put on a clean dress after she's eaten."

He dropped a kiss on the heads of both children. Then he brushed his cool fingertips against the bare skin of my upper arm and also kissed my cheek. Goosebumps erupted over my skin, and I felt a shiver skate up my spine.

He gave me a smile before striding off.

As I heard his car starting up in the driveway, I ran my hand over my cheek where he'd kissed it. Perhaps it'd been an automatic gesture, but that small moment of intimacy had sent a frisson of electricity through me.

I found it hard to focus, instead thinking about how his hand had lingered for a moment too long on my arm and his lips had touched my face. He had looked handsome and powerful in his dark suit, its sharp lines skimming the toned contours of his body, and his scent of soap and man lingered in the air.

We'd only been married a couple of days, but already I was finding it hard to disguise how his presence and touch affected me.

Shaking myself from my thoughts, I looked around me. And alone with the children, I felt a sense of trepidation come over me.

Adelina bustled in with some fresh toast. "Ma'am, I've fed Wilbur."

"Thank you, Adelina." I smiled at her. "I'll come and get him once the children have had their breakfast."

I looked around the table. I had spent time with Fee's kids, so I wasn't totally unfamiliar with children, but I still had the feeling that this was going to be a steep learning curve. "What do you both like to eat normally?" I tried.

Clara looked at me silently while Clemente ignored me as he continued to play with his toy car at the table.

After pondering what I should do, I decided to pour them both some cereal. However, while Clemente ate some, Clara barely touched hers. I also put some toast in front of them, and again Clemente finished over half of his, but Clara only took a couple of bites while she kept anxiously looking towards the door as if wondering where her father had gone.

I looked around at the room we were sitting in. It was a grand dining room, although not what I would have chosen for a family breakfast with young children. I knew that Lorenzo, however, would certainly not approve of his children eating breakfast in the kitchen with the housekeeper.

The table was laid formally with a fine china service. The antique off-white plates were very pretty, with an intricate pattern in gold and pale green around the rim. The cutlery was solid silver and highly polished, but I could see that the children found it awkward using the heavy pieces.

I wondered if this had always been the arrangement for meals even when their mother had been alive. My own family had usually dined more informally, and our dining room had always had a much warmer, more comfortable ambience.

When Adelina came in to clear the plates, I said to the children that they could go and play in the den next door while I spoke with the housekeeper about what she had planned for tonight's dinner.

As we spoke about the meals, I looked out at the lovely garden and tried the door handle but found it locked.

"Where is the key kept? It would be great for the children to play outside after breakfast."

Adelina shook her head. "Mr. Lorenzo keeps this door locked because he doesn't like the children going into the garden from the reception rooms. He says they always bring dirt back inside. If they want to go outside, they need to go through the kitchen, via the pantry, via the laundry room, via the back hallway, and that will finally bring them to a side door."

"Children have short attention spans. They would probably lose interest in going outside before they even got to the side door. Where is the key kept?"

Adelina pointed to a drawer in the sideboard. "But he likes this door to stay locked."

"We'll see about that," I murmured.

Afterward, I went to the den. Now that breakfast was over, I wondered how I was supposed to fill my day with the children. I knew that I also had to get Clara to put on clean clothes, but I decided I would need to get her to trust me a little before attempting that—if her father hadn't been able to convince her, then I would have my work cut out for me too.

CHAPTER 18

ANNUNCIATA

The children had switched on the TV in the den and were watching a cartoon. I knew that they would definitely benefit from some time outdoors after breakfast, but I would have to let them get used to me first.

"How do you usually like to spend your days?" I asked them both.

Neither child replied, their gazes fixed on the screen in front of them.

I bit my lower lip, wondering what we should do. "I still need to unpack everything for my cat, Wilbur, so perhaps you could help me with that?"

There hadn't been time to introduce Wilbur to them last night, and the mention of my cat caught their attention.

I collected the boxes and brought them into the den. Then I went to the kitchen and scooping up Wilbur into my arms, I brought him to meet the children.

Clemente giggled when he saw Wilbur, running over. "Cat!" he shouted. Clara's brown eyes grew big in wonderment, although she hung back, still unsure.

"Don't worry, he won't hurt you. He's very gentle." I showed Clemente how to stroke his fur. "Would you like a go too, Clara?"

But she shook her head as she continued staring at him.

"Maybe you'd like to help me unpack his things?"

Clara thought about this and then nodded. "Okay," she whispered.

Clemente, Clara, and I started taking things out of the boxes. There were cat beds, blankets, toys, a scratching post, more cat food, and lots of other things.

Clemente happily rummaged through the items, interested in all the new things, while Clara picked up one of the brushes I had for Wilbur and looked at it intently.

"That's for brushing Wilbur's fur," I explained.

She looked up at me solemnly.

"If you like, you could help me?"

She nodded at me, and I took it as a positive sign that she wanted to interact with him.

"Wilbur, time to get your fur brushed!" I called.

And upon hearing my voice, he scampered over quickly. Since arriving here, he'd been spending his time investigating the mansion and learning his way around his new home.

He loved having his fur brushed and obediently sat in front of me, waiting for the soothing strokes of the hairbrush upon his thick, white coat.

Clara sat quietly by my side, watching as I glided the brush over Wilbur.

"Would you like to have a go, Clara?"

But Clara shook her head. She seemed happy enough to watch, so I carried on brushing while she looked on. Clemente was sitting and playing with one of Wilbur's toys.

"Wilbur's fur coat is what he wears every day because cats don't have clothes." I stole a glance at Clara as I spoke to her. "He likes to have his fur coat brushed each day as it keeps it clean and tidy, just like humans put on clean clothes every day."

I could tell that Clara was thinking carefully about what I was saying.

"Do you think you might like to put on another dress so that you feel clean and tidy too?"

Despite my casual suggestion, Clara quickly shook her head as if she could see straight through what I was trying to do.

With all of Wilbur's things unpacked, the den was starting to look a little chaotic. I made a mental note that I'd have to tidy up all these things before Lorenzo came home later. I was sure he would be displeased if I didn't keep his house in order.

After a couple of minutes, Clara wandered over to one of her toy boxes. A few moments later, Clara returned holding a blue ribbon. She came and stood next to me, handing the ribbon over to me.

My brow furrowed. "Do you want me to put this in your hair?"

"No," she whispered.

I wasn't sure what she wanted. I looked at the ribbon and then saw her watching Wilbur. "Do you want me to put it on Wilbur?"

She nodded.

I gave it some thought. "Wilbur has a blue collar on today, so you think the blue ribbon would look nice tied to it?"

Clara nodded again. I attached the ribbon she'd picked and tied it into a small bow. I thought to myself that Clara seemed to like the color blue.

"Pretty cat," she commented when I had finished.

"Is blue your favorite color?"

"Yes," she replied.

Perhaps she thought that brushing the cat's fur was similar to a human brushing their hair, and that was why she had brought the ribbon to me.

"You know, Clara, you could let me brush your hair, and you could choose another blue ribbon and I could put that in your hair." I adopted a casual tone again, just like when I had when I suggested a couple of minutes ago that she put on a clean dress.

I could see Clara thinking about my suggestion, although she didn't look entirely convinced.

"See how handsome Wilbur looks after he's had his fur brushed and especially after you chose such a beautiful ribbon?"

Clara wandered back off to the toy box and then returned with another blue ribbon which she gave to me.

I smiled to myself as she sat in front of me. "Let me just get a comb, okay?"

"Okay," she said softly.

I hurried upstairs to grab a wide-toothed comb before she changed her mind.

When I came back to the den, Clara was sitting patiently. I got to work on her hair, taking my time and working the knots out from the bottom upwards. Her hair was the same color as her father's—a rich shade of the deepest brown.

"Wilbur likes having his fur brushed every morning. I think he's going to like it even more now if you choose him a fresh ribbon each day as well."

By the time I had got all the tangles out of Clara's hair, it looked so much tidier and shinier. I gathered the top section and tied the ribbon around her curls in a bow. Picking up Clara in my arms, I held her in front of the mirror over the fireplace to show her how she looked.

"Do you like it?" I asked her.

Wilbur let out a 'meow' in approval. He was an intelligent animal and often tried to talk to me and answer any questions I asked, although his responses were rather limited.

Clara giggled at Wilbur's reply and gave me a smile. "Like it," she said.

"I think Wilbur likes it too, especially because you are wearing matching ribbons."

She carried on looking at her reflection for a few moments and then wriggled to get down from my arms.

I watched Clara and Clemente play with their toys, letting Wilbur roam around the room at the same time so that they could all start getting used to each other. Clara, in particular, was taken with my cat. And after what she had done with the ribbons, I had an idea.

"Let's all go to the mall. Wilbur's collar is getting a bit old and shabby. Why don't we pick him up some new ones and you can also choose some ribbons for him? Then each morning you can choose which collar and ribbon he should wear."

Both children looked enthusiastic about my suggestion for an outing. I helped them to brush their teeth and wash their hands and faces. Then, with Adelina's help, I located the children's shoes and got them ready to go out.

We went from the hallway through the connecting door to the garage. A number of vehicles were parked there with their keys in their ignitions. Picking an SUV that already had child seats in the back, I got the children in and buckled up.

I could see the control to open the automatic garage door, so I started the car and drove down the driveway, coming to a stop when I reached the perimeter gates. The gates were closed, and there were two soldiers on duty—one older and one younger.

I'd noticed other various soldiers providing a security detail around the outside of the property, and those soldiers seemed to change throughout the day. Adelina had told me that the soldiers came and went depending on what duties Lorenzo assigned to them—if they were needed elsewhere, then they would leave as long as a set minimum number of soldiers remained at the house.

As I came to a halt, both the gate soldiers walked toward me.

Rolling down the window, I spoke to them. "I'm just taking the children shopping."

"Do you know where to go, Mrs. Marchiano?" asked the younger one.

"I've looked it up on the internet where the local shopping mall is and programmed it into the satnav. It looks close by."

"You'll have to take a bodyguard with you," said the older man in a no-nonsense tone. He nodded at the other soldier. "Giuseppe will accompany you. I'll call one of the other soldiers to come and take his place at the gate."

"Okay," I said reluctantly. I never had to take a bodyguard to go shopping in Venetiville. But then Venetiville had its own department store within the gated community—the wealthy Mafia families meant that the store did extremely well despite our community being so small.

Giuseppe looked at me and spoke hesitantly. "I should drive, ma'am. That way, if there's any trouble, I can take control of the situation."

I suppressed a small sigh, slightly irritated. I'd been allowed to come and go around Venetiville freely. However, realizing that Giuseppe's suggestion was probably a sensible one, given that I had the children with me, I got out of the driver's seat, making my way around the car to the passenger seat where Giuseppe was holding the door open for me.

When we got to the mall, the first place we went to was a large department store. As Giuseppe tailed us, completely failing to blend into the background and looking every inch a bodyguard, I made my way to the homeware section.

After looking around, I found what I was looking for. "Look Clara and Clemente." I picked up a plate. "Don't these look fun?" The children's plate was decorated with rabbits.

Clara looked at it with big eyes. "Pretty bunny rabbits," she murmured, pressing her fingers to the rabbits decorating the border of the plate.

Clemente pointed to another plate on the display stand. "Tigers," he said, jumping up and down.

"Yes, that's right, Clemente, they're tigers. Why don't you both choose a set and we can use them at mealtimes?" The plates had matching bowls and cups, as well as matching lightweight cutlery in a miniature size which was much more suitable for the small hands of young children.

Clemente had already made his decision as soon as he saw the plate with tigers. Clara, on the other hand, took her time looking through the different designs on display. Finally, she pointed to another one of the designs, this one with pictures of kittens around the border of the plate.

After paying for our purchases, Giuseppe volunteered to carry the bags. "Thank you, Giuseppe," I said. It was odd having a stranger keeping an eye on me. If I'd needed to take a bodyguard with me in New York, one of my brothers or cousins was always available to accompany me. That was the advantage of having such a big family.

So far, Lorenzo's interactions with his wider family had been rather limited. His home definitely didn't seem the type of place people could visit without an invitation; in that respect, it was very different from my childhood home where my sister and other family members would drop in unannounced throughout the day.

Walking to another department, we looked at the ribbons on offer. There were a myriad of colors, sizes, and designs.

"If we have two of each color, then you and Wilbur can wear matching ribbons." I was hoping that if Clara helped me with brushing Wilbur's fur each morning and chose a ribbon for him, she might then let me brush her hair and put the matching ribbon in it.

Clara gave a happy smile as she and Clemente picked out ribbons in various colors.

Next, we went to a pet store in the mall. "Can you help me pick out some new collars for Wilbur?"

Both children nodded enthusiastically. Adelina had told me that they had no pets of their own, and so far Wilbur was a novelty to them and capturing their interest.

I noticed how much Clara liked the color blue, picking out three collars all in different shades of blue, while Clemente picked out collars in red and yellow.

I sensed that both children were starting to tire and get fractious, and I decided it was time for us all to return home.

When we got back to the mansion, Giuseppe carried our packages into the mansion and then returned to his other duties.

For lunch, I asked Adelina to prepare sandwiches and a platter of fruit and vegetable sticks. Clemente was ravenous after our trip to the mall. Clara, however, only picked at her food and kept looking toward the door.

The children spent the afternoon playing with their toys in the den. Adelina told me that neither child had an afternoon nap anymore. Clemente looked like he could have done with one judging by how often he rubbed at his eyes, but he resolutely ignored my suggestion that he have one.

Clemente was into everything and running around. Clara, on the other hand, was more subdued, and there was a hint of sadness hanging over her all the time it seemed.

I unpacked our shopping from earlier as the children played. "Wilbur is going to look so handsome in his new collars." As I spoke, an idea flitted through my mind. "You know, perhaps we should go online and buy you both some new clothes, and that way you'll look just as smart as Wilbur?"

However, upon the mention of clothes shopping, Clara's eyes widened and she started to cry, while Clemente proceeded to have a tantrum. The little boy was in dire need of an afternoon sleep, but he still refused to let either me or Adelina put him down for one.

Once Clemente calmed down, I suggested that the children have some quiet time with their picture books, while I went online and selected a local store that offered same day delivery.

It was hard to shop for Clara because I wasn't sure what she liked, although I knew that she liked the color blue. In the end, I picked out a new blue dress for her, a pair of blue shorts, a couple of t-shirts, jeans, and a blue sweater. For Clemente, I ordered jeans, shorts, a t-shirt with cars on it, and a t-shirt with little planes all over it after remembering how much he enjoyed playing with his toy planes.

When the clothes were delivered in the late afternoon, I showed the items to the children. I also asked Clara if she would like to try on the new blue dress.

She looked at me from underneath her eyelashes and then shook her head from side to side.

"That's okay. I'll put them in the dresser in your bedroom, and they'll be there if you would ever like to wear them."

Before Lorenzo arrived home, I took the opportunity to ring Ma.

"Annunciata!" I smiled as I heard her voice.

"Hi Ma. How are you all?"

After she filled me in with what had been going on in Venetiville, she asked me how things were in Chicago.

I ran through my day with her, including Clemente waking three times last night, his tantrum at the mall, and then his refusal to have an afternoon nap.

"Annunciata, children are like puppies."

"Er...what does that mean, Ma?"

"It means they need lots of exercise and fresh air—particularly boys. Then they sleep better at night. You are right that the children should spend time outdoors each day. At Clemente's age, if he sleeps well at night, then he will be fine without a nap."

I also spoke to her about Clara's refusal to wear a clean dress this morning.

"You will find, Annunciata, that small children spend a lot of time not wanting to do things—get undressed, get dressed, get in the bathtub, get out of the bathtub, go to sleep, eat their food, and so on. The more content a child is, the easier it becomes. Continue the way you have started—you will learn as you go along. You have a big heart, and that means you cannot go far wrong."

Ma's words reassured me a little, and it felt good to be able to talk through my day with her.

That evening, I was disappointed that Lorenzo didn't make it home in time for dinner. He hadn't said that he would be late, and I had assumed that we would all eat together as a family.

Adelina had cooked ravioli filled with sweet potato and parmesan cheese, telling me that both children liked this dish. We used the new plates and cutlery that I had bought for the children this morning, and I hoped that this might make the children more enthusiastic about their food.

Clemente ate his food happily, though he was also enjoying making a mess with it. I noticed, however, that Clara ate less than her brother and yet again, she kept flicking her gaze toward the door.

Halfway through the meal, we heard the front door open and footsteps in the hallway. Clara looked up from her plate expectantly. As the footsteps came down the hallway, she kept her eyes peeled on the dining room door.

A few moments later, Lorenzo came into the room, walking over to the children and kissing them both on their heads.

He paused after kissing Clara and stared at her. "You've brushed your hair. It looks really beautiful, especially with the bow. Did Anni put the ribbon in for you?"

She nodded, giving him a shy smile, as he ran a hand over her dark curls.

Lorenzo fixed his gaze on Clara's plate, obviously taking in how much she had eaten—which wasn't much, especially compared to Clemente who had almost finished his plate.

At that moment, Lorenzo's cell rang. "Excuse me," he murmured as he walked out of the room.

I got up and followed him into his study because I wanted to speak to him out of the earshot of the children.

As he spoke into the phone, his eyes raked over my whole body, his attention making me feel lightheaded and breathy. I shook myself mentally, remembering what I needed to talk to him about.

When he'd finished his call and hung up, he turned to me, a frown marring his brow. "I'm concerned that Clara isn't eating enough."

I plucked up the courage to ask him what I needed to know. "Lorenzo...why are there no photos of your first wife around the house?"

He fixed an icy gaze on me. "That's none of your concern."

"If I knew, it might allow me to understand the situation more and how to help the children deal with their grief and related issues like their appetite. It's obvious that they are still grieving for their mother."

"Don't bring this up again, Anni." His voice was low and threatening.

I tried to stay strong, despite his obvious hostility to me. "I think it would help if you were home for dinner more." Despite his scowl, I continued. "I think Clara has some separation anxiety. She seems to be wondering all the time about when you will be returning, and that anxiety may be causing her to lose her appetite."

Lorenzo paused to think about what I had said. "Fine," he said tersely. "I'll try to be home for meals more. And I'll stay for breakfast tomorrow morning."

I was about to tell him that I had got the children some new clothes today, but then I thought that he would just point out that Clara wasn't actually wearing the new clothes, and so I just kept quiet and returned to the children in the dining room. Lorenzo and I were virtual strangers but somehow we had been thrown together and were now raising a family. It was going to take time to learn how to work with each other, especially as Lorenzo was such a closed book.

Another evening lay ahead of him being holed up in his study, while I was left alone with only the children to talk to. Although I was loving spending time with them, I was climbing the walls after only a few days due to the lack of adult company.

Our evening routine seemed to consist of Lorenzo working in his study and only communicating with me if it was regarding the children.

Going to bed alone that night, I thought how I'd been right in the first place when I'd thought that becoming a Mafia wife at the age of twenty was a very bad idea. But even then, I'd never imagined when I'd got engaged to Lorenzo that my marriage would be in any way lonely.

I'd been brought up in a big, loving family, where there were always people to talk to and plenty of affection from my parents, siblings and extended family. Since my marriage and coming to Chicago, the most interaction I'd had with any adult so far had been with Adelina. Was this how my whole marriage was destined to be?

Added to that, thoughts of my kiss with Lorenzo on our wedding night kept flitting through my mind. And although I wouldn't admit it to anyone, I started to let myself wonder what it would be like to have him kiss me again.

Each morning and evening, I admired his body when he wasn't watching, thinking about what it would be like to run my hands over his muscles and bare chest, and how it would feel to have him touch and kiss me in my most sensitive places. What would it feel like to have his body cover mine?

Shaking my head, I pushed these ideas away and tried to think about something else. I didn't know why I kept having these strange thoughts, and why these musings made my body heat and feel uncomfortable, but I told myself it was solely because I was starved of adult company.

CHAPTER 19

ANNUNCIATA

When we woke the following morning, I looked down at Clara who was in our bed again.

Clara had woken twice last night, as had her brother.

After I'd showered, I got dressed in a fitted blouse and a skater-style flippy skirt with polka dots which came down to mid-thigh length. I didn't wear dresses or skirts that often, but I liked this particular skirt.

When Lorenzo saw my outfit, I felt his eyes trail appreciatively over my bare legs, making a shiver ghost along my spine.

I saw to getting Clemente dressed, while Lorenzo tried to coax a reluctant Clara to get dressed.

"Damnit," said Lorenzo to me. "I put Clara's dress on to wash last night but forgot to set it to dry as well." He looked down at his daughter. "Clara, sorry, but your blue dress isn't dry. You'll have to wear something else."

"Wear blue dress," she pleaded.

"No, you can't. You can't wear wet clothes."

Big tears started to silently fall down her pale cheeks.

Lorenzo ran his hands through his neatly brushed hair. "Look, why don't you wear your pajamas for now, and then Anni can get your dress dry in a while?"

Clara looked uncertain about his suggestion but took Lorenzo's hand so that he could take her down for breakfast. I followed with Clemente who babbled away, seemingly oblivious to his sister's upset.

As we went down the staircase, I couldn't help my eyes wandering from Lorenzo's almost-black hair downward to his dark suit, his clothes perfectly tailored around the defined muscles of his toned body. I looked away, though, before he caught me staring.

Last night Lorenzo had promised to eat breakfast with the children this morning. However, as we reached the bottom of the staircase, his cell rang and he excused himself to take the call.

I took the children into the dining room for breakfast, and as I helped them up onto the antique chairs, Clara looked at me and whispered, "Cat?"

"Wilbur has to have his breakfast in the kitchen."

"Cat lonely," she murmured.

Wilbur was in the kitchen, probably getting spoiled by Adelina, and I got the feeling that it was Clara who was likely to be missing him more.

"He's a cat and your daddy wouldn't like him eating in here." Lorenzo would probably have a fit if he saw Wilbur's food bowl on the pristine, polished wood floors of his formal dining room.

Adelina brought in toast and a dish of scrambled eggs. I poured cereal for the children and plated up some toast and eggs for each of them.

Clemente began eating straightaway, but Clara didn't eat and kept looking at the door as if wondering whether her father was going to come back.

I tried to swallow down my frustration with Lorenzo. Surely the call could have waited half an hour if his presence meant that Clara ate something. An idea came to me. "Let's go to the kitchen and get the cat."

"Cat?" said Clara hopefully.

"Yes, sweetie. Wilbur."

And, at my words, she gave me a beautiful smile.

While Clemente remained in the dining room, Clara and I went to the kitchen. I scooped Wilbur into my arms. "Good morning, handsome," I said to him. He purred in happiness as I stroked his ears.

"Clara, why don't you bring his bowl to the dining room?"

Adelina had just set down the bowl with his food onto the floor.

"He hasn't eaten his breakfast yet, Mrs. Anni."

"Don't worry, he can eat with us in the dining room."

Adelina almost dropped the plate she was holding. "But what about Mr. Lorenzo? Surely he will not eat in the same room as the cat?" She had obviously sensed his intense dislike for the animal.

"If he ever gets off his phone and decides to eat with the children, then they'll be in the dining room with me and Wilbur."

Back in the dining room, I settled Wilbur in the corner with his food while Clara sat back in her seat. The little girl looked instantly happier. She didn't do well being away from those she cared for—and it was obvious that she had already started to form an attachment to Wilbur.

Clara watched him while he ate his food, and she giggled when he paused to lick around his mouth and whiskers. "Cat likes," she laughed.

"Yes, he does like his breakfast."

Clara carried on watching him while she stirred her spoon around her cereal bowl and avoided eating any of the actual cereal.

After a couple of minutes, she pulled the plate with toast and eggs toward her. "Kittens," she said, pointing to the pictures on her new plate.

"Yes, they're kittens. I think the kittens might also like eggs."

She looked at her plate for a long while, turning it around slowly to look at the pictures of the kittens scampering around the border of the plate. She may have not been eating the food, but at least she hadn't pushed it away yet.

Clara then carefully picked up her new matching fork and put the tiniest amount of eggs into her mouth.

I held my breath, trying not to watch her or make her self-conscious. Out of the corner of my eye, I saw her raise another small forkful to her mouth and chew it very slowly.

"Clara likes," she commented quietly.

I gave her a small smile of encouragement.

At that moment, Lorenzo strode into the dining room, his deep brown eyes zeroing in on Wilbur. "What's he doing in here?" he barked.

"Clara wanted Wilbur to join us."

He looked up at his daughter but stilled as he watched her bring another small amount of eggs to her mouth.

He sat down at the head of the table, and drinking his coffee, he kept watching Clara as she ate. She didn't touch her cereal or toast, but she ate over half the eggs on her plate.

Adelina came in with Wilbur's water bowl, and with a wary look toward Lorenzo, she set it down on the floor. Wilbur instantly lapped at the water, obviously thirsty after his meal.

Lorenzo scowled. "Your cat is really noisy when he drinks."

Jeez, he really was uptight.

The children finished before Lorenzo, so I took the key from the dresser drawer and unlocked the door. "Why don't you play outside for a little while until it's time to get ready to go to your grandmother's?" The kids were spending the day with Lorenzo's mother today. Lorenzo had said that they liked spending time with her and it would be a break from me so as to not overwhelm them with too much, too soon.

"That door is supposed to stay locked," Lorenzo clipped, as Wilbur trotted outside and raised his face to the sun. Clara and Clemente followed him and immediately ran off across the lawn.

"It's good for the children to get some fresh air."

I took my cup of coffee into the garden and was pleased to see Lorenzo follow me. The children looked happy to be outside.

"I spoke to Ma yesterday, and she said that children are like puppies and they need lots of fresh air and exercise."

Lorenzo's jaw dropped. "You ma compared my children to *dogs*?"

"No," I said, barely suppressing my sigh. "You know Ma loved the children when she met them at the wedding, She meant that it helps them to sleep better at night."

"If they don't hurt themselves first." Lorenzo nodded to Clemente and strode over to him, with me on his heels.

In the distance, Clemente had started to climb a tree and had scrambled up it very fast.

"Clemente, come down now!" Lorenzo called. "You are too small to be climbing so high."

"Stuck!" wailed the little boy. "I'm stuck."

He was about seven foot up the tree and just out of Lorenzo's reach. Clara stood at the base of the tree and looked up anxiously at her brother.

"Hell," cursed Lorenzo, looking down at his pristine suit. But as he started to remove his jacket, I began to climb the tree.

"What on earth are you doing, Anni?"

"What does it look like? I'm going to Clemente, and I'll guide him back down."

I'd had plenty of practice climbing trees when I was younger, and the position of the branches made this tree look relatively easy to climb, which was probably why Clemente had managed to scale it so fast even at his young age.

As I reached Clemente and started to guide him down, I heard Lorenzo growl below me. "For God's sake, Anni, I can see your panties."

"I get it now," I retorted. "That's why you always say you want me to wear a dress."

I heard a huff of irritation from him in response.

When we reached the ground, Lorenzo crouched level with his son. "You're not to climb so high until you're much bigger and older, understood?"

Then Lorenzo came and stood next to me.

He bended his head so that his mouth was next to my ear. "And you're to make sure that no one else ever sees your panties, except me. Otherwise, I'll be confiscating your panties again—after I've ripped them off and spanked you so firmly that your ass cheeks will be burning. Understood?"

But I wasn't able to reply as a hot blush rushed up my face and a liquid heat gushed between my legs.

I hurriedly changed the subject, telling the children that it was time to go inside and get ready to go to their grandmother's. While we'd been eating breakfast and been in the garden, I'd put Clara's dress in the dryer. Once we were back indoors, I took the children upstairs to wash their hands and clean their teeth.

"Would you like to wear one of your new outfits for your grandmother?" I suggested to Clara.

"No." She shook her head resolutely.

I contained a sigh. I knew she was not going to be easily convinced. Instead, I took her to the laundry room to check if her dress was dry yet.

"There's still a few minutes left on the drying cycle," I explained to her.

"Okay," she said, kneeling down in front of the dryer. It was one of those machines that had the drum door at the front so that you could see the clothing inside. Clara watched her dress spin around and around the drum, transfixed by the sight.

As I watched her, I thought how I kept seeing glimpses of sadness in her—similar to the glimpses I saw in Lorenzo when he wasn't being angry about something.

Once the machine beeped at the end of its cycle, it didn't need ironing thankfully, so I handed her the dry dress and she happily changed into it.

In the den, Clara brought me Wilbur's brush and a new sky-blue ribbon, while Clemente chose a yellow collar for Wilbur to wear today. Clara watched while Clemente and I brushed his fur. Then Clara handed me her comb, and I gently combed through her curls. Next, I tied matching sky-blue ribbons in her hair and on Wilbur's collar.

While we did this, Lorenzo tapped his foot impatiently, flicking though e-mails on his cell phone while he waited for me to finish getting the children ready so that he could drop them at his mother's house. "Can't you deal with the cat later?" he gritted out.

"Clara likes for her and Wilbur to have matching ribbons."

Lorenzo just looked at me like I was mad.

CHAPTER 20

ANNUNCIATA

Finally, once the children were all ready, Lorenzo drove them to his mother's house on his way to work. He said he was due to visit one of the Fratellanza's nightclubs today and that he would see me tonight.

After they had all left, the house felt very quiet. The only other person in the house was Adelina, and she was busy with the housework while Wilbur had gone up to my bedroom for his post-breakfast nap.

I wasn't used to such a lack of company. In my parents' house, you'd be lucky to get an hour to yourself before someone dropped in. My father, brothers and cousins were in and out of the house all day, while Fidella and my Aunt Priscilla were also frequent visitors.

I decided to ring Ma and catch up with her. Like yesterday, I used my cell rather than the house phone, not knowing if calls on the house phone were recorded by Lorenzo—I didn't want to have to watch what I was saying to Ma.

"Hi Ma."

"Annunciata!" she shrieked when she heard my voice, causing me to hold the phone a little away from my ear.

After Ma had told me some Imperiosi gossip, I asked for her advice about Clara's lack of appetite.

"You should try my homemade cotolette di pollo." Ma's chicken parmesan cutlets were out of this world. "They are very good at tempting the appetites of young children. The secret is to mix plenty of parmesan cheese in with the breadcrumbs and don't forget the garlic and parsley for seasoning," she advised.

"Thanks, Ma. I'll make them tonight for dinner. I know there's going to be no quick fix, but I want to start experimenting to see what might work with her."

"You're going to make a good mom to those kids, Annunciata. I hope Lorenzo appreciates what you are doing for his kids."

"He only seems to find things to grumble about. I got Clara to eat her scrambled eggs this morning, but all he did was complain about how noisy Wilbur was."

"Give it time, Annunciata. Made Men are a strange species."

"Ma, I wanted to ask you about speech as well."

"Speech?"

"Yes. Clemente is two and Clara is four. But their levels of speech are almost identical—both speak in only one-word or two-word phrases. Shouldn't Clara be speaking more by now, or do you think that Clemente is just advanced for his age?"

"No, you are right, Annunciata. Clara should be able to speak much more than that."

"Perhaps she's just shy and reluctant to speak around me because I'm a new person? But if things don't improve soon, I think I might take her to see a speech therapist."

After talking some more Ma told me she had to go and I promised to call her again tomorrow.

Hanging up, I looked around myself and wondered what I was going to do to pass the time today. I was up-to-date with my college assignments. Without the children here and with Wilbur still asleep, I had time to think, and thinking made a pang of homesickness hit me.

I knew I had to keep myself busy to stop myself feeling like this, so I got up and went to the kitchen to see Adelina.

"I thought I'd cook tonight, Adelina, if that's okay with you?" I didn't want to step on the housekeeper's toes, especially as I wanted us to be friends—I could really use at least one friend here in Chicago.

"Of course, Mrs. Anni, whatever you wish."

I checked on what ingredients were already in the fridge and kitchen cupboards, and made a list of what I'd need to buy from the grocery store.

Going into the garage, I picked the same SUV I'd taken yesterday. I really didn't want to have to take a bodyguard again with me though. It was awkward having one of Lorenzo's soldiers looking over my shoulder at all times, and my homesickness made me even more adamant that I didn't want a stranger trailing me today.

Lorenzo hadn't actually *told me* that I needed to take a bodyguard with me when I went out. I'd taken one with me yesterday, but I told myself that was because I'd had the children with me.

I checked my watch and saw that it was 10.50 a.m. I'd noticed yesterday that the soldiers switched duties every two hours, rotating between gate duty, perimeter duty, and other security duties.

Looking out of the window of the garage, I hoped that there would be a changeover at 11.00 a.m. My luck was in and, on the hour, the two gate soldiers headed to the guardhouse at the rear of the property to switch over.

While they were gone, I drove down the driveway. Upon reaching the gate, I put in the eight-figure code that I'd seen Giuseppe enter yesterday—I'd always had a superior memory when it came to numbers. After a moment, I smiled in triumph as the electronic gates opened for me.

Although my exit would probably be logged on the security system's electronic log, the gate guards hopefully would think it was just one of Lorenzo's soldiers leaving the property since the soldiers seemed to come and go throughout the day.

As I drove away from the mansion, I couldn't help thinking about the days since my wedding.

Coming into this marriage, I'd thought that the children would probably be the most challenging aspect of my new marriage—I'd heard so many times that the stepmom-stepchild relationship was a really hard one to navigate. And although the kids did have issues I needed to deal with, they were really lovely children.

The main issue I had was Lorenzo's distant attitude. How were we supposed to raise a family together if we didn't communicate properly?

Okay, so we hadn't exactly gotten off on the right foot, but I'd apologized to him for that on the day of the engagement party.

Maybe he was comparing me to his first wife? Although since he never actually mentioned her to me, I didn't really know if this was the case.

I headed to a nearby strip mall we had passed yesterday when Giuseppe had been driving. I'd seen a grocery store there and that would be the best place to get the things I needed for dinner.

Leaving the SUV in the parking lot out front, I made my way into the store and took my time browsing the aisles.

After collecting some of the ingredients I needed for dinner, I stopped in front of the magazine stand and flicked through a couple of magazines. It was really nice to be out of the mansion and just doing something without having someone looking over my shoulder all the time like Giuseppe had been doing yesterday. I was sure that Lorenzo would have asked him for a full report yesterday of what I'd done and how the children had been with me.

The store had a toy aisle and, walking past it, I saw a white toy cat among the stuffed animals for sale. I'd noticed that Clara had loved stroking Wilbur yesterday and had also spent a lot of time this morning running her hands over his soft fur. Picking up the toy cat, I also selected a stuffed tiger for Clemente.

"What are you doing here?" a deep voice demanded from over my shoulder.

I spun around, my hand flying to my chest.

Standing behind me was Lorenzo's brother, Aloysius. "Oh my God, you scared the living daylights out of me! What are you doing here?"

"That was *my* question." His dark eyes were fixed on me.

"I came to get some groceries." I tried to divert his attention away from me. "Er, are you shopping for groceries too?" Which was a really a stupid question given that he looked completely out of place here. In his black suit, black shirt, black tie, and with a black scowl on his face, he looked every inch a bad man—not to mention that he had waves of danger practically rolling off him.

He silently stared at me. "Does Lorenzo know you're here?"

"I'm, um, not sure."

"I'll take that as a 'no' then—especially as you are out unaccompanied. You know you need a bodyguard when you go out, right?"

"I just wanted to get some space," I said quietly.

He glanced down at my shopping cart, and after a few moments, he said more gently, "You need to be careful, Anni. This isn't Venetiville."

I nodded.

"Have you got much more shopping to do?"

"I just need to get some chicken and parmesan cheese, and then I'm done."

"I thought food shopping was Adelina's job?"

"It is, but I thought I'd make chicken cutlets tonight in the hope of tempting Clara to eat more."

"She's still not eating enough, huh?"

"Yeah. I asked my ma for her recipe, but we didn't have all the ingredients, so that's how I ended up here."

"Okay. I'll stay while you finish up."

After collecting the chicken and cheese with Aloysius following me, we went to pay. As he stood at the checkout next to me, I thought how I'd only talked with him briefly at the wedding and today was probably the longest conversation I'd had with him so far.

He was almost as tall as Lorenzo, although his body was leaner, and he had jet black hair and almost-black eyes. He definitely seemed a bit friendlier than Lorenzo.

I noticed that he didn't have any purchases to pay for. "So, what are you doing here if you're not grocery shopping?"

"I was on my way to your mansion, and I saw Lorenzo's SUV in the parking lot. I'd just left him at the club, and I knew it couldn't be him. He'd also said that the kids were at our mother's, and that you were spending the day at home, so I thought I'd better check it out."

If I ever snuck out on a grocery run again, I'd have to go somewhere further from the mansion and with a parking lot that wasn't visible from the main road. "Ah, so my plan wasn't so clever, after all," I said, in an attempt to make light of the situation. "I'm going to have to sharpen up my sneaking-out skills."

"Seriously, Anni, you need to be careful. There are bad people around and Lorenzo has plenty of enemies." He kept his voice low as we were in public, but I could tell that he meant what he said. "You shouldn't be driving yourself. If something were to happen, your bodyguard has advanced driving skills and will be better equipped than you to get you out of danger."

After I'd paid, Aloysius followed me out to the parking lot as I returned to my SUV.

"Where do you think you're going now?" He quirked an eyebrow up at me.

"Back to the mansion."

"Not by yourself you're not. Come on." He took my arm and purposely led me over to his vehicle. "I'll drive you home and get one of my men to bring your vehicle back to the mansion." He held his palm out. "Keys," he demanded.

"Honestly, I'm fine. I really don't need a bodyguard just to go the short distance home."

"You're Lorenzo's now," he stated. "You don't get a choice."

It was clear he wasn't going to take no for an answer, so I handed my keys over to him.

Although Aloysius was bossy, at least he was easier to talk to than Giuseppe had been. Giuseppe hadn't said anything to me yesterday apart from 'yes, ma'am', 'no, ma'am', and 'I'll carry your bags, ma'am'.

When we arrived back, Aloysius went to drop some money in the safe in Lorenzo's study and then left.

During the afternoon, I passed the time by playing with Wilbur and unpacking more of my belongings.

Then in the early evening, I started to prepare the cutlets. Lorenzo was picking up the children from his mother's and bringing them home in time for dinner.

When dinner was almost ready, Lorenzo arrived home. And crossing my fingers, I took a deep breath and hoped to myself that tonight's dinner would be a better success than yesterday's.

CHAPTER 21

LORENZO

I had just picked up the children from my mother's house.

Mother said that the children had been fine but that Clara hadn't eaten much for lunch again. I was glad that at least she had eaten the eggs this morning. I had hoped that she was getting her appetite back, but the eggs must have been a one-off.

I frowned as I noticed how old and shabby her dress was getting. Although her hair had been looking much better since Anni had been brushing it.

"Your hair looks so pretty when it's brushed and you've got a ribbon in it."

"Wilbur matches," she whispered.

"Yeah, I guess he does." Maybe that was why Anni was brushing the cat's fur this morning and putting the ribbon on his collar—to get Clara to have her hair brushed? Perhaps Anni was starting to get the hang of how to deal with the children.

When we got back to the mansion, Clara and Clemente went to find Anni. I followed them into the kitchen, wanting to check up on what my wife was up to.

"Anni!" Clemente said in greeting.

"Hi Clemente. Hi Clara."

Clara didn't respond, but she did give Anni a small smile.

"What's all this?" I questioned. "Where's Adelina and why isn't she making dinner?"

"I thought I would cook tonight. Why don't you get the children to wash their hands and get seated. I'll just be a couple of minutes and then I'll bring the food in."

I swallowed a sigh but did as she asked. I liked Adelina's cooking and had been looking forward to my meal.

A couple of minutes later, Anni carried in dishes of food. She had already laid the table with the formal dinner service for me and her and the kids' plates for Clemente and Clara. I didn't understand why we couldn't all just use the same plates. The brightly colored kids' plates certainly didn't go with the grandeur of my dining room.

"I thought Clemente and Clara might like to try my ma's recipe for Italian chicken cutlets—she's famous throughout the Imperiosi for it." She put some chicken and mashed potatoes onto the children's plates and then passed the dishes to me so that I could serve myself.

I looked suspiciously at the food.

The stupid cat was also standing next to his bowl in the corner of the room, waiting for his dinner. I'd have to do something about moving the animal back into the kitchen. As soon as Anni put some chicken in his bowl, he started eating straight away.

"Cat likes," said Clara to no one in particular.

"He sure does. This is my ma's recipe and everyone who has tasted it loves it, including Wilbur."

As Anni helped Clemente cut up his chicken, I saw Clara take a tentative bite of her chicken and chew it thoughtfully. After finishing it, she had another small mouthful.

I took a bite and was pleasantly surprised. "This is pretty good." As I ate, I couldn't help frequent glances toward Clara. I smiled to myself, pleased that she was eating.

As dinner went on, I relaxed a bit, and I even had a second helping. Although Clara didn't finish all her food, she definitely ate a lot more than the night before. Anni was a good cook if the cutlets were anything to go by, and perhaps she would be able to get Clara to eat more.

After dinner, I retreated to my study to finish some work. Anni was about to take the children upstairs to bathe them when I heard the front door open and someone come in.

I stuck my head out of his study door and frowned.

"Aloysius, what are you doing here at this time?"

"Your wife left this in my car earlier," he said casually.

I looked at what was in his hand.

It was Anni's purse.

I looked at Anni and noticed that she paled under my gaze. What had she been up to now?

My shoulders tensed as I faced Anni. "How did that end up in my brother's car?"

Anni hesitated, and I felt my blood heat.

"Anni?" I said in a hard voice.

"I was dropping off some money in your safe, and Anni wanted to go to the grocery store," Aloysius interrupted. "There wasn't a free soldier to accompany her," he said easily, "so I took her in my car."

"It was a lucky coincidence," she added.

I paused, staring at my wife. Then I nodded. "Good. You can go out, Anni, as long as you take a bodyguard. I don't want you going out by yourself."

"Okay. Um, the children are waiting for me to run their bath. I better go and see to them." With that, Anni hurried up the stairs.

"I better be going," drawled Aloysius as we watched Anni disappear up the stairs.

"Yeah, see you tomorrow."

I returned to my study, but instead of getting on with my work, I sat staring out of the window.

Anni had definitely been lying.

I spun my chair back around to my laptop screen and pulled up the security footage for the garage. Neither Aloysius nor Anni had said what time they went to the store, so I started the footage from when I'd left the house this morning.

I fast-forwarded through the recording until I saw Anni enter the garage and get into my SUV. Aloysius and my soldiers were nowhere in sight.

I didn't even bother trying to calm my rage as I switched to the gate footage.

From the time lapse between Anni getting into the car and then going through the gates, I could tell that she had deliberately waited to leave until the gate guards were switching duties.

Those fucking soldiers shouldn't have left the gate unattended even for a second. I'd be showing them my displeasure after I'd dealt with my wife.

I carried on forwarding through the recording, drumming my fingers on my desk while I searched for when Anni returned home.

When she came back, though, she wasn't in the same SUV. Instead, she was in Aloysius's vehicle. What the fuck?

I snatched up my cell and speed-dialed my brother.

"Lorenzo," he answered.

"You just lied to me," I spat out. I didn't even bother with pleasantries.

"Look, calm down. She went out without a bodyguard."

"What are you talking about?"

"I was coming over to your house and saw your SUV. It was parked in the strip mall on the main road. I'd just left you at the club and knew it couldn't be you, so I checked it out. She was grocery shopping and hadn't taken one of the soldiers with her, so I stayed with her while she finished shopping and then drove her home."

"You shouldn't have covered for her. Why would she go out without a guard?"

"I don't know…but she said she wanted some space. Maybe she's finding her new life a bit much? Lorenzo, you need to relax. She's taken on a lot. She's young and she's suddenly a wife and looking after two young kids who are pretty traumatized after losing their mom."

At least Aloysius had the sense to bring her back. "Thanks for bringing her home. But next time, don't lie to me."

"I won't."

I hung up and went upstairs to read a bedtime story to the children.

Once I'd kissed them goodnight, I went to find Anni who was in the master bedroom, putting clean laundry away.

I came to an abrupt halt as soon as I stepped into the bedroom. There was a suspicious white fluffy mound on my bed.

"What the hell is that cat doing on the bed?"

"He likes to sleep here during the day. Don't worry, he'll go back down to the kitchen tonight."

"I'd rather he spent all his time in the kitchen. I don't want him in or on my bed." After shooing the animal off the bed and out of the bedroom, I clenched my jaw, thinking back to the reason I'd wanted to speak to her. "I know you were lying to me before. You went out without a bodyguard, but Aloysius saw you and brought you home."

Her mouth dropped open. "How...did you find out?"

"I'll always find out if you lie to me," I growled as I stalked over to her.

CHAPTER 22

LORENZO

Anni had asked how I'd found out that she'd lied. "You said it was a coincidence that Aloysius was there when you needed a guard. My job has taught me that there's no such thing as a coincidence."

"You really are paranoid," she murmured.

I ran my gaze over her body and down to her bare legs. "For good reason, it appears. What were you thinking, going out without a bodyguard?"

"I thought it would be fine. I was just going to the store down the road. I took a guard when I went out with the children yesterday, but today I thought I'd be fine without one." She turned her back to me as she went back to putting away the laundry.

My muscles were coiled with tension. "You are my wife now. That means you're a target for my enemies. I'm not a good man and a lot of people would like to harm my family and me."

She kept her back to me and didn't acknowledge what I'd said.

I strode over to her, grabbing her arms and spinning her around to face me. "I don't care what your papà allowed you to get away with, but now you do as I say," I said in a low voice. "Is that understood?"

"Perfectly," she gritted out. Her jewel-like eyes sparked as she spoke, and I couldn't help but notice how pretty she looked. I softened my tone slightly. "Why did you go out by yourself in the first place?"

She shrugged. "I was bored, I guess. So, I thought I'd make dinner, but I needed some ingredients from the store." It looked like she wasn't going to confide in me that she might be finding things difficult like Aloysius had suggested.

"That's not enough of a reason to go out without a guard. Anyway, I thought you had your cat to keep you company."

"Wilbur always likes to go back to sleep straight after breakfast."

"He goes back to sleep straight after breakfast?" I couldn't keep the incredulity out of my voice. "I'm out all day working my fingers to the bone while your fucking cat spends his day lying around my house, eating food my money pays for, and sleeping in my bed?"

"It's *our* bed now. And he likes to sleep here as it makes him feel close to me."

Letting go of her arms, I tried to swallow my irritation with her and her animal.

Almost everything that girl and cat did annoyed me.

This marriage was supposed to make my life easier, but all it had done so far was make my head throb and my balls ache.

The thick air sparked between us. I ran my gaze from her pouted lips to her slender neck and down over her body. An urge ran through me to lick my tongue down that same path, from her mouth to her throat, to the top of her full breasts—and not stopping there.

We still hadn't consummated our marriage and my feelings of frustration regarding this were contributing to my bad moods.

I had been about to go back downstairs to my study. Instead, I grabbed her arms again and pushed her up against the wall, causing her to exhale as her back hit the plaster.

I pressed my lips against her soft mouth.

She resisted for a few moments, pushing her small hands against my chest.

But as I coaxed her mouth, she sighed and yielded to me, meeting my tongue with exploring strokes of her own.

Although she hadn't been ready for sex on our wedding night, the look in her eyes and the way she had kissed me back that night had told me that she desired me. And over the last couple of days, I hadn't missed her checking out my body when she thought I wasn't looking, particularly in the mornings when she would run her gaze over my bare chest.

I didn't let up with my kisses, making them demanding and aggressive, which was how I felt now that I had her in my arms.

Her hands, which were now resting against my torso, grasped the fabric of my shirt as tension built within her.

I ran my hands down her back, along her hips and over her ass, feeling her tempting curves. I could feel through the fabric of her skirt that she was wearing a thong. I couldn't wait to rip it off her and expose her pussy for me to feast upon.

But before that I moved my hands up to cup her generous breasts. I molded my hands around them as I ran kisses from the shell of her ear down to the base of her throat.

She moaned as my mouth connected with her neck. As I left a trail of hot kisses, I started to unbutton her shirt, starting at the top and slowly exposing her bra and her torso.

As her shirt opened, it revealed a silk and lace white bra. The see-through material teased a glimpse of her nipples, making my erection become even stiffer.

Reaching behind her to unclip her bra, I pulled it off and finally let my eyes devour what I'd ached to see.

Even since seeing her in that silky nightdress on her first night in Chicago, I'd been wondering what color her nipples would be. They were a dark pink, and my mouth latched onto the beautifully thick nipples, pulling at the hard tips in turn and making them lengthen as Anni arched her back and pushed her head back up against the wall.

She looked so sexy standing there in just her mid-thigh length skirt, with her legs bare and her breasts naked.

Grasping her hand in mine, I tugged her toward the bed. She followed behind me, not resisting for once. Once we were at the bed, I spun her around and pushed her back onto the bed, making her exhale in surprise.

I didn't pause, instead ripping off my jacket and kicking off my shoes before prowling over her body, my arms and legs caging her in.

I kneaded her breasts in my hands and sucked a nipple into my mouth. I gave it a gentle bite before soothing it with my tongue while twisting the other nipple in my fingers, enjoying feeling the sensitivity of her tits to my hands and tongue.

By now I'd stripped off my shirt and dress pants. Looking her in the eye, I pushed down my boxers.

Her eyes widened as she took in my rock-hard cock, and she slowly licked her lips.

I bent over her again and brought my mouth to her ear. "You're killing me," I whispered, nuzzling her neck.

As she squirmed under me, her skirt rode further up, but still not enough to show me what I wanted to see. I pushed up my hands under it and bunched it up around her waist.

Grabbing her ass cheeks, I ground her body into my cock which was pressed up against her, letting her feel its hardness against her thong.

Pushing my dick downward so it caught between her legs, she moaned as it rubbed against her clit.

Fuck, the silk fabric of her thong was dark with her pussy juices and I could feel the slickness of it against my bare erection.

My lips moved down her body, licking and nipping at her perfect skin, marking it as mine. As my mouth came level with her pussy, she held her breath.

I looked up at her and could see her need in her dilated pupils.

That was all the permission I needed to continue.

Pressing small kisses against her thong, my tongue flicked against the thin, soaked silk, giving me my first taste of her juices. It was like honeyed nectar and I could have come right then.

As she wriggled under my lips and her thighs parted, I could see that the wetness had started to escape from the edges of her thong and cling to the tops of her inner thighs.

Forcing her legs further apart and holding them firmly open with my large hands, I pushed my nose into her slit and inhaled her scent and her desire.

My face moved up to the top edge of her thong and I snagged the waistband with my teeth. With my mouth I yanked the thong away from her body, making the fabric rip loudly and revealing her complete nakedness to my eyes.

Her body was perfection—big tits, a full ass, and a slim waist. She had the sort of body that would give grown men wet dreams.

When my teeth had ripped away her thong, she had closed her thighs in shyness.

"I won't let you hide your body from me," I said sternly as I pushed her thighs apart again. "Your body belongs to me now."

I gazed at her slit, making her face flush pink, before bending my head and slowly licking all the way from her ass to her clit. She whimpered like a kitten as I sucked her sensitive nub between my lips and swirled my tongue around it.

Gripping the sheets beneath her, she closed her eyes.

I stopped abruptly. "No, keep your eyes open," I commanded her. "I'll stop if you close them. I want you to watch as I make your pussy mine."

A blush ran up her cheeks. But I didn't care if it embarrassed her—I wanted her to watch every second of it and have images of this memory etched into her mind forever.

She reluctantly opened her eyes.

"Good. Now keep them open," I said in a rough tone.

I lowered my face back between her warm thighs, my mouth watering at the swollen, wet pussy before me. I swiped my tongue around her folds, teasing her relentlessly, but I didn't touch her clit again.

Her hands reached for my hair as her delectable thighs clamped around my head. She tried to push me toward her clit, grinding herself against my face, but I wasn't going to let her tell me what to do.

Spearing my tongue, I played with her opening, imagining how soon I would be sinking my cock into her tight hole.

Finally, I returned to her clit, nibbling at it and nipping it gently, causing her to cry out. I sucked at it again and let my tongue make love to it.

Looking up, I saw she had closed her eyes again.

"Eyes open," I demanded in a hard voice, making her jump and quickly open her eyes.

"Good girl," I growled. "I like it when you obey me."

She kept her eyes open as my mouth gorged on her pussy, my fingers pulling at her taut nipples at the same time, making her gasp and moan with pleasure.

I only stopped when I sensed her climax was near. Crawling back up her body, I kissed her mouth hard. "This is what you taste like. And it's a taste I'm going to want every single day now. Do you understand?"

"Yes," she breathed, her obedience pleasing me and making precum leak from the head of my dick.

"When you're in my bedroom and you've got my cock inside you, you're no longer a defiant little kitten. Understand?"

She nodded.

"No—I want to hear you say it," I ordered her.

"Please put your cock inside me," she begged. "I promise to be a good girl."

Fuck me. She was pure perfection.

I never expected to have her begging me to take her virginity. "You're so responsive and submissive in the bedroom. I want to chain you up naked in here and never let you go."

I loved when she was like this: subservient to me and doing as she was told. Since the first time I'd met her, I'd imagined what it would be like to have her compliant and yielding to me as she lay under my body, but I never thought I'd be able to tame her this well.

Grasping my dick at the base, I lined up to her entrance.

She closed her eyes again as if preparing for the pain.

"I've already told you that your eyes are to stay open." My voice was hard and unforgiving.

She opened her eyes and looked right at me.

I stroked the palm of my hand softly over her cheek. "That's it, kitten."

Her face pushed into my caress.

"I want you to watch as I drill my dick into you, as I pump my cum into you, and as I coat the walls of your pussy with my seed."

Although she was soaking wet and fully aroused, I could also see her nervousness.

"I'll make this pleasurable for you—as long as you keep being a good girl." My tone was stern, warning her not to defy me again.

She nodded and kept her eyes fixed on my rigid tool.

Pressing my erection against her folds, I moved my hips back and forth, massaging the head against her clit and making my precum mix with her creamy juices.

She began to move her hips, seeking the friction of my dick as it slid between her folds.

"That's it, kitten—give in to your desire," I told her in a deep voice.

As we moved against each other, I pressed the swollen head up against her opening, toying with the sensitive nerve endings there but still not entering her.

Kissing her passionately, I braced myself on one arm and reached down between her legs with my other hand. My fingers massaged her clit, making her breath come in pants.

Her slickness was making my fingers slip readily around her swollen nub, creating the most delicious friction for her as the head of my erection continued to massage her opening with a little more pressure each time I surged my hips forward.

My fingers could feel her clit becoming even more swollen in response to my ministrations. Sweat beaded her forehead and her cheeks were flushed.

I held my weight above her, creating enough of a gap between our bodies so that she could clearly see my hardness sliding through her folds and against her pussy entrance.

"Tell me what you want, kitten," I commanded her.

"Please, Lorenzo," she said in a strained voice as she continued to make herself keep her eyes open and fixed on what I was doing to her. "I'm being a good girl for you. Please reward me. Please let me have your cock."

And that was it—I couldn't hold back any longer. Not when she begged me so keenly, not when she looked at my dick with such desire.

As I continued to massage her clit, I entered her, slowly stretching her channel. I held back my desire long enough to let her get used to the size of me.

When she pulled back slightly, I slowed my pace, giving her what she needed.

I didn't stop fondling her clit, and I could see on her face the mixture of pleasure and pain—and I could see that she liked it.

I moaned as I felt her muscles grip me tight. "Take it in all the way like a good little kitten."

"Yes," she breathed obediently, as she slowly took the whole length of me.

Although I was all the way within her, I fought the urge to take her in the merciless way I wanted. Instead, I withdrew my hardness slowly before filling her up slowly with it again and continuing in this rhythm.

I could feel her slick juices coating my cock and her tight muscles gripping it with such intensity. I wanted to come already, but I didn't because I wanted to make this good for her.

Continuing to move my dick in and out of her while playing with her clit, I brought my mouth down to hers and kissed her with the savagery I wanted to fuck her with, pushing my tongue inside her mouth the way I wanted to plunge my dick inside her.

Then I moved my lips down to her breasts and sucked hard on her luscious, rock-hard nipples, making her moan out loud in pleasure.

As I tongued her tits, I could feel her inner muscles tightening and at the same time her grip on my forearms became harder as she clung to me. I looked back up at her, not wanting to miss the emotions flitting across her face.

Speeding up my cock, I drove in and out of her relentlessly with no letup either for her pussy or her clit.

"Please, Lorenzo, I need to come," she pleaded. "Please let me come."

Her begging me so sweetly was my undoing. No longer careful, I pounded my hardness in and out of her and pinched her clit, making her cry out as she orgasmed on my dick, her cream gushing around my dick.

The spasm of her muscles contracting around me set off my own climax and as I came, I drove my copious amount of cum into her.

And as her pussy squeezed every last drop of cum out of my cock, I bent down and kissed her full on the lips. "That's my good girl," I said in a thick voice.

Once my breathing had slowed down, I went and grabbed a washcloth from the bathroom. "Let me clean you," I commanded.

And as I sat down and put my hands on her legs, she obediently opened her thighs for me and let me wipe away the mixture of blood and cum from the inside of her thighs.

Tossing the cloth onto the nightstand, I laid down beside her and wrapped her in my hold, slowly stroking her hair as she fell asleep in my arms.

And I thought to myself that I loved it when she was like this—as sweet as an angel.

CHAPTER 23

ANNUNCIATA

The days started to pass quickly, and I fell into a routine with the children.

Although Lorenzo was still somewhat emotionally distant from me, our closeness had improved after the first time we'd had sex and each time after that.

I was enjoying having Lorenzo explore my body and discover what aroused me. He was skilled at lovemaking, and I was eager to learn from him.

The following week, Lorenzo stayed to have breakfast with the children every day. Also, as promised, he was home for dinner almost every night.

I noticed how much less worried Clara seemed when her father was at home. And that night as we undressed for bed, I decided to speak to Lorenzo about my concerns.

"Lorenzo, can we talk about Clara?"

"What about her?"

"I've noticed that Clara seems to do much better when you're at home. I'm finding her apprehension increases when you leave for work, and she always appears to be anxious about when you are coming back."

"She's still getting used to you. It won't happen overnight."

I took a deep breath. "I don't think I'm being unrealistic with my expectations—I realize that it will take time for the children to get to know me and trust me. But it's more than that. I still think Clara is experiencing separation anxiety." I wanted to add that it might be an after-effect of losing her mother, but I decided not to lead the conversation into unsafe territory.

He looked carefully at me as he considered my words. "What would you suggest?"

I licked my lips. "I was thinking that perhaps you might be able to work from home sometimes?" Before he could dismiss my idea, I carried on quickly. "My papà always worked from home when he could, and I know my siblings and I enjoyed having him around."

He considered my words. "Okay, I'll see what I can do. Rita didn't like me working at home, but I have no problem working out of the study when my schedule allows for it. But I'll only be able to do this on occasion since I'll still need to visit our various businesses and enterprises."

I was shocked that he had even mentioned Rita to me, but I didn't comment on that. Instead, I gave him a smile in thanks and told myself that things were slowly improving—and that as the situation with the children improved, so would my relationship with Lorenzo.

After our discussion, Lorenzo began working from home at least a couple of days each week. I knew that the children liked having him around more, particularly Clara, and I hoped that this was a sign that things were starting to get better.

***

I still wasn't getting Clara to eat as much at lunchtime as I would have liked. Lorenzo was never normally home for lunch except on the days he worked at home, and I knew I had to do something to try and distract Clara from her anxiety when he was at work.

I had the idea to take the children to a nearby playground I'd seen when Giuseppe had driven us to the mall. I'd seen picnic tables there, so I was going to ask Adelina to prepare a picnic lunch which we could eat there after the children had played and had a runaround. Clara might eat more if lunch was a fun activity like a picnic.

After getting the children ready and loading the picnic hamper into the back of the SUV, I drove to the gate.

Getting out of the driver's seat to make room for our bodyguard, I greeted Giuseppe. "Hi Giuseppe. Can you assign a guard to come with us to the playground?" I didn't dare go out without a guard again, especially since I had the kids with me.

"I'm sorry, ma'am. We've no spare soldiers at the moment. The boss needed some extra men today, so we only have the minimum number at the mansion today and they're all required to keep the property secure."

I let out a small breath of exasperation as I leaned against the car door.

Another black SUV had just pulled into the gate, and its blacked-out window rolled down.

"Hey, Anni." It was Aloysius.

I smiled at him. "It's you again."

"I work pretty closely with my brother so I'm in and out of the house all the time." He noticed my expression. "What's going on?"

"Nothing now." I sighed. "I was planning on taking the children to the playground for a play and then a picnic, but there isn't a spare soldier to accompany us there. I'm going to have to postpone the outing and disappoint the children."

"I can take you," he immediately offered.

"Really?" I smiled at him. "That would be great. I really don't want to have to disappoint the children. Are you sure it wouldn't be too much trouble?"

"It's no problem at all. I just need to drop these papers to Lorenzo's study and then I'll be with you."

He got back into his SUV and drove up to the mansion, and I waited while he did what he needed to do in Lorenzo's study.

When he came back out, he walked back over to me. "We'll take your vehicle as the kids are already strapped in."

He got into the driver's seat and turned to look over his shoulder. "Hey, kids."

"Hey!" Clemente chortled, while Clara gave him a shy smile

"I hear we're off to the playground today."

Clemente gave a giggle. "Yay, playground!"

It was only a short drive to the playground, and once we got there the kids ran off happily to play.

I went to get the picnic hamper out of the back.

"I'll get that for you," offered Aloysius, taking the hamper from me and carrying it over to one of the tables.

He was a nice guy—relaxed and approachable. He'd be a good person to get friendly with and on my side, I thought, and then perhaps he'd give me some more details on what had happened to Lorenzo's first wife. If I knew exactly what had happened, it would make it easier for me to know how to help the kids deal with it.

"They like it here," I observed as we sat on the bench, watching them squealing as they came down the slide.

"Yeah, they used to come here quite often. I'm not sure if they've been recently—Lorenzo's been busy with work and the wedding, and Mother's hip has been troubling her so she usually looks after the kids at her house rather than taking them out."

We watched the children play for a while, and although we didn't talk more, the silence between us was relaxed.

"Are you sure you have time for this?" I asked.

"Absolutely. Family comes first." He then gave a slight frown. "Well, as long as there's enough food for me as well?" He indicated toward the hamper with a nod of his head.

"Yeah, there's plenty. I know Adelina packed enough to feed an army."

"Good," he laughed.

Clara scampered over, clutching her ribbon which had come out of her hair. "Ribbon out," she said with a sad face.

"That's no problem. I can fix it for you."

She sat in front of me and I gathered the top section of her hair and tied the ribbon around her curls. Today she had chosen matching teal blue ribbons for her and Wilbur to wear. "All done," I said.

"You look beautiful," said Aloysius to his niece, earning a cute smile from her.

"Are you hungry yet?" I asked.

She shook her head.

"Okay, tell me when you get hungry, and we can have our picnic then."

She nodded at me and then ran back to Clemente on the seesaw.

Aloysius watched her as she played. "She's still not talking much, huh?"

"No. I've noticed that her and Clemente's speech are around the same level, despite their two-year age difference." I was careful what I said, not wanting the wrong thing getting back to Lorenzo.

"She used to be able to talk much more." Aloysius's tone was more serious now.

"Really?"

"Yeah, like full sentences and stuff."

I didn't say anything else, not knowing how to phrase what I wanted to ask.

Luckily, however, he carried on speaking. "That was before her mom died. After that, she started talking much less, like in one-word or two-word phrases."

"Yes, that's what it's still like at home." As he'd brought up the topic of Rita's death, I probed a little further. "Did the children go to their mom's funeral? You know, to say goodbye to her properly?"

"No, they didn't go. Lorenzo didn't want it. He didn't want them hearing people talking about their mom and how she died."

The hairs rose on the back of my neck. If Lorenzo didn't want the kids hearing that, then there must have been something suspicious about the way she died—and the cause must have been something other than pneumonia.

Clemente ran over and interrupted us, meaning that I couldn't ask any more questions. "Eat now?" he asked with a tired grin.

"Sure, we can eat now. Call your sister over, and I'll get the food out."

Adelina had packed a picnic blanket with the food, and the children decided they wanted to sit on the grass rather than at the table. I got out the sandwiches which had a variety of fillings and were cut into neat triangles. There was also a chicken salad, slices of chocolate cake, fruit juice, and a flask of coffee.

The children had worked up an appetite by running around and Clara ate a good amount of lunch, although I knew I still had some work to do on getting her to eat more.

After lunch, the children went back to play on the slide again. Aloysius and I talked some more, but the subject of Rita didn't come up again, and I didn't know how to bring it up without it sounding too obvious or nosy.

Then the children wanted a push on the swings, so Aloysius and I were kept busy—me pushing Clara, and Aloysius pushing Clemente.

All too soon, it was time to go home. I was conscious that I was keeping Aloysius from his work, and I didn't want to get him in trouble with Lorenzo. Especially after he tried to cover for me last week and got found out.

Once we were back at the mansion, I turned to Aloysius. "Thanks for taking us out today."

"No problem, Anni." He gave a wave. "Bye kids."

Clemente was already running inside, lured by the prospect of his toys, but Clara was still at my side. "Bye-bye," she said. I could tell she liked her uncle, and I was glad that the kids got to spend some time with him today.

LORENZO

That evening, I was home in time for dinner.

I noticed that Clara ate a good amount at dinner tonight, and that made me happy.

"I have to go back out to work," I said to Anni. "I'm meeting Aloysius and we have some business to take care of at the club. I'll be back late."

"Okay. I'll read the children their bedtime story after I've done their bath time and gotten them into bed."

I was relieved that Anni had learned some of these things fast. I'd never expected to take on a new wife who had no child-rearing experience, and I definitely needed someone who could help me take care of the children.

Stooping down, I gave her a lingering kiss on her luscious lips. When I moved my mouth away, her eyes reopened, and I could see that her pupils were dilated with arousal. I was already looking forward to my return tonight and having her underneath me in bed.

***

I picked up Aloysius from his apartment as it was on the way to the club.

As I drove, I looked across at my brother. "Anni said you took her and the kids to the playground today."

"Yeah, there was no one available to accompany them, so she was going to cancel their outing."

"I'm glad to see that she wasn't planning on going out without a guard again."

Aloysius looked thoughtful. "I don't think she would take that sort of risk with the kids." He paused for a moment, before continuing. "I know it's only been a couple of weeks, but she seems to really care about them. And she's helping them, you know. She wanted to take them out so that Clara could work up an appetite, and she also had the idea of a picnic lunch so that Clara would find eating more fun."

"And did it work—did Clara eat more?"

"She ate a good amount. She definitely seems happier to me since Anni's arrived."

After we'd dealt with the business at the club and I'd dropped Aloysius back to his apartment, I headed home.

It had been a long day, and I was tired. Going home for dinner meant that I had to go back to work afterward to finish off a couple of things.

Anni was adamant, however, that Clara ate more if I was home and that Clara had some sort of separation anxiety.

When she'd told me that, it had made me feel even guiltier about Rita's death. And since Anni had mentioned this, I'd made a conscious effort to be home for mealtimes more. I tried to be there for breakfast and dinner, although I rarely made it home for lunch.

Reaching the mansion, I parked in the garage and went through the connecting door into the house. I started to head up the staircase when I saw that a light had been left on in the dining room.

When I went to turn the light off, I was surprised to find Anni asleep over her laptop and a pile of books.

I shook her gently by the shoulder.

"Hmm?" she murmured, her eyes still shut.

"What's all this?"

Upon hearing my voice, her eyes flew open and she jerked upright. "Lorenzo..."

"Well?"

"Um, I was just looking up a couple of things on the web." She was hurriedly gathering together the books around her. It was clear she didn't want me to see them.

I put my large hand firmly over her smaller one, making her stop what she was doing. With my free hand, I turned one of the books around so that I could read the title: 'Linear Algebra and Applications'.

"I thought you'd already graduated high school?"

"I have."

I flicked through the pages of the book. "Anyway," I said slowly, "this looks too advanced for high school."

Anni didn't comment.

I looked hard at her. "Explain."

She lifted her chin. "I'm studying for a college degree."

"What?"

"I have a brain and I want to use it. My major is in math."

"And you didn't think I had a right to know this?"

"It doesn't affect my duties as your wife."

"Really?"

"I never study when I'm looking after the children, so it's not harming them."

"I'm your husband." My tone was terse. "You should have informed me of this and sought my permission instead of sneaking around like this."

"I'm hardly sneaking around," she sighed, wearily gathering up her books and heading for the stairs. "I'm too tired to argue about this right now. If you want to talk about it, we can talk in the morning."

My jaw tightened as she brushed me off. When would this girl stop defying me?

CHAPTER 24

ANNUNCIATA

I'd been right when I'd thought that Lorenzo would disapprove of me studying for a college degree. We hadn't talked any further about it, but I knew after what he'd said that he wasn't happy about it. I had been avoiding doing any college work since he'd found me asleep over my textbooks, but it meant that I was falling behind on my studies.

His views were out of the dark ages. That probably shouldn't have surprised me given that he was a Made Man—they had an archaic view of women, thinking that her sole functions were to be loyal to her man, warm his bed, and produce heirs for him.

The whole virgin tradition was proof of that. The men were free to have sex with as many women as they wanted pre-marriage, while the women had to say pure and untouched for their future husband. And then the woman had the humiliation of having her husband asked the morning after the wedding to confirm her virginity.

***

A few days later, I noticed how tired Lorenzo looked. Whenever he was home he would stay in his study and work, only coming to bed when it was very late, by which time I was usually asleep given the broken nights we had with the kids. Each night, without fail, Clara would wake, and then Clemente would also get woken up. It took a long time to get them both settled again.

Lorenzo and I weren't spending much time together, and I was also still missing my family. Married life was a difficult adjustment, and Lorenzo and I were just muddling through the best we could.

This morning, Marco came over for breakfast as Lorenzo needed to speak to him about business.

In the past, Lorenzo would have just skipped breakfast and had an early meeting, so I was thankful that he was, at least, keeping to his promise to be home more for mealtimes. He was always home for breakfast and dinner now, and if he was going to miss one of those meals, he always rang to let me know.

This sort of stability in the children's routine was really good for them, particularly for Clara with her anxiety issues. When her father was home, she always looked much happier and ate more. She still needed to eat a bit more at lunchtimes, but I was working on that.

While Lorenzo and Marco discussed business, I talked quietly with the children and helped them with their breakfast, careful not to interrupt the men's discussion in any way.

After breakfast, Marco and Lorenzo left for work, and the children went to play in the den.

Ten minutes later, I was in the hallway after coming out of the kitchen.

I started as someone came in through the unlocked front door, my hand flying to my chest.

"Didn't mean to startle you," drawled a cold voice. It was Marco. His dark hair and charcoal eyes gave him a threatening aura, not to mention the fact that he never smiled. "Just forgot my phone."

"Oh...I...thought you'd gone?" I found Marco Marchiano downright scary. To be Capo, a man had to be brutal and merciless, and everything I'd heard about the Capo so far fitted that description.

Marco strode into the dining room and retrieved his phone which was still on the table. Adelina hadn't cleared the dishes yet, so no one had noticed that his cell was still there.

I wondered if I should ask him if he'd like another cup of coffee before he left, but then thought to myself I'd rather he just went as soon as possible. I'd never been left alone with him before, and I really didn't like the vibe that came off him.

He turned to leave but then spun back around and stared at me.

My pulse beat erratically as he looked intently at me.

He rubbed his hand across his jaw. "Why don't you bring the kids to dinner tonight?"

"We can't," I blurted out. "I mean...the children are looking forward to having dinner with Lorenzo tonight."

"Lorenzo's coming to mine for dinner tonight—it's already arranged. If you bring the kids, they can see him there. Wouldn't want to disappoint them, after all."

I felt irritation rise in my veins. Lorenzo had promised he would be home for dinner as much as possible, and if he wasn't going to make it, he'd tell me in advance so that I could manage the children's expectations. But he'd already made plans for dinner without telling me or the children. It was probably going to be another one of those nights where Clara would refuse to eat much, being worried because her dad wasn't home for dinner like he'd promised he'd be, and instead she'd spend the meal looking at the door and wondering if her father was actually coming home. She'd already had her mom snatched away from her, and she was terrified that the same thing would happen with her dad.

"Okay," I agreed. "I'll bring the children."

"6 p.m. I'll see you then."

With that, he turned around and left.

I headed into the den. "Clara, Clemente, tonight we're all going for dinner at your cousin Marco's."

Clara suddenly looked alarmed, her eyes pooling with tears.

"Don't worry, your father will meet us there too," I said gently.

"Really?"

"Yes, sweetie, really. We'll have dinner together, and you'll also get to see Marco and the others."

After making sure Clara was alright, I wandered into the kitchen to get another cup of coffee. Then I was going to get the children's art equipment out and we were going to do some painting and crafts this morning.

"Are you okay, Mrs. Anni?" Adelina noticed that I was deep in thought.

"I was just thinking about Clara. She seems so sad sometimes."

"Yes, the poor thing."

"I know that the children didn't go to their mother's funeral, so I was wondering if maybe that has affected them—you know, because it would have been their last chance to see their mother and say goodbye to her. What do you think?"

"Mr. Lorenzo didn't want them at the funeral. He thought it was for the best. Anyway, it was a closed casket funeral, so they wouldn't have gotten to see their mother again anyway."

A cold shudder ran through me.

The Mafia tradition was that funerals had an open casket unless the body was not in a fit state to be viewed—usually because the person had come to a violent and bloody end. The open casket was so that relations and friends could leave parting gifts to the deceased. The women would place handfuls of fresh flower petals in the casket, in order to give sweet and pure blessings to the departed. The men would each place a bullet next to the body, to represent their protection of the dead person's honor.

If Rita had died from pneumonia, there would have been no reason for the closed casket.

"Why...was there a closed casket?"

"I'm sorry, Mrs. Anni." She spoke hurriedly, as though realizing that she'd said too much. "We shouldn't be talking about this. I don't want to get in trouble with Mr. Lorenzo." There was a definite fear behind her words.

I nodded, not wanting to pressure her into talking when she clearly felt uneasy.

I picked up my coffee and made my way back to the den to get the paints out.

I was left feeling frustrated, as though I was deliberately being left in the dark. Lorenzo didn't even mention his first wife or have a single photo of her in his home, and everyone else seemed to avoid mention of her.

What I had learned today meant that Rita had probably been killed by the Fratellanza because she had betrayed them.

And out of all the people she could have betrayed and been killed by, the most likely person was Lorenzo. I wondered if she had cheated on him or if she had betrayed him in his business dealings?

I'd always known that Made Men had no qualms when it came to killing wives or family members who betrayed them. The thought, however, still made my blood run cold as I wondered what I'd gotten myself into by marrying this man.

CHAPTER 25

ANNUNCIATA

We left home a little before 6pm.

Marco's estate was nearby apparently, and Giuseppe was assigned to drive us there.

When we pulled up at the estate's perimeter, Giuseppe rolled down his window. "Got a visitor for the boss," he said to the soldiers, all of whom were armed with AK-47s. Although Lorenzo's gate guards were also armed, they were more discreet with their weapons.

The soldier walked around to my side of the car and signaled for me to roll my window down.

"State your business," he barked at me.

"Um…I've been invited for dinner?" I don't know why it came out like a question, but his weapon was making me very nervous, particularly with the children in the back. The guards at Venetiville were *way* friendlier.

"Name?" he demanded.

"Anni…"

"Surname?" he snapped.

I thought it best not to say 'Oakley'—he didn't seem like the type to be able to appreciate a joke. "Er...Marchiano?" Why did everything come out as a question?

"Marchiano?" The soldier looked at me in surprise. "You're Lorenzo's wife?"

"Yeah." A blush ran up my cheeks. I still found it weird being referred to as his wife.

"Sorry, Mrs. Marchiano, I didn't know it was you. Go straight through. I'll ring the Capo and let him know you're here."

"Thank you," I murmured, rolling my window back up.

Giuseppe drove from the perimeter gates up to a large modern mansion. The grounds appeared to be extensive, with expansive green lawns which stretched into what looked to be a wooded area. At the side of the property, I spied a helipad complete with a chopper, as well as an impressive glasshouse containing an indoor pool. The whole estate was grand, as befitting the home of a Capo.

As we reached the house, I couldn't help staring at the enormous statue of the Virgin Mary on the front lawn, standing out in blatant contrast to the modern house. It must have been nearly ten feet tall.

We came to a halt, and as I helped the children out of the back seat, Marco opened the front door.

"Anni," he nodded at me without a smile of any sort. When he looked down at the children, however, a warmness spread through his features. "Hey Clemente. Hi Clara."

Clemente gave him a wave and then pushed past him into the house. Clara hung back by my side and didn't reply to him.

"Hey, don't I get a smile from my favorite girl?" he asked, picking her up gently in his arms and giving her a small kiss on the cheek, eliciting a chuckle from her.

"Tickles," she giggled, as the scruff on his chin rubbed against her soft cheek.

"You like tickles?"

She shook her head.

He cocked his head to one side. "Well, I know you like playing with Debi and Danio, right?"

"Here?" Clara's eyes lit up at the mention of Marco's sister.

"Yep, she's definitely here. She was over the moon when I told her you were visiting today. It's been ages since you last came and she got to see you."

"See her?"

"Sure. She's in the living room."

He carried Clara into a huge living space while I followed behind. The room had a large seating area with couches on one side, a dining room on the other side, and a kitchen just behind; all three areas were open plan to each other.

When we walked in, Clemente was already running around and exploring, and Clara wriggled to get down from Marco's arms to join in.

"Hi Anni," said a young girl.

I remembered meeting at the wedding. "You're Debi, right?"

"Yes, I'm Marco's sister." She gave me a friendly hug.

At a table sat a teenage boy, whom I recalled was one of Marco's many brothers. "Hey Anni," he greeted with a warm smile. He was wearing jeans and a hoodie, and he was working on two laptops simultaneously.

"Hi Danio." I was glad that I could remember some of their names.

"Yard?" Clemente said to no one in particular, pointing at the glass doors that led out to a huge backyard.

"Sure," said Danio, pushing back from the table and standing up. "Do you wanna come too, Anni?"

"Okay." I smiled at him. At least Danio and Debi were friendlier than their older brother. I really didn't want to be forced to stand around and make small talk with Marco. Even though he had invited me today, I still found him scary and intimidating.

Out in the yard, Danio kicked a ball around with the kids while Debi got out a bubble wand that fascinated Clara.

I crouched down to Clara's level. "You dip the wand in the special bubble mixture. Then you wave the wand and bubbles appear." I guided her hands to make the actions. As bubbles appeared around her, Clara gave a delighted giggle.

Just then Clemente fell over in his haste to get to the ball and started howling.

Running over to him, I picked him up in my arms. "Hey, sweetie. Where does it hurt?"

He carried on crying but pointed to his knee.

There was no graze, so it was just a bump. "You know what will make it better?"

He shook his head.

"If your sister blows bubbles on it."

I carried him over to Clara. "Hey Clara, can you blow a special bubble on Clemente's knee to make it all better?"

She nodded and, with a look of deep concentration on her face, she slowly dipped the wand in the mixture and then waved the wand how I'd shown her.

Clemente instantly forgot about his knee, fascinated by the bubbles and scrambling to get down from my arms so that he could have a go too.

"It's great you could bring Clara and Clemente over today," commented Debi. "We haven't seen them since your wedding."

"And we hadn't seen them for a while before that," added Danio. "Which is a shame as we used to see them all the time. They're our only cousins who live close by, although technically we're only second cousins."

"The children definitely seem to enjoy spending time with you," I observed. Clara and Clemente seemed happy and relaxed here. "Now that the wedding is out of the way, hopefully Lorenzo will have more time to bring them over, or I could bring them by sometimes and you could come over to our place."

Debi grinned. "That would be awesome."

"Lorenzo's just texted to say he is pulling up in the drive now," hollered Marco from the open doorway. "Let's get dinner started—I need to go back out to work afterward."

As we sat down at the dining table, Marco's other two brothers joined us. I had met them briefly at the engagement party and wedding. Alessio, who was his deputy and Consigliere, had a serious, intense gaze which, quite frankly, creeped me out. The other brother, Camillo, looked like a thug—he had thick muscles, huge arms and endless tattoos.

I got Clemente and Clara seated and had just sat down myself when I heard footsteps in the hallway and Lorenzo appeared.

He halted as soon as he saw the children, his gaze darting around and then lasering in on me. "Anni, explain what you are doing here," he demanded.

The stern censure in his voice carried through the room, making everyone stop what they were doing and look at me in the ensuing awkward silence.

Before I could formulate a response, Clara slipped out of her chair and scampered toward to her father, her arms reaching up to him.

He scooped her up into his arms with ease. "My precious," he crooned at her, his voice immediately softening when he spoke to her.

She snuggled deep into his hold, happy to see him and finding comfort in his arms.

Carrying her back over to her chair, he set her down on the seat and kissed the top of her head.

Then Lorenzo strode over, took my arm and pulled me to my feet. "I need a word with my wife..."

CHAPTER 26

LORENZO

As I dragged Anni down the hallway and into Marco's study, she tried to pull her arm away from me. "You're hurting me."

Pushing her into the study, I slammed the door shut. "What the hell do you think you're doing?"

"Marco invited us for dinner."

"So you just thought you'd come here without telling me first?"

"I didn't think I needed your permission. Anyway, Marco told me that *you* had already arranged to come here for dinner—something you forgot to mention to me, like you're *supposed* to do if you're going to miss dinner at home."

"I don't need to ask my wife permission for anything I do."

"No, you don't. But you do need to let me and the kids know, so that Clara won't worry something's happened to you and think that you might be snatched away from her."

Her words made me hesitate for a moment, but then my anger at her made me carry on. "I don't want the children coming to any Fratellanza gatherings."

"This isn't a 'Fratellanza gathering'. This is your *family*, Lorenzo. You told me that Marco is practically a brother to you."

"I don't want them to hear any gossip about their mother. I'm trying to protect them from the ugly rumors."

"And what exactly did happen to their mother?" she asked carefully.

"That's not your concern." A muscle ticked in my jaw.

"Of course it is! I'm trying to help the children, and that includes helping them cope with their grief. How am I supposed to do that if I don't even really know what they're going through and what gossip you're trying to protect them against? Lorenzo, you have to start trusting me, whether it's about me studying for a degree or knowing about what's happened so that I can help the children and you. And maybe you need to forgive yourself for whatever happened with Rita..."

"I wish it was that easy." My voice was a harsh whisper. And feeling an unwelcome flood of emotions that I usually fought so hard to repress, I turned on my heel and strode back to the dining room, leaving her to follow me.

Back at the table, everyone was busy either eating or talking. Two large lasagna dishes sat on the table, together with a platter of garlic bread and a large salad.

As I sat down, Marco looked at me carefully. "Everything okay?"

"It's fine." My tone made it clear that this was not something I was going to discuss here.

I was sat next to Clara, and I felt her small hand find its way under the table into my grasp. I looked at her and saw the relief apparent on her face, making guilt creep into my conscience, although I quickly brushed it away.

Danio passed me the lasagna, and I served myself a helping.

As we ate, I was glad to see that Clara was making inroads into her portion and that Clemente was also eating away, although he was also making a big mess.

Marco turned to Anni. "How are you finding your new role as a mom?"

I really didn't want a discussion on the topic of Anni's child-rearing skills. Couldn't I just eat in peace? I shot Marco a death stare, but he just ignored me—the fucker.

"There's a lot to learn, but I'm liking it."

"I remember the shock of being thrown into the deep end," replied Marco.

"You have kids?" Her mouth gaped open. "Sorry, I just mean that I knew you weren't married, but I hadn't realized that you had a baby-mama tucked away somewhere."

Her words made Marco grin. "Nah, I haven't got a baby-mama hidden away. After our parents died, me and Alessio had to bring up our younger siblings."

Anni stared at him with wide eyes. It was clear that she couldn't see him as the sort of person to have the patience to bring up a child or teach them right from wrong. "That must have been...an adjustment for you all." She was attempting to be tactful in her choice of words.

"Yeah," Marco shrugged, "but we managed. Like you will."

Once dinner was finished, I called Giuseppe to come and pick up Anni and the kids. "I have to go back out with Marco to deal with some stuff. You'll have to read the children their bedtime story."

"Of course," Anni replied stiffly, making me feel a pang of guilt that I was missing the children's bedtime.

Kissing the children goodnight, I gave Anni a nod and then headed out with Marco.

As he drove us in his SUV to a meeting with a couple of our men, he looked across at me. "She's helping the kids, you know."

I was silent for a moment. "I take it you're talking about Annie Oakley."

"Yeah. You should cut her a break."

I didn't say anything in response. I really didn't want to talk about Anni right now.

Marco, however, wasn't one to be put off. "I watched her playing with Clara and Clemente. I was surprised at how well she did after you told me that she didn't actually have any childcare experience."

"Yeah, well, she's had to learn fast. She had no choice as it was too late to do anything about Ma Veneti's blatant lies."

Everyone kept telling me that she was helping Clara and Clemente—first Aloysius and now Marco.

But they didn't have to live with her—or nearly get shot by her, or tricked by her ma, or put up with her fucking feline.

I sighed to myself. But maybe they were right—perhaps I should give her more of a chance. And maybe I'd been too harsh with Anni tonight.

I remembered the look Clara had given me tonight when I'd arrived at dinner. Anni had been right when she'd told me that Clara was worried something might happen to me like it did to her mother.

That thought cut me to the core. As a Made Man, I'd hurt many people, but I feel little guilt over the things I did in the course of my work. Causing pain to my child, however, was a whole different ballgame. And each time I saw how much the kids missed their mother, it made profound guilt prick at my conscience.

CHAPTER 27

LORENZO

The next morning I made sure that I stayed for breakfast
I had to make mealtimes with the children a priority—even if it did mean eating in the same room as that fucking cat.

"More eggs?" Clara said to me, after watching the creature devour his whole breakfast and then rub against Anni's legs in an attempt to get some more.

"Of course you can have some more eggs." I spooned another portion onto her kitten plate, and she gave me a beaming smile in return. Anni was right when she'd said that Clara ate more when I was home.

"Me too," Clemente demanded, banging his tiger fork onto his matching tiger plate.

"Say please, Clemente," Anni said gently.

"Peeze," he said with a cheeky grin.

"Good boy," I praised him, as I added more eggs to his plate.

Clara was wearing the old blue dress yet again, but at least Anni had it freshly washed and ironed every single morning—which was more than I used to achieve. Adelina retired after dinner, and it had been my job to remember to put Clara's dress on to wash each evening; by the time I'd got the kids to bed, though, I'd often forgotten. That was one job that Anni had taken off my hands, and I was glad that she was remembering to do it every night. Even though Clara was insisting on repeatedly wearing the same dress, at least it was clean for her every morning.

"I'll be home for dinner tonight," I said to Anni.

"Okay."

"We've had a problem with the bakeries." I didn't normally talk about my work with her, but I felt I owed her an explanation for the early starts and late finishes I'd been doing recently.

"The Fratellanza own bakeries?"

"Yes, we have a monopoly over the independent bakeries in Chicago and the surrounding areas. People love their artisan bread, and it's a cash-only business." Anni would know that this meant they were used as a front for laundering our dirty money.

"What sort of problems have you been experiencing?"

"Someone is stealing from the business. It's hard to know who, though, as the bakeries are a fairly big operation with lots of people involved in it."

"Are they taking a lot of money?"

"Some, but it's more that if someone is disloyal enough to steal from us, it's only a matter of time before they take the next step and shop us to the Feds in return for a nice government pay-off." The kids were too young to understand what we were talking about, so I could talk freely in front of them.

"Do you really think they would go to the Feds?"

"Once someone is disloyal, they can no longer be trusted within the organization. Too much is riding on it to run that sort of risk."

It was nice to be able to talk to her about my work, I thought. Rita had always refused to hear anything about it.

When everyone had just about finished, I dropped a kiss on the heads of both children. "See you at dinnertime," I said, earning a big smile from Clara.

Anni had just gone to get something from the kitchen, and I passed her in the hallway as I went to the front door. Putting my arms around her, I pulled her into me and gave her a slow kiss on her lips. She was deliciously responsive, and I was looking forward to getting home later and sharing my bed with her.

***

After a shitty day of more running around trying to deal with the issue at the bakeries, I arrived home just in time for dinner.

As I walked into the hallway, Adelina greeted me. "Hello Mr. Lorenzo. I will have dinner on the table in ten minutes."

"Thank you, Adelina."

Clara's head popped out of the den. She must have heard the door and my voice. She scampered forward but stopped in front of me. "Hi," she said shyly.

I felt a pang of sadness, remembering how before her mother died, I would come home from work and she would launch herself at me and run into my arms.

I gave her a smile. "Hi, yourself." I scooped her up in my arms and gave her a hug. I frowned as I looked at her, noticing that she was wearing a different dress from the one she'd put on for breakfast this morning. "Is this a new dress?" For once she wasn't wearing her old blue dress.

She nodded and then wriggled to get down from my arms. I set her down, and she did a slow twirl in front of me.

"You look beautiful," I said softly. And she really did. The new dress was a similar shade of blue to the old dress, but it fitted right and looked smart rather than shabby.

Just then, the cat strode in like he owned the place. He began to weave his body around Clara's legs in a figure of eight.

"Careful he doesn't trip you up," I warned.

"Cat hungry," she said in her small voice.

I felt like saying that the fucking cat would just have to wait for his dinner like everyone else. Instead, with forced pleasantness, I replied, "Adelina told me dinner will be ready in a few minutes."

Clara reached down and stroked his snowy fur.

As I watched them, I noticed that Clara and the cat were wearing matching ribbons. Anni had been brushing Clara's hair every morning—which I still didn't know how she'd achieved—and tying a ribbon in it. The cat had exactly the same ribbon tied to its collar in a bow. The cat looked fucking ridiculous, but I kept my thoughts to myself.

She stroked his ears, earning a deep purr from him as he rubbed his head against her hand. "Nice cat," she murmured.

I knelt down to her level. "Can you say Dadda?"

That's what she had always called me. She hadn't been able to say Daddy to start with and had called me Dadda, and then Dadda had stuck. I hadn't heard her call me that in over a year.

Clara didn't say anything.

"Dadda," I said slowly.

She looked at me in with her solemn, brown eyes.

"Just try to say it once," I pleaded with her.

But as I was met with resolute silence, I realized that I wasn't going to hear her call me that today or anytime soon.

And the thought made my heart ache with such an intensity that I thought it would burst.

Clara continued stroking the cat, and knowing that she was concentrating on him and not on what I was saying, I stood back and said quietly, "Mia preziosa, forgive me for what I did to your mother."

A moment later I heard a noise, and looking up, I saw Anni walking toward us.

CHAPTER 28

LORENZO

Anni had come out of the laundry room. "Hi," she said with a small smile.

I looked carefully at her, but she didn't seem to have heard me talking to Clara.

I didn't want her to know that I'd just been trying to get Clara to say Dadda. I concealed my emotions and moved my mind to a safe topic. "Where did the new dress come from?"

"I took the children to choose some new clothes a couple of weeks ago. I know it's taken a while to get Clara to wear the new things, but—"

"But nothing," I said firmly. "I'm pleased to see the new dress. Good job."

Anni's eyebrows shot up at my praise, and I realized that I probably hadn't given her much credit since she'd arrived and started taking care of the children. She was more mature than I'd given her credit for, and I probably hadn't appreciated her enough so far.

The cat trotted off toward the kitchen, probably to try the same thing on Adelina to get a snack from her. She also, for some reason, seemed obsessed with the animal.

The cat looked over his shoulder as he heard Clara follow him, and after waiting for her to catch up, they both went into the kitchen side-by-side. Clara spent a lot of time with the cat—maybe he was good for her in some way, although I didn't understand it.

Adelina came through to put the food onto the dining table, Clemente at her heels, and then we all sat down to eat.

"Did you manage to get any further with the problem at the bakeries?" enquired Anni. Although she was making conversation, she seemed distracted. She must have had a busy day, I thought.

"No. Aloysius and I have been working on it for a while now, looking at all possible avenues, but we keep drawing a blank."

"What signaled it in the first place that there's a problem?"

"A contact of mine at our bank told me that one of our guys, Alberto, has been depositing large sums into his account. He works for us, overseeing a lot of the stuff going on at the bakeries. There's no way he could have that sort of income. The idiot should have used a different bank, but he knows that our bank doesn't ask questions which is why they are safer to use. He didn't know that we keep tabs on the men's accounts."

"Where do you think his extra money might be coming from?"

"We thought he might be doing a sideline, like working for the Bratva or Cartels as well and earning money from them. But we've had him followed and all his online activity tracked for over two months now, and we've come up with zilch. Which means he must be taking money from the bakeries business—that's the only business he's closely involved in."

A small frown puckered Anni's forehead. "Are the bakeries losing money?"

"That's the thing. They are making less money than they used to, but that's all explainable due to higher overheads. Our accountants have gone through all the accounts, but nothing is showing up as suspicious—it's all as it should be."

"What are you looking into next?"

"I really don't know. I've brought a set of accounts home with me tonight to have another look through it. Aloysius's coming over after dinner so we can go through it together—two heads are better than one. But I don't think the problem is there. I'm beginning to think that maybe Alberto is taking a small cut from a number of bakeries."

"That would be harder to detect, right?"

"Yes, because smaller amounts are easier to hide. But the bigger worry is that if this is Alberto's mode of operation, he must also have quite a few of the bakery employees working with him—so we're looking at not just him betraying us, but also betrayal from a number of our associates who are working in the bakeries. We can't run a money laundering operation through a business containing so many disloyal men. The only reason we have the bakeries is for laundering purposes. The whole thing is a complete nightmare."

It was good to be able to talk this through with Anni, and she seemed genuinely interested. Rita would have forbidden any such business talk, hating all the illegal things that went on within our organization.

"You don't mind me talking about business at home?"

"No, my papà and brothers were always talking about their work during mealtimes, so I've grown up used to it."

ANNUNCIATA

We had just finished up our meal when Lorenzo headed into his study to take a phone call.

The children had gone into the den to finish watching a cartoon and then it would be time to take them upstairs for their bath time. I was just about to go into the kitchen when Aloysius arrived.

"Hey Anni."

"Hi Aloysius."

Lorenzo saw Aloysius in the hallway through his open study door. Covering the mouthpiece of his phone, he said, "Just give me a couple of minutes to take this call, Aloysius."

"Sure thing," he replied in a casual tone.

"Can I offer you a cup of coffee," I asked, trying to remember my manners when I was, in fact, distracted by other matters. I had heard Lorenzo earlier when he'd said to Clara, *"Mia preziosa, forgive me for what I did to your mother."*

Those words had sent a chill through my veins. What had he done that he was apologizing for? My sixth sense told me that whatever it was, it wasn't good.

"That would be nice, thanks, Anni," replied Aloysius.

I led Aloysius into the dining room. On the sideboard was a coffeepot and cups since Adelina always brought in coffee after dinner. Pouring a cup for Aloysius, I decided to join him and poured another for myself.

Sitting down at the table, we sipped at our drinks.

"Lorenzo said you were coming over tonight to talk about the problem at the bakeries."

"Yeah, that's right. It's proving to be a bit of a headache."

"Yes, Lorenzo said pretty much the same thing."

"I'll be glad when we finally get to the bottom of what's going on."

I liked Aloysius. He was relaxed and easy to talk to, and we were getting on well.

Stealing a glance through the open dining room door and seeing that Lorenzo was still on the phone across the hallway in his study, I lowered my voice. "Aloysius, what exactly happened to Rita?" Lorenzo had told me never to ask about this again, but I needed to know what had happened.

"What do you mean?" he asked smoothly, although I detected his body stiffen slightly.

"No one talks about her, and there's not a single photo of her in the house, not even in the children's bedroom. Lorenzo didn't want the kids at the funeral, and there was a closed casket." I took a deep breath. "Who killed her and why?"

"You've found out quite a lot," he observed, but he didn't answer my question.

"If I knew what happened to her, it might make it easier for me to understand what the kids are going through and try to help them deal with their grief. You said yourself that Clara has stopped talking as much since her mother's death—she just seems so sad a lot of the time, and I don't know how to help her."

"You shouldn't ask questions about Rita," he warned in a low voice. "You're doing fine with the kids—they've improved since you've arrived, so just keep on doing what you're already doing."

"But—"

"But, nothing." His tone was stern for once. "Rita's death isn't something I can talk about. And if you know what's good for you, you'll stop asking questions. Lorenzo won't like it, and you don't want to incur his anger."

"Is that what Rita did—incur his anger?"

"Anni, I have work to do," he said gently before standing up and heading to Lorenzo's study. "Thanks for the coffee."

Chapter 29

ANNUNCIATA

When I went to bed that evening, Lorenzo was still in his study with Aloysius.

I was frustrated that no one would tell me what had happened to Rita. The fact that everyone was so secretive about it was enough to tell me that her death was not an accident or through natural causes. I knew for sure that someone had killed her.

A cold shudder ran through me as I wondered whether her murderer had been Lorenzo or someone else.

My thoughts wandered back to just before dinner when I'd met Lorenzo, Clara, and Wilbur in the hallway.

I had just been about to come out of the laundry room into the hallway when I'd heard Lorenzo speaking to Clara. He'd been trying to get her to say Dadda.

"*Can you say Dadda as well?*"

His question had been met with silence.

"*Just try to say it once,*" he'd urged. "*You used to say it all the time.*" And, when he'd said that, I'd heard the profound longing in his voice—longing to have back the happy little girl Clara had once been.

I'd hung back, not wanting to intrude and not wanting him to know that I'd heard.

I had done some research on the internet and read that speech regression in children should be assessed by a professional. Aloysius had told me that previously Clara had been able to speak in sentences. I didn't know whether she could still speak in sentences and just didn't want to, or if her speech skills had regressed.

When Lorenzo came to bed, I made up my mind to discuss this with him.

I waited until he'd undressed and climbed into bed before broaching the subject. "Lorenzo, I was thinking that perhaps we should take Clara to see a speech therapist."

He remained silent as we lay in the darkness, so I took that as a cue to continue.

"Aloysius told me that Clara used to be able to speak more."

"She can speak. It's just that she doesn't want to."

"But we don't know that, do we? And I've been doing some research and read that if a child's speech regresses, they should go and see a professional."

"Clara doesn't need any help." His tone had become defensive, and I knew I had to tread carefully with what I said next. I definitely didn't want to mention that I'd heard him trying to get her to say Dadda earlier.

"I just think that maybe if Clara had better speech skills, she might be able to express her grief better, and that would help her to come to terms with it better."

He considered what I'd said for a few moments. "Okay, I'll think about it. But I think she's maybe a naturally quieter child."

It was clear I wasn't going to completely bring him over to my way of thinking tonight. Things had been going well between us today, and not wanting to rock the boat by pressing the issue, I let it drop for now.

Lorenzo pulled my body toward him and ran his hands under my chemise, pushing it up so that he could thumb my nipples as he kissed me deeply. I let my mind wander from this evening's events, not being able to stop my body's reaction to his skilled touch.

I wasn't wearing any panties and soon felt his hands between my thighs and fondling my labia, running his fingers up and down my folds and using my wetness to make his fingers sensuously glide against the entrance to my sex.

Soon I was writhing against his fingers, wanting to feel their pressure on my most sensitive nub. But frustratingly, his strokes avoided that.

"Please, Lorenzo," I begged. "Please touch my clit. I need to feel your touch there."

His eyes darkened further at my words. "If you want to feel my touch on your clit, you can have my mouth there."

I sank back against my pillow with relief that he was finally going to give me what I needed.

He hauled me up and took my place against the pillows. "No, kitten. If you want my tongue on your pussy, you're going to have to ride my face."

I swallowed hard. Ride his face? He had always taken the lead when giving me oral, leaving me to lie back and enjoy his tongue as it swirled between my thighs.

I licked my lips. "I don't know how..." I wasn't sure how I was supposed to do this and that thought made me feel vulnerable. "But I want to please you...by learning how to do it," I said quietly.

His nostrils flared with desire. "That's my good girl," he growled, making arousal practically leak down my thighs. Something within me sought and responded to the approval in his deep voice. "Kneel over my face so that you can rub your pussy against my mouth."

His words made me flush. I began to move my body but then stopped. "Which way around should I be?"

Having to ask these questions made me feel slightly stupid, but he stroked my leg to reassure me. "Whatever way you like, kitten."

After thinking for a second, I bent over him on all fours with my head facing his rigid cock. Then I slowly backed my body toward his face, looking down between my legs to see when my sex was level with his mouth.

His eyes were glued to my core, and he was breathing heavily in anticipation. "Lower yourself onto my face," he commanded. "I want your pussy on my face."

I felt so exposed like this but it also felt incredibly hot.

As I crouched my hips onto his face, his hands came up and grabbed me, holding me in position as his tongue swiped from my ass to my opening, and down to my clit, his lips finally latching onto my clit and making me cry out in pleasure.

His mouth sucked at my swollen tissues and his tongue massaged it. As he ate my pussy, I looked down between my legs and watched his mouth. The sight was nearly enough to make me come, but sensing that, he slowed down.

"You're pussy is so fucking wet, just the way I like it." His breath tickled against me as he spoke and then I felt something thick penetrate me.

Looking back down between my legs, I saw that he was plunging three large fingers in and out of me. Oh God, the friction inside me was so good, his fingers making me feel so full.

He continued fucking me with his fingers as he tongued my clit, making me whimper as I approached my climax.

But then he stopped moving his fingers, making me pant with need as his tongue kept working my clit.

Eventually he started plunging his fingers inside me again, thankfully bringing me toward orgasm, the pressure of his digits against my pussy walls being what I needed to take me over the edge.

But as I was about to come, he again stilled his fingers, leaving them positioned inside me and making me want to scream with frustration. He kept bringing me close to my climax and then deliberately backing off.

Lifting myself onto just my knees, I started to move my whole body back and forth, lifting my vagina off his fingers and then plunging back down on them, again and again, to mimic what he had just been doing to me.

And each time I pushed back down on his fingers, I ground my clit against his mouth, getting the delicious friction I so wanted there.

Now I understand why it was called riding a guy's face. I looked over my shoulder as I sank back down onto his fingers and mouth, seeing the profound desire in his gaze as it focused on my pussy, his face wet with my juices.

As I looked forward again, the sight of his cock as hard as steel made my mouth water and I couldn't help myself from taking it in my mouth for the first time.

I slipped the silky tip between my lips and then took as much of his length in my mouth as I could, tightly massaging the rest with my fist.

This was the first time I'd taken him in my mouth. As I continued moving my hips over his face while plunging my mouth up and down his cock, I heard his voice behind me. "Good girl," he said in a hard voice.

After a while he pushed me off his body, flipping me over onto my back and filling me with his huge cock in one harsh movement, making me cry out in pleasure.

"You're such a good girl that I didn't even need to tell you to suck my dick," he growled as he pounded my pussy. "I love that you're such a good girl but such a dirty girl at the same time."

He penetrated me relentlessly and this time didn't back off, instead bringing me to an intense orgasm which made me cry out loudly, before he surrendered to his own climax, grunting into my neck as he pumped me full of his endless cum.

Afterward he dragged me onto his chest and stroked my arms and kissed my hair. "Go to sleep now," he murmured, as I let my tiredness claim my body.

CHAPTER 30

ANNUNCIATA

The next day, I went back to thinking about Clara's speech. Whichever way I looked at it, I knew it might be difficult to get Lorenzo to realize that Clara could benefit from professional help.

I recalled seeing a book about how to do speech therapy at home with your child, and I went back onto my laptop and went through my search history to see if I could find it again. Finding the website, I made a note of the name of the book and then found an online copy to buy.

I was taking the children to the playground this morning, and I decided to start reading the book while I was watching the children there.

After Giuseppe had driven us to the playground, I settled on a bench where I had a good view of the children and started the book.

It began by outlining different types of speech issues and then moved on to the speech therapy technique that the book would teach. As I read through it, I wondered if this technique could help Clara develop her speech?

The technique involves expanding the child's single words into two-word phrases, then three-word phrases, then four-word phrases, and continuing this expansion until the child could speak whole sentences. This could possibly help Clara because so far I'd never heard her say anything longer than two or three words together.

Clara came over at that point. "Drink, please," she asked me.

I wondered how I could use the technique with her. After thinking about it for a few moments, I said "*Want* drink, please?" emphasizing how a longer phrase would sound if she used it.

And she nodded in reply. So, she understood what I said, but I needed to get her to start saying these longer phrases and sentences.

"Here you are." I handed her a bottle filled with water.

"Like drink," she said after drinking a third of the bottle.

"*I* like drink," I modeled for her, just like the book suggested I do.

She nodded again but didn't repeat my longer phrase. I knew that there would be no quick fix and that I needed to study the technique in more detail, but this was a start, and I was determined to work with Clara to help her.

I didn't need to tell Lorenzo, though, especially as it might not work. I would be careful not to use the technique in front of him.

"Thanks," Clara said.

"Thanks, *Anni*," I modeled for her.

And she nodded back at me with a smile.

***

That afternoon, the children wanted to make a camp in the den. I set up their pop-up tent, and we brought down pillows and blankets from their bedrooms to put inside. They then proceeded to bring some toys to play camping with. Clara got out lots of her stuffed animals and arranged them in a neat line, while Clemente wanted to put his toy cars in the tent next to him.

On my way back from getting some snacks from the kitchen, I noticed that Lorenzo had left out some papers on the dining table.

Out of curiosity, I went to have a look.

It looked to be a copy of accounts, and when I looked at it more closely, I saw that it was the accounts for the bakeries.

Scooping up the papers, I took them back with me to the den. After giving the children the snacks, I sat on the couch and started to look through the papers.

Figures and math had always fascinated me, and there was a lot of information contained in the accounts. Grabbing some drawing paper and a pencil from the children's art supplies cupboard, I began taking some notes as I went through the papers.

And that's how Lorenzo found me when he came home for dinner that evening.

Walking into the den, he raised his eyebrows as he looked at the toys, pillows, and blankets everywhere.

"Sorry." I jumped up from the couch. "I'll have this all cleared up in the next ten minutes." I knew he really hated mess around the house.

Clara and Clemente waved to their father from inside the tent.

"Looks like the kids are having fun."

"Yes, they've really enjoyed playing camping. Come on, children, time to tidy up and then we can have dinner."

I picked up the papers, hoping he was distracted by the kids enough that he wouldn't notice what I was holding.

I should have realized, though, that I wouldn't get anything past him.

"What's that?" His gaze lasered in on the papers.

"Um, you left some accounts for the bakeries in the dining room. I was taking a look through them—you know to see if I could find what might be causing the issues you mentioned."

"You wouldn't understand them."

"I can read profits and loss accounts, and I also understand balance sheets."

He looked at me carefully. "Where did you learn that?"

I shrugged. "I taught myself a while back."

"You taught yourself?"

"These sorts of things interest me, so I started to look at some examples and explanations of what the different parts meant. It wasn't that hard."

"I'll take those papers now." He held out his hand to me.

I handed them back reluctantly.

"Okay, let's go have dinner," he called to the kids, walking out of the den.

We ate dinner, and then I bathed the children, followed by Lorenzo reading them their bedtime story.

He went back to work in his study afterward.

Plucking up courage, I knocked tentatively at his door.

"What do you need?"

"I just wanted to talk about the accounts for the bakeries."

"I've got a new team of accountants reviewing them." He didn't look up from his paperwork. "You don't need to worry about it," he said dismissively.

"Actually...I think I may have found the problem."

He stilled, then sat back in his chair.

"You've found the problem?" He raised an eyebrow at me.

"Yes."

He looked at me carefully. "Go on."

I licked my dry lips. "There's too much money allocated to raw ingredients at times." I walked over to his side, and opening the accounts to the appropriate page, I pointed to the price listed for wheat purchases. "See, in this month for example."

He gave a sigh. "I've noticed that already. And Alberto's explained it due to the bakeries buying in extra wheat supplies before grain prices went up." He turned the page to the following month and showed me where there was an increased wholesale price for wheat. "It's standard practice when prices are due to go up."

"Yes, but grain prices didn't rise that month. They actually fell."

That grabbed his attention. "How do you know that?"

"I read the newspapers, including the business pages. And for some reason, my brain tends to like remembering numbers."

He didn't shoot me down, so I continued. "Although the extra wheat purchased is listed in the inventories, the reality is that the business didn't spend extra on it as claimed."

"And Alberto kept the money he claims the bakeries spent on the extra wheat," Lorenzo said slowly.

"Yes. And I've found another month when he did exactly the same thing. The accountants checked the figures, and the extra purchases would have tallied up with the physical inventories; but they didn't think to check the commodity prices listed under the quoted purchase prices."

He nodded, deep in thought.

"I know you think that I'm just a dumb girl."

"No, I don't..."

"Yes, you do. You think I'm brainless because I'm blonde and I'm cat-mad—and because I missed when I shot my gun at you."

He waved his hand at the accounts. "I think this has proved you have a brain—even if I didn't give you enough credit on that front to start with."

I took a deep breath. "And...has it convinced you enough that you won't mind me continuing studying for my college degree?"

He hesitated for a few long moments but then nodded. "You can continue with your studies as long as it doesn't interfere with looking after the children."

I resisted rolling my eyes at him. I hadn't let it interfere with the kids so far, and that wasn't going to change. "Good." I gave him a small smile. At least I could stop all the sneaking around I was doing with my books.

His mouth tugged up into a grin. "And, just for the record, I'm glad you missed that day, Anni."

And I could help myself from grinning back at him.

CHAPTER 31

LORENZO

The next evening, I arrived home late from work. It had been another long day, and I was tired.

I saw a light on in the dining room and went in to find Anni asleep over her textbooks again. She was wearing a silk nightdress and robe.

Now that I'd said she could continue with her studies, she was obviously not wasting any time in getting back to her assignments.

Looking down at her, I could see how exhausted she was. She'd spent all day looking after the kids, and once she'd put them to bed, she'd obviously got straight down to her studies. Appreciating how much effort she'd been putting into family life and taking care of the kids, I realized how lucky I was to have a woman like her in my life.

Gently taking a book from her hands and laying it on the table, I scooped her up in my arms.

"Lorenzo?" The movement had made her stir.

"Shh, kitten. Go back to sleep."

And carrying her soft body against mine, I slowly climbed the stairs and put her to bed.

I went in to check on the kids and both were fast asleep.

Clara was snuggled up with the stuffed white cat Anni had got for her. She had her arms tightly wrapped around it and looked at peace as she slept. Her cheeks were flushed pink, and her dark curls tumbled around her face. Bending down, I gave her a goodnight kiss.

I hadn't been too keen on the toy cat—in my opinion, it looked too much like Wilbur. Clara had wanted to take the *real* Wilbur to bed with her, but I'd put my foot down over that, explaining that cats slept in kitchens. He might have Anni and my daughter fooled with his 'I'm-just-a-cute-little-cat-act', but I wasn't a man who was easily deceived—and that animal was trouble with a capital T.

After my refusal to allow the creature to sleep in Clara's bed, Anni persuaded Clara to take the toy cat to bed with her instead. Anni had told her that the stuffed cat would look after her at night, and now Clara fell asleep every night stroking the toy. And, to my surprise, she was waking in the night much less, and she even managed to sleep through the entire night three or four times a week now. That was a huge improvement in her sleep pattern, and I knew I had Anni to thank for that.

Returning to the master bedroom, I stripped off my clothes, laid down beside Anni, and curled my body behind hers while cupping her silky breast with my hand.

And, as sleep overcame me, I thought to myself that having her in my arms just felt so right.

ANNUNCIATA

On my last trip to the mall, I had bought myself a new dress...a tennis dress.

I knew Lorenzo didn't want me having one, but I wasn't able to resist going to the sportswear store.

I loved playing tennis, and Lorenzo even had a tennis court at his mansion, so I didn't see why I should have to give up my hobby. I had already given up so many things when I married, and this wasn't going to be one of them.

At home, I hid the dress on the top shelf in the closet. After what Lorenzo had said about my keeping secrets from him when he found out about my college course, I was going to have to be careful about how I broached the subject with him.

A couple of days later, the kids were at Cosima's, and I knew that Lorenzo was working in his study.

Taking down the tennis dress, I quickly got changed. It was similar to my last one: white, sleeveless, and most definitely short.

Next, I found my racket which was still packed in one of my boxes sitting on the floor of the closet. I pulled my hair into a short ponytail, just like I always did when I played tennis. After checking my reflection in the mirror, I made my way downstairs and knocked on the study door.

"Come," he drawled in his deep voice.

Even though he could tell it was me by the way I knocked, he still refused to drop his formal tone as he called for me to enter.

Taking a deep breath, I pushed the door open and sauntered into his office.

"What do you need?" He flicked his deep brown eyes briefly up from the documents he was working on, but his pen didn't stop writing until he clocked what I was dressed in. He stilled and then sat up straight. "What are you wearing?" he growled.

"Hello to you too," I murmured.

I walked toward him and watched as he threw down his pen and leaned back in his chair, his eyes traveling down the tightly fitted dress and coming to rest on my bare thighs.

Making my way slowly around his desk, my racket swinging at my side, I perched my ass on the edge and faced him. "I need someone to play tennis with me."

"Do you now?" His voice held a dangerous edge. "I thought I told you no more tennis dresses."

"That was because you didn't want other men looking at me. This dress is for your eyes only. Unlike the Venetiville tennis courts, your court is secluded and no one can watch who's playing."

"There are security cameras there, so my men can still see you," he gritted out, as his large hand ran along the sensitive skin of my inner calf and stroked up my thigh.

Goosebumps pebbled on my upper arms. I bit my lower lip, trying to concentrate on our discussion rather than on the caress of his calloused fingers on my skin. "If you play with me, you'll be there to protect me, so the cameras on the court can be turned off." My voice came out breathy, and I was acutely aware of the dampness pooling between my legs.

"And if I win, what do I get?"

"Whatever you want." I played regularly, and I knew that Mr. Tennis-Hater here wouldn't beat me. "And if I win, I get what I want." *Like being allowed to play tennis whenever I wanted.*

He regarded me before standing up. "Stay here," he commanded.

I watched while he exited the room and went upstairs. He returned a few minutes later, dressed in black shorts and a fitted black tee.

He clicked on an app on his cell phone and pressed a couple of buttons. "Security cameras overlooking the court are off now. I'll just let the guards know not to disturb us there." I watched his fingers fly over the screen of his phone before he pocketed it and held out his hand to me.

"You don't have a racket," I pointed out.

"I'll collect one on the way."

Before we left the house, he opened a storage closet which was full of sports equipment. Moving aside a bag of golf clubs, he selected a racket, zipped it into its carry-case, and slung it over his shoulder. "All set," he announced.

We walked out to the court and coming up to it, I admired the well-kept green grass. Although I had seen the court, this was my first time actually on it, and it felt really good.

After collecting some balls, he walked over to the other side of the net. "I've got time for one set," he called.

My face fell slightly. "Only one set?"

"Yes. I've got things planned for this afternoon."

I would have liked to have spent the whole afternoon out here, but I wasn't going to argue. The very fact that he had let me keep the dress on and had agreed to play with me was a huge step forward in itself.

After a warmup of hitting the balls back and forth, each practicing our forehands, backhands, serves, and volleys, we got ready for the first game.

My first shot was an ace, making me shoot a triumphant smile at my husband. "You're going to have to move faster than that if you want to beat me," I called in a saucy voice.

He scowled but walked to the other side of the court to get ready for my next serve.

My serve was out of the lines, so I hit a less aggressive second serve, which he was easily able to return straight down the line and out of my reach.

"Good return," I said in surprise.

We continued playing, and each won our own service games until the score was four games each. I quickly came to realize that he was, in fact, pretty good at tennis. He'd fail to ever mention that, and I was beginning to regret saying he could have whatever he wanted if he won. I knew I had to make sure I won the set.

It was my service again, and I won my first two serves.

But then Lorenzo won every single point in the rest of the game, taking the score to 5-4 to him.

He got ready to serve. "If I win this game, I win the set," he said cockily, as if I needed reminding.

I hunkered down, ready to receive his serve.

But he aced it before I barely got moving.

His next shot was also an ace, putting him 30-0 up.

The next serve I backhanded down the line, and although he managed to return it, I ran up to the net and lobbed it out of his reach. 30-15 now, but he was still in the lead.

His next serve was keenly fought by both of us, but he managed to get a shot past me, making it 40-15.

"I've got set point," he called. "I hope you're ready to give me my reward."

"You haven't won yet," I huffed out, still out of breath. The arrogant bastard.

And, as if to prove his point, his next serve flew me and gave him an ace.

"Game, set, and match to me," he drawled, stalking over to me with a dark look in his eyes.

CHAPTER 32

LORENZO

Prowling over to Anni's side of the net, I kept my eyes on her.

Sweat beaded her neck, making me want to lick her there.

When I reached her, I bent my head down toward her, skimming a kiss at the base of her throat.

She shuddered at my touch. I'd been exploring Anni's body every night for the last few weeks, and I had been very pleased at her response to me and my touch.

Lifting my mouth, I whispered into her ear. "Time for you to pay the penalty."

Taking her hand, I tugged her reluctant body toward the two chairs at the side of the court which were used for water breaks during longer matches.

"I said that the winner gets a *reward*," she reminded me as she dragged her feet, "not that the loser has to pay a penalty."

"It's the same thing in my eyes."

Not letting go of her hand, I sat down in one of the chairs and then yanked her toward me.

My quick motion caught her off guard and as she lurched forward, I pushed her down.

"Ohhh!" she cried out.

"Don't worry, I'm not going to let you fall," I said in a low voice as I pushed her firmly onto my lap, her head facing downward and her legs on the opposite side.

She immediately tried to get up, but I held her down, my hand pressing hard into the small of her back.

"What are you doing?" she gasped.

I smoothed the short skirt of her dress over her ass. "I can see your panties like this."

"Lucky the cameras are off then," she retorted.

Lowering my hand to her pert cheeks, I moved my hand over them in smooth circles. "Yes, but you knew that I didn't want you wearing a tennis dress at my house."

As my fingers inched closer to the apex of her thighs, her voice became breathy. "But only you can see me, Lorenzo."

I deliberately didn't stroke where I knew she wanted me to touch her. "You disobeyed me," I growled. "I don't like it when you break the rules I've made."

"I didn't—," she began.

I lifted my hand and brought my palm down hard on her ass. Whack! The sound cracked through the air.

She gasped. "What are you doing…?"

I didn't answer. I rained two more swats to her behind, every muscle in her body tensing as I savored the sound ringing through the silence.

She grimaced in pain and began to struggle.

I merely looped one muscled arm around her back and ribcage, firmly clasping her body to mine, while my other hand continued to punish her. "Don't fight me!" My words whipped through the air as I smacked her cheeks again. Whack!

"Lorenzo…" she panted, the back of her sweet thighs turning pink.

I flipped up her skirt and yanked her white lacy panties down her thighs. "This. Dress. Is. Too. Short." Five sharp smacks punctuated each of my words.

She cried out, and a dark satisfaction suffused my body.

I soothed her naked flesh with a slow caress. "When your bare ass is bent over my lap like this, I can see your pretty pussy peeking out." I traced a finger over her pussy lips.

As she fought to get up and her face turned toward me, I relished the flush of embarrassment and fury on her face. My dick was already rigid and seeing her like this made it as hard as steel.

She started to grapple, using her small hands to try and free my hold off her body.

I grabbed both her wrists and used one hand to anchor them into the small of her back and immobilize her arms.

"Stop struggling and take your punishment like a good girl," I said in a stern voice while admiring the deep red imprints my large hands were leaving on her delicate skin.

But she continued to writhe against my lap.

"I told you to stop struggling!" Letting her go for a moment, I grabbed my racket carry-case and unclipped the leather strap from it.

Free of my hold, Anni scrambled up, her panties still around her lower thighs.

Before she could get away, I stood up, hauled her back to me and completely pulled off her tennis dress. I sat back in the chair and pushed her face down into my lap again.

"Don't tie up my hands!" She pulled her hands away the furthest she could get them from me.

"Don't worry," I said in a smooth tone. "I'm not going to tie your hands, kitten."

Taking a knife out of the ankle holster I wore under my black sports socks, I cut through the straps of her white bra and dragged the fabric away from her. "You won't be needing this."

"Lorenzo!"

I doubled over the leather strap in my hold. Raising it in my hand, I brought it down on her bare ass cheeks in a series of rapid slaps.

"Ow! What—ow, ow, ow!" she shrieked out. She turned her head and looking at the leather strap, she cried, "What are you doing?"

"I told you. You disobeyed me by buying another tennis dress." My breathing had accelerated. "Now you're receiving your punishment."

She tried to kick her legs, but they were constrained by her panties which I had tugged down to her knees. I liked seeing her powerless and at my mercy. But I knew that right now she hated being naked and exposed to me like this.

I continued to strap her ass cheeks, overlapping strikes down to the top of her beautiful thighs before running back up and occasionally interrupting the smacks to fondle her pussy lips and the entrance to her sex.

She wouldn't stop fighting to get out of my hold, angering me further.

I brought down the strap on her pussy lips, making her scream out in shock and pain.

Her face was turned to the side and I could see tears leaking out of her eyes as she cried out upon each slap of the leather against her swollen pussy.

But despite her tears, running my fingers between her legs, I found her pussy drenched with arousal.

"I'm bringing the strap down hard enough to teach you a lesson but know that I can use it much more harshly on you if you continue to struggle." The strikes were enough to sting harshly but not to cut her delicate skin there.

Heeding my warning, she stopped thrashing her legs and tried to stop squirming in my lap. Her eyes were screwed shut. "I'm sorry...I'm sorry I disobeyed you."

Grabbing her short ponytail, I jerked her head up, making her look at me. "I'm glad to hear you've seen the error of your ways, kitten."

"Please will you stop now?" she begged, her eyes wide and beseeching.

"No. So behave and take your punishment like a good girl," I said in a rough voice.

And as she slowly stopped fighting me, her body softened and accepted the strikes.

The punishment of the leather cracking against her skin was music to my ears, and her submission to me was pure arousal for my cock.

Dragging the strap through her slit, I jerked her head by her ponytail to face me again, and then I licked the leather. "You taste divine." I pushed the strap in front of her mouth. "See how good you taste."

Her small pink tongue darted out and she ran it along the strap which glistened with her juices.

"Your pussy is fucking soaking. Don't tell me that your body doesn't like what I'm doing to you."

To reward her for complying with my commands, I pushed two thick fingers into her tight pussy, making her cry out with pleasure. "You're such a good girl submitting to your punishment. And see what good girls get?" I said in a low hum.

"Thank you," she breathed, pushing her hips back into the thrust of my fingers.

"I love when your pussy is soaked—it's just how I like it when I want to pound my dick inside you."

Her pouting mouth was panting, and her naked ass and pussy were on display in front of me. I was rock hard and wanted her.

Letting go of her hair, I pushed a hand under her to palm her breasts. As I fondled them, she raised her chest up. The friction of her tits against the coarse fabric of my tennis shorts had made her nipples into large nubs which were as hard as rocks. She whimpered as I pinched each nipple.

Freeing my rigid member, I pushed her back down and adjusted her position.

She took me in her mouth without any further bidding. "That's it, kitten. Eat my dick. Take it all the way down your throat."

She ground her hips downward, trying to get the friction she desperately wanted on her clit but not in the right position to get it.

She used her hands to grip tightly around the base and plunged her mouth up and down my stiffness. Despite struggling to fit my girth into her mouth, she didn't slow down and set the rhythm exactly as I liked it. She was a natural at sucking my dick and loved being at my mercy and wrapping her pretty mouth around me.

I stroked her fair hair. "I like it when you're being good, kitten." And she practically purred when I praised her like this.

As I pounded three fingers from one hand in and out of her tight hole, her mouth moaned out loud around my erection.

Her channel was gripping my fingers tightly and trying to pull them further in. I needed my dick in her. Suddenly standing and lifting her body with my arms, I spun her to face the chair I'd been sitting on. "Bend over and grip the chair with your hands," I ordered her.

She immediately did as she was told, her small hands seizing the seat of the chair and her exquisite ass in the air.

I crouched down and pulled off her panties which were still around her knees.

"Spread your legs." My tone was abrupt and she obeyed straightaway.

I stroked her ass cheeks over the red marks left by the leather strap, making her shudder.

"You know what good girls get, don't you?"

She looked over her shoulder at me, her pupils dilated and shook her head.

"They get fucked good and hard," I growled. "I'm going to take you roughly. I'm not going to go easy on you. Don't let go of the chair. Understand?"

"Yes," she breathed.

Without any further warning, one hand tightly held her hip and the other grabbed her ponytail. And I shoved my whole length inside her, making her cry out. But I didn't slow down. I swiftly withdrew and then slammed into her again and again.

With each thrust, I pulled her hips into me and heard my balls slapping against her clit as I drove into her.

"Please fuck me hard," she gasped.

I tightened my hold on her ponytail. "I love it when you beg like a good girl."

She did as she'd been told and kept hold of the chair in front of her.

I watched as my cock disappeared inside her tight pink hole with each penetration, each of my thrusts making her moan, both from ecstasy and from the pain of my body slamming into her stinging ass cheeks.

Her legs were soon quivering and her sounds became more high-pitched as she approached her climax.

And as I felt her clench and spasm as she came around my cock, I didn't stop my pounding and quickly brought her to a second orgasm, making her scream out.

I finally gave into my own need and allowed myself to let go and come in her pussy, my cock pumping my seed deep inside her.

Dripping with sweat, I pressed my chest against her back and kissed her neck.

Once her breathing had slowed, she reached for her discarded panties and tried to clean herself with them.

I snatched away the fabric and shoved them into the pocket of my shorts along with the scraps left of her bra.

"I need to clean myself," she protested. My thick seed was trickling out of her pussy and down the insides of her thighs.

"No," I growled. "You're going to wear my cum for the rest of the day."

She opened her mouth to argue but then thought better of it. Instead, she started to get to her feet.

"Stay there," I ordered. Bending her over my lap again, I firmly held her body down.

I pulled out a small tube of lotion I'd put in my pocket when I'd changed into my shorts and t-shirt. I'd known I would win the match—I regularly played tennis with my personal trainer—and I'd planned to punish her like this all along.

Squeezing lotion onto the palm of my hand, I gently soothed it onto her ass and pussy lips, making her flinch.

Her face was pink with embarrassment, but I wasn't going to let her go until I'd taken care of her.

"This will help with the sting caused by the strap. I'll get you some painkillers when we go inside."

I stood up and set her on her feet.

Picking up her tennis dress which lay on the ground, I put it over her head. "Arms up."

She lifted her arms tiredly. After I helped guide her arms through, I pulled the dress down over her body and noticed her wince as the fabric skimmed over her red ass.

Then picking her up in my arms. I carried her back to the house.

"You won't be able to return the dress now that you've worn it. So, you can keep it for when we play tennis again."

She raised her head in surprise. "You'll let me play tennis?"

"Yes, but only with me."

She smiled.

"And you're never to wear panties with your tennis dress again. Understood?"

"Yes, I understand," she said earnestly, snuggling into my chest. "And thank you."

That evening, my mind kept wandering back to what had happened on the tennis court. Each time I thought about it, I smiled to myself. And it wasn't just the physical side that made me happy, although that had been great; it was also how much closer emotionally I was starting to feel toward Anni.

After Rita, I'd always been adamant that I wouldn't let myself get close to another woman or let someone into my heart. Although I'd agreed to the marriage to Anni, it had been for the sake of the alliance and to give my kids a mother-figure in their lives.

I had never imagined that my second marriage would turn out like this—a relationship where I actually wanted to spend time with a woman on a deeper level and where I wanted to get to know her more. So many things about Anni fascinated me: her intelligence, her caring nature, her beauty.

Perhaps I'd been wrong in my initial estimation of her? Maybe I'd been wrong to hold myself back so much from her? I hadn't wanted to let her get close to me, but that was what was happening now.

Not many women in the Mafia world were interested in studying and using their intelligence—simply because they knew that the main role expected of them was as a wife and mother. Anni, however, was determined to combine her studies with looking after a family, and something in me admired that trait in her. And it felt really good to be able to talk about my work with her—she was genuinely interested and had shown that she had a valuable contribution to make.

But most of all, she was so good with the children, particularly Clara. She had shown endless patience, care, and willingness. It was easy to forget that she was only twenty and that she had no real experience outside her overprotective life growing up in Venetiville.

And the thing was...I felt so damn attracted to her—to her beautiful mind, to her sexiness, and to her willingness to submit to me.

CHAPTER 33

LORENZO

A couple of weeks later, Anni's parents invited us to Staten Island, and we decided to head there for the weekend.

We hadn't been back to New York since the wedding and took the children with us as well, and it was nice to see them excited about the trip. Personally, I would have preferred to have stayed in Chicago, but I wanted to make an effort with Anni and do something together that would make her happy.

We took our private jet and then picked up a car to drive from the airfield to Staten Island.

As we drove across the Verrazzano-Narrows Bridge, Anni gave a satisfied sigh. "Whenever I come across this bridge, it always feels like coming home. It's the best view in the whole wide world."

Today she was wearing a white strapless jumpsuit that had an enormous white bow around the waist, plus white stiletto heels. I considered asking her to wear something more conservative and suitable for her new role as my wife, but given that we were just visiting her family, I decided that they must be used to her strange dress sense by now and so let it go.

We arrived just before dinner. After drinks in the drawing room, Napoleone announced that dinner would be at the clubhouse tonight.

"At the clubhouse?" I asked.

"Yes. It's the monthly Mexican Night, and I know you wouldn't want to miss that."

I stilled. "I thought your monthly Mexican Night is held at the end of every month?" I had purposely asked Anni about this and then deliberately scheduled our trip for the start of the month so that we would avoid the Mexican Night and fucking sombreros.

Ma Veneti shot me a devious look with her beady eyes. "We postponed the last one—especially so that you would be able to enjoy it with us when you visited." I had the distinct feeling that she was gleefully inflicting another Mexican Night on me because of my refusal to wear a sombrero at the engagement party.

We made our way to the clubhouse. Although the children had been in the clubhouse for the wedding reception, tonight it felt different to them with the richly colored papel picado decorating the walls and the band playing lively Mexican music.

Clemente clapped his hands in glee, loving the energetic atmosphere and eager to explore his surroundings. Clara, who had taken a shine to Ma Veneti, sat between her and Anni, and allowed the older woman to keep her occupied with the contents of her purse.

Anni's older brother, Christian, was sitting across from us. "Seeing your kids is making me broody," Christian remarked.

"You, broody?" Anni laughed at her oldest brother.

"Yeah, I need to have an heir one day, so why not?" Christian had the same green eyes as Anni and most of the other Venetis, but his seemed menacing for some reason.

"You'd need to find yourself a wife first, and you've always said there's no one in the Imperiosi families who interests you."

"Now we have this alliance with the Fratellanza, I could find a girl from Chicago."

That was never going to happen, I thought to myself. Napoleone was easy enough to work with as he was getting on in years and wanted a quiet life. Christian, on the other hand, was hungry for power and ruthless enough to do whatever was required to get it. I couldn't see any

Fratellanza man entrusting their daughter in marriage to Christian, alliance or not.

A little while later, I caught sight of Napoleone arguing with Anni's other brother, Leoluca.

"What's that about?" I asked Anni, my voice quiet.

Anni's brow creased with a frown. "I love my papà, but he's always been too hard on Leoluca."

"In what way?"

"Papà always says Leoluca is a bitter disappointment to him and Ma."

"He seems to be doing a good job to me. From the little I've seen of him, he appeared every inch a typical Made Man in terms of what he does and what he achieves."

"But he's a *reluctant* Made Man, and that pisses Papà off to no end."

"And your ma is disappointed about that too?"

"Oh no. Ma always wanted Leoluca to be a priest. She prayed feverishly for it. Until the day Papà had to break the news to her that Leoluca liked bedding women far too much for him to be suitable for the priesthood. So Leoluca was a bitter disappointment to our parents: to Ma because he didn't want to be a priest, and to Papà because he didn't want to be a killer."

I knew my wife hailed from a family of lunatics, but this was a new level of crazy.

"He works in the business but he's a reluctant participant, and Papà is always on his case because of that."

Clemente ran around our table, thoroughly enjoying himself. Although I still refused to wear a goddamn sombrero, the children happily joined Anni and the rest of the clubhouse in donning the supplied hats.

A variety of appetizers were served, and although Clemente enjoyed a number of the dishes, Clara was much more cautious. She was pleased, however, when Ma Veneti took her and Clemente over to play with a pinata shaped as a donkey.

For the main course was a dish with slow-cooked chicken, brown rice, and avocado, as well as spicy empanadas.

After dessert was served, Ma Veneti asked Leoluca to take down a row of the papel picado and she showed them to Clara. She was fascinated with the jewel-like colors and intricate design of the decorations. "It's pretty paper," she said softly, looking up at Ma Veneti.

"Yes, it's so pretty, just like you," Ma Veneti replied.

Another girl, whom I'd remembered as being one of Anni's bridesmaids, was also playing with Clara. "Who's that girl?" I asked Anni.

"That's Nicki. She's another one of my cousins, although she's more like a sister to us."

"I thought you only have the one sister, Fidella?"

"I have, technically. But Nicki's mom died when she was young, and then her dad and brother were killed by the Cartel, so Nicki's lived with us since then."

"That was good of your parents to take her in, especially as your papà could have ordered any of his men to take her into their family."

"He could have, but he saw it as a debt of honor—her dad and brother died protecting Papà when the Cartel tried to assassinate him."

"She seems nice, and Clara appears to like her."

"Yeah, she is nice," she said with a smile. "And it's nice to be able to catch up with everyone." After that, Anni went to greet various relatives around the room while I stayed at the table and kept a close eye on the kids and attempted to engage in as little polite conversation as possible.

Checking my watch a while later, I realized that Anni had been gone for a while. I scanned the room for her and saw her talking in a corner with Christian. They were deep in conversation, and when I finally managed to catch Anni's eye, she looked back at me with a guilty edge in her gaze.

I tapped my watch to signal that it was time we returned to our hotel for the night. The children were tired after the trip today and all the excitement of the evening. We would be returning tomorrow to spend the day with the Venetis before jetting back to Chicago in the evening.

Anni returned to the table, and after bidding goodnight to everyone, I drove us to the hotel.

"What were you talking to Christian about?"

"Um, nothing, really."

"You were talking to him about 'nothing' for a long time."

She sighed. "He was just asking how my marriage with you was going, and I was just filling him in."

Something about Christian niggled at me.

Although we had an alliance with the Fratellanza now, we'd made that with Napoleone. Christian, as the oldest son, would take over from him one day. Christian was a devious bastard, however, and I didn't know if I would ever fully trust him.

***

The following Friday, I finished work early and arrived home about an hour before dinner. I said hi to Anni and the kids and then went up to take a shower.

Coming back downstairs afterward, I walked into the den where Anni was relaxing with the children.

It had been a long week, especially with dealing with the fallout from the issue with the bakeries and the treachery from Alberto. After Aloysius and I had tortured details of his accomplices out of him, Alberto and his two accomplices came to a grisly end at the old meat-packing plant we'd bought to use for such purposes.

I picked up Clemente and swung him around, eliciting a giggle from him.

"I've brought home some brownies."

"Yay!" Clemente yelled.

"They're from the Blackbird Bakery just down the road—it's one of the bakeries owned by the Fratellanza," I explained to Anni.

"I like brownies," said Clara in her quiet voice.

"And there's plenty for all of us. They're a thank you, Anni, for your help with the accounting issue. I remember you saying once that they are your favorite."

Anni gave me a warm smile, and I thought how much better things had been between us lately.

As I gratefully sank onto the couch, I reached for the TV control to switch to the news.

"Don't change the channel," said Anni, looking up from Clemente who was now sitting on her lap.

"I want to watch the news."

"You can't. Wilbur is watching the swimming championships."

I looked over at the TV which was on one of the sports channels. "He's a cat. And cats don't watch TV."

"Wilbur does. He loves watching the swim competitions and will be heartbroken if you change the channel."

I glared at the creature. He was, indeed, transfixed by the scene in front of him. "You know he probably thinks the swimmers are fish, and he's planning on how he can kill them."

"I'd figured as much. Anyway, so what? He's enjoying himself."

All that cat did was fucking enjoy himself while I slaved away running the business. "By letting him watch this, you're just pandering to his lethal tendencies."

"By carrying around a gun, you're pandering to your homicidal instincts, but such is life." Anni gave me a cheeky grin.

There were a number of TVs in the house, but I couldn't bring myself to leave the room. Next to Wilbur sat Clara. Although she wasn't watching the swimming, she stayed at his side, gently stroking his fur and captivated by him. I didn't want to change the TV channel if it meant that Wilbur would stalk off and disappoint Clara. For some reason, she liked him, and he made her happy.

I'd known since his arrival that Wilbur was utterly besotted with Anni. Today, however, I realized that the cat also loved Clara and that his love was unconditional; and that Clara loved him back too.

Whenever I went to check on the children after they'd gone to bed, Wilbur would insist on trotting up the stairs behind me and following me into Clara's bedroom despite my best efforts to keep him downstairs. Once there, he would perch his chubby paws up on the side of her bed and then look down at her as if checking to see she was alright. Once satisfied that she was okay, he would scamper back off downstairs to his basket in the kitchen. He was devoted to Clara and showed an unwavering loyalty to my daughter.

Everything felt right for once. Anni was finally beginning to settle into her role as a wife and mom, and the children were happy.

I'd also noticed that Clara's speech had started to improve lately. I'd known that all she needed was some time, and I was glad that she was speaking a little more now.

I had the feeling that things were going to work out between Anni and me, and that thought made me feel good.

I'd come to realize that I needed her—the pain inside me needed her. She was like a healing balm to my damaged heart. She could soothe the anger inside me—the anger that Rita had left me and the children. Rita's actions had shattered my heart and robbed my soul, but Anni was slowly mending me and mending my children.

She gave me a kind of love that pushed my walls down. Her love was like a drug—something that soothed the damage within me and made me happy again.

Anni leaned her head against my shoulder as she sat next to me, and I savored her closeness and sweet scent. I never imagined that we would even remotely get along after our first meeting, nor that she would ever let me touch her after our wedding night, but things were working themselves out.

I surveyed the scene around me: my wife curled up next to me on the couch with Clemente in her lap while my daughter and the cat sat snuggled up together at her feet.

Something akin to contentment passed through me...and I realized that it had been a long time since I'd last felt like this.

CHAPTER 34

ANNUNCIATA

In the weeks that followed our trip to Venetiville, things between Lorenzo and I were going well.

In bed one evening, I decided to broach the subject of Clara's speech with Lorenzo.

Lorenzo had just turned off his nightstand lamp, and we were lying in the dark. "Lorenzo, can we talk about Clara please?"

"What about Clara?"

"You know how she's been speaking more lately?"

He paused. "Yes."

I took a deep breath. "Well, a couple of months back, I read up about a speech therapy technique, and I've been using it with Clara."

He immediately sat up and snapped his lamp back on. "And you didn't think to tell me?"

"I wanted to see if it would work first." My words came out in a rush.

"What does this technique involve?"

I sat up as well. "The technique involves expanding the child's existing words and phrases. When I speak to Clara, I've been modeling speech to her based on her current capabilities. I've been demonstrating to her how she can extend single words into two-word phrases, then three-word phrases, then longer phrases; and I wanted to continue this expansion until she started saying whole sentences."

He nodded slowly. "And it appears to be working."

"Yes," I agreed. "It's just that Clara has expanded now to four-word phrases. But that's where I've gotten stuck. She hasn't progressed at all in the last four weeks."

I could see he was carefully considering what I'd just told him.

Before he could shoot me down, I carried on quickly. "I think now would be a good time to get her assessed by a professional speech therapist. I think she's gone as far as she can with the technique I've been using, and now she needs some help from someone more qualified than me."

"I don't think she needs to see anyone."

"But what harm will it do? If she could speak more, then she could speak about her grief as well."

"Please, Anni, stop interfering," he said in an anguished tone.

"I just thought—"

"Go to sleep, Anni. And don't bring this up again." His words whipped through the room and stung deeply.

Lorenzo switched off the light and laid back down.

I slipped back down under the covers, unable to hold back my silent tears of frustration. All I wanted to do was help Clara. Both children were beautiful little people, and I knew I had fallen in love with them both. And that love meant that I only wanted the best for them, and it hurt when Lorenzo shut me down like this and dismissed my concerns.

LORENZO

The next morning, as I shaved, last night's conversation with Anni kept running through my mind.

Anni kept insisting that Clara needed help with her speech and her grief.

Deep down, I knew Rita's death and Clara's issues were all my fault.

My chest was feeling tight, and I rubbed my hand across it, but another uncomfortable twinge flitted across my chest.

I'd been having these pains more frequently recently. Rita's birthday was coming up soon, and that had been playing on my mind, making my guilt niggle away at me even more than usual.

Once Rita's birthday had passed, then these feelings in my chest would pass—I was sure of it.

ANNUNCIATA

Today the kids were spending the day with Lorenzo's mother.

Lorenzo was going to be out working all day, so I planned to spend the day studying. Getting out my laptop and textbooks, I started an assignment which was due the following week. I was too unsettled, however, from our conversation last night to concentrate.

Throwing down my pen, I opened an online news site on my laptop and let that distract me for a while. Then, under the local news section, an event caught my eye: the Chicago Cat Convention was taking place today in the city.

I had heard about Cat-Con in the past but never thought I'd actually be in Chicago to attend it. Excitement started to bubble inside me. The convention would have all sorts of cat-themed exhibitors, and as I read through the list of what was scheduled, I knew I had to go to it.

And I had the perfect thing to wear to it: I had a fluffy white cat costume which I had once bought because it looked just like Wilbur's fur, but I'd never had the opportunity to wear it. Lots of people dressed up as cats for Cat-Con, so I'd fit right in.

I hurried up to the walk-in closet in the master and dug around in the boxes which I hadn't yet unpacked. As my hands ran across the plush, white fur of the costume, I felt a sense of excitement run through me.

Between my new marriage, studies and childcare, I'd had little time for doing fun things since arriving in Chicago. I made a mental note to rectify that as soon as possible—I needed some downtime if I was going to cope with Lorenzo and my new role as his wife.

After I'd dressed, I grabbed a small backpack and added a bottle of water, my phone, and wallet. In the garage, I picked out an SUV and drove it toward the front gate. Reaching the gate, I came to a stop as I saw Giuseppe walk toward me.

Although I was dressed in my cat costume, the large fluffy white head with blue eyes lay on the passenger seat since wearing it would obscure my view while driving. I rolled down the blacked-out window just enough so that Giuseppe could see my face but not what I was wearing—given how uptight Lorenzo was, I thought he'd want as few of his men as possible to see me dressed in my costume.

"Good morning, ma'am."

"Hi Giuseppe." I smiled at him. "I'm headed out to the city center today. Could you allocate a guard to go with me please?" The bodyguard would see my costume, but I'd warn him that Lorenzo would be deeply unhappy if he mentioned it to any of the other soldiers.

Giuseppe hesitated. "Does Mr. Marchiano know about this?"

"No."

"You'll need his authorization before you can go into the city."

"His authorization? Of course, I don't need his authorization. I'm his wife, not his possession."

"Just a minute, ma'am."

He pulled out his cell phone and made a call. "Boss, just ringing as per your orders. Your wife wants to go to the city center… Yeah, got it, Boss… Understood."

He looked up at me apologetically. "I'm sorry, ma'am, but Mr. Marchiano says that you're not allowed to go."

"Not *allowed* to go? What do you mean?"

Giuseppe looked uncomfortable as he tried to explain. "All your trips out so far have been to places a short drive away, like the mall and playground. Heading to the city center would pose more risks as it will be a lot busier around there. I think that Mr. Marchiano doesn't want you in any danger."

"What reasoning did he give *exactly*?"

Giuseppe moved from foot to foot as he didn't respond.

"Answer my question, Giuseppe," I said coldly. I had learned a thing or two by having a Capo as my papà.

He reluctantly spoke up. "He didn't give a reason. He just said under no circumstances were we to let you leave to go into the city."

What the hell?

And he'd been able to spare me just five seconds. If he was going to say no, he could at least try to first understand why I wanted to go out.

It was as if I was just another one of his annoying business issues that he was being forced to deal with. And he was dismissing this problem—and me—as quickly as possible.

But then this whole marriage had been just a business arrangement for him all along.

I was fuming at the fact that he'd ordered his soldiers to report such matters him.

I wasn't a schoolgirl who needed her parent's authorization to go on a freaking excursion. I was a twenty-year-old adult woman.

And if Lorenzo thought me old enough to be his unpaid nanny for the children and his unpaid whore for his bed, then I was damn well old enough to go out wherever and whenever I wanted.

I took a deep breath before schooling my features into a neutral expression. This is just a misunderstanding."

I pulled out my own cell and pretended to dial Lorenzo.

"Hi *honey pie*," I said in a syrupy sweet voice. Lorenzo and I weren't at the stage yet of having pet names for each other—and judging by last night, we would probably never be—so I used the name Ma called my papà. "As the children are at your mother's today, I thought I'd pop into the city center. I promise I'll be careful."

I paused, pretending that Lorenzo was speaking to me.

"Sure, I was planning on taking a guard with me, but I'd much rather you take me. We could have lunch together and some, you know, *private time* without the kids." I shot a look at Giuseppe, whose face had gone bright red as he listened to our personal conversation.

I paused again, waiting for the fake Lorenzo reply.

"You're nearby? That's great. Yes, I know where the bakery is—it's the one where you got the brownies from. I'll meet you there in five minutes." I paused, then carried on, "Yes, I definitely know where it is and can drive myself there. *Love you, honey pie!*" I added a girlish giggle for good measure.

I lowered my phone and smiled at Giuseppe. "All sorted. My husband is going to take me. He's at the Blackbird Bakery down the road and told me to meet him there."

I crossed my fingers, hoping that Giuseppe didn't know Lorenzo's movements today—and praying that Giuseppe didn't know that Lorenzo wasn't actually at the Fratellanza-owned bakery down the road.

"I'll just get another soldier to take my place at the gate, and then I'll drive you to the bakery, ma'am."

"No, it's okay. Lorenzo said it's fine for me to drive myself there. I mean, it's two minutes straight down the main road, so nothing is going to happen to me on the way there."

Giuseppe gave me a hard look. "The boss has given us clear instructions that you're not supposed to go *anywhere* without a guard."

"Oh, yes, he's said the same thing to me—that's meant for when I'm taking the children out."

He pulled out his cell phone again. "I'll have to ask the boss."

"He's told me repeatedly that he doesn't like to be bothered with domestic trivialities," I said firmly.

Giuseppe wavered, but I could see his fingers poised over the keypad and ready to dial.

"Fine, Giuseppe, but don't blame me when he's pissed..."

Giuseppe put his phone away. "I'll open the gates, ma'am."

"Great. Thanks, Giuseppe."

Driving through the gates, I smiled in triumph. Chicago Cat Convention, here I come.

CHAPTER 35

LORENZO

I came home in the early afternoon to collect some cash from the safe. Aloysius was with me, and after this stop we were heading to one of our clubs.

As Aloysius drove us, I noticed that his mind was not on what I'd been discussing with him. "You've been a bit preoccupied lately."

He shot me a sharp look.

I decided to venture a guess. "I thought that perhaps you've met a girl?" Women seemed to fall over themselves for his laid-back charm, and he was always happy to take advantage of this.

After a moment, he drawled. "You know me, I've always got a few different girls on the go." He wasn't giving anything away.

"I thought that maybe there might be a special one, given that sometimes your mind is on something—or someone—else?"

He grinned at me. "Maybe there is someone. But it's not at the stage yet of me introducing her to the family."

"I was right. I knew it." The girl must be Italian if she was suitable to be introduced to the family in the future, although she might not be from a connected family.

I knew that I wouldn't get anything more out of Aloysius today, so I let the subject drop. Anyway, we had reached the mansion now.

The house was quiet when I let us in, and we went straight to my study. After dealing with the money, I went to find Anni to tell her that I would pick up the kids from my mother's on my way home this evening.

Anni wasn't anywhere downstairs. Not finding her upstairs either, but finding Adelina, I asked the housekeeper where my wife was.

"She said she was going out, Mr. Lorenzo."

I knew that she hadn't gone to the city center, as I'd vetoed that trip, but I didn't know where she'd decided to go instead. "Where was she going?"

"I'm sorry, sir, but she didn't say."

"Never mind. I'll check with the soldiers at the gate. They'll know who drove her and is guarding her today."

Aloysius was waiting for me in his car. He drove us back up the driveway and stopped at the gates. After speaking to the soldiers, we'd head to the club.

I found Giuseppe and another soldier on gate duty.

"Giuseppe."

He nodded at me. "Boss."

"Who's guarding my wife today?"

"Er...who's guarding Mrs. Marchiano?"

"Yes, that's what I said." It wasn't like Giuseppe to be so obtuse. "Well?" I demanded when I received no answer.

"Boss, she said you were going to accompany her today..."

I was silent for a moment. "I was going to accompany her where?"

"To the city center. She said that you told her to meet you at the Blackbird Bakery, and from there you'd go together."

My hands curled into two tight fists.

What the fuck was she playing at? She'd obviously lied.

"Which soldier drove her to the bakery?" I snarled.

Giuseppe looked like he wanted to be anywhere but in front of me right now. "She said that you gave permission for her to drive herself to meet you at the bakery—"

"For fuck's sake!" I roared. "She's a twenty-year-old girl and you let her go into the city without a guard?"

"I...I'm sorry, boss," he stuttered.

"She can't have gotten far," drawled Aloysius, infuriatingly calm. Nothing ever seemed to ruffle him.

"We need to find her," I said.

"We should split up. I'll get some of my men on it as well. With us all scouring the city, we'll find her soon."

"Giuseppe," I barked. "Which car did she take and what was she wearing?"

"I didn't see what she was wearing..."

"Fucking Christ! I pay you to be fucking observant and on top of your job!"

"I don't like to stare at her, boss," he tried to explain. "I know you wouldn't like it. And she only rolled the window down a bit."

"Get the fuck out of my sight before I do something I regret."

Giuseppe scurried off, knowing it was in his best interests to get as far away from me as possible in my current state of mind. I'd deal with him later.

Aloysius headed off in his car, firing orders into his cell as he drove off, and I strode back to the garage to get another car.

As I walked to the garage, only one thought consumed me: once I found my errant wife, she'd be sorry that she ever dared to defy me.

CHAPTER 36

ANNUNCIATA

I was at Cat-Con and the atmosphere was just awesome. I'd never been with so many like-minded cat fans, and everywhere I looked were so many exhibitors I wanted to speak to.

I'd already visited a number of stands and had purchased some new cat toys for Wilbur and got various cat-themed goodies for myself and the children.

A number of people had stopped me to tell me that they loved my costume. Another lady stopped me. "Oh my gosh, your cat costume outfit is great! It's just so adorable," she gushed.

I beamed at her. "Thank you. I moved to Chicago just recently, and this is my first time at Cat-Con."

Despite my excitement, I was keeping a very close eye on my watch.

The time was passing fast, and I'd already been here for three hours.

All I had to do was make sure that I went back to my car in time to pick up the kids from their grandmother's house and get home before dinner—and Lorenzo wouldn't be any the wiser. I was wearing shorts and a tee under my costume, so I could just strip off my costume and hide it in the trunk once I got back in the car.

There were a couple thousand people here at least, all of them as excited as me to be attending. Chicago Cat-Con was a huge deal and got lots of media attention every year.

I was looking at the products at a stand when I heard a commotion coming from behind me.

I looked around and saw people dressed up in cat outfits. They were in a spirited mood and having a good time, I thought at first. But something about their demeanor was off.

I quickly realized that they were some sort of protesters invading the convention center.

They charged toward a stand which sold a famous cat food brand. "This company's owner wears real fur!" one of them yelled. The protesters were all shouting at the same time. "She doesn't really care about animals!"

Someone hurled a can of red paint over the stand and the people manning it.

A number of people began hurrying toward the exit and people started getting bumped into or pushed out of the way.

There must have been over a hundred protesters running through the center. They were all shouting and hurling red paint.

I was frozen to the spot, watching the drama unfold around me, before deciding I needed to get the hell out of here.

Security had been called and was dashing in at the same time as people were trying to get out.

A media crew who'd been filming some shots for a local news channel was blocking the exit I'd been heading for, making people turn back on themselves as they clambered to get to an alternative exit.

I was being pushed from all directions as I tried to get to an exit.

Soon I heard police sirens. Thank God the cops were here—the in-house security were completely overwhelmed and had lost control of the situation.

As the cops stormed in, I heaved a sigh of relief.

Someone grabbed me by the arm. I saw it was the lady who'd told me earlier that she loved my cat costume. "She's one of them!" she yelled.

What?

"She's one of the protesters," she screamed as she pushed me into the arms of a police officer.

Oh shit... She thought I was a protester because I was dressed in a cat outfit like them. "No wait," I cried. "I'm just here for Cat-Con! I'm not a protester!"

"You're under arrest!" the cop shouted. He clinked shut a pair of cuffs around my wrists, patted me down, and dragged me away as he read me my rights. "You have the right to remain silent. Anything you say can be used against you in court—"

"No, you're making a mistake!" I screamed.

But it was to no avail and my pleas fell on deaf ears as I was hauled toward a police car.

Oh God, what had I got myself into?

Chapter 37

ANNUNCIATA

When we got to the police car, the officer pushed me into the back seat.

"Officer, please, I wasn't part of the protest—this is all a big misunderstanding."

"Lady, save it for the judge," he responded in a cold tone. "I hear the same excuses all day long."

He'd taken my backpack from me when cuffing me and now he was searching it.

"My name's Anni," I gabbled. "I have a husband, two children called Clara and Clemente, well, technically stepchildren, plus a cat called Wilbur." That's what you were supposed to do when you were taken against your will, right? To get the person to empathize with you?

Wait, maybe that was when you were taken by a serial killer?

I was trying to stay calm but in reality I was on the verge of a full-blown panic attack.

"Do you have pets?" I prattled on. "Like, maybe a cat?" If he was an animal-lover, then he might understand why I was at Cat-Con dressed up as a cat, and that it wasn't because I was an animal-rights protester.

His eyes darkened at me in response. I took that as a no.

"Or a dog?"

He scowled at me.

"Or…a gerbil?"

He glared menacingly at me. He definitely wasn't a pet person.

After checking my backpack contained no weapons, he tossed it into the trunk, slammed my door shut and clicked the locks in place.

I sat there for a few minutes, alternating between hyperventilating and trying to figure a way out of this. Maybe the filming by the media crew showed that I was just a regular girl visiting the convention, and that I had nothing to do with the protesters and paint throwing?

A sharp tap on the window made me jump.

Looking up, I saw a pair of dark eyes watching me.

And my heart pumped full of relief.

Thank God and all the angels in heaven!

It was Aloysius. He'd be able to call a lawyer for me to help get out me of this mess.

The officer opened the door, pulled me out, and uncuffed me. There was only one other officer standing nearby as most of the cops had already set off for the station or were still inside the convention hall. "Don't worry about him," said the officer to Aloysius. "He's my partner and he'll keep quiet about this."

"How did you find me, Aloysius?"

"We have contacts in the police force." His voice was low as he quickly ushered me away. "Lorenzo found out that you'd gone out without protection, and we came to the city center to search for you. I was nearby when the officer saw your surname was Marchiano from your credit cards and driver's license in your wallet. He gave me a call, and I came straight away."

The officer had searched my backpack, and my wallet was in there with my keys and phone. I hadn't thought about that—thank God he'd seen my name was Marchiano and called Aloysius.

I climbed into Aloysius's car and slumped back against the seat. "This day has turned into a disaster," I groaned, sinking my face into my hands.

"I'll have you home soon," reassured Aloysius. As he started the ignition, he spoke into his cell phone. "Call off the search. I've got her. I'm bringing her home now."

As I listened to the ensuing conversation, I realized he was talking to Lorenzo, and it was obvious my husband was absolutely furious—especially when Aloysius mentioned that I'd been arrested.

CHAPTER 38

LORENZO

Aloysius had called to let me know that he had Anni. He was bringing her home, and I was heading back to the mansion at the same time.

As I approached the gates, I saw Marco's car heading toward the gates too.

Great. He'd obviously already heard what had happened. Although I would have informed him about today's events, I would have preferred to have had things out with Anni first.

We both parked in the drive and got out of our vehicles.

"I hear your wife got herself arrested," he gritted out. I could tell he was pissed.

"I've got it under control."

"You obviously don't have *her* under control," he snapped.

"Nobody questioned her and the Feds got nowhere near her."

"When is she getting back?"

"Aloysius is about twenty minutes behind me."

We went in through the front door and as I walked in, I nearly tripped over the fucking cat who was gazing at himself in the hallway's full-length mirror. The dumb animal was utterly vain and loved to look at himself.

Then I caught sight of him kissing himself in the mirror. I swear the fucking creature would marry himself if he could.

The cat flicked his cold blue eyes to me and looked at me in disdain as if I had disturbed him in his self-admiration session.

"That cat always looks at me like he wants to kill me," I muttered as we made our way to my study. "When I look at him, it's like looking straight into the eyes of a killer."

"Don't be such a fucking wimp, Lorenzo," Marco barked at me.

"I'm a Made Man—I know a killer instinct when I see one."

"Jesus Christ, Lorenzo. I don't know if it's the cat, your new wife, or a combination of them both, but you seriously need to get a fucking grip. It's just an animal." Marco clearly wasn't feeling in an empathetic mood.

"It was your idea that I marry the girl in the first place. Her cat, not to mention her whole family, are bat-shit crazy."

I poured us both a glass of whiskey as we waited impatiently for Aloysius and Anni to arrive.

A while later I heard the front door open, and then Anni and Aloysius entered the study, knowing that I'd be waiting for them there.

I glared at Anni but said nothing as she came in. I was sitting behind my desk while Marco stood at my side.

"Boss," Aloysius said, nodding at Marco.

"Sit," I ordered my wife, nodding at the chair in front of the table.

She was wearing a fucking fluffy white cat costume. As she sat, I noticed some spots of red on the white fur. I clenched my fists—I'd kill any fucker that had hurt her.

"It's not blood," said Aloysius, following my gaze. "It's just red paint that was thrown by protesters."

Anni looked up at Marco and me. "I'm sorry—" she began.

"I'm not interested in fucking apologies," snapped Marco. "Do you know what would have happened if Aloysius hadn't arrived?"

"I never thought—"

"Once the cops saw your name, the Feds would be all over you before you could even blink." He wasn't letting Anni get a word in.

"The—"

"And how long do you think you'd last under the Feds before they started to get information out of you?" he demanded. This was a completely different Marco to the guy who invited her to a family dinner a few weeks ago.

"I wouldn't—"

"For fuck's sake, Anni! They wouldn't just be asking about the Fratellanza—they'd be interrogating you about your own family too," yelled Marco, thumping the table in front of her.

Anni visibly flinched. I could tell that she was frightened of him. He was a scary fucker when he was in a good mood; when he was in a bad mood, he was terrifying.

"Get her under fucking control," Marco growled at me, before striding out of the room and taking his leave.

"I better be going too." Aloysius shot Anni a sympathetic look.

"Thanks for your help today," I said to my brother. "I really appreciate it."

"Sure, anytime," he said easily.

It was just me and Anni left in the room.

"What the hell are you wearing?"

"Lots of people dress up for Cat-Con, so I just wanted to join in..."

"What the fuck were you thinking?" I was unable to hold in my anger any longer. I'd been forced to let Marco, as Capo, take the lead while he was here, but now that he was gone I could finally say what I wanted to say to Anni.

"I'm really sorry." And she did look sorry, but I didn't care.

I strode over to her side of the desk.

Yanking her out of her seat, I gripped her arms as I towered above her. "Never leave this house without a guard ever again."

Her eyes widened at my tone.

"That is—if I let you out of this house ever again."

She swallowed. "I thought it'd be safe," she tried to explain. "Chicago Cat-Con is a big deal. I just...wanted to see what it was all about," she added lamely.

"You remember what curiosity killed, right?" My voice was hard and uncompromising.

"Yeah...the cat," she whispered. She hugged her arms more tightly around herself as if fearing I might burn her fluffy white cat outfit like I did her tennis dress. Between Wilbur and her costume, the fucking cats in her life were driving me insane.

"Just go to bed." I was frustrated at her inability to think things through properly. I needed her to stay safe, but I couldn't do that when she did things like this.

She picked up her backpack. "What about the children?" she asked quietly.

"They're spending the night at my mother's. I didn't want them walking into this commotion."

She nodded and then left the room and hurried up the staircase.

I was too worked up to say anything more. What I really wanted to do was put her over my lap and spank that sweet ass of hers. Jesus, why did she make me feel like this? I was furious with her, but all I could think about was feeling her sweet ass cheeks under my hands and then fucking her until she screamed and submitted to me.

Sitting back down behind my desk, I tried to calm myself as I answered a few urgent e-mails that I hadn't been able to deal with earlier due to Anni's disappearance.

As I typed out a response to one of my captains, I felt a tightness in my chest again.

I stretched my chest muscles, hoping that would help relieve the tightness, but it didn't seem to have any effect.

This had been happening more and more frequently lately.

CHAPTER 39

ANNUNCIATA

I fled up the stairs to our bedroom. I didn't want Lorenzo seeing me cry.

I was shaken by what had happened at the convention, my subsequent arrest, and what had happened when I'd arrived home. Everything I did lately seemed to be the wrong thing.

Going into the bathroom, I stripped off my clothes and had a long shower, letting my tears of frustration mingle with the hot water. I felt chastised and treated like a child by Lorenzo.

I really wouldn't have gone to the convention and gone without a guard if I had known something like this might happen. I mean, what were the chances?

And I certainly wouldn't have let anything slip to the Feds.

Getting out of the shower, I pulled my white robe around my body and then looked in dismay at my cat costume. There were spots of red paint all over the side of it. I set to work on trying to get the paint off, but it wouldn't budge, upsetting me further. I carried on trying to get the paint off, wiping away my tears as I scrubbed at the fluffy fabric.

A while later, I heard a voice through the door. "Anni." It was Lorenzo.

"I'm busy," I called. "I'm having a shower." I didn't want him seeing my red eyes.

"I heard the shower stop half an hour ago. You've been locked in there for ages. Come out of the bathroom."

I didn't say anything and stayed where I was on the edge of the bathtub.

"Anni, open the door." His voice was harder.

"I'm not dressed yet." That much was true—I only had my robe on.

"I don't care if you're naked. Let me in."

I hated the way he thought he could just command me to act.

"You've got until I count to three then I'm going to break this damn door down! One..."

I wanted to shout at him to leave me alone. But I couldn't deal with any further arguments today.

I reluctantly clicked the lock open and then returned to cleaning my costume, keeping my eyes down.

He stalked over to me and lifted my chin in a hard grip with his hand. "You've been crying."

"Not really. I just can't get the red paint off," I murmured.

"Don't lie to me," he gritted out.

"What do you want me to say then?" I cried. "Everything I do is wrong, whether I go out somewhere or want Clara to see a therapist. I've been trying so hard since we got married, I really have, but nothing I do is good enough for you."

I'd been holding in my frustrations and insecurities for so long that they all just came tumbling out.

LORENZO

I was taken aback by Anni's words.

Usually, she was so strong and confident in everything she did.

"You don't trust me with anything. You don't trust my opinion with the kids, and you don't trust me when I ask for a guard to take me into the city. What else did you expect when you denied me permission to go out today?"

Her words stung me, and I went on the offensive. "I expected you to be obedient," I growled. "I was trying to keep you safe today."

"You were being dictatorial!" she cried. "The way you're acting, you're smothering me. You second-guess everything I do or want to do. You undermine my opinions on the children and my attempts to help Clara. You don't want me taking the children to visit your cousins, or Clara to visit a therapist."

The tears ran silently down her pretty face, and I couldn't help noticing that her blonde hair was in two braids, like the first time I'd met her.

"You thought I wasn't looking out for the children when I took them to Marco's house for dinner. We're married, and now Clara and Clemente are my family too. I *love* those kids—I wouldn't ever do anything to harm them or put them in danger. Why can't you understand that?"

I ran my hands through my hair. "I never wanted to make you cry," I said gently.

She tried to wipe away her tears with the back of her hand. "I'm doing whatever I can to help the children, but you won't even help me understand their grief by telling me what happened to their mother. You don't trust me, and I just don't see how this marriage can work without trust."

She wasn't just talking about today; she was talking about the state of our whole marriage. Her words sent a shot of alarm through me. "You'd hate me if I told you what happened to Rita," I said slowly.

"My father and brothers have killed traitors before, so why would I hate you for doing the same? But I need to know what gossip the children might hear so that I can support them through what they're going through now and what they might go through in the future."

"You think Rita was a traitor?" I asked.

"I know she had a closed casket funeral, so it's pretty obvious to me. Just like it will be to the children when they're older and hear people talking about it. I know you're trying to protect the kids from hearing about it, but once they start school, they'll come in frequent contact with the other Fratellanza families—they're bound to hear about it sooner or later."

I hesitated for a long minute.

Did I want my marriage to work? I'd already failed at one marriage. I had to decide if I wanted my second marriage to have a different fate.

"Rita wasn't a traitor." My voice was low and toneless.

A frown pulled at Anni's pale brow. "I don't understand. Was she killed in an accident?"

"No," I said slowly, looking up and meeting Anni's eyes. "You were right in the first place. I killed my wife."

CHAPTER 40

ANNUNCIATA

Although I'd known that Lorenzo was the person most likely to have killed his wife, a big part of me had hoped that it wasn't true.

His dark eyes met mine, and I felt a shudder run through me.

He held out a hand to me. "Come. It's time that I explain things."

I'd said that I wanted to know the truth; now that the moment was here, however, I held back, not taking his outstretched hand. I just looked at it, knowing that he had killed so many people with it, including his own wife.

He firmly gripped my hand and led me back into the bedroom, walking me toward the bed.

Once I was standing in front of it, he pushed at my shoulders, forcing me to sit down.

He remained standing in front of me, forcing me to look up so that I could watch his expression and discern his mood.

An icy coldness had taken over his entire being.

"Rita never accepted our way of life, nor my role in the Fratellanza."

My heart was beating erratically.

"Her own mother had a very religious upbringing, and that rubbed off on Rita while she was growing up."

"But Rita's father was part of the Fratellanza?"

"Yes, he was, but her mother's family wasn't. That's the problem of marrying an outsider. Her mother was Italian, but that wasn't enough to understand what we do—what we *have* to do. Rita took after her mother and could never accept that killing came with my job, nor that it helped fund our lifestyle."

"So, Rita betrayed you to the authorities?" My voice was laced with horror. Everyone knew how important *omerta* was in the Mafia: the code of silence which demanded that we didn't talk to or cooperate with law enforcement or the authorities.

"No." His voice was strained. "*I betrayed her.*"

My blood froze in my veins. I couldn't breathe. "What do you mean?" I forced my words out, my voice hoarse.

"She couldn't cope with her life with me. I knew she was struggling—that she'd always struggled with it."

I stayed silent, confused, but not wanting to interrupt him when he was finally opening up to me.

"She was worse after Clemente was born. She had postpartum depression. I thought she'd get better. We had two beautiful children, and she had given me an heir when Clemente was born. It was my fault that she killed herself."

"She committed suicide?"

He nodded. "I guess she decided she couldn't go on anymore. She'd pleaded with me to leave this life behind, that we could start afresh somewhere."

"But she knew, deep down, that was never possible," I said softly. "We all know that. None of us can leave this life." Anyone walking away from the Mafia held too much knowledge and was too much of a danger to those who remained; therefore, the only way to leave the Mafia was through death. The only way Rita had been able to escape the Mafia life she despised was by killing herself.

"I couldn't leave," Lorenzo carried on, "even though I knew she was struggling so much. She said I was a monster because of what I do: killing people."

"But she would have known neither of you could ever have left. Marco and the Fratellanza would never have allowed it."

"I couldn't even talk about it to Marco. He's Capo, and me even thinking about leaving could have been classed as a betrayal."

"Did she get any professional help?"

"No. I blame myself. I repeatedly urged her to see someone, but she always refused. I should have insisted more. If I had, then her death could have been prevented."

"You can't blame yourself, Lorenzo."

"Yes, I can! I was her husband. She was my responsibility. I let her down."

"I don't understand why you didn't tell people what really happened and how she died? The closed casket would make everyone assume that you must have killed her—that she must have disobeyed you or betrayed you. Why would you let people think that?"

His features hardened. "It's better my men think me a strong Underboss—someone who doesn't hesitate when it comes to killing traitors, even if that traitor is his wife."

"You surely can't mean that?"

"It was better than the alternative—that they think me a weak man who couldn't even control his woman and make her be a good Mafia wife."

I opened my mouth to argue, but deep down, I knew that he was right. People in our world believed that men should be able to control their wives. Even to the extent of forcing their wife to support her husband in whatever he did and whoever he murdered.

***

Following Lorenzo's revelations, I decided to go to bed early. I wanted some time to myself to think about what he'd told me.

I'd never considered that Rita might have killed herself. When I thought about the kids maybe finding this out one day, my heart broke for them.

But would it be better for them to think that their father killed their mom? I really didn't think so. Lorenzo would have to tell them the truth when they were older, but I didn't know what his thoughts were on this, and his revelations tonight were still too raw to discuss this.

What I did know, however, was that I felt closer to Lorenzo now that he'd finally confided in me what had happened to Rita. It also helped me to understand his fierce overprotectiveness, particularly when it came to Clara and Clemente—in his own way, he was trying to protect them.

I felt unsettled after everything that I'd learned today.

But I was sure of one thing: now that Lorenzo had shown his trust in me, I was willing to put everything into making this marriage succeed.

When Lorenzo came to bed later that night, he took me into his arms and kissed me hard. I could tell that he was still angry at me after what had happened today, but also behind his kiss was raw passion.

And I knew that this marriage was worth working for, worth fighting for, and worth loving for.

CHAPTER 41

ANNUNCIATA

During the weeks that followed, I felt closer to Lorenzo after he'd confided in me about what had happened with Rita.

Lorenzo had finally agreed that we should take Clara to see a speech therapist. The therapist saw Clara once a week, and in between that, I worked with Clara, using the new techniques the therapist had shown me.

One weekend, I was about to go into the den when I heard Lorenzo talking to Clara.

"Dadda," he said. "Just try to say it."

I peeked around the door and saw Clara looking at her father with her big brown eyes.

"Dad-da," he said more slowly. "Just repeat after me." He paused, then carried on in a quiet voice, "You used to say it all the time."

I knew it hurt him that she still didn't say it.

So far, she hadn't attempted to say Dad or Dadda. Whenever she wanted to get his attention, she would tug gently on his sleeve, and each time she did that and reminded Lorenzo of her speech issues, I would see the pain in his eyes.

Even though Dadda was such a small word, after what Lorenzo had told me about his wife's suicide, I could see how much he needed to feel love from the kids. Clara saying Dadda would mean so much to him after all they'd been through.

Every though she was having professional input now, I could still see how much Clara struggled at times, and how upset she would get when she couldn't express herself. If she could deal with and process her grief better, I reckoned that would help her anxiety and thus help her speech.

That night, in bed, I turned to Lorenzo.

My voice was tentative. "Lorenzo, I know the children didn't go to Rita's funeral, but do they ever visit her grave at the cemetery?"

"No." His answer was short and abrupt. But I didn't let that put me off.

"I think it would help the kids, especially Clara, if they could see where their mom is and perhaps even talk to her."

"That's not a good idea."

I knew him well enough by now to know that he wasn't going to budge in his view, so I let it go for now.

***

A couple of days later, after showering, I dressed in denim shorts and a striped tee, and then made my way down to breakfast.

The children had spent the previous night at Cosima's house, and I was going to bring them home after lunch. Their grandmother loved spending time with the children, and they were great company for her as she lived alone.

I'd just come out of the kitchen after checking on breakfast with Adelina, and as I walked toward the dining room, I sensed Lorenzo coming down the staircase.

Looking up at him, I stilled.

He'd taken a couple of steps down the stairs, then sank down onto a step.

"Lorenzo?" When he didn't respond, I hurried up the stairs.

"It's...nothing," he rasped.

He grabbed the handrail and hauled himself to his feet. He tried to take another step but his legs gave way and he sank back down to the stair.

His breathing was labored, and he couldn't catch his breath.

"What's wrong, Lorenzo?" I said urgently, watching him as he tried to take a breath.

"Need to...catch my breath. Just give me...a minute." His voice was hoarse and his hand was pressed against his chest.

I hovered in front of me. "Should I call someone—the doctor?"

"No!" he forced out. "Just...need a minute."

After gathering himself, he stood up but collapsed back down before he could even take a step. "Fuck!" he rasped.

What was happening? He wasn't even doing anything taxing—he was just coming down the stairs, for God's sake!

CHAPTER 42

ANNUNCIATA

"Adelina!" I yelled. "Adelina!"

Adelina, hearing the urgency in my voice, came hurrying out of the kitchen.

"Mrs. Anni, what is it?"

Upon seeing Lorenzo hunched down on the stairs, his breaths coming out in harsh gasps, she dashed to the foot of the stairs. "Mr. Lorenzo! I'll call the doctor."

"No doctor." He made his voice as firm as he could. Beads of sweat had broken out on his forehead.

"Help me get him down the stairs, Adelina. We'll get him to the couch in the den."

Adelina and I stood on either side of him and helped support his weight as we slowly came down the stairs. I could tell he wanted to refuse our help, but he knew as well as us that there was no other way he could manage.

Once we got to the couch, he gratefully slumped down onto the cushions, trying to get his breath back.

"I'm calling 911," I said quickly. "You need an ambulance."

"No!" He closed his eyes. "Ring...for doctor," he conceded. His breathing was getting worse, not better.

I dashed to the phone, trying to control my panic. I needed to stay calm but calm was the last thing I felt.

Resisting the urge to call 911, I instead dialed the number for the doctor used by the Fratellanza. I explained to him what had happened as quickly as possible and he told me that he was on his way.

As I spoke on the phone, Adelina brought a glass of water for Lorenzo but he wasn't able to drink it.

The doctor lived close by and was with us in less than twenty minutes although the wait felt a lot longer.

I followed the doctor as he strode into the den.

"I think it's my heart, doc," croaked Lorenzo.

"Your heart?" I cried. "If I'd known that, I definitely would have called 911!"

"Don't worry, Mrs. Marchiano," soothed the doctor. "Based on the symptoms you described, I called for a private ambulance to meet me here, just as a precaution."

"Too much stress lately," gasped Lorenzo. "Too much talk...about Rita. Too much worry about...kids..."

My heart plummeted as I heard Lorenzo's words. "Is he having a heart attack, doctor?" I felt so helpless as I stood there.

And I knew in my heart of hearts that I couldn't bear for anything to happen to Lorenzo...because I loved him.

How could I not fall for a man like him? He was powerful, insanely handsome, and my heart melted each and every time I saw him with his children. He might not be perfect, but he was an amazing father to Clara and Clemente, and I could see that his world revolved around them. Not all Made Men were so devoted to their families, and I knew I was lucky that with Lorenzo I might eventually be able to have the sort of relationship my parents had—a relationship where my partner genuinely cared about me and respected me.

"The ambulance has pulled up outside," declared Adelina, standing at the doorway and wringing her hands.

"We need to ease your breathing first, Lorenzo," the doctor instructed in a calm voice. "He used his cell to call the paramedics in the ambulance. "Bring in your portable nebulizer please."

A minute later, two paramedics hurried in with some equipment, and they and the doctor quickly hooked up Lorenzo to it, fixing a face mask over his mouth and nose.

"Just take slow, deep breaths," advised the doctor. "This should hopefully allow you to get your breath back."

"What's happening to him, doctor? He seemed fine yesterday and when he got up this morning." I was used to seeing Lorenzo strong and full of energy, not weak and struggling to breathe.

"We'll take him to the private clinic. That's where I usually treat more serious cases."

"Doesn't he need the hospital?" I protested.

Lorenzo grabbed at his face mask and pulled it away from his nose and mouth. "No hospital!"

"You need to keep that on, Lorenzo." The doctor turned to me. "Mrs. Marchiano, the clinic has just about everything we could potentially need. The paramedics will take him straight there, and I will stay with him in the ambulance. You should follow in another vehicle. Lorenzo's men will know where to take you."

"I can walk," Lorenzo gritted out when the paramedics wheeled in a gurney. He argued with the doctor until they compromised on Lorenzo being taken to the ambulance in a wheelchair. And he'd only given into that suggestion because his breathing was still labored, although it seemed a bit better than before.

I kissed Lorenzo on the mouth before the paramedics closed the rear doors to the ambulance.

After the ambulance had left, I grabbed my purse. Giuseppe was already behind the wheel of a vehicle, waiting to drive me to the clinic.

"Do you know where to go?" My words came out in a rush.

"Yes, ma'am."

As he sped down the road, I willed my racing pulse to slow down.

Lorenzo had seemed to be breathing better when he'd got up to leave, and he'd taken the couple of steps from the couch to the wheelchair by himself. That had to be a good sign, right?

LORENZO

On the way to the clinic, the doctor asked me a whole raft of questions, instructing me not to speak and instead to nod or shake my head in response. I still had the mask over my nose and mouth, and he told me not to remove it.

Once we got to the clinic, the doctor immediately did an ECG on me.

"Good news, Lorenzo," he said afterward. "There are no signs that you have suffered a heart attack."

"Are you sure?" I was incredulous. "It sure felt like I could be having one."

The doctor asked me more questions, asking where I'd visited lately, who had come to my mansion, if I'd met any new people, and if I'd changed any brand of medication.

He got the nurse to prepare for more tests and asked me to lie on my stomach. He disinfected a section of skin on my back and proceeded to prick me with needles.

"You may have had a reaction to something," he explained. "We need to rule that out."

"I'm not allergic to anything, so you won't find anything there. What will you check once you've ruled that out? What do you think is causing this?" Now that I was breathing easier, I was feeling a sense of frustration and impatience. I didn't like my men seeing me weak, and that's exactly what I'd looked like when I'd been taken out to the ambulance in a wheelchair.

"Let's just take one step at a time, Lorenzo."

After a few minutes, the doctor said I could sit up. "I've solved the mystery. It was an allergic reaction."

"I've already told you, doc, I'm not allergic to anything. I think you should do another ECG on me."

"Lorenzo, have you recently gotten yourself a pet cat?" the doctor asked.

"No, I haven't fucking *gotten myself a pet cat*," I snarled, not liking where this conversation was going. My hand automatically twitched as it rested on my gun holster which was lying by my side on the examination bench.

The doctor took a step back. "Er...what I meant was...have you recently, perhaps, bought your daughter...or son...a pet cat?"

"No," I snapped. "I wouldn't be so stupid."

The doctor took a swallow. "Have you, maybe, gotten yourself—I mean, your children—a pet which is an animal from the cat family, like a...lion or tiger?"

He looked extremely uncomfortable and was getting on my nerves, so I put him out of his misery. "No. But my wife, on the other hand, has no such sense. *She's* brought a cat into my home."

"Ah, there we have it," the doctor said in relief. "You've had an asthma attack due to your allergy to cats."

"I don't have asthma," I declared. "I'm a fucking Made Man."

The doctor looked over the top of his glasses at me. "Lorenzo, it clearly says on your medical records that you are asthmatic, and I know that I, personally, have also prescribed you inhalers in the past." He was talking to me like I was an errant schoolboy.

"I barely have asthma," I argued. "It doesn't bother me at all. And these pains have been different to what I've had in the past."

"Symptoms have flared up due to your airways becoming inflamed as a result of your cat allergy. I always advise my asthmatic patients that they really should avoid having pets in their home," the doctor continued in a lecturing tone.

"It wasn't my goddamn idea to have Wilbur in our home!"

The doctor retreated further away from me as he ran through the treatment options, keeping his gaze carefully fixed on me and my weapon. "I'll prescribe you a course of prednisolone which will bring down the inflammation in your airways and bring your breathing back to normal."

As the doctor ran through the other medications, I quietly seethed.

"Um...can I ask, Lorenzo, is 'Wilbur' a domesticated pet, or is he...a wildcat?"

I glared at him.

He carried on quickly. "It's just that I have to let you know, er, that I don't feel comfortable doing house calls to homes containing wild animals like lions, tigers—"

"Get the fuck out!" I roared.

He hurried through the door. "I'll just go and explain the situation to Mrs. Marchiano," he called over his shoulder.

"You do that and then tell her I want to see her," I growled.

I tried to get my temper under control while I waited for Anni to make an appearance.

I didn't have to wait long.

"Hi Lorenzo!" She came into the room, all relaxed and smiling.

A nurse followed her in. "Hi Mr. Marchiano," the nurse purred. "The doctor asked me to bring in your medication for you." She fluttered her eyelashes at me as she passed me some pills and a cup of water.

She began to tuck the sheets around me, letting her hand linger too long by my thigh, earning her a dark look from Anni.

"Is there anything else I can get you?" the nurse asked with a seductive smile.

"No. I just want to get out of here."

"I'll get your prescription filled for you and then you'll be all set to go. Where are you headed next?"

"Work," I said abruptly.

"Oh, and where do you work?"

"Here and there." Her small talk was really irritating.

"Is it nearby?" I really wanted to get rid of her so that I could speak to my wife.

"Sort of," I replied vaguely. "How long until you can get my script filled?"

"I'll do it right away, sir," she said, her tone sultry and her hips sashaying as she left the room.

Anni shot her a disparaging look as the door closed.

She turned to me with a beaming smile. "What good news! The doctor told me you haven't had a heart attack, and it's just an allergy."

"Just an allergy?," I repeated incredulously. *"Anni, not only did you try to kill me again, but that fucking feline was in on it too!"*

She tilted her head to one side as she looked at me. "You're being a drama queen," she said calmly. "How was I to know that you're allergic to cats—you didn't even know it yourself until the doctor told you today."

"That's not the point," I blustered. "I've had as much as I can take of your cat. He has to go."

"Now you're being a real drama llama." Her tone was patient. "Wilbur's not going anywhere. The children, particularly Clara, would be heartbroken if he did. The doctor says that you just need to use an inhaler daily—as you *should* have been doing already."

I clenched my jaw. It was true, I didn't use my preventative inhaler—because I usually felt fine without it. Anyway, a Made Man couldn't carry around an inhaler—it was a sign of weakness and I didn't want my enemies to know of any physical frailties that I had. "It's weak to admit I have an allergy or that I have to use an inhaler."

"My brother, Christian, takes antihistamines for his allergies—he makes no secret of it, and no one thinks any less of him as a Made Man."

"What's he allergic to?"

"Just about everything, according to him," Anni responded.

"Yeah well, I'm not like your weird family. And while I'll use the inhaler, as I've got no choice now, I won't be mentioning it to anyone."

CHAPTER 43

ANNUNCIATA

Lorenzo was released from the clinic that same day.

We needed to pick up the children from Cosima's on our way home and headed there after we left the clinic. Or so I thought.

Although we had been headed in the right direction, after a while I noticed that we were traveling in circles and that Lorenzo was checking his rearview mirror even more than usual.

"What's wrong?" I asked, looking over my shoulder.

"Nothing."

"I thought we were going to Cosima's?"

"We are. But first, I need to make another stop concerning a business issue."

"Don't you think that you should rest today like the doctor advised?"

"The doc is an old woman. I'm perfectly fine now, and I've already missed nearly an entire day of work. I need to check on some things, otherwise they won't get done."

I knew he wasn't going to be persuaded otherwise, so I sat back and tried to stop my exasperation at him from showing. This man, who'd thought earlier that he was stressed and might be having a heart attack, was refusing to go home and rest. Instead, we were repeatedly circling some dodgy neighborhood while Lorenzo checked that we weren't being tailed.

Eventually, we pulled up at a shabby industrial estate, stopping in front of a factory.

"What is this place?"

Lorenzo stared at me. "Curiosity killed the..."

"Cat," I finished. "Yeah, I get it." After how mad he was with Wilbur causing him to have an asthma attack, I knew that I should keep my mouth shut. He'd probably been exaggerating when he'd said at the hospital that Wilbur had to go, but I wasn't taking any chances.

"Don't get out of the car, Anni, and keep the doors locked. This isn't the safest area. I'll be back in about twenty minutes."

I nodded. I didn't need to be told twice. The factory looked half-derelict, and it gave me the creeps.

After a quarter of an hour, getting bored with the wait, I called Christian on my cell.

"Hey, Mrs. Marchiano," my brother greeted me.

I rolled my eyes, even though he couldn't see me. "Hey, Christian. What are you up to?"

"Oh, you know, just admiring the view over Staten Island." I resisted a snort—Christian was always working and plotting on how to increase the influence of the Venetis. "And what are you up to, little sister?"

"Just sitting in some parking lot, waiting for Lorenzo. We've just come back from the doctor's clinic. Turns out he's allergic to cats, including Wilbur."

Christian laughed out loud. "Good old Wilbur, I knew he wouldn't let down the Veneti name!"

I couldn't help a little smile at that. "I'm telling you as I thought you might be a little more sympathetic given your own allergy issues. Anyway, it's not funny—he threatened today that Wilbur has to go, but I told him that my cat isn't going anywhere."

"Lorenzo is an annoying fucker, so it's not easy to feel sympathy for him, especially as he's such an ass toward you sometimes." Christian was suddenly more serious. "Has anything improved on that front?"

"At times, I think we're getting closer and that he's starting to trust me more; at other times, though, he still seems so closed off toward me. I just hate that we don't have an equal partnership, particularly when it comes to the children." I remembered how quickly he shot down my suggestion two days ago that the children visit their mom's grave. "He doesn't always value my opinions or my views on how to deal with things."

"Are you saying that Lorenzo doesn't appreciate your *unique* personality and approach to life?"

"Haha, very funny. I'm not that weird."

We chatted for a while until I saw Lorenzo exiting the factory. "I better go. Lorenzo's back." He started to walk over to our car. "By the way," I added quickly, "don't mention that I told you he has a cat allergy—he doesn't want anyone thinking he's weak in any way."

"Okay, sis. Just let me know if he ever threatens to get rid of Wilbur again, and I'll sort the fucker out for you."

"Thanks, Christian," I said drily. "Love you."

"Yeah, love you too, Anni."

At the same time as Lorenzo appeared, Aloysius pulled up outside the factory and got out of his SUV. He walked over to talk to Lorenzo, and then they both walked toward the car.

I rolled down the window as Aloysius approached the passenger side and smiled at me.

"Hi Anni."

"Hi Aloysius. It's good to see you. Lorenzo didn't tell me that you'd be here as well."

"I wasn't due to be here today—I was just saying to Lorenzo that one of our men, Tommaso, told me that Lorenzo hadn't made it to the factory today, so I thought I'd drop by and check on things."

"See, Lorenzo—you didn't have to stop by. Aloysius would have taken care of things here for you." I tried to keep the exasperation from my voice.

"I wasn't expecting to see you here, Anni," commented Aloysius.

"We were on our way back from the doctor's clinic, and Lorenzo insisted on making a stop here." I wrinkled my nose as I looked around at our less than salubrious surroundings. "He brings me to all the best places."

"That's my brother for you," he laughed. "How are the kids?"

"They're good, thanks. They stayed at your mother's house last night, and we're going to pick them up now and take them home. Why don't you come by for dinner tonight? They'd love to see you."

"I've got quite a bit of work to handle today. But I'll come by later in the week, for sure."

"Great. We'll look forward to it."

Lorenzo got into the car, and as he drove away, he looked over at me. "Who were you talking to on the phone?"

"Just Christian."

"And what were you talking about?"

"Family stuff—nothing important." I tried not to sound guilty as I said that—I knew I shouldn't have told Christian about Lorenzo's allergy, but I really couldn't see what harm it would do and it had just slipped out.

Since leaving the clinic earlier, Lorenzo hadn't mentioned anything again about Wilbur having to leave—but I could tell that he was still really pissed at him.

***

The next morning, I double-checked with Lorenzo that he had taken his medication and inhalers.

He grudgingly admitted that he had and that his breathing was definitely getting easier.

After he'd told me about what had happened to Rita, I'd thought that would bring us closer together. And it had a little, but Lorenzo still seemed so distant at times as if he were carrying the weight of the world on his shoulders. I wondered if his distance was just due to the whole thing that had happened with Rita, or if something else might also be bothering him? I really didn't know, though, as he was such a closed book most of the time.

This morning, after Lorenzo had left following breakfast, I got out the children's art and crafts supplies, and they happily set to work on their creations.

I had various appointments to schedule for the children, and I had made a note to myself to check if they were up to date with their immunizations. Lorenzo wasn't sure what shots had and hadn't been done. As it was my job now to take care of these things, he had given me a folder which contained various medical papers for both kids.

Sitting on the couch in the den, I sifted through the medical papers while keeping an eye on the kids at the same time.

I quickly found Clemente's immunization record and checked it off to see what he'd had and what was due.

I then carried on going through the papers and looking for Clara's record.

I was halfway through the file when I found an appointment card in Rita's name. The name of the doctor was Dr. Lois Fontaine. There was a contact telephone number, but no further details. The date of the appointment was one week before she died.

This file was supposed to contain the children's papers. The card must have been filed in the wrong place.

After turning the card over again and again in my hands, I got out my phone and searched for a Dr. Lois Fontaine in the Chicago area. I found a match, and the website I was led to listed Dr. Fontaine as a psychologist specializing in helping patients suffering with depression, including postpartum depression.

I got up and went to the dining room.

Using my cell, I rang the number on the appointment card.

"Good morning. Dr. Fontaine's office. How may I help you?"

"Oh, hi," I said. "I wanted to make an appointment with Dr. Fontaine. I saw her quite a while ago, so I'm not sure if I'd need to book an assessment appointment or a follow-up appointment?"

"Sure, ma'am. May I take your name, date of birth, and the date of your last appointment with Dr. Fontaine please."

I took a deep breath. "The name is Mrs. Rita Marchiano." After giving Rita's date of birth, I crossed my fingers and said that my last appointment was on the date listed on the appointment card I'd just found.

"Yes, I've found you on my system. Your last appointment was more than a year ago, so you would need a new assessment with the doctor. That appointment will be longer than a standard follow-up appointment." It was clear no one had notified this doctor's office that Rita had passed away, and that was just what I needed so that I could pretend to be Rita and get some information.

"Can you remind me how many appointments I had with her in total last time?"

"Sure. Let me just check."

I held my breath as she checked her records.

"You saw the doctor for a total of seven appointments then."

"Okay, that's helpful. I'll ring back when I have a clearer idea of when I'll be free to attend an appointment. Thanks for your time."

Disconnecting the call, I sat back and thought about what I had just learned.

Lorenzo had told me that Rita had never sought professional help and that he blamed himself for that. This, however, cast a different light on past events.

LORENZO

That evening, after Anni had bathed the kids and I'd read them their bedtime story and tucked them in, Anni came to see me in my study.

Walking in, she hovered at the edge of my desk. "Hey," she said.

I looked up with a tight smile. "Can this wait? You know I have to go back out to the factory and I'm already running late. Being at the clinic yesterday took up most of the day and I still haven't caught up."

The factory housed the Fratellanza's drug lab where we tested product we'd purchased and then processed it by dividing up the raw product and repackaging it in the appropriate size for selling.

"It's important, Lorenzo. I found the children's immunization records today."

"Good." My voice was curt.

"I also found this." She reached into her pocket, taking out an appointment card and pushing it across the desk toward me.

I reached for it. And, when I saw Rita's name on it, I froze.

CHAPTER 44

ANNUNCIATA

"Boss," said Giuseppe, coming to the study door.

"What?" Lorenzo barked at him.

"We're ready to leave."

He closed his eyes for a moment. "Go without me. I'll follow in ten minutes."

"Got it, boss."

Waiting until he'd heard the front door close, he turned back to me. "Where did you get this?"

"I just said, I found it with the children's immunization records. It must have been filed in the wrong place. Have you heard of Dr. Fontaine before?"

"No." He snatched up the card and tossed it into his desk drawer, slamming it shut. "Anything else? I have to go." He was clearly dismissing me.

"I looked up the doctor on the net and rang the number on the card."

"What?"

"The appointment date was one week before Rita's death."

"I'm well aware of that."

"It's just that you said Rita never got help for her issues, and you felt guilty that you should have helped her get some more support," I said quickly. "Dr. Fontaine is a psychologist, specializing in depression and postpartum depression. Don't you see, that means Rita did get some help?"

"You don't know that she ever actually went to the appointment," he said tersely.

"I do." I hesitated. "I rang the clinic and pretended I was Rita."

He sat up very straight, like a predator getting ready to pounce. "You did what?"

"That was the only way they'd give me any information. And they told me that Rita did go to that appointment and that she attended seven appointments in total with Dr. Fontaine."

"This is none of your business."

"But don't you see, Lorenzo? Rita *did* get help. So, you shouldn't blame yourself."

He said nothing but was breathing heavily.

"You need to be less hard on yourself, and you need to forgive yourself."

His nostrils flared. "Is that what you think?"

I nodded. "I do."

"I didn't marry you to think and give me your opinions," he snapped. "I married you so that I would have someone to be a wife and look after my children."

I was taken aback by the aggression in his voice, and when he said 'my' children something inside of me broke. "You don't see me as your wife and a part of this family," I retorted. "You treat me like a whore—you have sex with me and expect me to do as I'm told."

"You're being ridiculous. Of course I don't treat you like a whore."

I gave a brittle laugh. "No wait, a whore actually gets paid for her services."

His eyes flashed at me, and he clenched his jaw hard.

I stormed out of his study and ran upstairs. Going into the master, I grabbed what I needed and then marched to a guest room.

I was done with him treating me like this: like I wasn't part of this family, like I didn't love the children, and like my feelings didn't matter.

He clearly didn't understand the bond I'd formed with the children, nor did he care. And that really hurt—because I loved the children now as if they were my own.

I sat on the bed in the guest room, tears rolling down my cheeks. The room was kept spotlessly clean by Adelina and there were always fresh sheets on the bed. But it was cold and empty—just like my heart was feeling right now.

LORENZO

I needed to be at the factory, but I couldn't move.

I just sat in my study, my head in my hands, staring at the appointment card.

I don't know how long I sat there, memories of my marriage to Rita replaying in my mind—some good times, but mostly the bad times. The times when she could barely get out of bed, the times she refused to leave the house, and the times she begged me to leave the Fratellanza.

I was supposed to be at the factory tonight.

But, for once, I couldn't face work. I couldn't face doing the thing that had driven a wedge between me and Rita, driving her so far away until she'd completely left me.

When I went up to bed that night and realized that Anni had moved into a guest room, I felt an impenetrable red mist descend over me.

I'd been right when I'd thought she was too young and too wild to be my wife. She was completely unsuitable. She wasn't tameable—I needed someone who would obey me and just get on with what I needed her to do.

I should have followed my gut in the first place, and I should never have allowed myself to fall for another woman again.

***

I was asleep alone in my bed when my cell beeped. The notification sound told me that it was the app connected to the mansion's security system.

I'd missed some calls earlier and not returned them. That was completely out of character for me, but I knew that if there was anything urgent, the caller would get hold of Aloysius who would handle it as my second-in-command.

Security, however, wasn't something I would ever ignore or be complacent about.

I snatched up my phone to check the notification. Someone had entered the house via the front door. It was 1 a.m.

What the fuck?

I flung back the bedcovers and grabbed my gun.

Creeping downstairs, my eyes were immediately drawn to my study. The light had been switched on in there.

Silently prowling toward the open door, I aimed my weapon.

"Aloysius?" I said in surprise.

My brother was removing money from the safe. He spun around when he heard my voice, shock all over his face.

"Lorenzo? What are you doing here?"

I lowered my weapon. "I think that's my question, little brother. This is my house, and it's 1 a.m.," I drawled. "What's going on?" The gate guards knew to let in Aloysius automatically, and he had his own key to the house and the code for the safe. He was in and out often, leaving and collecting cash from my safe.

"I thought you'd been arrested."

My nerves pricked. "What are you talking about?"

"The Feds raided the factory tonight and arrested everyone there. We thought you were caught up in the raid. You said you were going to the factory tonight and you haven't been answering your phone."

I strode over to my laptop and flipped it open, downloading the security feed from the factory. "I was supposed to be there. But I got delayed and never made it."

I pressed play on the footage.

"Federal agents! Put your hands on your head now!"

Men and women dressed in suits and FBI jackets swarmed into the factory, their guns raised and aimed at our men.

"Spread out," the lead agent yelled. "Everything goes—seize those computers and all files!"

Our men were being cuffed.

"You're under arrest!"

But before I could see anything else, the footage was disconnected.

"Fuck! Who did they get?"

Aloysius reeled off a list of names, including two of my best Captains and Giuseppe. "That's our best guess. We haven't got a complete list yet—I've got one of my guys going through today's security footage from earlier, seeing who arrived and who left, and compiling a list of who we think was still in the factory when it was raided."

"Fuck, fuck, fuck!"

"I came to collect cash to give to the lawyers," Aloysius explained. "Bail will be set in the morning and then we can get everyone out. We kept large amounts of cash in our safes for this very reason. The lawyers also will want to be paid daily in cash—in case our assets are frozen. Our lawyers are already at the station, trying to get more information on who was arrested."

"And, let me guess, the cops aren't being very helpful."

"Correct. Christ, Lorenzo, I thought you'd been arrested too. Thank God you weren't caught up in it."

"I would have been, but something came up here at home. How the fuck did the Feds find out about the factory?" I snarled. I was in charge of the factory operation. Only a tight circle of our men had knowledge of the factory. We had deliberately kept it on a need-to-know basis to prevent unnecessary risks. "It's been working well for the last eighteen months, and there've been very few changes in personnel since we established it."

"Maybe someone let something slip inadvertently?" Aloysius suggested.

"Everyone who works there knows to keep their mouths shut. They've all proven their loyalty. Who's the newest person we have there?"

"Tommaso. He's been there fourteen months, and he's worked for us for six years now. We pay him very well, and I can't see him as ever being disloyal," Aloysius mused. "However, he's the last person to be told about the factory's existence."

"But he's not," I murmured.

CHAPTER 45

ANNUNCIATA

Since coming into the guest room earlier, I hadn't been able to stop thinking about my argument with Lorenzo.

Lorenzo had never treated me like a person with a brain, and he didn't listen to any of my views or opinions concerning the children.

Each time things started to improve between Lorenzo and me, something would set us back again. It was like one step forward and two steps back.

Lorenzo wanted a doormat for his wife, not a smart woman who could stand by his side and help him when he needed it.

I knew I should never have married this man. I should have listened to my gut instinct right at the start, that marriage to this man was going to end up being a disaster, and I should have tried harder to persuade my papà of this.

Eventually, sometime after midnight, I fell asleep. But even that was stressful, with my dreams involving being chased through a forest and not being able to get away.

At some point in the night, the bedroom door opened and Lorenzo came in, snapping on the light switch.

"Lorenzo?" I squinted my eyes into the bright light.

He'd obviously come to apologize for his earlier behavior, although I didn't know why he had to switch on the overhead light while I was still barely awake.

But once my eyes had adjusted to the brightness, I could see that he hadn't come to apologize. He was obviously still angry, his eyes dark and his body tense.

He prowled toward me. "Who did you tell about the factory?" he demanded.

"The...what?" I struggled to sit up in the bed. "What are you talking about?"

"The factory," he gritted out. "Who did you tell?"

"The one you visited on the way back from the clinic?" That was the only factory I thought he could be talking about.

"Don't play dumb. Answer my question."

"I...didn't tell anyone."

"Really?"

"Yes, really," I sighed.

"Not even Christian?"

"Christian?" I rubbed at my eyes. They felt gritty and tiredness tugged at them. "Why would I tell him about the factory?"

"You tell me," he snarled.

"I really don't know what you're talking about." I was irritated that he was talking in riddles, and I was beyond annoyed that he hadn't come to apologize for earlier.

"You were all cozy and talking to your brother when I came out from the factory, just like when we went back to Staten Island. What did you tell him?"

"Nothing," I said. My tone was defensive in the face of his aggression. But then I remembered telling Christian about Lorenzo's allergy, and I felt a sense of guilt wash over me—Lorenzo definitely hadn't wanted anyone knowing about his allergies.

"I know you're lying." His voice had risen, and although he'd close the door behind him, I still worried that he'd wake the kids. "You told the Feds somehow, or you told Christian and he told the Feds."

"The Feds?"

"Or was it when you were with the police at Cat-Con before Aloysius found you? What did you say to the cops?"

"Nothing. They arrested me and put me in the back of a cruiser. They didn't get as far as questioning me."

"What did you tell the Feds?"

"Why would I tell the Feds anything?"

"So that they could raid our factory, shut us down, and arrest our people. And you knew I was headed there tonight, but you didn't realize that I didn't actually go."

My body froze as realization dawned on me. "There was a raid by the FBI?"

"Cut the bullshit, Anni."

"I didn't tell anyone, I swear. Maybe one of your men spoke to the Feds—"

"I trust my men." His voice was as hard as nails.

"And, what, you don't trust me?" I don't know why I was asking this. After everything that had happened recently with Rita, it was clear he didn't trust me.

"We told the details and location of our drugs factory to no one in the Imperiosi. The alliance was still too new to trust them with that level of information Then the raid was the day after *you* found out about the factory—there's no such thing as a fucking coincidence."

Before I could say anything else, he grabbed my cell phone from the nightstand and stormed out of the room.

I wanted to run after him, to ask him what was happening and why he thought I was involved, but my limbs couldn't move.

His anger toward me had been scary. And the fact that I didn't understand what was going on was even scarier.

I wanted to call my papà or Christian, but Lorenzo had taken my cell.

I hurried out of bed and down to the den but he'd already taken my laptop and tablet. I checked all the landline phones in the house but he'd disconnected them and taken all the phones away. Damn!

I could see a line of light shining from under his study door and could hear him talking to someone.

Silently padding closer, I put my ear against the door and recognized Aloysius's voice.

Slowly making my way back up to the guest room, I told myself that at least Lorenzo and Aloysius hadn't been arrested. I shuddered and wrapped my arms around myself. If the raid had happened yesterday when we'd all been there, then I would have been arrested as well as them.

I didn't fall asleep again that night. Instead, I racked my mind, trying to put together the few things Lorenzo had told me, trying to work out why he thought I'd leaked information to the Feds. I alternated between trying to figure this out, succumbing to tears, and raging that he trusted me so little.

I'd never wanted to become a Mafia wife at the age of twenty, but that's what I'd become. And although I'd never admitted it to anyone, it had brought a whole new sense of purpose into my life. I'd become not just a wife to Lorenzo, but also a stepmom to two beautiful children. Two children who needed me—they needed someone to help them to pick up the pieces of their grief and lives and put them together into something meaningful again. And I suspected that even Lorenzo needed me...just like I needed him now.

Lorenzo was convinced that I was the leak...which meant he would probably kill me after this. But instead of thinking of myself, all I could think about was Clara and Clemente losing another parental figure from their lives and the devastating impact that would have on them.

And the other thing I kept thinking was that if Lorenzo killed me, then I also wouldn't have him in my life anymore, and that made the tears start to fall again.

LORENZO

I was on the phone with Marco and had just explained to him about Anni being the leak.

"You're sure it wasn't anyone else?" he asked, his tone serious and terse.

"I don't have any proof yet, but she has to be the leak. There's no one else it could be. She says it's just a coincidence that the raid was the day after she found out about the factory. But we all know that there's no such thing as a coincidence when it comes to our business dealings. Once I get confirmation it was her, then I'll deal with her."

"Would she have made such an effort with your family if she was planning to shop you to the Feds all along?" Marco mused.

"Her family probably hadn't let her into their plan at that stage, knowing that she wouldn't be able to hide any such deception. You should have seen her when I asked her outside the factory what she'd just been talking on the phone to Christian about—she had guilt written all over her face. She must have mentioned something about the factory to her brother; even if she didn't tell him the exact location, all he had to do was triangulate the location of her phone to find out where the factory was."

"Okay. Get me proof and we'll take it from there."

I hung up my phone.

Raking my hands through my hair, I thought about the woman who was upstairs, rage burning inside me.

She'd never been cut out to be my wife. I'd been right all along. She'd allowed herself to be easily manipulated and persuaded by her family to turn on her husband and she'd never even really thought through the repercussions. She didn't understand the meaning of loyalty—loyalty to me, and loyalty to the Fratellanza.

Anni clearly didn't have the level of maturity needed to be a Mafia wife. This wasn't just a game of pretend; this was serious and real life. She had jeopardized everything I'd worked for since the day I'd been initiated into the Fratellanza.

I'd let my guard down, just like I had with Rita, and this is what happened when I let someone in and let them get close to me—they hurt me.

I slammed my fist on my desk. I should have known better—I should never have started to believe in love again.

And when my contacts confirmed that Anni was the leak, then I knew there could only be one outcome for her.

CHAPTER 46

ANNUNCIATA

In the morning, Lorenzo was already gone when I got the kids up.

I was surprised that he hadn't already hauled me off to his torture rooms or, at the very least, locked me in the bedroom.

"Did Lorenzo say where he was going?" I asked Adelina.

"He said he had to go see the Capo."

That made sense.

Adelina looked at me with worry in her eyes. "Did Mr. Lorenzo say when Giuseppe would be released?"

"Giuseppe?"

"Yes, ma'am. The men are saying that Giuseppe was one of the men arrested in the raid last night."

Shit. I rubbed my hands over my tired eyes. "No, he didn't say. I'll let you know if I hear anything."

After breakfast, one of the soldiers came to the front door. "Ma'am," he said, an icy look in his eyes. "I've been instructed to take the children to their grandmother's house today."

"To Cosima's? By whom? That wasn't the plan today."

"By the boss."

"Lorenzo?"

He nodded, looking like he wanted to end my life there and then. Did everyone think that I was the leak?

I got the children ready while the soldier stayed by the door. Luckily the kids were excited about the impromptu visit and didn't sense that anything was amiss.

After the children left, I thought about what I needed to do today. Not being able to settle on anything, I decided I needed to get out of the house. It felt like everyone here thought that I was the leak, making the atmosphere around me oppressive. I would do something normal, like getting the groceries, and hopefully the small change in scenery would help me clear my mind. I grabbed my purse and went into the garage to get a car.

Driving up to the gate, I rolled down the window. "I need to go get some groceries. Could you assign a guard to go with me please?"

The soldier on gate duty fixed me with a steely stare. "The boss says you're not to leave the property."

"He said what?" I was open-mouthed with shock.

The soldier didn't respond. I might not have been locked in the bedroom, but it was clear I was now a prisoner in my own home.

Turning the car around, I seethed while I returned to the garage.

Back in the house, I went to the kitchen and wrote out the list of groceries I had in my mind. I would have to send Adelina to the store. She was upstairs cleaning, but she could go later on.

As I made the list, I heard a notification beep from her cell. It had come from her purse.

I bit my lower lip in thought. I really needed to talk to Christian. I could ask Adelina to use her cell—but I didn't want her to get in trouble with Lorenzo.

I went into the hallway. Listening to the sound of the hoover running, I knew she was still upstairs.

I returned to the kitchen and opened her purse and took out her phone, promising myself that I would go to church and mention this misdeed in confession.

Quickly checking over my shoulder, I punched in Christian's cell number. The thing about having a mind good with numbers was that I could easily remember multiple phone numbers and pin codes.

"Yeah?" Christian answered.

"Christian, it's me, Anni."

"Hey, Mrs. Marchiano," he answered with his usual greeting for me. "Have you got a new number?"

"No. Christian, I have to make this real quick. A Fratellanza drug factory was raided by the Feds last night. Lorenzo thinks I might have leaked to the Feds, which means he might want to kill me." I was only half-joking—even though I knew that I wasn't the leak, I still had to convince Lorenzo of this somehow. "I need you to tell me the truth: did you or papà find out about the factory's drug operation and leak it to the Feds?"

"No, we didn't." He didn't hesitate before answering—but then, he was a good liar.

"You're sure?"

"One hundred percent. Anni, if Lorenzo is being an asshole and trying to blame you, then I should come down and talk to him."

"No, don't worry, Christian. But I'll call if I need you."

"Anni, are you sure?"

"Absolutely. It's just a misunderstanding and I'll be able to sort it out."

I heard Adelina coming down the stairs. "Sorry, gotta go. I'll call you again when I can." Then I hung up and shoved the phone back in Adelina's purse before she came back into the kitchen.

"Mrs. Anni," Adelina nodded at me.

"Hi Adelina. Would you mind getting some groceries from the store for me please?"

"Of course, Mrs. Anni."

After handing over the list, I went to the den to think.

Now that I knew that the Imperiosi wasn't behind the leak, I just had to prove that someone else was.

***

I paced back and forth in the den all morning, trying to work out what had happened.

Lorenzo's words kept running through my mind: everything he'd said last night about me interfering in what had gone on between him and Rita, telling me that Clara and Clemente were *his* children, and then accusing me of being a snitch to the FBI.

I slumped down on the couch and buried my head in my hands.

It couldn't get any worse than last night—my own husband accusing me of leaking intel to the FBI. That he really had that low an opinion of me shocked me to the core.

I shook my head, trying to clear my mind. I had to stop dwelling on the issues in my marriage; instead, I needed to focus on what had happened at the factory last night and work out who had leaked to the Feds.

I remembered what Lorenzo had said: there's no such thing as a coincidence.

I thought back to my visit to the factory. Lorenzo normally didn't take me along when he was on business. He had taken me because he'd been running significantly behind schedule that day after his trip to the doctor's clinic. Going to the clinic was the only out of the ordinary thing I could think of that Lorenzo had done in the couple of days preceding the raid.

That had to be it: someone at the clinic must have followed us.

Why would they do that, though? They obviously knew who he was...so they must have decided to get some dirt on him in a way to make money. The Feds would have paid handsomely for a tip-off about someone as powerful as a Marchiano.

Now I just had to work out who it was at the clinic that had tipped off the Feds.

I knew the only way I could do that was by looking up on the internet who worked at the clinic and seeing what else I could dig up on them via online credit checks and stuff like that. That was what they always did in the cop shows: look at who was in trouble financially and would therefore most benefit from going to the Feds.

I thought back to the nosy nurse, and a groan escaped from me. With hindsight, it was so obvious. Thinking back, her questions had been suspicious. She'd been flirting with Lorenzo right in front of me, probably to distract both me and him, and then she'd asked him about his work. Surely she knew enough about the clinic's clientele to know he was a bad man and that asking him about his work wasn't a good idea?

I needed access to Adelina's cell again so that I could access the internet and do some digging. I knew I could just ask Adelina to borrow her phone, but I really couldn't bear for her to get into trouble with Lorenzo. He'd be furious with her if he discovered that she'd helped me, and she'd become such a good friend to me since I'd come here that I didn't want to risk getting her fired.

Instead, I headed to the kitchen and hung out there for the afternoon, keeping an eye on Adelina and waiting for her to leave the kitchen for a few minutes so that I could sneak a look at her phone.

"Mr. Lorenzo will calm down, don't you worry," soothed Adelina, thinking that this would all blow over.

She obviously had more faith in him than I currently had. I didn't think he'd calm down at all unless I could find out who the real leak was.

I hung around the kitchen all afternoon, no doubt getting under Adelina's feet, but she didn't complain once.

Adelina had decided to spend the afternoon making her homemade tomato spaghetti sauce. That required simmering fresh tomatoes and herbs on the lowest possible heat for at least three hours to let all their richness seep out. I really wished she'd chosen another day to do this.

The only times she left the kitchen was to use the bathroom, but that wasn't enough time to do any real research on her phone apart from looking up a list of the clinic's personnel. I found the nurse's full name and committed it to memory.

By the time Lorenzo arrived home, I was no further in my research and knew I'd have to wait until tomorrow to use Adelina's phone again.

LORENZO

When I got home that evening, I was greeted by the rich aroma of Adelina's homemade tomato and garlic pasta sauce. I went into the kitchen and found Anni there with Adelina.

"Shall I serve dinner now, Mr. Lorenzo? Have you collected the children from their grandmother?"

"No, Adelina. They're spending the next couple of days there."

"But they haven't got their clothes, toys, and other things," Anni worried.

"My mother always keeps a supply of things for them at her house, so they'll be fine," I said tersely. "I can send a soldier with anything else they need."

"Bring my dinner to the study please, Adelina."

Adelina nodded, knowing that it was wisest to make no further comment given the tension in the air.

I stalked to my study and slammed the door shut, collapsing into the chair behind my desk and closing my eyes.

My cell rang.

"Marco," I answered.

"Come over this evening." He didn't even greet me, such was the seriousness of the matter. "I need an update on your investigation into who the leak was."

"I'll be there within the hour."

As I hung up, Adelina brought in dinner.

After wolfing it down, I headed to Marco's.

***

At Marco's mansion, I stood in the study as I updated my Capo. "I've put feelers out with my contacts among the Feds. There are no leads yet, except for one of my guys confirming that someone in our organization leaked to the FBI." Tiredness was numbing my body—I hadn't slept since I'd found out last night about the raid.

"Fuck, that means that there's definitely a leak."

The Feds shutting down our main drug factory was costing us an obscene amount of money each day until we could get a new operation up and running. Marco had spent the day dealing with the lawyers while putting me in charge of investigating the leak and Aloysius in charge of sourcing a new location for our factory operations.

"The only new person to know about the factory *in months* was Anni," I gritted out. "She is the most obvious suspect."

But even as I said the words, something inside was niggling away at me.

"I should feel relief that we know who the leak is," I said to Marco. "But something inside me makes me feel that this isn't right."

"What isn't right?"

"That Anni is the leak."

Marco stared at me. "But you've already told me that she is and that you're completely convinced of it."

"That's just it. The facts point that way, but something inside me keeps niggling away. This isn't how I do things normally—I never doubt my decisions and actions. But something deep inside of me tells me that there was no way that the Anni I've come to know would have shopped me to the Feds."

Marco looked at me sharply. "What makes you think that?"

"This is a woman who has tried her hardest since she's come into my family's lives to make things better: to make the children's grief better, their sleep better, their meals better, their anxiety better, and their confidence better. She's made *me* better. I've always told myself that she was too young, but I now know that isn't true. She's got a wise head on her shoulders. She's handled becoming a wife and mom with a level of maturity that has, quite frankly, surprised me. She's a strong woman and I don't believe that she would let herself be so easily manipulated by her family. I believe in her loyalty to me, to my family, and to the Fratellanza."

Confronting Anni about being the leak should have made me feel better. If she had allowed herself to be manipulated by her family and if she had leaked to the Feds, then that would have proved what I'd thought all along—that she was too young and too immature to be a Mafia wife to me.

But I didn't feel any relief or triumph.

Instead, all I felt was that I'd made a terrible mistake in accusing her. And it was all my fault: it had been my choice to accuse her and my choice not to believe her.

Now that my initial anger had passed, I had done nothing but turn things over and over in my mind. Doing an about-face now by telling Marco that I had changed my mind and that she couldn't be the leak, especially when I had no proof about who actually was the leak, was making me look like a weak and indecisive Underboss. Just like telling everyone about Rita's suicide would have made me look like a weak Underboss to my men after she had died.

But this time I wasn't going to let my pride stand in my way.

No, I was going to fight for what I believed in—and what I believed in was Anni and the family she had created with me, Clara, and Clemente. She was the other half of me, the woman who made me feel whole again.

After what had happened with Rita, I'd always sworn that I'd never trust another woman again or let a woman inside my heart. I'd agreed to marry Anni for the sake of our alliance with the Imperiosi, but I'd never agreed to give her my heart—I'd been determined to protect that at all costs and not open myself up to heartache and loss again.

But that is exactly what I was left with now—heartache over losing the woman who'd brought so much light and love into my life and into my family. Because after I'd accused her the way I had, she would want nothing further to do with me.

I knew I couldn't lose Anni—not now, not after I'd fallen for this woman.

"She's fucking smart, Marco. She's much more intelligent than I originally gave her credit for. She understands business issues—actually takes an interest in them. I told you how she figured out the bakeries' problem after our highly-paid accountants failed to do so. I thought before that she'd been manipulated by her family into revealing information about our operations. But now I realize that she's far too smart, and far too loyal, to let herself be manipulated in such an obvious way."

Marco regarded me carefully. "If you really believe in her, then you know what you have to do." I could see in his eyes that he agreed with me about Anni.

"Yeah, I know. I have to find out who the leak really was."

CHAPTER 47

LORENZO

After arriving back from Marco's, I had spent the evening holed up in my study, trying to figure out who the leak might be.

Anni was spending the night in the guest room again, adding to my bad mood.

I was rewatching the footage of the FBI raid to see if there were any clues I had missed, but finding no new information, I closed the video on my laptop and sighed in irritation.

I clicked on the folder for the security cameras around my mansion and the grounds.

Although I'd turned the main security cameras off when I'd taken Anni to the tennis court, I'd kept on the cameras that only I had access to. And clicking on the file from the day of the tennis match, I viewed the footage.

I watched as I spanked her, strapped her, fingered her, and then fucked her, zooming into her face and closely watching her emotions.

Fuck, she'd been just as turned on as I had been. Although my kitten liked breaking the rules sometimes, she also liked being forced to submit to me.

Getting to the part when I finally penetrated her with my dick, I watched while she tightly gripped the seat in front of her.

The harsh thrusts of my cock forced her whole body forward and made her full tits bounce up and down, her nipples erect with arousal. The sound of my balls slapping against her pussy with each thrust was mingled with her labored gasps.

Just watching it made me want her all over again.

Saving the file to my cloud, I closed my laptop and strode upstairs.

I entered the guest room without knocking, making Anni jerk up in surprise.

She'd been lying in bed. "Lorenzo? What's wrong?" She was wearing silk sleep shorts with a matching camisole top.

I sat on the end of the bed. "Come here, kitten," I said in a low, dangerous tone.

I waited to see if she would obey me.

And I was rewarded by the sight of her crawling across the bed and kneeling beside me.

"I've got something to show you."

She licked her lips as she looked down at the tablet in my hands. "What is it?"

"You'll see." I clicked on the video I wanted her to watch.

"What are we watching?" She frowned in confusion.

The video started from when I had pulled her down across my lap.

I watched the expressions flitting across Anni's face as she watched the footage of me yanking her panties down her thighs and spanking her ass hard.

A flush crept up Anni's face. Finally finding her words, she spoke to me. "But the security cameras were turned off..."

"The main ones, yes. But not the cameras that only I have access to."

"You recorded us?" she asked, incomprehension suffusing her words.

"You're *my* wife, so I can do whatever I like—can't I, kitten?"

She swallowed hard. "Turn it off," she said abruptly as she reached for the tablet at the same time.

I held it away from her. "No, kitten, I want you to watch the video." It had reached the part where I'd started to strike her ass and pussy lips with the leather strap from my racket case.

I'd edited the footage to zoom into the view of her pussy glistening with her juices as I punished her.

She covered her face with her hands, but I pulled her hands away and forced her to watch. "See how much you like it when I punish you like this?"

The picture zoomed into my fingers spreading her wet arousal over her swollen folds and clit.

"You like to disobey me sometimes. But you also like to receive your punishment like a good girl, don't you? Although sometimes I have to persuade you to comply with my plans."

"Please turn it off." Her voice softened into a pleading tone.

But I could see now how her pupils were dilating with need. "You can deny it all you like, kitten, but you're turned on just as much as I am by watching this video."

Now her eyes couldn't leave the screen as she watched me pushing two thick fingers into her tight vagina.

I pulled her into my lap and she didn't resist, and we continued to watch as the recording reached the part where she'd taken my huge dick between her plump lips.

As we watched and she sat on my lap, I parted her legs and inched my fingers under her silk shorts. "Good girl," I growled with approval at what I found. "You're soaking wet and so ready for my cock, aren't you?"

I closed the tablet just before it got to the part where I penetrated her with my dick.

Anni looked at me. "Please let me have your cock," she begged. *She was back to being my sweet angel.*

Pushing her onto the bed, I dragged her shorts down her legs and pulled her camisole over her head, leaving her completely naked before me.

"Get on all fours," I ordered as I unzipped my pants and grasped my aching hardness.

As soon as she turned onto her hands and knees, I shoved her thighs apart and sunk into her with one hard thrust, eliciting a strangled cry from her as I forced apart her sensitive walls.

"Please, I need you," she whimpered.

"This should be a punishment fuck," I growled, "for your disobedience over going to the conference." I continued to slide my dick in and out of her. "But I'm not going to punish you tonight." I didn't explain further, but I knew that I wanted to pleasure her and to show her how much I wanted her and needed her.

Gripping her hips, I set a slow, deep pace. My hardness massaged every part of her vagina as I buried my cock up to my balls inside her again and again.

I bent my head over her shoulder and whispered into her ear. "I love the view of you bent over on all fours for me, your legs spread wide and your greedy pussy obediently taking in every inch of my dick."

I could practically feel her pussy gushing at my words. She got off on all this just as much as I did.

Her pussy was so wet that with each thrust of my cock, more and more of her cream leaked out of her and coated her thighs and my balls. And this sound of her wet arousal was my undoing.

Speeding up, I pushed myself against her front wall, increasing the friction in that delicious spot for her.

Her breaths were coming in pants now, her back damp with sweat and her hands trying to keep her body from slipping on the sheets with the force of my thrusts. "Please let me come," she begged. "Please, Lorenzo. I've been good and watched the video."

I buried myself in her yet again, slamming my balls against her swollen pussy lips. "And did you like watching the video?" If she wanted to come, I first wanted to hear her admit that she'd liked it just as much as me.

"Lorenzo, please…"

"Answer me!"

Then she said what I wanted to hear: "Yes…I loved watching you punish me. I loved seeing you teach me a lesson with your hands and your cock."

"Fuck, kitten," I gritted out as my fingers reached round her front to find her clit.

And fondling that bundle of nerves as I pounded her tight channel was enough to send her over the edge into an orgasm that made her cry out in ecstasy.

Her clenching muscles made me come hard, and I buried myself deep inside her as I marked every bit of her pussy walls with my thick cum.

After I recovered my breath, I reluctantly pulled out of her and rolled her onto her back.

She tried to close her legs but I forced them apart again. "Lorenzo, I can't…"

My nostrils flared. "You'll take whatever I give you."

Spreading her labia back open with my fingers, my tongue dove between her folds and I ravaged her pussy with licks, bites and sucks, feasting on her clit and forcing her to come two more times at the mercy of my mouth.

And to finish off, I kneeled over her and pumped my hand up and down my hard dick, releasing white ropes of cum over her smooth body with a guttural moan and then kissing her deep on the lips.

We stared at each other for a few long moments, and then I got a washcloth to clean her up.

When she was clean, I lifted her limp body under the covers and laid down beside her, taking her in my arms and stroking her hair as she fell asleep.

CHAPTER 48

ANNUNCIATA

The next morning, Lorenzo had already left when I woke up.

I immediately thought back to last night. Lorenzo was right when he'd said that I got off on submitting to him, but the thought still made me blush. I didn't really understand what had happened last night. I thought Lorenzo would want to punish me, but he didn't do that and he didn't explain why, adding confusion to the jumble of emotions inside my head.

I got up and showered and then went downstairs.

Without the children here, the house was too quiet. After a quick coffee, I hung around the kitchen and waited until Adelina went upstairs so that I could sneak her cell phone out of her purse.

As I rummaged through the capacious bag, I frowned, not being able to see the cell. I looked through it more carefully, taking my time to search all the pockets, but I still couldn't find it.

I heard Adelina coming back down the stairs, so I hurriedly put the bag back where I'd found it.

As Adelina came in, holding a vase of flowers that needed its water changed, I casually asked, "How are your grandkids doing?"

Her face lit up as she told me the latest news of them.

"I'd loved to see some more photos of them. Do you have any new ones on your phone?"

"Yes, my daughter sends me pictures almost daily." I had known this, of course, but used it as an excuse to find out where she had put her phone.

Adelina picked up her purse and looked through it. She sighed. "I must have left my phone at home."

My heart sank. I had been counting on using her phone to gain access to the net so that I could do some research on the clinic's employees.

Noticing my disappointed expression, she added, "Don't worry. I'll remember my phone tomorrow and show you the photos then."

I felt bad for deceiving her, so I mustered up a smile. "That sounds great."

I wandered back to the den and thought about how else I could prove who the leak was. I couldn't just sit here and do nothing while Lorenzo continued to think that I was a traitor.

Apart from Adelina, I wondered who else I could ask for help. Cosima wouldn't go against her son to help me, not that I had any way of contacting her without access to a phone.

Then I thought of Aloysius. Why hadn't I thought of him before? He was always willing to help me. All I had to do was keep an eye out for anyone arriving at the house today. He was in and out of our mansion all the time, so, hopefully, he would pop by today.

I got my college books out to do some reading in the hope of taking my mind off the current situation. That was the only college work I could do without my laptop.

I set my study materials out on the dining room table, and although I tried to read, my mind couldn't concentrate with everything else that was going on.

If I could tell Aloysius my suspicions about the clinic employees, then he could do the background checks on them, focusing on the nosy nurse. He could get one of his men to do a financial check on her, and I was sure that would tell us all we needed to know, including showing a nice big pay-off to her from the Feds.

I knew that there was a good likelihood of Aloysius coming to the mansion today and an even better chance of him agreeing to help me.

It had to be the nosy nurse who had followed us and then leaked the factory location to the Feds. As Lorenzo was always saying, there was no such thing as a coincidence.

I kept hoping that Aloysius would come by today, but as the hours passed and it became late afternoon, he still hadn't appeared. I checked the time again. If he came by, I really needed to be able to talk to him alone before Lorenzo arrived home.

I told myself that there was still another couple of hours during which Aloysius could appear before Lorenzo came home and that Aloysius was sure to help me. He was always turning up and helping me—like when I snuck out to the grocery store at the strip mall, and when there was no guard to accompany me and the kids to the playground, and the time I got arrested at Chicago Cat-Con.

There's no such thing as a coincidence.

Lorenzo's words rang in my ears, and I stilled.

Aloysius was always appearing when I needed help—was that just a coincidence?

CHAPTER 49

ANNUNCIATA

When Lorenzo arrived home for dinner that evening, he had dinner in his study like the previous day.

Even though I knew he was busy working, I needed to talk to him. Knocking once, I entered the room.

"I've been thinking about who the leak might be," I began. Before he could accuse me again, I hurried on. "I thought it might be the nurse from the clinic—you know, the one who was flirty with you and was asking those questions about where you work. I thought that maybe she followed us from the clinic to the factory—"

"That's not likely. I made sure I wasn't followed."

"I know. I understood that after I thought about it some more. You were circling the area for ages before pulling up at the factory, and I realized that the ditsy nurse didn't seem the type to have a grand plan to follow us."

"Is that all, Anni?" Lorenzo's exhaustion was clear to hear in his voice.

"No, it's not actually. You said that there's no such thing as a coincidence. That got me thinking." I paused, licking my dry lips. "Aloysius seems to always be around…is that just a coincidence?"

Lorenzo sat up ramrod straight. "You should have proof before you accuse anyone in my family like this."

"It's just that he's always around," I said quickly. "He was there that day when there was no guard available when I wanted to take the kids to the playground. And then there was that day when he found me at the strip mall—"

"That was hardly a coincidence. You were in a bullet-proof SUV with my number plates, parked in a strip mall on the main drag on his way to the mansion."

"I know, so maybe those couple of times *were* a coincidence. But what about Cat-Con?"

"What about it?"

"There were thousands of people there. Out of all the people you had looking for me, he was the one to find me."

"And you should be glad he did since, if you remember, you'd gotten your sorry ass arrested."

"I'm grateful he found me. But is it a coincidence that he's always finding me? I'm just saying how did he find me so quickly when it was chaos there?"

"He told us: his police contact called him when he saw that you were a Marchiano."

"But I never told him my name."

"You must have," he said carefully.

"No, I didn't. They didn't ask me, and they normally don't take down details like that until they're booking you in at the station."

"You said that day that the officer searched your backpack. Your wallet had your driver's license."

"But I've thought about it really hard, trying to remember step-by-step everything that happened. And I'm positive that the officer didn't look in my wallet. He did a search of my bag, but it was real quick because he was just checking to see if there were any weapons." I took a deep breath. "Lorenzo...is there any reason Aloysius might have wanted you arrested at the raid by the Feds?"

Lorenzo pierced me with his dark gaze. I couldn't tell what he was thinking. "He's my brother," he gritted out.

"I know," I said quietly, "but that doesn't answer my question."

He just stared at me, and I could tell there was something he wasn't telling me.

"Aloysius turned up that day you took me to the factory. I remember him mentioning that he wasn't due to be at the factory that day. And I thought that maybe it wasn't a coincidence that he was there at the same time as us. And when he saw me at the factory and realized someone else now knew about the existence and location of the factory, he knew he could leak intel to the Feds and blame it on me."

"Why would he do that?"

"That's what I don't know. But I think you might..." My voice trailed off as I watched an array of emotions cross Lorenzo's face.

"Anni, he's known about the factory since it's been operational, so well over eighteen months." Lorenzo's voice had become less hard as if he was wavering. "If he wanted to frame me, he could have done it at any time before now."

"But maybe he didn't have someone else to point the finger at—not until he saw that I now knew about the factory. Didn't you tell me that all your men who worked there had known about the factory for many months by now?"

"He's my brother," he said again, his voice hoarse.

"Why won't you trust me?" I asked softly. "Why won't you let me in?" I knew that Lorenzo was holding something back.

"I've been wondering for a while if Aloysius has been holding something against me." Lorenzo ran his hands over his weary face. "He hasn't said or done anything specific, but there's a little niggle at the back of my mind—a sense that something isn't quite right between us as brothers."

"What could he be holding against you? You've always seemed so close."

"We are close and always have been. But I've been wondering if Aloysius heard something that he shouldn't have."

"Like what, though?"

"Like I'm not our father's rightful heir and successor."

I went very still. "What do you mean? You're the oldest son, so everyone knew when your father passed away that you were the one who would take over his position as Underboss."

"I was the oldest son, but I wasn't my father's son."

I went cold. "I don't understand..."

"My mother was pregnant by someone else when she married my father. Neither of them knew until after the marriage. My father didn't throw her out; instead, he brought me up as his own son. My real father was an associate of the Fratellanza, but he never knew that my mother had become pregnant by him. My parents told everyone I was a honeymoon baby and that I'd been born two months premature. I was a small baby, so apparently no one questioned it."

"Your father did that?" I asked in disbelief. Made Men were notoriously proud, not to mention totally obsessive about the purity of their bloodline.

"Yeah. He was already in love with my mother by the time he found out."

"When did you find out?"

"When my father was on his deathbed two years ago. He'd been really ill for a couple of months by then. I don't know if it was all the painkillers making him less inhibited in what he said or whether it was a genuine need to unburden his concerns, but he told me everything."

I was completely stunned. When I'd felt that Lorenzo was distant and closed off, I never imagined that he was keeping a secret like this from me. "What did he say to you?"

"He said how even though I wasn't his son, he was proud of me and knew I'd make a good Underboss. He told me that he didn't want me to ever find out about my parentage from anyone else and that he wanted me to never doubt my own strength and capabilities. He also said that no one else could ever know the truth because, if they did, it would destabilize the whole Fratellanza. The whole organization is built on bloodlines and loyalty. If anyone found out that he was weak enough to let his wife get away with such a betrayal and allow a bastard son to take over from him, people would start to question how strong the organization's internal leadership really was."

"Perhaps if your father hadn't been an Underboss, then it wouldn't have mattered so much," I suggested. "Did Aloysius know about this too? And since then, he's been hostile toward you?"

"No, my parents never told Aloysius. My father made my mother and me swear to him that we would never tell him. He was afraid of what it would do to our family if Aloysius ever found out that he'd been cheated of his rightful inheritance of being Underboss."

"But Aloysius found out somehow?"

"The day my father told me in his bedroom, I thought I heard someone outside the room. But when I checked, no one was there. I didn't think any more of it—not until the last six months or so. I've sensed something different within Aloysius, but sometimes it's hard to tell if I'm imagining it or if it's really there."

"Lorenzo, I'm one hundred percent certain that the police officer didn't see my ID and didn't know my name through that." I repeated my assertion in the hope that it would persuade him to take my suspicion about Aloysius seriously, which was even more plausible given what he'd just told me. "Do you believe me, Lorenzo?"

I held my breath, waiting for his reply.

"Yes, I believe you. Because I love you and I trust you, Anni."

I stilled, before slowly smiling at him. "You telling me that you love me doesn't surprise me—because I've felt it, and because I love you too. But I'm still not sure if you trust me yet."

"I trust you, Anni. It's taken a while, but I do trust you. I need to deal with Aloysius first, and then we'll sit down and talk."

I nodded. I desperately wanted to talk to him about everything, but I knew he would be distracted until the issue with the leak was resolved.

"I want to bring down all the barriers between us, Anni—all the barriers that could get in the way of my love for you."

My heart lifted knowing that he loved me and that he trusted me. He'd trusted me enough to tell me of his illegitimacy and that he wasn't the rightful Underboss—something that was at the center of his life and defined the very person he was.

And even more importantly, I knew now that he loved me, in the same way that I loved him. And he was no longer afraid to admit it.

CHAPTER 50

LORENZO

Talking to Anni made me feel a sense of overwhelming relief.
I'd had a choice to either put the organization and my role as Underboss first, or to tell Anni the truth so that together we could work a way out of this mess.
And I'd chosen to let Anni in and work with her. I'd trusted her enough to believe in her innocence and to entrust her with the secret of my illegitimacy.
I'd told her something I'd never admitted to anyone else. And I'd kept it secret until now not just for the sake of the Fratellanza, but also for my sake, because it revealed a deep flaw in me—my illegitimacy.
It shouldn't matter in this day and age that I was illegitimate, but I knew it did matter within the organization, and it mattered a lot. Because it meant that I was not my father's lawful offspring, and I was not the rightful Underboss.
I was admitting that my whole life was a lie, and I was tearing apart my whole identity as an Underboss. I'd been raised ever since I could remember to be Underboss one day and to protect the Fratellanza at all costs, but now something else mattered: Anni.

After my conversation with Anni, I went straight over to talk to Marco. We had to figure out what to do about Aloysius and how to protect the Fratellanza.

I set out the facts to my Capo, including the situation regarding my illegitimate birth and Aloysius being the rightful successor. Marco looked hard at me. We were in his study together with his brother, Alessio. I'd brought Alessio, as Consigliere, into the conversation too.

"Have you got Anni's cell phone with you?" Alessio asked.

I nodded and got it out of my pocket, setting it on the desk in front of me.

Alessio picked it up, and taking a small tool out of a drawer, he removed the sim card and the back of the phone. After inspecting it, he looked up at us. "There looks to be a device implanted in the phone. My guess is that it's a tracking device." He walked to the door. "I'll get on it now and let you know what I find."

Alessio shut the door behind him.

"So, now you know everything," I said into the tense silence.

"You never thought that you had a duty to tell me, your Capo, all this?" Marco roared.

There was nothing I could say. In hindsight, maybe I should have told Marco. We were as close as brothers, but it hadn't felt right telling him and not telling Aloysius, especially as the person most affected by it was Aloysius.

"The only reason I'm not shooting you in the head right now," snarled Marco, "is that your reasons for keeping this all secret was so as not to destabilize the Fratellanza."

"I'm not going to try and defend what I've done," I said quietly. "The whole thing's fucked up. It's fucked with my head so much over the years, and it fucked up my marriage with Rita. The only thing I can do to try and make it up to you is to work even harder for you and show you my loyalty."

Marco paced up and down his study. "You can show me your fucking loyalty by helping me deal with Aloysius," he snapped. "There won't be any second chances for you." I knew this wasn't an empty threat from him. Marco was volatile and had a short fuse—I would have already been dead if they'd been any other whiff of past disloyalty, but my record working for the Fratellanza was exemplary and I knew I was Marco's best Underboss.

"Yes, Capo," I nodded. I knew it would take me some time to earn back Marco's trust, but I was willing to put the work in and do whatever it took.

"Our organization is built on trust, honesty, and loyalty." He gave a harsh exhale. "In the end, you did what you did in loyalty to the Fratellanza. Your father was right—the traditionalists in the organization would have had a field day with the news that he kept on a disloyal wife and that he allowed his heir to be a man who was not his son. Some of the men would have genuinely felt that your father's actions demonstrated he was too weak to be Underboss; other men, however, would have stirred things up to force your father to lose his position, in the hope that they could take it over for themselves. We can't have any of this shit surfacing now. I've got too many problems with the Bratva to be dealing with infighting and discontent within the organization."

"Tell me what you need me to do," I said to him.

"First, we need unequivocal proof that Aloysius was the leak. Fucking hell, what was he thinking? What he's done affects the whole organization."

"What's happening with the FBI and their investigation?" I asked.

"The judge hearing the initial motions is someone on our payroll. We've managed to get the arrests kicked out due to a technicality on the search warrants—really, that hearing shouldn't have gone our way, but having the judge on our team meant we got what we needed. Bad news is that there's obviously no way we can get the drugs operation up and running again in the same location, and we're having to start from scratch. It's costing us millions each month we're not fully operational."

Alessio had come back into the room. "I've given the phone and tracking device to Danio. He's the tech genius, so he'll be able to best deal with it." He looked at me. "Have you heard the latest about the Società alliance?"

I looked at Marco. "You've come to an agreement with the Società in L.A.?" Marco had been in discussions for some time with this Italian Mafia organization based on the West Coast.

Marco nodded. "Finally."

I could tell he was still furious with me, and I knew that would last for some time, but this was business we were now talking about.

"The Bratva are all over our asses," Marco said tersely. "They've been taking away power from not just us but from all the Italian Mafia organizations, and the Russians' growth is not slowing down. We're stronger now that we have the alliance with the Imperiosi in New York, but that's not enough. By also making an alliance with the Società, we'll be increasing our power dramatically. As much as I hate those fuckers in L.A., we need each other at the moment."

I nodded. "I don't trust anyone, but if it's a choice between trusting the Russians or the Italians, I'd go with the Italians every time."

"The Russians are savages," added Alessio. "The Società, at least, share the same values as us. Did Marco tell you his happy news?"

"You agreed to marry someone from the Società?" I asked. In forming this alliance, there'd been discussions about Marco marrying a girl from a Società family.

Marco sat down and leaned back in his chair, crossing his arms behind his head. "It's the best way to cement the alliance. I'm looking forward to meeting the young virgin they've decided to sacrifice to me." He gave an evil smirk.

"You mean the girl they've decided to promise in marriage to you," corrected Alessio.

"It's the same thing, though, isn't it?" he drawled. "She's Società, and she'll have to obey me once the engagement contract is signed."

As close as I was to Marco, I still couldn't help thinking that a man would have to be insane to agree to marry his daughter to my Capo. Marco was unpredictable, ruthless, brutal, and the complete opposite of what someone would look for in a future husband. I just hoped that the girl and her family knew what they were letting themselves in for.

***

Arriving home late that night, I handed Anni a new cell phone.

"What's happened to my old one?" she asked.

"Alessio thought we should check it. When we took it apart, we found a tracking device in it."

"A tracking device?" Her voice rose in confusion.

"Aloysius must have planted it in your phone. That's how he found you at Cat-Con, and how he knew you'd gone to the drug factory that day."

"But how did he..." Her voice trailed off, and she closed her eyes. "The day I left my purse in his car on the way back from the grocery store. My phone was in it. Do you think he planted it then?"

"Probably. And then when I had everyone searching for you the day you went to Cat-Con, he would have used the tracker to find your location, and that's why he was the one to find you. At least the tracker came in useful in letting us get to you before the cops took you to the station."

"He was so nice that time he found me at the strip mall, like he genuinely was concerned for my safety because I was out in public without protection."

"He probably was concerned about you that day. It was probably only after you left your purse and phone in his car that he came up with the idea of the tracker and making you the scapegoat for a leak to the Feds."

"Does Marco believe that Aloysius is most likely the leak?"

"Yes. Everything points to that, particularly after we found the tracker in your phone. We just need to get concrete proof now, and then we can confront him."

CHAPTER 51

LORENZO

The next couple of weeks were tense.

I had to act as normally as possible around Aloysius but also watch him carefully for any clues he might give away confirming that he was the leak. At the same time, Anni had to lie low so that Aloysius still believed she was under house arrest. I'd told him, however, that the kids had come home as it was too unsettling for them to be away from me for too long.

The breakthrough came two weeks later. We'd been having him tailed twenty-four hours a day, plus planted listening bugs in his home, car, and phones.

He was a slippery bastard, that was for sure. But he finally slipped up when he dumped a burner phone in his trash. The team trailing him retrieved the phone, and we were able to recover the deleted call history to see that he had spoken several times to the FBI agent who'd been in charge of the raid at the factory.

Once we had the proof in place, Marco let me be the one to confront Aloysius.

"Hey, bro," said Aloysius when I arrived at his apartment. "You didn't say you were coming over today." Normally we met at my house.

"I had something I needed to talk to you about."

My tone made Aloysius stop what he was doing and look up at me. "And what's that?" His tone was casual, but I could tell it was forced.

"We know that you are the leak—that you leaked the factory location to the Feds."

Aloysius's gaze hardened, and he didn't say anything for a moment. "How did you find out?"

I was glad that he was according me enough respect to not even try to lie his way out of it, not that there was any way he'd be able to do that given the evidence we had gathered of his betrayal.

"The burner phone you used to call your FBI friend. You heard our father that day didn't you, when he was telling me that he wasn't my real dad?"

"Yeah, I did."

I nodded. "I thought I heard someone that day, but when I checked, there was no one there. If you heard us, why didn't you just say something?"

"Father died the next day and then there was the funeral and all that shit to deal with. I thought you would talk to me. But you didn't—you were happy to carry on lying to me."

"Why not just be a man and have it out with me face-to-face?"

"What?" he sneered. "Like you told me to my face that you weren't the rightful Underboss?"

"I was following our father's wishes."

"Like hell you were!" he yelled. "You just wanted the Underboss position for yourself when you knew it should have been mine all along."

"I never wanted the position. We were brought up being told that I would be Underboss one day and you would be my second-in-command. That's just the way it was. I never had a grand plan to be Underboss."

"But you didn't refuse the position, even when you knew you were a bastard and it wasn't rightfully yours."

"Christ, Aloysius, you know what I went through with Rita—how she wanted me to leave the Mafia life behind and start somewhere else afresh. You know that being in this life is what drove the mother of my children to kill herself. How can you think that I saw the Underboss position as being something so special that I had to have it no matter the cost? I would have willingly given up my role if I could have done so without destabilizing the Fratellanza and everything our father had built up over the years."

"Yeah, it's all about you, Lorenzo, just like it's always been. You keep harping on about how your life's been affected, but what about mine? I'm the one who was cheated out of his rightful position, the one who's had to make do with less power and influence within the organization, and the one who's always had to play second fiddle to his superior brother."

This wasn't getting us anywhere. "I thought you were preoccupied because you were involved with a girl, but now I realize you were actually preoccupied with revenge. Christ, how did I not see it? And why did you target Anni?"

"After she left her cell in my car, she was easy to set up to take the fall for the leak to the Feds. All I had to do was bide my time until the opportunity arose, and that happened the day you took her to the drug factory. It's a shame, because I liked the girl, but it was business." He frowned. "I'm curious. How did you figure out that she wasn't the leak and that it was me?"

"There were too many coincidences."

He gave a harsh laugh. "You always were a paranoid bastard."

"For good reason it seems." I shook my head. "I just can't believe that you did this—that you shopped me and the whole organization to the Feds. Didn't us being brothers mean anything to you?"

"Brotherly love works both ways," he retorted. "How did you expect this conversation to turn out? For me to say that it's all okay and that I don't mind that you've cheated me?"

"I expected you to have some remorse at least. I've always felt bad that you weren't Underboss, but there wasn't anything I could do to change it. If our men knew that our father had stayed married to our mother after finding out she was pregnant with another man's child, our family name would have been weakened forever in the eyes of the rest of the organization. What was I supposed to do?"

Suddenly, a gunshot rang out through the room and Aloysius's body reeled backward.

Withdrawing my weapon, I spun around and found Marco standing there, his gun aimed at where Aloysius had been standing.

"What the fuck, Marco?" I whipped my head back around and ran over to Aloysius.

He lay there, a bullet through his chest and struggling for breath.

"What have you done?" I yelled at Marco.

I fell to my knees and hauled Aloysius into my arms, cradling his body against me. "Hold on, little brother! We're getting a doctor, you're going to be okay, just hold on."

"It's...too late," he croaked.

"No, damnit, it's not!"

"I deserve...this," he said. "I b-betrayed...the Fratellanza."

"No!" I roared.

But I could do nothing as his body slumped in my arms and all life seeped from his veins. "Call a fucking doctor," I shouted at Marco.

Marco walked over slowly. "He's gone. He signed his own death warrant the moment he betrayed us to the Feds—you know that. I killed him so that you wouldn't have to do it."

And I did know that, but that didn't stop the grief from pouring out of me.

"Santa Adelina, Madre di Dio, prega per noi peccatori, adesso e nell'ora della nostra morte," I murmured in a choked voice. These were the words a Made Man said upon a death, but I never thought I'd be saying them upon the death of my own brother: 'Holy Mary, Mother of God, pray for us sinners now and at the hour of our death.'

***

News of Aloysius's death quickly circulated among the Fratellanza, together with details of his betrayal.

As expected, Marco wanted to make an example of what would happen to any person inside the Fratellanza who turned against the organization. Marco, however, didn't reveal why Aloysius had acted as he'd done, and people assumed it was a case of a jealous younger brother trying to get rid of his older brother so that he could take over his position. My illegitimacy remained a secret, Marco agreeing that the truth would have too much of an unsettling effect on the organization.

The funeral was a quiet affair, with just myself, my mother, Anni, Marco, and Alessio attending. Whenever I thought about what had happened, I felt numb. I'd never wanted things to turn out this way.

***

The day after the funeral, Anni and I had just finished putting the children to bed.

We had done it together, and as I turned off the light, I took a last look at Clara. She was already asleep, having succumbed to her tiredness before I'd even finished the bedtime story.

She looked so little in her huge bed. She was lying practically on top of the stuffed cat toy Anni had given her, and Wilbur was tucked up next to her with her arm snugly around him. I had finally given in to Clara's pleas to take Wilbur up to bed with her. He would do anything for Clara and let her spend hours stroking his fur, and she seemed to get a lot of comfort from stroking him as well as from stroking her toy cat. I was just glad that Clara was happier and coping better with her grief.

Ever since Anni had gotten the stuffed cat toy for Clara, her sleep had gradually improved to the point where she rarely woke at night now. And her not waking also meant that Clemente didn't get disturbed and he, too, slept through almost every night.

I went downstairs with Anni, and we sat down to finally talk.

"Regarding the raid, deep down I didn't want to believe you were the leak, but I had to do my job as an Underboss. I couldn't ignore the fact that the raid was the day after you'd found out about the factory. My head and heart were telling me different things."

"I get that. But I need you to trust me," she said seriously, "particularly when it comes to the kids."

"I know. And, for what it's worth, I do trust you with the kids. You don't know how glad I am that I have you in my life, not just for the kids, but also for me."

She smiled at me.

"I've been thinking about what you said when you told me that you'd been taking Clara to see a speech therapist. I know I didn't like it at the time, but now I can see that you were right."

"Really?" she asked carefully.

"Yeah, really. I know I've been an asshole about the whole speech therapy thing. You've done wonders with Clara's speech since you came to live with us, and I haven't shown you enough appreciation for what you do."

"I don't need appreciation; I just want your trust."

"You have it," I said seriously. "The next appointment, we'll all go to the session together."

"If you're busy with work, I can take Clara by myself..."

"No, I've left you to do too many of these things by yourself up until now. We're a family, and I want us to do these things together." I closed my eyes for a moment. "The business is a mess right now with the raid happening and everything else, and the Aloysius thing isn't something I know how to sort out."

"You'll deal with it, just like you deal with everything else thrown at you, and I'll be right here at your side."

"I haven't dealt with things well in the past. Everything in my life has been about my role as an Underboss in the Fratellanza, a role that wasn't even rightfully mine. And what has it achieved? A brother who was out to get me and is now dead, a first wife who hated what I did so much that she couldn't carry on with life, and a job that means I have to suspect my own wife of wrongdoing if the facts point that way despite what my heart might tell me. Has it all been worth it? Is it worth it now?"

"But look at all the other things that you've achieved in that time: Clara, Clemente, and us."

I shook my head. "My role is interfering with my relationship with you, and I hate that. My heart tells me that you would never do something disloyal to me, the children, or the Fratellanza. But my mind is so messed up sometimes with everything that has happened in the past, making me doubt myself and the things I've done. What if I'd come clean to everyone right after my father had died, telling them that Aloysius was the rightful successor? He would have made a good Underboss, and the Fratellanza would have been no worse off—and maybe Rita would still be alive and the kids would still have her in their lives. That's the really hard thing—the thing that's so hard to forgive myself for. Every time I see the grief in Clara's eyes, that just kills me to my core."

Anni put her hand on my arm. "You have to focus on the future, on healing, and on happiness. Not one of us can change the past, but we can change the way we deal with it. I'm not saying forget what's happened. But let the kids have photos of their mom around the house," she said gently, "and remind them of her love for them and the happiness that you had together. Because there were happy times, but right now you're focusing on the bad times and what went wrong. We can't control life, but we can control our response to it—if we're going to let it beat us down, or if we're going to embrace everything that it throws at us and come out stronger on the other side of it."

"I just keep wondering what if I had gotten out of this life, if that would have made a difference somehow?"

"*What if*—the words we all say and think. And it's okay to think about it, but don't let those thoughts overwhelm you. No one can control what fate throws at them, and it's futile to try otherwise."

I pulled her into my arms. "You're so good for the children and for me. We were so lucky the day you burst into our lives. I've always believed that there's no such thing as a coincidence. It was fate that brought us together that day when you tried to shoot me after I growled at Wilbur."

"I was only trying to protect him."

"Yeah, I was pretty angry when he scratched me just after you'd shot at me for the first time. I can get why you were trying to protect him."

"Does that mean you're coming over the dark side: to a life where cats rule supreme?"

"Yeah, that's not going to happen anytime soon, but I know I'm never getting rid of Wilbur. I may be stubborn and obstinate, but even I know that there's no arguing about that with either you or Clara—you and Wilbur have completely corrupted her."

"In a good way," she added, resting her head against my chest.

"Yeah, in a good way. She's at her happiest now, and that's all because of you coming into our lives with your determined rays of sunshine. With you in our lives, part of me knows that the kids—and me—are going to get all the love we need to thrive. And I want to give you that love back and show you how much you mean to me."

EPILOGUE

ANNUNCIATA

A few weeks later, I walked into the bathroom with some clean towels. Clara followed me, eager to help me with putting the freshly washed laundry away.

We came across Lorenzo standing in front of the basin and holding my cat costume.

"What are you doing?" I asked.

"Getting the red paint off." He was cleaning the white fur with a special solution.

Clara stood next to him and watched him. She tugged on his sleeve.

"Yes, presh." *Mia preziosa, my precious*, and *presh* were all variations of the endearment Lorenzo called his little girl.

"Please could I have cat costume too?"

A frown pulled at his brow. These were obviously not words he wanted to hear from his daughter. "You want a fluffy white cat costume like Anni's?"

She nodded. "I think I would look cute," she said earnestly, making him smile.

"With that reasoning, how can I say no?" he replied.

"Thank you," whispered Clara.

"Let me finish this, and then I'll come downstairs and we'll have a look online to see if we can find a cat costume in your size."

With that, Clara happily skipped away, and I heard her go down the staircase.

"That was nice of you to say yes," I commented.

"She asked so nicely, and I didn't want to refuse her. And, just to be clear, I might be allowing her to have a cat costume like you, but there's no way I'm ever letting her practice shooting a gun. Your papà and brothers may have allowed you to do that, but my little girl will never fire a weapon if I have anything to do with it." Changing the subject, he said, "Her speech is coming along well, don't you think?"

"Absolutely. The speech therapist has helped a lot, and the new techniques she's suggested we use at home with Clara are great." I looked down at my costume in his hands. "I've tried everything already to clean it. But I can't get the paint off." I watched him as he continued to scrub at the red paint. "It looks like she's bloody and hurt—it actually makes me really sad to see my cat costume like this."

"I don't like to see you sad."

"I know it's a costume, but she means a lot to me."

"And you mean a lot to me. I remember the first time I set eyes on you. You were so cute, standing there your messy blonde pigtails and scowling at me."

"I've told you, they were *French braids*!" I gave him a playful push on his shoulder.

"I've spent a lot of time getting blood off things. A little bit of red paint isn't going to defeat me. I'll get it as good as new for you."

"You'd do that for me?"

"Yeah, of course."

It was such a small gesture, but it made me feel warm inside. Lorenzo cared about my feelings now—he cared about *me*.

I'd never thought that we'd get to the stage where we could have an easy relationship rather than clashing heads over everything.

We had the children in common, but I realized now how much I needed him to appreciate who I was as a person. I wasn't just a wife to him or a mother to the children; I was my own person, with my own likes, dislikes, and opinions.

I looked more closely and saw that the red paint was faded. "Is it coming off?" I asked in surprise.

"Yep. It'll take a few more scrubs, but I should be able to get it all out."

I beamed up at him. "If you do, I might have to give you a reward."

"An incentive, eh?"

"An incentive," I agreed.

"Like letting me fuck that sweet little pussy of yours?"

I gave a saucy smile. "I mean like...a chocolate-chip cookie."

Lorenzo's gaze darkened. "I think your ass might need a spanking before I get to your pussy," he said, striding toward me.

I squealed as I ran back into the bedroom, but as I reached the bed, he caught my arm and spun me around.

"How about a kiss to make it up to you?" I purred.

"Depends on how good a kiss it is..."

I stood up on tiptoes and pressed my lips against his, instantly opening my mouth to accept his tongue while pressing my body up against him.

"Hmm..." He considered the kiss and then pushed me hard. "Not good enough," he growled.

I fell back onto the mattress.

Instantly he was on top of me. "I've got you where I want you now," he said in a low voice as he nuzzled kisses into my neck, making me instantly wet. "And I know exactly how we're going to spend the next hour."

LORENZO

The following day, a guard at the gate rang my cell. "Boss, the Venetis are here to see you."

"The Venetis?"

"Yeah, boss."

"Which ones?" I demanded.

I heard muffled voices as he asked them. "Boss, it's Napoleone Veneti, Christian Veneti, and a lady who says she's called...er...Ma Veneti."

My heart sank. I felt like asking what they wanted before I decided whether to let them in, but I knew I couldn't treat my in-laws like that. "Let them through."

Anni had heard the conversation. "Have my family come to visit?"

"I don't know, Anni—you tell me."

She just shrugged her shoulders, at the same time smiling in anticipation as the doorbell rang and following me down the hallway.

I opened the front door to find Ma Veneti standing there—with a baseball bat.

And Napoleone and Christian stood behind her.

"To what do I owe this pleasure?" I asked through gritted teeth.

"You wanted to kill Annunciata!" Ma Veneti shrieked.

"Huh?"

"Because you thought she leaked to the Feds," added Christian.

"That all happened a couple of *months* ago," I said.

"I happened to mention it to Ma this morning, so she's only just found out about it," shrugged Christian.

"Christian," said Anni, "I told you that it was sorted out. It's really sweet of you to come check on me, but you didn't need to come all the way to Chicago."

"You know what Ma's like once she gets an idea in her head," drawled Christian. "She insisted on paying a visit to check on things herself."

"I never actually said I wanted to *kill* Anni," I said, trying to hide my irritation. "And, as you can see, she's still here, so I haven't killed your daughter just yet. Which means you can relax and stop worrying."

"Relax? Relax, he says!" She jabbed a finger toward me. "Don't think that my son hasn't told me all the things you've done to my Annunciata."

I looked at Christian; he'd already lost interest in his ma's ramblings, however, and was flicking through messages on his cell phone.

My gaze swung to Napoleone, but he too looked disinterested and was checking his watch as if wondering how long until he could leave.

"And what else am I supposed to have done to your daughter?" I asked, completely baffled at her attitude toward me.

"You threatened to get rid of Wilbur!"

I scowled at her. "Yet I didn't—he's still here. Unlike you, who got rid of the family cat as soon as Anni moved here," I retorted.

"Nonsense! Annunciata was Wilbur's favorite person. He would have *pined* for her if I hadn't sent him to Chicago. I loved that cat, and it was a *selfless* act letting him go and sending him to Annunciata's new home instead."

"Ma," interrupted Christian, "you know that's not true. You don't even like cats."

"You don't know what you're talking about, Christian," she huffed.

"You called him the 'fucking furball' when Anni wasn't around," he pointed out.

"It was a term of endearment," she snapped, waving a hand dismissively at him as if he were an annoying kid. "I loved that cat with all my heart—I was *inconsolable* when I had to let him come to Chicago to be with Annunciata."

"Look, Fantasia—," I began.

She tightened her double-handed grip on the baseball bat. "I've told you already," she screeched, "you're to call me Ma!"

"Ma," soothed Anni, "you've had a long journey. Why don't you come in for coffee and see the children? And you'll be able to see for yourself that Wilbur is doing fine."

Anni's mother needed no further invitation and pushed past me into the house. Walking past the den and seeing the kids, she shrieked, "Bambini!"

Clara and Clemente's faces lit up as soon as they saw her, and they dashed into her outstretched arms. I really didn't know what my children saw in this mad woman.

We all went through to the drawing room, and Adelina served coffee. Clara sat in Fantasia's lap, cuddled against her, as the older lady passed her another piece of biscotti.

In the hope of getting rid of our uninvited guests, I went into the kitchen and gingerly picked up Wilbur.

He shot me a look that told me I was interrupting his spoiling session with Adelina.

I carefully carried him into the drawing room, holding him as far from my body as possible and using a firm grip in the hope that he wouldn't assault me with his claws which looked alarmingly sharp.

Clara had got down to play on the floor, so I went to put Wilbur in Fantasia's lap.

"Keep that animal away from me," barked Fantasia.

Swallowing down a sound of exasperation, I dumped him in Anni's arms instead. "As you can see, the cat is alive and thriving in my household," I said through clenched teeth.

I had to endure another hour of sitting with Anni's family before I could get rid of them. Luckily, the men had to be back in New York by evening, so I didn't have to tolerate an overnight stay.

"People shouldn't just drop by uninvited," I grumbled to Anni, as I closed the door on them later.

"It wasn't so bad. The kids loved seeing Ma."

"Yeah," I conceded. "I guess they did. Your ma is good with children, especially Clara. Maybe I'll put up with a very occasional visit from your ma if it makes Clara happy."

"And me?"

I smiled at her. "If it makes you happy, I'll do it for you too. But next time she comes without the baseball bat. Christ, not only is your ma a pathological liar, but she's also a thug."

"Thug? Says the Made Man..."

"Come on, how many Mafia moms do you know that carry around their own baseball bat? Although perhaps I should have expected something like that from her after the pepper spray thing on our wedding night."

"She's not all bad," protested Anni. "I get my math talents from her, you know."

"Your ma is good with numbers?" That surprised me.

"She is. Didn't you know that she's been banned from all Upstate New York's casinos because of counting cards?"

"Your ma *counts cards*?" I was incredulous.

"Yeah, she's just lousy at hiding it. Papà has even banned her from his casino."

"I don't know if that makes my opinion of her better or worse."

Anni rolled her eyes at me in response.

I gave her a playful swat on her sweet ass. "You know when you roll your eyes at me like that, it makes me want to spank you."

"Promises, promises."

I gave her a wicked grin. "Just you wait until I get you alone tonight."

***

After Aloysius's death and funeral, the only thing that took my mind off the recent events was spending time with my family.

My relationship with Anni kept going from strength to strength, and for that, I was thankful.

I decided to talk to Anni about what she had found out from Rita's psychologist.

"The only things I found out," said Anni, "are what I've already told you: that Rita saw a psychologist who specializes in depression and postpartum depression and that she saw the psychologist a total of seven times, including the week before her death."

"I'd like to see if I can find out more. Patient confidentiality means that the doctor won't be able to tell me anything, so I'll have to threaten her. That will make her talk."

Anni sighed. "You can't just go around threatening people to make them do what you want."

"How else am I supposed to get anything done?"

"You can try talking to her, appealing to her compassionate side. Perhaps the patient confidentiality duty isn't as absolute once the person has passed away?"

"I think my way will get better results—"

"No," Anni said firmly. "I'll make an appointment, and we'll go and speak to her together."

"I don't want to argue with you, Anni, so we'll try it your way first. But if it doesn't work, then I'm threatening her."

***

We made an appointment to see Dr. Fontaine the following week.

In the doctor's office, we sat across from the psychologist. She was smartly dressed and looked to be in her forties.

"Mr. Marchiano," she said, "your request for information is an unusual one. This is not how we usually do things." She was choosing her words carefully, no doubt aware by my surname and by what Rita had told her that I was part of the Mafia—the Marchiano family was notorious throughout Chicago.

"We understand that, Doctor," I said, "but is there anything you are able to tell us that might help me understand better what drove Rita to take her own life? I know that she was probably suffering from postpartum depression and that she was getting help from you. I also know that she found her life difficult due to her religious beliefs. I'm just trying to fill in the gaps if I can."

The doctor nodded. "Unfortunately, I'm still bound by doctor-patient confidentiality. However, I can say that Rita was brave enough to come forward and seek help. You and your children should seek comfort in the fact that she wanted to get better, not just for herself, but for you and your children. Her family was very important to her."

"I've read a bit about postpartum depression, but I'm still not clear on what causes it?" I was keen to find out anything which could improve my understanding of what Rita had gone through.

"Postpartum depression is often caused by the imbalance in hormones after a woman gives birth. Pregnancy and birth result in a surge of various hormones within women. It's an emotional time for women, and some individuals can continue to struggle for some time. It seems that everything became too much for Rita, but the one thing she told me repeatedly was how much she loved you and the children and how much she wanted to get better for you all."

As we drove home, I turned to Anni. "I'm glad you convinced me to just talk to the doctor rather than threaten her. After hearing what she had to say, it's made it easier for me to understand what happened so that I can try to consign it to the past. I need to focus now on making sure that the children are happy after everything they've gone through and also that you're happy—because I love you and the kids, and I want us all to be happy together."

Anni smiled at me. "I want us all to be happy as well."

"I'm so lucky to have you, Anni, and so are the children."

"And I'm lucky to have found you. I never imagined I would get married at twenty and have a readymade family, but it's all worked out and I love being a mom to Clara and Clemente."

I'd come to fully appreciate just how good Anni was with the kids. I'd recently agreed with her idea to put photos of Rita around the house. At first, I'd worried how the children would take it. But after seeing their positive reaction, I knew Anni had been right. Just this morning, I'd seen Clara touch a photo of her mother and say, "Momma was so pretty and happy." I wanted the kids to have good memories of her.

"Clara's been so much happier since you've joined our family," I continued, "and you were right when you said she would feel less frustrated if she could articulate herself better. I'm glad we've been going to the speech therapy sessions together—I'm glad that we're doing things as a family." And when I said the word 'family', Anni's face lit up, making my heart sing with love for her. She'd not only accepted me and the children, but she *wanted* to be with us, and that was the best feeling in the world.

ANNUNCIATA

The following Saturday, after lunch, Clara came up to Lorenzo with a ball in her hands. She was wearing her new white cat costume, while Clemente was running around in his new striped tiger costume.

"Will you play with me?" she asked her father.

"I'd love to play with you. You look very pretty in your cat costume." It was an exact replica of my costume, just in a smaller size, and Clara had a blue ribbon tied in a bow around her neck, matching the ribbon Wilbur had on his collar today.

"Can we play outside, Dadda?"

My eyes immediately shot to Lorenzo, and I saw him go very still. He was completely stunned and overwhelmed. She'd called him *Dadda*.

"Of course, we can, mia preziosa." His voice was hoarse and his eyes glassy, but I could tell he was trying not to make a big deal of it.

Clara hadn't called him Dadda since before Rita died, and I knew that had really hurt. I smiled at Lorenzo, knowing how much this meant to him, and he gave me a dazed smile back.

Later that afternoon, I sat down with Clara to do her daily speech therapy exercises.

Clemente sat down on the floor as well—he enjoyed the therapy games we played and often joined in. I made the sessions as fun as possible so that it wouldn't feel like work to Clara or make her self-conscious about her speech skills.

I had noticed some issues with Clemente's speech lately, and Lorenzo had immediately agreed when I suggested we take him to be seen by the speech therapist. We had an appointment next week for Clemente, but I wasn't worried because I knew that Lorenzo and I would work through any speech issues with Clemente in the same way as we were doing with Clara. Lorenzo and I were a team now.

To my surprise, Lorenzo came and sat on the floor of the den with us. "Can I join in?"

"Sure," I said easily. Usually I did the exercises during the day while he was working, meaning that he didn't usually take part, although he continued making time to come to the appointments with the therapist.

"What are we doing today?"

"I thought we'd play the game about who we love in the family." Clemente clapped his hands, and Clara gave her sweet smile. They both loved this game. Although it was one of the early therapy games I'd done with them, and Clara could already master these simple sentences, I still played this game with them sometimes.

"What are the rules?" asked Lorenzo.

"We go around in a circle, and each person makes up a sentence about who loves who. You have to start your sentence with the last name spoken."

"Okay," he agreed. "I think I can do that."

Clemente wanted to start. "Clemente loves Grandma."

Lorenzo had his turn next. "Grandma loves Clara."

Clara then had to start the sentence with her own name. "Clara loves Dadda," she said shyly. Unlike earlier, Lorenzo didn't even try to hide his reaction. After a stunned moment, he pulled her into his lap and gave her a kiss on her forehead. "Mia preziosa," he murmured to her, his voice full of emotion, "and I love you—always and forever." As he spoke, he couldn't help his voice cracking with emotion.

Clemente wanted to have another turn. "Dadda loves Ma Veneti." Lorenzo's face fell at that, and I had to hide a smile.

We carried on, and soon we'd exhausted most members of the family. It was Lorenzo's turn, and he had to start his sentence with, 'Dadda loves...'

"Dadda loves...pizza," he said.

"No Dadda," said Clara seriously. "You have to say someone in our family."

"But I've used up all the family I can think of," protested Lorenzo.

She shook her head. "No, you haven't. You can say, 'Dadda loves Wilbur'."

I could see the struggle in Lorenzo's expression. But seeing Clara's earnest expression and not wanting to upset her or discourage her speech therapy, he said what she wanted. "Dadda loves Wilbur," he gritted out, earning him a beaming smile from his little girl, her reaction somewhat mollifying him.

Clemente added another sentence: "Momma loves Clara." Momma was what they called Rita. I'd heard Clara tell Clemente about their mother, plus he was always interested in looking at the photos of Rita we now had up around the house.

Clara then added, "Clara loves Mom."

"Mom?" said Clemente with a frown.

Clara pointed at a photo of Rita by the TV. "That's Momma." Then she pointed at me. "Anni is Mom." She turned to me. "Mom, you love us, don't you?" she asked.

I felt tears well up. They'd never called me anything but Anni, and I'd been perfectly fine with that. But to hear Clara call me Mom made my heart clench with so much emotion that I thought it would burst.

"Yes, I do," I choked out. "I love you to the moon and back."

"Mom take us to moon?" asked Clemente hopefully.

"No, silly, the moon is far," Clara said gently to her brother before I could reply. "We're going to the zoo tomorrow. No time for the moon."

"Ok," replied Clemente. "No moon."

This made me and Lorenzo laugh, and I surreptitiously wiped away the couple of tears that had spilled over.

Once we finished the game, the children ran off to find Adelina so that they could have a snack, Wilbur following on Clara's heels.

I snuggled up to Lorenzo on the sofa. "Thanks for joining in."

"I didn't think I was going to have to declare my love for the cat," he grumbled.

"You were a good sport."

"Well, I didn't mind saying it if it made Clara happy."

"It definitely made her happy," I said, resting my head on his shoulder, with a sigh of contentment.

"You've worked wonders with the children...and with me. When I first got engaged to you, I was worried that you were going to be too wild to settle down and that I was going to end up with someone else to look after. But I've come to realize that you were actually an angel coming into our lives, rescuing us from our grief and allowing us to become a family again—a family that wouldn't be complete without you in it."

His words made my heart clench. I loved him and the children so much and would do everything in my power to protect and care for them—and to know that he felt the same about me meant that I had everything I needed to be happy.

***

That night, Lorenzo gathered me in his arms after making love to me.

We were still using birth control because I didn't feel ready to have another child yet. We had talked about it, and although we both wanted more children, I was happy having my hands full with Clara and

Clemente for now. I was only twenty, and I wanted to have enough time to be able both to complete my college degree and to take care of the two children I already had.

And that was how I truly felt—that Clara and Clemente were *my* children, just as much as if I'd given birth to them myself.

"Thank you," Lorenzo said in a low voice, "for everything you do for me and our children." Lorenzo always said 'our' children now, and I knew that he really meant it. Every time he said it, my heart would beat faster.

"You just being here more for mealtimes and stuff has really helped the kids too," I replied.

"The kids are definitely happier." He paused. "Clemente has always dealt with Rita's death better, but I reckon that's because he's too young to remember her really."

I was thoughtful as I pondered what he'd just said.

"What are you thinking about?" he asked.

"Sometimes I think that Clemente has coped better because of the way Clara is toward him. She's really protective of her little brother. If he takes a fall, or if he's grumpy and having a bad day, she's instantly at his side, playing with him and reassuring him. I think that's helped Clemente so much more than we could ever know."

"I've noticed how Clara is with Clemente," remarked Lorenzo, "but I've never thought about how that could have helped him in the aftermath of Rita's death."

"Your daughter is strong in her own way."

I felt him nod his head in agreement. "Anni, I don't ever want either you or kids to feel that you're not strong, or that talking about your problems is a weakness." His voice was serious. "I wish Rita had been able to talk to me more. I wish I could have talked to you more about my problems when we first married. Instead, you were thrust into being a wife and mom, and I didn't make things any easier for you."

"I'm just happy that you're listening to my opinions now."

"Well, you were right about having pictures of Rita up around the house. Having photos of her with the kids during happier times is good for the kids. It gives them something to focus on instead of just their grief."

"You know, Lorenzo, as long as we all keep talking to each other, then I have the feeling that we're going to be okay."

"We're going to be more than okay, Mrs. Marchiano," Lorenzo replied. "Because if I have anything to do with it, then we're going to live happily ever after."

Thanks so much for reading. See here for a free **BONUS EPILOGUE** if you are already missing Anni and Lorenzo: https://BookHip.com/SLMBMMZ

Continue reading for a sneak peek of **MAFIA AND TAKEN**...

SNEAK PEEK

**MAFIA AND TAKEN
A DARK ROMANCE
(MARCHIANO MAFIA SERIES)**

CHAPTER 1

*Santa Adelina, Madre di Dio, prega per noi peccatori, adesso e nell'ora della nostra morte.
Holy Mary, Mother of God, pray for us sinners now and at the hour of our death.
— the words every Made Man recites upon a death.*

CATE

"Caterina, it's time you were married. You're twenty-one years old now and people are starting to ask why you're not even engaged," said my father, in his usual commanding tone.

He was the only person who called me 'Caterina'. Everyone else in my life called me 'Cate'. We were eating dinner at my father's house—how I hated these weekly dinners. They were nothing like the family dinners we had when I'd been younger—when my mom and brother had still been alive.

I clenched my fingers more tightly around my cutlery before answering my father. "Father, I don't want to marry anyone yet, especially not a Made Man."

A Made Man was what we called a man initiated into the Mafia. My father, Ovidio Russo, was a Made Man—he was a Captain in the Fratellanza Mafia here in Chicago.

As we spoke, his forehead creased in annoyance. "It's not a matter of what you want, Caterina. You know that in our world you are expected to marry to further the strategic bonds of your family and, just as importantly, to provide heirs for the Fratellanza."

So, there we had it. I was expected to spread my legs to carry on the distinguished line of Made Men in the Fratellanza.

"Father, you know how I feel about our world and what goes on in it—"

"You've made your feelings quite clear, which is why I have allowed you to have a job and live in your own apartment since you turned eighteen." My father's irritation had made him interrupt me in a harsh tone. "Most families and fathers would not permit those freedoms to their daughters, especially to the daughter of a high-ranking Captain."

Although it was unusual that my father permitted me to live in my own apartment, his soldiers still kept watch over me and guarded me closely every day, even when I went to work each day as a teacher's assistant in kindergarten.

My father pierced me with his gaze. "Now it is time for you to do your duty."

Duty. I was sick of hearing that word. It was used as an excuse for everything in our world. For business, for crimes, for murders. Anything could be justified in the Mafia by declaring it to be a duty.

"I have been approached by another Fratellanza Captain. He is looking for a bride and I think you would make a suitable match. After all, you are the daughter of a Captain and understand the responsibilities that come from being part of such a family."

I felt like shouting out that I wouldn't do it, but my mom had brought me up to be polite at all times, no matter the situation. Even though she was gone now, I didn't want to let her down. I answered as calmly as I could, "Father, I'm not ready to marry anyone just yet." And when I did marry, I definitely wouldn't be marrying someone from the Mafia world—I'd seen firsthand how it could only lead to tragedy and heartbreak.

"Caterina, you're twenty-one years old. In the Mafia world, the 'two' at the front of your age means that people expect you to be married by now or, at the very least, engaged. People are beginning to talk." To not be engaged by the age of twenty was scandalous in our world.

"They are just a bunch of gossips," I blurted out. "All they do is talk about the nearly-weds and the newly-deads. The women in the Fratellanza like nothing more than to speculate about who might be promised to who, and which families are trying to unite through strategic marriages. They haven't got anything better to do." I couldn't help the bitterness seeping into my words.

My father pierced me with his gaze. "Your mom was married long before your age. She was married to me by the time she was seventeen."

That sounded scarily young to me. "Father, I want to choose my own husband when the time comes, not be told who I am to marry."

"You know that arranged marriages are the usual method of matrimony in our world, given that we do not marry outsiders. We don't let anyone else into our circle. It is far too dangerous to let in people who do not understand our ways and the Mafia's codes of honor."

Every Saturday, I was required to attend dinner with my father at his house. My grandmother, Nonna, was normally at these dinners, but this week she was visiting her sister in Florida. I was missing not having Nonna here tonight to fill in the awkward silences and to act as a buffer between my father and me. Without her presence, my father was hounding me even more than usual.

Coming here once a week meant that my father left me alone for the remainder of the week. I just had to get through this meal without having an argument with him.

I looked down at my outfit. I was wearing a shift dress and heels. My father expected me to dress formally for dinner, rather than in the more casual clothes that I preferred. I wore my auburn hair loose over my shoulders and had applied some light makeup—just some eyeshadow, mascara around my hazel green eyes and some pale lip gloss.

"As Nonna isn't here, I was thinking I wouldn't stay the night like I normally do and skip church in the morning."

After dinner here each week, I would stay the night before going to church with my grandmother on Sunday morning. Then I was free to go back to my apartment and my life for another week.

"Nonsense. You will stay the night and I will go to church with you tomorrow."

I suppressed a sigh. I wasn't sure what the point was of my father going to church. He wasn't particularly godly in his beliefs, and it would take him at least a decade to confess all his sins.

After we finished our meal, I excused myself, saying I was tired and wanted to go to bed. My father went into the drawing room, but I always avoided that room as much as possible because on the mantelpiece were my mom's and brother's ashes.

The ashes had been there since I'd been fourteen years old. Just seeing them always brought a lump to my throat as memories of my mom and brother would come flooding back to me. My mother had always wanted to be cremated so that her ashes could be scattered back in her homeland. My father wouldn't allow me to do this by myself, and he had never gotten around to scheduling time for us to make the trip together—as always, work was his sole priority and came before everything else for him.

I climbed the stairs to my childhood bedroom. It was still the same since Father had not changed it after I moved out three years ago and Nonna kept it as clean as a whistle.

I took a long shower before putting on a strappy satin nightgown that fell just above my knees. I climbed into my childhood bed and pulled the covers up to my chin, but it took ages to fall asleep as always.

This house no longer felt like my home—it hadn't felt like my home since I'd been fourteen years old. But I blocked all those memories from my mind. I couldn't go there tonight.

I watched the stars outside my bedroom window, seeking comfort from their light in the darkness, and eventually I fell asleep.

***

I woke abruptly to loud voices coming from downstairs. Squinting into the darkness, I checked the clock and saw that it was after 2.00 a.m.

Father must be talking to some of his men. They sounded angry with him, but it was odd for someone to raise their voice at my father since he was a Captain.

For some reason, the loud voices made the hairs on the back of my neck stand up. I decided to go downstairs to check with my father that everything was all right.

This house always made me feel uneasy now, but the loud voices were making me more nervous than normal. I reached for my robe. It was thin, but it would cover up my nightgown.

I silently crept down the stairs toward the voices coming from the drawing room. That was strange as well since my father conducted business in his office at the front of the house.

I slowly approached the drawing room, catching sight of my father surrounded by several men dressed all in black with their weapons drawn. My heart started to race.

They weren't Fratellanza. *They were the enemy.*

How had they gotten past the soldiers guarding the gate? If these men were in our home, that could only mean that our soldiers were dead.

And that meant that the intruders probably wanted to kill us too.

I suddenly felt cold, but at the same time felt a bead of sweat trickle down my back, making me shiver. My father was pleading with the intruders. "Please, Dmitri, it wasn't anything to do with me, I swear!"

The man he was talking to raised his gun to my father's head.

I cried out. The man with the raised gun turned and saw me.

And seeing the look on his face, I didn't think. I just ran.

I had a petite frame and ran to keep fit, so I was quick on my feet. I raced toward the front door, but another man dressed in black was coming through that door.

I spun on my heel as I made for the stairs in the opposite direction. There was a bathroom near the top of the stairs, and it had a lock on it. I only had to get that far.

I grabbed the wooden handrail, leaping onto the first step and rushing up the stairs.

I urged my legs to move faster but it felt like my whole body was moving through deep water. The man who had seen me was behind me—he was chasing me.

I stumbled on the stairs. I used my hands to push my body up and forward. It sounded like the man was close to me and I could hear his heavy breaths right behind me.

But I didn't have time to look around behind me. I had to keep moving forward if I was to get away from him.

I had gone up and down these stairs so many times during my childhood but my ascent up them had never felt so difficult. I was breathing in huge gulps of air as I saw the top step come into my line of sight—only three more steps to go, two more steps.

Then I felt my foot touch the top step.

Once I reached the landing I didn't pause for breath. I turned back on myself and bolted for the bathroom. Despite being fit from my regular running, my breath was coming in short pants and my body felt jittery.

I made it into the bathroom, whirling around and pushing the door shut at the same time.

The door bounced off a man's hard body.

In slow motion I saw the face of the man as he came toward me.

With each step he took toward me, I took a step away from him trying to keep him from me until my back hit the bathroom wall and there was nowhere left for me to go.

His face snarled as he looked at me. I didn't recognize him.

But he knew who I was. "Cate Russo...you're even more beautiful than I had imagined."

His complexion was pale, and his hair was light brown. The slight trace of an accent in his voice made a shudder run through my body.

He was Russian—which must mean that he was *Bratva*, part of the Russian Mafia. My father had called him Dmitri. This could only be Dmitri Petrov, head of the Chicago Bratva.

I was standing still but my breaths were coming in heavy gulps and needles of terror were piercing my skin.

He reached out his hand toward me. I tried to push past him but his arm caught my body and his other hand yanked my head back with a violent tug at my hair.

I cried out as pain ripped through my scalp and neck, but he held my head back at an awkward angle and forced me to look at him, into eyes which were dark and menacing.

I saw his hand moving toward me from the corner of my eye. "Oh Cate, how I've been looking forward to meeting you."

As I tried to scream, he forced a damp cloth against my mouth. I struggled against his hand smothering me, fighting the sickly chemical smell that was threatening to overwhelm me.

But it was no good.

The chemical was taking over the air I was inhaling, slowly stealing me away from my body and making me fall down into a deep black hole of unconsciousness.

ALESSIO

I faced my brother, Marco Marchiano, in the kitchen of the mansion we shared.

"Ovidio Russo's men have alerted me that he didn't show up for a meeting this morning and the soldiers at his home weren't answering their cellphones. They checked his house and the two guards there had been shot dead."

"What happened?" Marco growled. Marco was twenty-seven years old and Capo—the boss of the Fratellanza. I was a year younger than him, and I was his Consigliere—his second-in-command and chief adviser.

"They checked the security footage from the house and grounds—it was the Russians. Dmitri Petrov was there."

Marco frowned as he considered what I had said for a minute. "What the hell?"

"Well, I'm thinking that both us and the Russians have been having problems with bad drugs over the last few months. It's strange for us both to have the same problem, at the same time, given that we have completely different drug suppliers."

We'd been having problems with bad drugs. Someone had mixed some shit into our drugs, and the resulting impure product had caused numerous deaths, meaning that we now had the FBI sniffing around us.

"Go on," said Marco.

"Ovidio oversees our drug shipments when they arrive, so he has access to all our drugs. Now it appears that he is also involved with the Russians in some way, otherwise why would they take him? So, it seems that Ovidio is the common denominator in this whole story. The Russians have recently started having the same problem of bad drugs in their supply chain, causing lots of deaths too among the drugs they sell."

Marco understood now and summed up my theory. "Goddamnit, if he's been diluting our drugs with some other shit, that would increase the overall weight of the drugs. Then he could sell the extra weight to the Russians, making himself a tidy amount of money on the side."

I nodded. "He might have gotten away with it if the drugs hadn't started causing so many deaths, alerting the Russians and us to the fact that there is a problem with the chemical makeup of the drugs."

Marco grimaced. "It seems like he got greedy." He shook his head. "Traitors always eventually get tripped up by their greed."

"What are bad drugs?" asked our younger sister, Debi, who had come into the kitchen.

"Nothing for you to worry about, shortcake," I said gently. We always shielded our fourteen-year-old sister from the details of our business. Of course, she knew what we did, but I would protect her from the more sordid aspects for as long as I could. "Why don't you take the dog out for his walk?"

"Okay, Alessio. Come on, Mr. Fluffy, do you want to go for walkies?" The dog didn't need to be asked twice, and he started barking excitedly, bounding toward the door to the garden.

I waited for Debi to go outside before carrying on. "We need to get Ovidio back, to find out what he's been up to, who else is involved, and then to deal with him ourselves. Plus, the security footage also shows that his daughter was taken too. Ovidio's men told me she's twenty-one and her name is Caterina."

"Why on earth did they take the daughter?" asked Marco. "The Bratva don't usually target the families."

"The CCTV from the house shows Dmitri Petrov asking Ovidio where the money is and saying something about the daughter's bank account."

"Christ. Well, it looks like we need to talk to the girl as well. The whole family might be involved in this shitshow."

"I'll get on it right away."

I went to the office to start work on tracking down Ovidio and his daughter. My blood was boiling like a blazing inferno—we expected absolute loyalty from our men, and nothing else was acceptable. The whole Fratellanza was built on this.

For a Captain to betray us was shocking, but even worse, it made me wonder how many other traitors were lurking among the Fratellanza.

Upon the death of our father, Marco had taken over as Capo at the age of eighteen, and I had been seventeen when I became his Consigliere. We had taken over an organization that was fraught with infighting and corruption, and it had taken many years and us working our asses off to turn it around into the success it was today.

Betrayals and treachery had the potential to bring the whole organization down, and I would do whatever was required to prevent that, dishing out whatever retribution was required to set an example to the rest of the Fratellanza.

My brothers and I were known as the Kings of Chicago. Our family hadn't gotten to its position today by being careful and respectful of others—we had gotten here through brutality and being merciless.

I couldn't even think about Ovidio Russo without my insides churning up with fury. I couldn't wait to get my hands on our deceitful Captain and anyone else he had been working with. The adrenaline started to course through my veins as I thought about the punishments we would dish out, about the violent ends they would meet.

For her sake, I hoped the daughter wasn't involved in any betrayal.

Because even if she was a girl, the Fratellanza treated all traitors the same.

CHAPTER 2

CATE

I tried to open my eyes, but my eyelids were so heavy like I was struggling to wake from a deep sleep. My head was pounding, and my mouth felt dry.

I could feel movement around me, as if we were in a moving car, perhaps. I didn't know what was going on, but my head was hammering too much to even think. I must be dreaming, I thought, letting the drowsiness take over.

But then I heard that voice again. It was the voice with the accent—the man my father had called Dmitri. Dmitri Petrov. I had never seen him until today, but even I had heard the name of the most feared Russian in Chicago.

I forced my eyes open, and panic engulfed me as I remembered what had happened. I tried to say something, but my brain was all foggy and I could only manage a low moan.

The car stopped and a blast of cold night air rushed in as the doors were ripped open. Dmitri pulled me out of the car and marched me towards a warehouse on a derelict industrial estate while another man dragged my struggling father. I saw that his mouth was gagged, and his hands were tied behind his back with zip-ties.

After we entered the warehouse, Dmitri tugged me along as he crossed the building, and I stumbled as I struggled to keep up with him.

He reached down, grabbed my arm, and hauled me to my feet before continuing toward his destination. He opened another door, and I felt a coldness penetrate my bones as he led me down a set of stone steps into a basement. The smell of damp stung my nostrils and the iciness in the air made me shiver.

"Where are you taking me?"

"You'll see." He didn't give anything away.

"What do you want with me?" I pleaded.

He pushed me up against a wall. I felt the cold of the brick seep through my thin nightclothes.

"What do I want from you? Oh, the things I want to do to you...What do you think you could do to please me, to make me go easy on you?"

I shuddered.

He ran the back of his fingers across my cheek. "I could torture you...But what I really want is to see you on your knees in front of me with my cock stuffed in your mouth, begging me to spare you."

I felt the blood drain from my face.

"Have you ever sucked a cock?" he smirked. "Oh, angelic Cate, I know you haven't, which will make it all the sweeter when you suck mine. After all, the Fratellanza keep all their daughters as pure virgins until their wedding day, to make it all the more satisfying to finally break them in, don't they?"

I tried to swallow the terror balling in my throat, but I felt a tear betray me and slide down my face.

"Will your pussy get wet when your tongue wraps around my cock?" His harsh laugh echoed in the emptiness of the building. "I can't wait to find out."

He seized my arm and I couldn't stop the scream from leaving my mouth.

He pushed me onto a hard chair, binding me to it with my arms tied behind me, the coarse rope cutting into my wrists and legs. I struggled to try and stop him, but I was no match for his strength.

"I like seeing you all tied up. No need to gag you though—there is no one to hear you and I want to hear all your screams."

I looked up and saw my father being dragged down the same steps and taken off into what looked like a different room further along. He was still fighting, trying to get out of his restraints.

I could see the fear in my father's eyes. Not much frightened him—he was a Made Man and was used to violence and death, but this was different. I didn't know what the Bratva wanted with us, but it could be nothing good.

Dmitri walked away to the room my father was taken into. My head was pounding, probably due to the drug they had used on me, and I was so tired. I forced my eyelids to stay open—I needed to work out a way to escape from here.

My mind raced, trying to work out how to get away from these men but whatever way my mind turned, I could see no way out.

I was powerless in this situation, and I needed to figure a way out of here; eventually, however, my mind blurred with a fog of wooziness and exhaustion, and I couldn't stop my eyes from closing.

***

The next time I woke, it was to the sound of a deep scream in the distance. I opened my eyes and held myself very still as I tried to figure out where the sound had come from.

Then I heard it again. It was my father. Terror crawled over every inch of my body–they were torturing him. But why? I tried to move, but I was firmly bound to the chair. My arms ached having been tied down for a long while by now. I wasn't sure how long I had been there.

As I saw Dmitri approach me, I tried to sink back against my chair. Perhaps I should try to distract him from whatever he had in mind for me. "May I use the bathroom, please?" I wasn't sure why I was being so polite to him, but it was my usual manner and I didn't want him to refuse.

He looked at me for a minute without answering.

He took a knife and came back toward me, his gaze fixed on me. The look in his eyes said he wanted to do something to me, and that thought made me shudder.

He slowly cut the ropes open, freeing my body. My legs were shaky as I tried to stand up. His hand roughly gripped my arm, and he dragged me forward and up the stairs. The restrooms must be on the ground floor, I thought to myself.

As we climbed the stairs, I suddenly jerked to a stop as I heard loud bangs—gunshots.

Dmitri ran up the remaining steps to the ground floor, shouting over his shoulder, "Stay here!"

He didn't try to tie me back up—I guess he thought that even untied there wasn't much harm a girl like me could do to anyone.

The screaming had stopped from the next room. I didn't know whether that was a good sign or not.

I wondered if I should try to escape. This might be my only chance while the Russians were distracted by the gunshots. I decided not to give myself time to think but to go with my gut.

I ran up the stairs and was almost at the top when the door burst open and one of the Russians appeared in front of me. He frowned as he saw me, but this was my chance now and I pushed past him.

My legs were still shaky and numb after being bound up for so long. He grabbed me but I tried to push his arm away.

Somehow, I lost my footing and felt myself fall back. My foot couldn't find the step. I tried to grab the handrail—it was just out of my grasp.

There was nothing for me to hold on to and I felt myself falling down the hard concrete steps. As I tumbled down one stair after another, each was another harsh blow to my body, sending sharp pains searing through me.

But I didn't care about the pain. All I could think was that my chance to escape was slipping through my fingers.

That was my last thought before my head hit the hard ground. There was a moment of intense pain, then everything went black.

CHAPTER 3

ALESSIO

We had tracked down the Russians to this warehouse through a combination of hacking into the Russians' cellphones and gaining illegal access to street camera footage. My youngest brother, Danio, was a computer genius and could get us access to all sorts of things.

If Ovidio Russo was indeed siphoning off some of our drugs and selling them to the Bratva, he deserved to be left to be tortured to death by them. However, we needed to find out the extent of his dealings with the Russians and what his daughter's involvement was—then we could decide their fates.

Marco and I had come to the warehouse with our soldiers. The Bratva were a tough opponent; however, we had the element of surprise on them.

After getting past the Russian soldiers on the ground floor of the warehouse, there was no sign of Ovidio or his daughter.

I turned to our men. "Split into two. Half search the top floor and the other half search the basement level."

Marco went with some soldiers to the top level while I headed with the remainder of our soldiers to the basement level.

I held my weapon close to my body as I made my way down the steps to the basement, checking my surroundings for any more of the enemy. My gaze immediately caught sight of the still figure lying at the foot of the stairs.

It was Ovidio's daughter—the girl that was likely involved with him in his betrayal.

I heard noises coming from somewhere in the basement. I signaled to my soldiers to carry on toward where the noise had come from while I stayed to check the girl. She was lying on her back with her head turned to one side, her hair covering her face.

I knelt down beside her and smoothed her auburn hair back from her face. I could see the rise and fall of her chest—she was still alive.

The thin nightgown and robe on her body were torn, and her skin was cold to my touch. I checked her over for broken bones. There were no obvious breaks as I ran my hand over the soft contours of her body.

I heard a low moan and as her body stirred, her torn nightgown fell open, exposing her full breast and a rosy pink nipple that had hardened in the cold, dank atmosphere of the basement.

Her eyes fluttered open, revealing exquisite hazel eyes that were an alluring combination of green and amber. When she saw me, her eyes widened with panic. "D-don't touch me," she cried, trying to push my hands away. She forced the words out, even in her weak state.

"It's okay, we've got you now." I watched the frown on her forehead smooth out in relief.

She thought I was her savior. She didn't realize that we knew what her father had been up to and her likely involvement.

I saw one of our soldiers heading back toward me. I didn't want anyone looking at her in her semi-naked state. I took off my leather jacket and quickly laid it over the girl.

The soldier gave me an update. "Boss, Dmitri Petrov and a couple of his men have gotten away, but we have the remaining Russians rounded up. Ovidio is still alive although he's been tortured and is in bad shape. Two of our men have also been injured and need medical attention."

I nodded at him and then looked back at the girl, but she had drifted back into unconsciousness.

Marco came down the steps into the basement, and I updated him. "Ovidio and the girl are still alive, although he's been tortured and the girl needs to see a doctor too."

"Okay, take them back to the garage block on our estate and we'll question them there," responded Marco.

The garage block was not just a normal garage. It was where we took people to torture information out of them.

From the front, it looked like a normal garage and matched the modern white exterior of our mansion. Behind the cars parked in it, however, was another door leading to our interrogation rooms.

"I'll take the girl with me," I said, scooping her up into my arms. She felt so fragile.

I couldn't forget, however. that she was a possible traitor. In fact, she had the perfect guise—no one would suspect a Mafia daughter of being involved in this sort of treachery.

As I wrapped my arms around her petite frame, I heard a whimper escape from her lips. I looked down at her face—she was obviously hurt and in pain.

But I knew that would make no difference to my treatment of her.

I carried her up the stairs and out of the warehouse to my SUV and laid her on the back seat before getting in beside her. I told one of my soldiers to drive the vehicle so I could stay in the back with her.

Marco would take Ovidio in his vehicle. Ovidio had been beaten badly but I felt no pity for him. It was unlikely he was innocent in this whole charade. Once we had gotten what we needed from him and his daughter, they would pay for their deception and betrayal.

As our SUV moved off, I decided to give the girl a more thorough check. I pulled out the medical kit that we kept in every vehicle, and as I felt her head for any cuts or bumps, I enjoyed the softness of her silky strands between my fingers. I noticed that she kept drifting in and out of consciousness, indicating that she might be suffering from concussion.

I noticed the bruises and scrapes on her arms and, more worryingly, around her throat. Her translucent skin had been marked at the hands of the Russians, and that thought stirred up more anger in me.

She belonged to the Fratellanza, and the Russians had no right to touch her.

CATE

I squinted as I felt a bright light being shone into my eyes, but it was hard to close my eyes because someone was holding them open.

The blackness in front of my eyes was lightening to a gray. I opened my eyes more widely to find myself looking up at a man who was checking my injuries.

I felt his fingers running through my hair, gently massaging my scalp. I'd recognized him inside the warehouse. He was Alessio Marchiano—the second-in-command of the Fratellanza. I had never spoken to the man, but I had seen my father speaking to him on a few occasions.

"You've got a bump on your head. I'll get the doctor to look at it." His voice was like a velvet caress.

The relaxing rhythm of his fingers against my scalp made me want to fall into the oblivion of sleep, but I fought to stay awake and focused on the man in front of me. Even though we were sitting down, I could immediately sense that he was tall and strongly built. I looked up at his hands checking me over, noticing his strong wrists, olive skin, and the dark hair that trailed up his muscled arms.

Thank God he'd saved me from the Russians. I shuddered at the thought of what would have happened to me at their brutal hands.

When he looked down at me, my eyes flitted over his almost-black hair and rich brown eyes.

"Where are you taking me?"

"I'm taking you home."

I breathed a sigh of relief. All I wanted to do was to be back in my own apartment. Back in the safe life I had built for myself away from this violent Mafia world.

I looked down at myself. A leather jacket was covering up my torn clothes. It hurt when I breathed; it hurt all over, my eyes ached, and my ears were ringing. Just being conscious hurt. "My father?"

He looked at me with narrowed eyes. "We've got him as well."

But he didn't say anything else about my father. His jaw was set in a hard line, and I felt like his dark eyes were searing into me. I felt unease prickle through my body. I had a bad feeling that my father had done something very wrong.

My father seemed to know our kidnappers. They certainly knew him and were determined to get some answers out of him—by torturing either him or me. As a Mafia daughter, I had been shielded from the finer details of our violent world, but even I knew that our kidnappers were the Bratva.

As the SUV turned a sharp corner at speed, I winced as my sore body was thrown against the car door.

"Take it easy with the goddamn driving," I heard Alessio bark at the driver. But all too soon, he drove around another bend, and I let out a cry as my badly bruised arm hit the passenger door.

"For God's sake," said Alessio. Before I knew what was happening, he had undone my seatbelt and tugged me into his arms, setting me in his lap and holding my body against his chest.

My pulse started beating too fast as I felt most of my body in contact with his, and I was acutely aware of how little I was wearing under his jacket.

Sometime later, we pulled up outside a modern estate and I realized that he wasn't taking me back to my own home—this was the Marchiano estate. "I want to go back to my own apartment."

"Not yet."

"Why have you brought me here?"

"We need the doctor to check you." He didn't look at me as he spoke.

I wanted to argue, but I didn't have the energy to. Everything either hurt with pain or ached with exhaustion. I didn't even want to have to think anymore.

As we reached the perimeter gate of the estate, Alessio rolled down his window and spoke to one of the soldiers on guard. "When Dr. Cotrone gets here and is done with Ovidio, tell him that I need him to take a look at the girl as well."

"Got it, boss."

The SUV pulled up in front of the mansion and I gazed at the modern white house surrounded by extensive grounds. But what caught my attention was the enormous stone statue of the Virgin Mary.

It was positioned on their front lawn, the traditional statue clashing blatantly with the modernity of the house. Italian-Americans had a custom of displaying a saint statue in their front yard. I wouldn't have taken the Marchianos, however, as being the godly sort who would follow this tradition. After all, they spent their lives killing people—and enjoying every minute of it.

After Alessio got out of the car, I followed and attempted to stand, but as my legs gave out under me, he caught me and scooped me up into his arms.

I felt too dazed to voice anything except for a small gasp, so instead I let my body sink into his comforting hold, and I relished the warmth of his body against mine.

He was tall, easily over six feet in height, and his whole body was a machine of finely honed muscle, from his broad shoulders down to his powerful thighs and calves. He was wearing dark combat pants, a black fitted top and boots.

Black was, of course, the clothing color of choice for most Made Men—no other color hid the bloodstains so well—however, together with his almost-black hair, dark eyes and his precise movements, he gave off the aura of a highly-trained assassin.

He carried me into the garage and headed past all the vehicles and through a door leading to more rooms.

Was this a back way to enter the house? After walking past the luxury exterior of the main house, these rooms were a harsh contrast with their stark emptiness and desolate air. "What is this place?" I asked, looking around in confusion.

He didn't bother to answer me.

He went into the first room we came to, put me down and closed the door behind him, the sound echoing with a sinister finality.

I felt unsteady on my feet, but that was the least of my worries right now.

The room felt a few degrees colder than the temperature outside. There was no heating or air conditioning, and the room only contained the bare essentials of a table, two chairs, and a storage closet.

My breath caught as the realization hit me of what this place was: the closet would be full of torture equipment.

"Why have you brought me here? What are you…you going to do with me?"

"That depends on you, on whether you cooperate." His words were casual but hinted at something darker beneath his careful veneer.

"I don't know anything," I said quickly.

He prowled toward me, his proximity unnerving me. "Didn't your parents ever teach you not to lie?" His voice was cruel now, in complete contrast to the man who had soothed me earlier, and I realized just how dangerous this man truly was.

My eyes swiftly swept around the room trying to figure a way out. My breaths were coming in shallow rasps. "I thought you came to save me from the Bratva?"

"So, you do know something—you know who your captors were."

I desperately tried to understand what was going on. "I know that my captor is now you," I said harshly. "And anyone would know that those other guys were Russians with the accent they had."

"What did they want with you?" As he fired questions at me, he was rolling up the sleeves of his dark top, revealing his strong forearms dusted with dark hair.

A bead of cold sweat trickled between my breasts, making me shudder. He was a Made Man: a man who had been brought up to torture and kill, a man who had no conscience, and a man who thrived on cruelty. I should have known that he wasn't my savior. I should have known that he was just like every other Made Man. He was a person who lived and breathed violence, and a person who could only bring pain and suffering into my life.

"I d-don't know. I was staying the night at my father's house and woke up to find them in the house. I don't know what they wanted with us."

He pierced me with his eyes, and I could sense his mind trying to figure out what I knew. "Tell me, what did they say to you?"

"Nothing, I swear. They barely said a thing to me."

He sighed. He knew I was lying...

CHAPTER 4

ALESSIO

She was lying.

I had dealt with enough deceit in my life to know when someone was not telling the truth.

Her body was shaking, and her eyes were wide. Her father was in a bad way, and we probably wouldn't be able to question him for a while, meaning that it was imperative that the girl talked and that she talked now.

Dealing with women was one of my least favorite jobs, but a traitor was a traitor, irrespective of their sex.

She was my captive now—and I would make her talk.

I walked toward her and watched her pretty face pale. She knew how this was going to go.

As I neared her, she tried to back away, her hazel eyes huge in her pale face, but after a few steps she came up against the concrete wall. She swiftly looked around herself and realized that there was nowhere left for her to go.

I slammed my palms on the wall either side of her petite body, caging her in. I knew what had to be done next.

But first I relished her being trapped by my body. I slowly brought my hand up to her pretty face, stroking the back of my rough, calloused hand against her face. As my skin made contact with hers, she flinched. It was going to be such a shame to ruin her pretty looks.

I cocked my head to one side, regarding her for a few moments. "Do I scare you?"

She didn't reply, however I knew the answer. She was trembling and I could almost smell the fear rolling off her.

The darkness within me burned as the knowledge that she was afraid of me called to my primal senses. That side of me thrived on her terror, causing desire to flair through my loins. She was my captive now—mine to do with as I wished.

"What did Dmitri Petrov say when he took you?" My hand continued to stroke her cheek. "I want to know exactly what was said." My voice was low, caressing the air between us.

Her answer was barely audible. "Nothing...he said nothing."

My hand suddenly leaped from her cheek to her throat, pinning her against the wall. My face was centimeters from hers, my eyes burning into her irises.

"Please don't—I don't know what you're looking for," she rasped. "I don't know anything."

"Do you want me to force it out of you, is that what you want?"

"No, please!"

"Then stop lying to me. Otherwise, you won't like the consequences," I growled.

"Please...I don't feel so good. My head's pounding and won't stop spinning."

She probably had a concussion, but I wasn't going to let her feminine pleas distract me. "The doctor can deal with it later. Now, talk."

She wearily shook her head at me.

I should have drawn my knife at this stage.

Instead, I spun her around and slammed her back against my chest, my hand gripping her windpipe and applying pressure.

Fuck, I had wanted to avoid this. But if I had to do this, I didn't want to see her face while I did it to her.

"What. Did. He. Say?" I steadily applied more pressure to her slender throat as I forced out each word through gritted teeth.

I could hear her gasping now, and her clammy fingers were frantically scrambling against my iron grip, trying to loosen my hold.

A hint of distaste soured my mind because I was doing this to a woman, but I also knew that was the reason why I was choking her rather than cutting her—if she came out of this, the choking would leave bruises but no permanent scars—no permanent marks to sully her beauty.

I released my hold a fraction, allowing her to gulp in a few small lungfuls of oxygen. I bended my lips to her cheek and saw that her flawless complexion was marred by hot tears. "Are you ready to talk now?"

"Please don't do this!"

I tightened my grip on her throat again, squeezing her delicate throat and feeling her body writhe against mine before giving her another respite for a few seconds.

"Tell me what I want to know."

She was sobbing. "Please...I think—"

Before she could say anything else, her body sagged, and she slumped in my arms as she blacked out.

"Damnit!" She was definitely unwell, probably as a result of the hit to her head.

Irritated, I got out my cellphone and rang Dr. Cotrone. "I need you to come look at the girl as soon as you're done with her father. She's passed out—it's likely a concussion. I need her conscious ASAP to carry on my questioning." I knew the doctor would be nearby in one of the neighboring interrogation rooms taking a look at the father.

After ending the call, I looked at her small body collapsed on the damp concrete floor. As I lifted her into my arms, she stirred and cried out as she saw my face.

"I need the doctor to look at you," I said tersely. All this was delaying me from my task at hand, namely extracting information from her.

For some reason, something in my gut told me to take her into our house. I exited the garage block and made for the front door of the mansion, turning sideways so as not to hit her body against the door frame as I carried her inside.

I then took her up the staircase, heading for my bedroom and putting her down on my bed. "The doctor will be here soon."

Her whole body trembled. "Is this your bedroom?"

"It is."

"I can wait for him in the garage..." She spoke quickly as she huddled against the headboard. She probably thought I had brought her here to rape her.

"Lie down," I ordered.

As she lay down on the bed very slowly, a wary look in her wide eyes, there was a knock at the bedroom door. I opened the door to see that the doctor had arrived and stepped out of the room to talk to him.

"I couldn't feel any broken bones, but she has a large bump on her head and there are cuts and bruises that need looking at. When we found her, it looked like she had fallen down some stairs, but I don't know what happened before that."

"If you can wait out here, I'll take a look at her now," replied the doctor.

I felt my eyes narrow at his words. "I'll be staying in the room while you check her."

"With respect, Alessio, you're not family and it wouldn't be appropriate for you to be in the room while I examine her."

"Fuck propriety. She's our captive now, and I'm staying with her."

The doctor sighed. "Fine. Let's take a look at her now."

I opened the bedroom door and allowed the doctor to go in ahead of me.

"Hello, Caterina. I'm Dr. Cotrone. Alessio has asked me to check you over. Is that okay with you?"

I don't know why he was asking her that, I thought. I was in charge here and if I said she needed examining, he just needed to goddamn do it.

She gave a slight nod, and he opened his bag and took out his equipment. I listened to his various questions, and I watched while he ran his hands over her body and checked the knock she had suffered to her head.

I impatiently paced up and down the bedroom while I waited for the doctor to complete his examination. I couldn't keep my eyes off his hands which were touching her small body. I wanted to break every one of his fingers, slowly and painfully.

By the time he was finished, Cate looked to have passed out again.

But I was taking no chances.

I pulled out the syringe I had stashed in my pocket.

Removing the cover, I pressed the end into her neck. I couldn't risk her waking up during what I was going to do to her next.

As the needle jabbed into her skin, she gave a slight moan, and then the drug quickly took effect.

I pierced the doctor with a stare. "Put a tracker put in her."

"Alessio," he sighed. "I know we sometimes put trackers in your prisoners when you're worried about them escaping. Unlike a trained enemy, however, this girl has no chance of getting past you or your soldiers. Plus, she's a woman..." It was obvious that the good doctor was reluctant to carry out such a procedure on a female.

"She may be a woman, but she is here with great reluctance," I snapped.

He closed his eyes briefly. "Very well."

The doctor knew I wasn't going to change my mind.

"I'll need your assistance. The best spot is between her shoulder blades. I need her laying on her front."

She had only my jacket and a sheet covering her torn nightgown. I didn't want to expose her body to anyone else's eyes. I rolled her body so that she was on her stomach, all the time making sure that her body remained largely covered by the sheet.

Then, pulling my jacket part of the way down, I took my knife and sliced through the satin fabric at the top of her back, exposing her delicate skin.

The doctor got a syringe ready and inserted it in the optimal position and then covered it with a small dressing. The tracker was the size of the lead tip of a pencil and was the ideal way for me to keep control of her. I would always know where she was, and she wouldn't be able to get away from me.

The idea of having control over her made my dick stir.

She looked so helpless and vulnerable in her current state...and I liked having her powerless in my bed like this...

To add **MAFIA AND TAKEN** to your Amazon TBR: https://www.amazon.com/author/isaoliver

Hi Lovely. I have lots of stories in my head about the Marchiano universe, and if there's enough interest, I'd love to write more books. If you enjoyed MAFIA AND ANGEL, please consider leaving a review (or even just a rating) on Amazon. Reviews help new authors like me SO MUCH, and I truly appreciate your support. Love Isa xxx Link to leave a rating/review at Amazon: https://www.amazon.com/dp/B0BQZ6DRPX/

Printed in Great Britain
by Amazon